MW01124284

Dragon Dojo Brotherhood

Reign of Dragons

Fate of Dragons

Blood of Dragons

Age of Dragons

Fall of Dragons

Death of Dragons

War of Dragons

Queen of Dragons

Myths of Dragons

Vessel of Dragons

Gods of Dragons

A Legend Among Dragons

Blackbriar Academy

The Trials of Blackbriar Academy

The Shadows of Blackbriar Academy

The Hex of Blackbriar Academy

The Blood Oath of Blackbriar Academy

The Battle of Blackbriar Academy

The Nighthelm Guardian Series

City of the Sleeping Gods

City of Fractured Souls

City of the Enchanted Queen

Demon Queen Saga

Princes of the Underworld

Wars of the Underworld

Sentinel Saga

By Dahlia Leigh and Olivia Ash

The Shadow Shifter

sive bonus novella from the Nighthelm Guardian series, *City of the Rebel Runes*, the prequel to *City of Sleeping Gods* only available to subscribers.

https://wispvine.com/newsletter/olivia-ash-email-signup/

Enjoying the series? Awesome! Help others discover the Dragon Dojo Brotherhood by leaving a review at Amazon.

FALL OF DRAGONS

Book Five of the Dragon Dojo Brotherhood

OLIVIA ASH

When I became a dragon, my magic evolved. The shift unlocked something *other*. Something far more dangerous—and deadly—than anyone expected.

There's an entirely new depth to my magic, and for the first time, I truly have no limits. There are no boundaries to what I can do—and that terrifies everyone who has been trying so desperately to control me.

The fact is, I'm a diamond dragon—the only one of my kind. The only other diamond dragons in history were the gods themselves.

So… what does that make *me?*

A war is brewing, and try as I might, I can't help but be in the center of it. The Knights want to use me as propaganda to fuel their anti-dragon message. The Bosses want to break me until I bow before them. Harper needs my help to stop this war before it destroys her entire family.

It's me and my men against the world, and thank the gods I have them—because in the blink of an eye, everything I ever believed in is destroyed.

Because, even from beyond the grave, my former mentor might have found a way to kill me.

Fall of Dragons is a full-length novel with a badass heroine, a riveting storyline, and an alternative relationship dynamic. Get ready for a heart-pounding story filled with a dragon shifter romance unlike anything you've read before.

Buckle in for heart-pounding action, breathtaking magic, dragon shifters, sexy bad-boys with badass weapons, deadly assassins, four drop-dead gorgeous leading men, and lots of toned muscles.

Most importantly—a young woman's journey of

justice, self-discovery, and freedom as she steps into the truth of who—and what—she is.

READ THE WHOLE SERIES

The Dragon Dojo Brotherhood: a riveting and addictive dragon shifter fantasy romance series.

Book 1: Reign of Dragons

Book 2: Fate of Dragons

Book 3: Blood of Dragons

Book 4: Age of Dragons

Book 5: Fall of Dragons

Book 6: Death of Dragons (Oct 2019)

Book 7: War of Dragons (Dec 2019)

Book 8: Queen of Dragons (Jan 2020)

Book 9: Myths of Dragons (Feb 2020)

Book 10: Vessel of Dragons (Apr 2020)

Book 11: Gods of Dragons (May 2020)

Book 12: A Legend Among Dragons (June 2020)

***Warning:** The Dragon Dojo Brotherhood is an adult urban fantasy series with explicit scenes and is meant for mature readers who enjoy spellbinding stories with a few fan-your-face moments in their fantasy fiction. Prepare for lip-biting, fist-pumping, and lots of "hell YES" moments.*

IMPORTANT CHARACTERS & TERMS

CHARACTERS

Rory Quinn: a former Spectre and the current dragon vessel. Rory was raised as a brutal assassin by her mentor Zurie, but escaped that life. When Zurie tried to force Rory to return, Rory was forced to kill her former mentor. Rory's newfound magic is constantly evolving and changing, and now that she has shifted, her magic continues to defy all known limits. Her diamond dragon is the only one of its kind, and the only other diamond dragons known to exist were the fabled dragon gods themselves. But Rory was born a human, so she can't be a *goddess*... can she?

Andrew Darrington (Drew): a fire dragon shifter.

Drew is one of the heirs to the Darrington dragon family. With no real regard for rules or the law in general, Drew tends to know things he shouldn't and isn't fond of sharing that intel with just anyone. Though he originally intended to kidnap Rory and use her power for his own means, her tenacity and strength enchanted him. They have a pact: if he doesn't try to control her, she won't try to control him. Drew sees her as an equal in a world where he's stronger, smarter, and faster than nearly everyone else.

Tucker Chase: a weapons expert and former Knight. Tucker's a loveable goofball who treats every day like it's his last—because it very well might be. His father is William Chase, current General of the Knights anti-dragon terrorist organization. Tucker was originally assigned to hunt Rory down and turn her in to his father, but as he spent more time with her, she became the true family he'd never had. To protect her, Tucker fed his father false intel about her abilities. When the Knights found out, his father tried to drag him back and reprogram the insubordination out of him in a failed attempt that ultimately destroyed one of the Knights' primary fortresses. It's now unclear what the General's stance on Tucker is, and whether or not the Knights have a kill-order out on him.

Levi Sloane: an ice dragon shifter and former Vaer soldier who went feral when his commander killed his very ill little sister. When he was feral, Rory saved him from a snare trap on the edge of the Vaer lands, and he has been by her side ever since. Feral dragons slowly lose touch with their human selves, but Rory helped bring him back from the brink. Though all dragons can communicate telepathically when they touch, Levi and Rory can also communicate this way in human form. To save Rory's life, he and his dragon healed their relationship, and Levi can once again shift and retain full control He's the only dragon to ever come back from being feral.

Jace Goodwin: a thunderbird dragon shifter and former Master of the Fairfax Dragon Dojo. Jace grew up in high society and has the vast network to prove it. A warrior, he used to operate as the General of the Fairfax army—and his only soft spot is for Rory. He gave up his position at the dojo to take her as his mate, and now his full attention is devoted to her. As Rory's mate, he is deeply connected to her and her magic, and he's the only person who can soothe her wild power. If she dies, his dragon will go feral, so he has quite a bit at stake if one of Rory's many enemies comes after her.

Irena Quinn: Rory's sister and former heir to the Spectre organization. She betrayed Zurie when she discovered her former mentor wanted to sell Rory as an assassin-for-hire, which would mean they would never see each other again. A brutal fighter, Irena's only purpose in life is to keep her sister safe and destroy the Spectres organization that almost killed them both. A powerful bio-weapon created by the Vaer gave Irena strange super-strength and bright green eyes that are eerily similar to Kinsley Vaer. Irena might develop magic or even a dragon of her own, though no one knows for sure what Kinsley's experiments have done to her.

Zurie Bronwen (deceased): former leader of the Spectres and former mentor to Rory and Irena. Zurie was a brutal assassin and held the title of the Ghost. Cold-hearted, calculating, and clever, Zurie considered both Rory and Irena as failed experiments—and she was determined to kill them both. The war she started between the Fairfax family, the Vaer family, and the Knights will have lasting consequences, and it's unclear if Zurie realized just how terrible the outcome would be. However, she was the greatest assassin in the world, and it's likely she has set an after-death contingency plan in place to destroy both Irena and Rory. The question is—what did she do?

Diesel Richards: a former Knight turned Spectre. With Zurie dead, Rory out of the picture, and Irena excommunicated for her betrayal, Diesel is now the Ghost. His incentive is to kill both Irena and Rory to ensure no one threatens his rule. He's helped Rory once and tried to kill her on other occasions, so Rory isn't sure what Diesel really wants or what game he's playing with her life.

Harper Fairfax: a thunderbird, the Boss of the Fairfax dragon family, and Jace's cousin. Harper is friendly and bubbly, full of life and joy, but Rory knows a fighter when she sees one. The young woman is smart and cunning. As Rory's first friend, Harper has a special place in Rory's life. She will do anything to protect her friend—including going to war to protect her.

Russell Kane: a thunderbird and new Master of the Fairfax Dojo now that Jace has stepped down. He endured brutal trials to earn his place as the new dojo master. He grew up with Jace and Harper in the dojo and has a deep love for both the castle itself and the people within it. He will do anything to protect the Fairfax dragons—and Harper, for whom he seems to have a soft spot.

Eric Dunn (deceased): a fire dragon and part of the Fairfax family, Eric was the one man Irena was beginning to let herself love. After a betrayal by someone she adored, Irena had shut down. Eric's death broke her, and she left Rory's side shortly after.

Brett Clarke: a Knight and the General's second-in-command. With the General still out of commission after his last run-in with Rory, Brett led the Knights' charge against the Fairfax Dojo. When the Knights lost, Brett was captured. Though he expected to be killed, the Fairfax took him prisoner and will treat him with respect—as long as he doesn't try anything.

William Chase: mostly referred to as the General. William is a former military man who was discharged from the army in disgrace for his terrorist connections to the Knights. He now runs them in a brutal regime that kills defectors, and he now has his sights set on his son Tucker.

Guy Durand (deceased): an ice dragon and former second-in-command to Jace Goodwin at the dragon dojo. Guy always wanted power. When he lost the challenge to Jace for control of the dojo, he joined the Vaer and gave over top-secret intel about Rory and the dojo itself. He was killed by Jace after he tried to kidnap Rory and return her to Kinsley.

Ian Rixer (deceased): a fire dragon, Kinsley Vaer's half-brother, and a master manipulator. Ian was smarmy, elitist, and arrogant. He was often referred to as honey-coated evil for his ability to speak so calmly and kindly, even while torturing his prey. He treated everything like a game, and playing that game with Rory cost him his life. He tried to control her and Jace's magic with specially designed iron cuffs to block their power, but Rory's magic can't be contained. She destroyed the cuffs—and him.

Mason Greene (deceased): a fire dragon and sadistic Vaer lord tasked with dismantling the Spectre organization. Irena gave him access to their sensitive Spectre intel in exchange for giving her and Rory a fresh start, but he betrayed them both. His attempt to kill Rory backfired massively and ultimately cost him his life.

Kinsley Vaer: an ice dragon shifter and the Boss of the Vaer family. Her power and cruelty make most grown men tremble in fear. She's utterly ruthless, cruel, vindictive, and vengeful… the sort to kill the messenger just because she's angry. She's increasingly frustrated that Rory has slipped through her fingers so often, and she's done giving her minions chances to redeem themselves. Now, it's personal—and Kinsley is coming after everything Rory loves.

Jett Darrington: a fire dragon, the Boss of the Darrington family, and Drew's father. He wants Rory for reasons not even Drew fully knows, but everyone's certain it can't be good. He disowned his son when Drew wouldn't hand Rory over, but he promised Drew everything he could ever dream of—including ruling the Darrington family—if he betrays her.

Milo Darrington: a fire dragon, Drew's brother, and current heir to the Darrington family line purely because he's older than Drew. Not much of a fighter, but an excellent politician and master manipulator.

He's been growing increasingly resentful of his younger brother's skill and charm.

Isaac Palarne: a fire dragon and the Boss of the Palarne family. A skilled warrior and empowering speaker, Isaac can rally almost anyone to his cause. He's a deeply noble man, but there's something unnerving about his eagerness to get Rory to come to the Palarne capital.

Elizabeth Andusk: a golden fire dragon and Boss of the Andusk family. Vain and materialistic, Elizabeth can command attention without even a word. She exudes power mainly through her beauty and has a knack for getting people to share secrets they wouldn't have shared otherwise. She's determined to obtain Rory and considers the girl to be nothing more than another object to control and display.

Victor Bane: a fire dragon and Boss of the Bane family. He's a brutal fighter, excellent negotiator, and never gets caught in his many illicit dealings. With his hot temper, he picks fights whenever he can. He has little direction and purpose, merely looking for the next thing—or person—he can steal.

Natasha Bane: a fire dragon and Victor's sister, Natasha has almost as much influence and control over the Bane family as her brother does. She's smart, clever, and cunning. A sultry temptress, she enjoys bending men to her whims. Though both demanding and entitled, she knows when to keep her mouth shut to get her way.

Aki Nabal: an ice dragon and Boss of the Nabal family. He's excellent with money and can always see three moves ahead in any dealings—both financial and political. Clever and observant, he can pinpoint a fighter's weaknesses fairly quickly, though he's not an exceptional fighter himself. He believes money is power—and that you can never have enough of either.

Jade Nabal: an ice dragon and Aki's daughter, Jade is young and not much one for words. As a silent observer who prefers to watch rather than engage, little is known about Jade. She and Rory have met once, only briefly, and Rory knows there's far more to Jade than meets the eye.

OTHER TERMS

The Dragon Gods: the origin of all dragon power. The three Dragon Gods are mostly just lore, nowadays. No one even remembers their names. But with the dragon vessel showing up in the world, everyone is beginning to wonder if perhaps they're a bit more than legend…

Dragon Vessel: According to myth, the dragon vessel is the one living creature powerful and worthy enough to possess the magic of the dragon gods. Rory Quinn was kicked into an ancient ceremony pit—the one Mason Greene didn't know was used to judge the worthiness of those who entered. With that ritual, Rory unknowingly brought the immense power of legend back to the world.

Castle Ashgrave: the legendary home of the dragon gods, said to be nothing more than ruin and myth. Drew believes he's found the location, but he's not yet sure.

Mate-bond: the connection only thunderbirds can share that connects two souls. The mate-bond is not finalized until the pair make love for the first time. Even before it's finalized, however, the mate-bond is powerful. The duo can vaguely feel each other's whereabouts and, if one should die, the other would go feral.

Magical cuffs: complex handcuffs that cover the entirety of a shifter's hands when they're in human form. These cuffs are designed to keep thunderbird magic at bay. The Vaer have designed special cuffs just for Rory, with the ability to block her magic. These cuffs come with a remote that allows the captor to electrocute their captive to help subdue them, as thunderbirds are notoriously powerful.

Spectres: a cruel and heartless organization that raises brutal assassins and hates dragonkind. The Spectres specialize in killing dragons and are known as some of the fiercest murderers on the planet, in part thanks to their highly advanced tech that no one else has yet to duplicate. They're a spider web network that spans the globe, all run by the Ghost. Often, Spectres are raised from birth within the organization and are never given the choice to join. Once a Spectre, always a Spectre—quitting comes with a death sentence.

Override Device: Spectre tech. Very frail and easy to break, it fits into USB ports and can grant access to sensitive files. Though imperfect and obscenely expensive to create, it *usually* works.

Voids: Spectre tech. Fired from a gun with special attachments, a void can force a camera to loop the last 10 seconds and allow for unseen access to secured locations.

The Knights: an international anti-dragon terrorist organization bent on eradicating dragons from the world. Run by General William Chase, they'll do anything and kill anyone it takes to further their mission. There are some rebel Knights organizations that think the current General is too soft, despite his brutal rampage against dragons and his willingness to kill his own family should the need arise.

Fire Dragons: the most common type of dragon shifter. Fire dragons breathe fire and smoke in their dragon forms. They're found in a wide array of colors.

Ice Dragons: uncommon dragons that can freeze others on contact and breathe icy blasts. Usually, ice dragons are white, pale blue, or royal blue. The only known black ice dragons belong to the Vaer family.

Thunderbirds: dragon shifters that glow in their dragon forms and possess the magic of electricity and lightning in both their dragon and human forms. They're the most feared dragons in the world, and also the rarest.

The Seven Dragon Families: the seven dragon organizations that are run like the mob. Each family values different things, from wealth to power to adrenaline. Usually, a dragon is born into a dragon family and never leaves, but there are some who betray their family of origin for the promise of a better life.

Andusk Family: sun dragons who prefer warm climates, almost all of which are golden or orange fire dragons. They're notoriously vain, focused on beauty and being adored. Fairly materialistic, the Andusk dragons hoard wealth and gems and exploit those in less favorable positions.

Bane Family: ambitious fire dragons who deal mainly in illegal activities. They view laws as guidelines that hold others back, while they aren't stupid enough to follow others' rules. They like to see what they can get away with and push the limits.

Darrington Family: the oldest and most powerful family. Darringtons are mostly fire dragons, and angering them is considered a death sentence. They're well situated financially, with a vast network of natural resources, governments, and businesses across the globe. They're notorious for thinking they're above the rules and can get away with anything... because they usually do.

Fairfax Family: a magical family known as the only one to have thunderbird dragons. They have innate magic and talent, but sometimes lack the drive it takes to use those abilities to obtain greater power. They prefer to think of life as a game, and the only winners are those who have fun. To the Fairfax dragons, adrenaline is more important than money, but protecting each other is most important of all.

Nabal Family: wealthy fire and ice dragons. Money and information are most important to the Nabal, and they have an eerie ability to get access to even the most secured intel. Calculating and cunning, the Nabal weigh every risk before taking any action.

Palarne Family: noble fire and ice dragons known for their honor and war skill. Ruled by their ancient dragon code of ethics, the Palarne family operate as a cohesive military unit. Their skills in war are unparalleled by any other family.

Vaer Family: a secretive family of fire and ice dragons, they're known to be behind many conspiracies and dirty dealings in the world. Some see them as brutal savages, but most fear them because they have no ethics or morals, even among themselves.

CHAPTER ONE

A new kind of magic rages within me, crackling like fire.

Fierce.

Bloody.

Mine.

I stand on a cliff overlooking the ocean as the warm night wears on. With no moon in the sky, there's barely any light—but I'm most comfortable in the darkness.

Far below, waves crash against the rocks at the base of the cliff. The roar of water against stone tangles with the low and distant rumble of brewing thunder.

The night is restless, and so am I.

Wind and magic dance over my skin as I tap into

the depths of my power, and my loose white dress practically glows in what little light there is. The silk brushes against my legs, soft and soothing—a blip of delight in the storm.

In the grumbling night, I have to confess I feel at peace. Something about the rage and brewing storm appeases the tension in my bones.

At peace, perhaps, but not at home.

I miss the dojo. My tower. But all of that lies in ruins, crumbled and charred as the Fairfax struggle to rebuild what the Vaer so brazenly destroyed.

All to get *me.*

And they *failed.*

I smirk in victory. Zurie, Guy Durand, Kinsley, even the General—they *all* failed.

But I didn't leave the battle without some scars. No one did.

In an attempt to block out the memory, I close my eyes. I try to focus on the magic coursing through my blood. On the powerful diamond dragon stirring in my soul.

My partner.

She stirs and hums with energy, loving my attention. She preens, and deep within me, I can feel her coil around herself with excitement. Life is still so new to her. Every sensation is a rippling delight.

The salt on the air. The way it stings my throat and fills my lungs.

The breath of the wind as it cuts along my face, dancing through my loose curls.

The surge of her vast, new power as it burns beneath my skin.

I grit my teeth as the white sparks fizzle along my fingers, aching for release. Back at the battle for the dojo, I tapped into magic—even used it to kill Zurie—but it was uncontrolled. Wild. Raw. Any more surges like those, and I risk killing the people I love.

I can never allow that.

A deep breath fills my lungs, and I hold it for a moment, trying to settle my mind as sparks race over my palms. A sharp pain shoots through my temple, and I wince. My ear rings a little—just slightly, quietly, but it's there. I'm still wounded from the war. Hell, those missiles nearly killed me, and it's going to take time to heal.

Even for me.

Deep within, my dragon stirs, ready for vengeance and utterly furious that someone tried to kill us.

The *nerve.*

Try as I might to suppress it all, the tiny little movement in my chest ignites a flurry of flashbacks.

The scream of dying dragons.

No.

I need to focus.

The dojo soldiers' bodies littering the forest.

I grit my teeth as a surge of guilt and shame tear through me.

I have to rein this in.

Brett Clarke's dark brown eyes, lingering a little too long as he's dragged away to his prison cell.

Explosions echo in my memory as I try to meditate, as I try to connect to my dragon and focus.

Sensations blur through me as the flashbacks shift.

Wind across my scales.

The thrill of flight.

The exhilarating sting of cold air through my lungs.

Roof shingles cracking beneath my claws as I land on the roof.

The deafening bellow of my roar as it cuts through the battlefield.

Being a dragon—now *that's* power. There's nothing like it, and I love my dragon more than life itself. I will protect her at all costs.

Because that's who—and *what*—I am now.

A *dragon.*

The pulse of my magic burns abruptly brighter, the energy surging through me like a wave. It's sudden and violent, and I grit my teeth to contain it. Fists tight, shoulders tight, I keep the surge at bay—but only barely. I grimace, reining in the wild magic as best I can, making it listen even though it wants nothing more than to break free and shoot through the sky.

To make itself known in a world that doesn't want me to exist.

My arms tremble slightly, like someone's pushing against them as I try to hold everything still, and I feel myself lift off the ground. It's a surreal sensation, one I can barely acknowledge as the magic takes my full focus. There's a tug on my navel, like someone's lifting me into the sky, and I feel unexpectedly weightless.

My toes are the last thing to touch the rock as I slowly lift into the air, but I keep my eyes shut.

I keep trying to focus.

If my focus slips—even a little—I will lose control.

This shouldn't be an issue, not anymore. And yet, somehow, I'm more powerful than ever—and I can only guess as to why.

Shifting into my dragon did something.

Unlocked something, far more than just the chains on my body.

As I try desperately to rein in the magic, my dragon takes a little more control to compensate. I feel something change in her, and with the small and subtle shift comes a surge of grief.

I couldn't save Eric. And because I failed to save him, I couldn't save Irena, either. Not in the way she needed to be saved.

My power surges, and once again, I can barely contain it. It pushes against me, aching to break free.

So many funerals.

So many good men and women, dead.

Sparks burn across my skin, pushing me to my limit, and I can feel myself begin to lose control.

I remember Irena's note—the two simple words that broke me.

I can't.

Once again, it shatters my heart—and breaks the last shreds of my control.

My magic surges, exploding into the sky as lightning strikes the water. Though my eyes snap open, I see mostly white. My body freezes, suspended in the air. My muscles tighten. Every inch of me screams for a moment of relief, to rest, to simply lie down—but I can't.

I can't even open my mouth. All I can do is grimace against the pain and let the magic run its course. The power consumes me, consumes everything around me, and all I can do is let this burn away.

Damn it.

When the surge finally fades, I fall to the ground—

exhausted, my chest heaving. I try to stand, but the most I can do is lean my weight on my elbows as I try to catch my breath. I briefly scan the world around me —the charred remnants of what were once trees. All that's left is black soot and rock. Holes have been burned into the white silk of my dress, and I hang my head in frustration.

This is just like when I first found my magic, back when I couldn't control this at all. I grit my teeth in anger, balling my hand into a fist as I try to figure out what I am. What I can do. What my limits even are.

And why everything *changed*.

The soft and gentle coo of my dragon deep within me soothes my soul, if only a little. She's here for me. She knows even as we're exploring this new life of ours, that everything will be okay. We'll handle this together, as a team.

There's a tug on my navel, a familiar reminder that my mate is near.

Jace.

With that gorgeous, half-cocked grin, he walks toward me from the darkness of what little forest remains after the surge. I sit up as he nears, ravenously scanning his body despite myself. His muscles pull against his shirt, his strong pecs clearly visible beneath the pale blue fabric.

The former dojo master grins as he sets his hands on his hips and looks down at me. "Are you trying to get us caught, or are you just showing off?"

Despite my exhaustion, I laugh. "Ass."

He chuckles and gives me a hand to help me up, and though I'm just fine and can do it on my own, I let him pull me to my feet.

"I'm just angry," I admit, looking out over the water, shaking out my hands as I try to suppress my fury. "I finally figured out how to control my magic, and now it's out of control again. All because I shifted."

"This is new territory for all of us," he says with a shrug. "You can't expect perfection of yourself when you don't even know what you can do."

"Fair point," I admit, crossing my arms, not really feeling it.

"Do you want to try again?" he asks.

I shake my head. I need a moment.

To catch my breath.

To calm my anger.

To figure out a plan, since what I'm doing obviously isn't working.

"That's fine," he says calmly, as if I haven't just destroyed an entire section of this little island we're hiding out on.

The two of us sit on the cliff, our legs dangling over the edge as we look out over the stormy water.

"How are Harper and Russell?" I ask, mostly to distract myself from my own irritation.

We haven't heard from them in two weeks, and I'm starting to get concerned. We've been moving from place to place, and they've been dealing with the political fallout of the battle.

Drafting soldiers.

Producing weapons.

Preparing for war.

"They're fine," Jace says coolly. "Busy. Harper's in Boss Mode, so everything else falls to the wayside when she's like this, including checking up on friends. She means well. You'll get used to it."

I smile. "She's kind of scary in Boss Mode."

"Yeah," Jace admits with a chuckle as he leans back on his palms. "But don't you dare tell her I said that."

With a laugh, I shake my head. "No promises. What about Russell? Are the prisoners from the battle cooperating?"

Jace wrinkles his nose in annoyance. "Not really. Most are passive but not saying anything. Only Brett is talking."

I shoot Jace a sidelong glance, wondering why he's being vague about this. "And what is the General's second in command saying? That seems *kind* of important, Jace."

The former dojo master frowns, hesitating for a moment as his gaze drifts over to me. "That he will tell us everything—but only if he talks to you first."

I scoff. "Like that's going to happen."

"Exactly. It's a bad idea, and I won't allow it."

I bristle at his audacity. He won't *allow*—and after everything we've been through, to think he would have the *nerve*—

I glare at him, ready to tear him a new asshole because I thought we were past this.

But he just winks.

Oh.

It was a joke.

Damn, I *am* tense, far more so than I realized.

I laugh, rubbing my temples. "You got me," I admit.

Jace chuckles. "I know you could take Brett. I'm not worried for you. But you do need to be careful." He gently grabs the back of my neck and possessively pulls me toward him as he kisses my forehead. "Brett's manipulative. We've seen signs of that in the interrogations. He's a clever guy who worked his way up to second in command for a reason, Rory. If you ever find yourself in the same room as him, just be careful."

"I know," I say. "We can't trust him."

"Come on," Jace prods, standing. "You're ready for a meditation. I want to try something. Let's test the depths of your power."

I roll my eyes. "You're so damn bossy, especially without a dojo to run."

"Insufferable," he agrees with a smirk as he helps me again to my feet. With his strong hands on my shoulders, he turns me toward the ocean as his deep, soothing voice rolls past me. "Close your eyes."

I indulge him, taking a calming breath as his touch sparks delight across my skin. My body leans impulsively toward him, and I let my back rest against his chest, leaning into him as his calming voice takes me inward.

"Don't question this," he says evenly, his tone calm and constant. "Dive inward, and let your dragon lead you. We don't need to access your magic. We don't even need to control it. We're just going to look."

Just looking.

Right.

In mere moments, I feel the limitless depths of my magic. It's like a pit, deep and unyielding, and I can feel my dragon with me.

Together, we dive into the abyss—into the depths of my power deep in my core.

And we fall.

All we're looking for is the bottom.

"Keep going," Jace's voice echoes in my ear, but it feels so distant.

I keep expecting the abyss to simply end, to hit the ground hard. Sometimes in these meditations, there's nothing but darkness and sensation; other times, there's imagery to experience, symbols to dissect and understand.

But here, right now, there's only my dragon and I, tumbling through the darkness.

We don't stop falling, and I'm beginning to think there's no bottom anywhere in sight. I keep preparing to hit the ground, to feel a limitation, to feel anything other than the endless dive.

But I don't.

It's a little overwhelming. There's no end to this. No end to my magic, not now that I've shifted. Not now that my dragon and I have each other.

The flickering worry of the unknown sparks more magic across my skin—it's an impulsive reaction, like a natural defense, and this time I feel something in my palm.

Impulsively, I shatter the meditation and open my eyes—only to find my fingers wrapped around a dagger made of white light. The magic in my hand sparks and fizzles, and it only takes a moment to recognize the design of the blade—a Spectre knife, but one somehow made out of my magic.

Despite the reminder of my past, I smile a little at the nostalgia—it was our safety blanket of sorts, and we were never supposed to be without one.

As I marvel at it, the dagger dissolves into the thin air and disappears as quickly as it came.

"Can thunderbirds do that?" I ask, looking at Jace as I lift my open palm in mild disbelief.

My mate stares at my fingers, his lips parted in shock, and it takes him a moment to shake away his surprise. Laughing, he runs a hand through his hair as his stormy gray eyes dart toward me. "That's just you, Rory."

There's a flicker of pride in discovering a new ability, but deep within that pride, I have to admit I feel isolated. No one knows what my magic can do or what I'm capable of. What my limits are—if I even have any.

The fighter in me loves that, of course. Limitless potential. Untamed power.

But there's so much we still don't know. It's daunting to realize I thought I'd mastered my abilities, when in fact I'd barely grazed the surface.

The gentle thud of footsteps captures my attention, and Jace and I turn just as Drew, Levi, and Tucker crash through the underbrush toward us. Each man frowns once he steps onto the charred cliff, a concerned and wary expression on each of their faces. The moment their eyes rest on me, however, all three relax.

"We saw a power fluctuation," Drew says, his brows knit in concern. "Are you okay?"

"Do we need to kill anybody?" Tucker adds, whipping out a handgun and cocking it.

I grin. Who am I kidding? I'm not isolated at all. I have a family that loves me, and that's everything I need.

And as for these new powers, I'm too damn stubborn *not* to figure it all out.

The question is simply where to *start.*

CHAPTER TWO

I take a deep breath as I lean back against Levi's chest, relaxing in the sun. The warm Florida light beams through the windows around and above us as we relax on a sofa in a southern manor's sunroom.

For the moment, I'm letting myself be at ease. Levi's chest rises and falls beneath my head, his strong arms wrapped around my body as he holds me in place on top of him, and I close my eyes. Right now, like this, all I can do is enjoy his powerful presence and the way he makes me feel so incredibly calm.

Tucker and Jace are on lookout, and it's my turn in a few hours. Drew's getting into trouble somewhere, I'm sure—spying on someone he shouldn't spy on, most likely—but I'm not about to stop him.

Like I even could.

The sad fact is we have to keep moving until we find Castle Ashgrave. Otherwise, we're sitting ducks. Without the protections of the dojo, we have targets on our backs—practically every dragon in the world wants a piece of me, and they'll use my men to get to me if I let them.

I won't, of course, but the risk is there.

Truth be told, I hate moving from safehouse to safehouse. It reminds me too much of my days as a Spectre. Of never feeling at home. Of not having a place to go back to. Of taking only what I can carry in a small backpack and nothing more.

Only the essentials.

After so long at the dojo, I'm spoiled. The thought of having a home base is more than alluring—it's almost necessary at this point. Required. Jumping from place to place just makes me feel like I'm not welcome in this world anymore, and that's not the life I choose to live.

Not now.

Not after everything we've been through.

My magic fluctuation the other day meant we had to leave that safehouse quickly, far sooner than we expected to. My magic is too distinct. Too easy to spot —and track. Anytime I have a fluctuation, we have to pack up and move instantly.

Fun times.

This new manor is in the middle of nowhere, deep in the Spanish oaks and moss-covered branches of the Florida panhandle, and no one even saw us arrive. We'll be gone in a week, and I'll do anything I can to keep my fluctuations at bay while we're here.

Absently, I pull my phone out of my pocket and stare at it. The dark screen calls to me, and I wonder if I should text Irena.

If her number is even still good.

After all, I haven't heard from her since I found out Eric—

I clear my throat. I can't even finish the thought as my mouth runs dry.

With a few taps of my thumb on the screen, I bring up her contact. My finger hovers over the call button, but I hesitate.

She's deep underground, networking and connecting among the Spectres, turning them against each other and doing everything she can to destroy them with their own technology. With their own intel. With everything Zurie foolishly gave her all those months ago.

I put the phone away and groan in frustration as I once more close my eyes and rest my head against Levi's chest.

"She's fine," Levi says, his deep voice growly and soothing. He kisses my hair. "Relax, Rory."

I chuckle. He knows me almost too well.

The thud of footsteps in the hallway catches my attention, and I recognize the gait.

Drew.

My fire dragon walks in, consumed by his phone, his thumb racing across the screen as he paces in front of us without saying a word. He doesn't even look up, but whatever he's doing makes him grimace and grumble to himself.

"Well, hello to you, too," I say sarcastically, grinning as I watch the Darrington heir continue to pace in front of me.

He doesn't seem to hear me. Instead, he rubs the stubble along his jaw, his brows furrowed with apprehension. "Damn it."

"What's wrong?" I ask, sitting up as I study his handsome face.

Without answering, he simply grabs the remote off the coffee table and turns on the TV, flipping through a few channels until he finds a national news station.

As the reporter leans forward, pressing his finger against his table, I see my picture in the top left screen.

My eyes go wide, and for a moment, I can't breathe.

"…and the truth has finally come out," the reporter finishes saying as we catch him in the middle of a sentence. "The world is buzzing with the recent release of new information regarding the famed dragon vessel. As I'm sure you're well aware, we humans have been kept in the dark about this important figure in dragon lore, and we have been hunting tirelessly for any information at all as to what her reappearance in this world means. We don't know who this girl is, why she's important to the dragons, or really anything about her past." He hesitates, a dangerous smirk spreading across his face as he stares into the camera. "Well, at least, we *didn't.* It seems the truth has come out at long last, and only here on Action News will you hear the report first."

He leans his elbow on his desk and lifts his chin, going silent as he waits for the report to start. In the brief silence that follows, a red headline flashes beneath him.

BREAKING: the truth about the dragon vessel.

My pulse thuds in my ear, and I realize I'm standing even though I don't remember getting up. I lean toward the television, consumed by the horror of what I'm watching.

I can't seem to get enough air in my lungs. Sweat

licks my palms, and my eyes go wide as I wait for whatever is about to happen.

This can't be real.

This has to be a nightmare.

With a quick flash, the screen shifts to some footage of trees as they sway in a gentle wind. The camera pans down as a news reporter with dark brown skin and a deep frown holds a microphone to his mouth.

"The reality of this situation is grim, folks," the newscaster says, shaking his head a little and really milking it as he gestures to the trees behind him. "I'm standing here on the outskirts of the Fairfax Dragon Embassy in Washington state—or, at least, what's left of it. Despite attempts from the Fairfax family to silence our report, we managed to capture satellite footage of a decimated embassy. It lies in ruins—the result of a war for the dragon vessel, a human girl we know next to nothing about."

He takes a few steps toward the camera, his smooth voice ensnaring me as he tells the world things he shouldn't know. "My sources tell me the dragon vessel is none other than a young woman named Rory Quinn."

"Sources?" I ask, my throat dry. "Who the hell—"

"He's exaggerating," Drew interrupts, frowning as

he stares daggers at the man. "I dug into his files, at least anything he stored digitally. As far as I can tell, he only had one viable source—someone I couldn't track down. They covered their tracks too well."

"Damn it," I mutter.

The reporter squares his shoulders as he stares into the camera. "Rory Quinn and her sister, Irena Quinn, are..." he pauses, trailing off, rolling his shoulders back as if what he's about to say is difficult. His jaw tenses slightly with fear, but he clears his throat and powers through. "The Quinn sisters are Spectres, and it would seem that they have enchanted and swayed powerful dragons to their cause, though no one is quite sure how."

"What the *fuck*," I say under my breath.

This can't be real.

This *cannot* be real.

The thought repeats in my head, but it doesn't stop any of this from happening.

It doesn't wake me up.

Because this *is* real, and I am so absolutely *screwed*.

A Spectre's greatest fear is to have her shadows taken away, and with that one, simple statement, mine are gone. I'm utterly exposed, and with Irena in the depths of the Spectre organization, trying so hard to dismantle it, she's just as vulnerable as me.

Maybe even more so.

"One of my sources put her life on the line to get us this information." The reporter pauses, taking a deep breath as if he's bracing himself for the worst, and I wonder who the hell "she" even is.

Harper would *never* tell anyone what I am, but she's the only woman alive who knows.

I frown, my mind racing with possibilities.

Could she have...

No. I square my shoulders, absolutely refusing to believe she would do this. I trust her.

But who else could *possibly*—

"You've seen this first on Action News," the news-caster says, interrupting my thoughts. "Here's the exposé, complete and uncut from none other than the girls' mother," he says.

"*What?*" Drew, me, and Levi say in unison, our voices dripping with disgust and confusion.

My mother is dead.

Zurie killed her when I was five and lied to me about it for most of my life.

So who the *hell*—

There's a brief pause, and I swear it goes on forever as they try to work the technical side to get the video running. But once the screen cuts to my so-called mother, I see only Zurie's face.

Zurie.

That *bitch.*

She sits at a kitchen table with her hands on the surface, her fingers daintily intertwined. Trees sway in the breeze through the window behind her, and the kitchen sink is barely visible in the corner. She wears a red and white patterned dress with a conservative, modest neckline, and her hair dangles behind her head in a simple ponytail.

Hell, she even put on makeup for this.

She milked it for everything it was worth, doing all she could to make herself look innocent—like an average American housewife.

And she *nailed* it.

So, this was her after-death contingency plan. Destroy us in the one way every Spectre fears—by exposing everything we are and every secret we have.

Shit.

"I don't know how to start this," Zurie says, her voice shaking a little as she really sells her trembling fear. "I haven't wanted to say anything because, well…" she trails off, looking away as her voice breaks. "They *are* my daughters, but the world deserves to know. *You* deserve to know the truth."

Zurie rubs her temples and takes a steadying breath. "Rory and Irena are loyal Spectres. They always have been. I love them and tried my best, but..." She trails off, shutting her eyes as if this has tortured her for her whole life. "But ultimately, I failed. I failed them as a mother, and I let them go down a dark path. I know I'll probably be killed for telling you this, but you deserve to know you are not safe as long as Rory Quinn is alive. Becoming the dragon vessel changed her. It made her angry. Cruel. Vindictive. I don't even recognize her anymore."

My former mentor's voice breaks as she squeezes her eyes shut in agony, and I hate how good of an actor she is. Anyone who doesn't know the truth will buy this.

Damn it.

"I don't know exactly what she wants," Zurie continues. "I only know that what I've seen is terrifying. I'll send over all the pictures I have with this video, since I know that I will probably not be able to expand upon any of this." She squares her shoulders, lifting her chin slightly in defiance, and if I didn't know her better, I would believe everything she was saying.

Zurie has always been an excellent liar.

"The Fairfax dragons know her association with the Spectres," Zurie continues. "And for whatever reason, they don't seem to care."

I frown, briefly wondering how Zurie could know that, but it's probably nothing more than a best guess. If nothing else, she's just weaving a more complicated lie—anything to screw over anyone associated with me at all.

"The Fairfax dragons obey both Rory and Irena," Zurie continues. "I don't know how or why, but that seems to be the case. These are my girls, and I wanted to think the best of them, but I have to face the truth. These two young women seduce men to do their bidding. They warp men's minds and bend them to their will. You cannot trust anything either of them say," Zurie adds, pleading, her eyes widening slightly as she looks deep into the camera.

"I wish I could kill her a second time," I mutter, my nails digging into my palms as white sparks dance through my fingers.

"All you have to do is look at the men she surrounds herself with," Zurie says, her voice a little breathless, as if she's scared to say all of this. "Drew Darrington is disgraced and disowned from his own family for his association with my daughter. She warped Jace Goodwin's mind and got the general of the Fairfax army excommunicated from his own dojo. Tucker Chase is an innocent human man, swept up in her charm, and there's no telling what other humans she's seduced to do her bidding."

I snort derisively, figuring she glossed over Tucker's connections to the Knights because it wouldn't make her report look very good.

"And Levi Sloane," Zurie continues, shaking her head slightly for effect. "He's the most terrifying of them all. A feral dragon who will rampage and murder at her command."

"I've never wanted to kill a dead person before this moment," Levi admits, gritting his teeth as he practically snarls at the television. "But I kind of wish I could dig up whatever's left of her just to destroy it."

"There's nothing left," I say darkly, wishing the same. "Just this video and a few piles of ash."

With every one of her lies, my rage burns brighter. I can feel my magic bubbling within me, pushing against me and trying to break free. White light flickers over my skin like the northern lights, but I'm consumed by the television and unable to pay much attention to anything else.

I'm too angry and furious from her lies.

"I accept my fate," she says calmly, staring at the floor as she leans back into the chair. "I know I won't be around once this goes public—hell, by the time you're watching this, I'm probably already dead." She pauses and looks up at the camera as another flicker of white magic burns through me, desperate to break free. "But it's worth it," she says simply.

And with her final words, just seconds before the camera cuts off, I see a little smirk at the corner of her mouth.

Her moment of victory from beyond the grave.

The moment she realized and knew without a doubt that she had absolutely screwed me over.

The television cuts back to the newscaster, and though I hear the murmur of his voice, I can't understand anything he's saying. Something about conmen and repercussions.

My magic sizzles in my soul, as if it's lighting me on fire from within. As the rage burns brighter, I know I won't be able to contain this much longer.

Furious, I charge outside. I don't even care where I'm going. I just need to burn off this energy. I vaguely feel Drew and Levi following, but I can't hear a thing they're saying. I can't hear their footsteps or see their faces.

All I can feel is rage.

All I can hear is my own pulse.

And all I can see is *red*.

I charge through the grass and southern trees as the humid air sticks to my skin. I have to find a safe spot to burn everything this time, to let my magic loose so that I don't hurt anyone or reveal where we are.

Because after this, the world is going to be after us.

Not just the dragons—*everyone.*

There's a flicker of pain in my chest as my dragon roars within me, asking to take over. In my blurred and hazy mind, I give in, and before I know it, I'm soaring through the air as we awkwardly take to the sky.

Thunder rumbles in my chest as I growl in hatred, wishing I could blow Zurie to bits all over again. It suddenly doesn't feel as satisfying to know she's dead because even from the grave, she might be able to kill me.

White sparks flit across my scales as I soar higher in the air, weaving through clouds and protected from view by a brewing storm. The longer I fly, the darker the clouds get. Rain mists across my skin, and before long, it becomes a pelting torrent. The deep rumble of a raging gale tumbles through the air, and a bolt of lightning cuts through the sky ahead of me.

I have to find Ashgrave.

We need a safe space, a spot where I know my men will be safe. Where Irena can stay between missions. Where no one can touch us.

My own little corner of the world, where no one else would dare venture.

Ashgrave.

The word just repeats in my head over and over as the anger, magic, and power swirl within me.

Ever stronger.

Ever more deadly.

The ringing in my ear becomes a pulse, and strangely it's not mine—or my dragon's.

My vision shifts, and though I can still see the storm clouds before me, I catch flickers of something else.

Another land. Another place. Another time.

As another bolt of lightning rips past me, I see a flash of snow. Of mountains.

Still fuming, still with my magic about to take over, desperate to break free and building, I don't fight this.

I give in.

I listen, trusting that my magic is here to guide me.

There's another flash of snow, and there—in the depths of a frosty mountain—I see the ruins of a castle.

A gate.

A stone pillar nearly lost to time and covered in snow, with a single open door in the middle.

The heartbeat is there, covered in frost and forgotten. The pulse is slow, but getting stronger. Weak, but willing to fight.

These snowy ruins feel like home, and my dragon instinctively knows what this is.

Ashgrave.

A vision, leading me home.

I wait for you, my master. The voice echoes in my mind, the words repeating over themselves so often that they blur together. I can't even tell if it's a man or a woman—or something else entirely.

I'm coming, I reply, wondering if Ashgrave can hear me.

With that, my magic takes over, and I don't hold back. I let it loose as thunder and lightning crash around me, my power masked by the storm.

I will find Ashgrave. I will make it mine.

And I pity the poor soul who tries to get in my way.

CHAPTER THREE

Naked and alone, I sit with my back to a tree deep in a forest far from the manor. This is a thick grove of ancient oaks covered in dangling Spanish moss. Cicadas buzz from the canopy, a constant hum of life that reminds me I'm not alone.

As the rough bark of the tree bites into the exposed skin on my back, I lean my head against the trunk. With one arm on my knee, I stare through gaps in the emerald green canopy at the stars far above.

I feel numb.

The flash of hot anger is long gone, but there's still a simmering rage that won't go away. It won't burn out, like I'm used to it doing. It won't fizzle into nothing like I expected, and it's painfully distracting.

Deep in my core, my dragon stirs as we both feel

Jace nearby. For the first time, we're both too angry to ache for him. We simply know he's there, and we're too irritated, too distracted to care. He's probably giving me space, and I wonder if he can feel my rage.

I want to go back to them all and brainstorm, but I need to calm down first. I can't make a decision or act out of fury, and I need to be able to think clearly.

But I've been out here for ages.

As the night wears on, I wonder when that will happen. When my head will finally clear. I stare at the dark sky through a gap in the trees above me, watching as the moon slowly creeps across the sky.

For hours, I don't move a muscle.

I simply sit.

And wait.

To *feel* again, anything besides the numbing rage. To *think* again, anything besides the same thought, over and over—I can't stop Zurie this time.

Because she's already dead.

There's no revenge, here. No way to get back at her. No way to slow her down.

A deep, soothing breath fills my lungs, and the first flicker of lucid thought returns. That's not entirely true—my greatest revenge against Zurie is to simply survive. To be everything she never wanted me to be. To thrive despite all the ways she set me up to fail.

To use her own weapons against her. If Zurie takes away my shadows, I'll step into the light—and I'll soar. No more hiding, not for me.

I have no idea what that means or what it would even look like, but in my vengeful anger, it feels right.

And, finally, to help Irena destroy the Spectres. Zurie's one legacy is being remembered as a truly terrifying Ghost, one of the greatest in history. If we can destroy the organization she ruled, there will be no one to remember her name.

Then, she will truly disappear.

Only then will she truly die.

My intuition flares, and I hastily study the shadows of the dark forest. Someone's nearby, and it's not Jace.

Effortlessly, I summon my magic into my hands, and this time it burns along my fingers like blue fire fueled by my anger. The cool blue light shines against my skin and casts a soft glow against the grass beneath me.

Well, *that's* new.

Even though there's someone in the shadows, I take a second to simply look at the blue fire flickering over my fingers. I wish I could control this—all this new power. I wish I knew what I was, or what this magic can do.

Movement in my periphery captures my attention,

and my eyes dart over toward a tall silhouette as it steps out from behind a tree.

The firelight dances across his face, illuminating handsome and familiar features as the shadow comes into view.

Levi.

I relax, and the fire dissolves with a hiss.

Wearing just a loose pair of shorts, he sits down next to me without saying anything. Together, we watch the sky in silence, his warm bicep brushing against mine as he silently lets me know he's here.

It's kind of nice to sit in silence. I'm not sure what I would say anyway.

I lose track of time as the clouds float by through the gaps in the trees, illuminated with a soft silver glow from the moon. I'm thankfully far from where my magic cut through the sky disguised as a storm, so hopefully no one even noticed my surge. Even if they did, we should be safe to sit a while.

For now.

"Ashgrave has to be our top focus," Levi says, his voice snapping me out of my daze. "We need to hide you for a bit, get you out of the limelight, but we can resume travel once we know where we're going."

He has a point. With no anonymity, the Bosses will

be after me more than ever. Some will come with a vengeance, thanks to their hatred for Spectres.

But I don't think he understands what just happened. Not really.

"No hiding," I say simply.

There's an odd silence, and now I can feel his gaze on my face. I don't look over. I think he's expecting me to explain myself, but I don't see the need.

He, however, seems to disagree.

"What the *hell* are you talking about?" he snaps.

I frown, tilting my head toward him as I study his face. His brows are knit with anger, and he watches me with an incredulous expression I've never seen on him before. His ice blue eyes are clear and focused, unwavering as he glares me down.

He's… *mad*.

It's such a strange thing to see on Levi. He's always so calm and collected, so poised and clear-headed. I don't think I've ever seen him angry with me.

I pause, thinking through what I'm about to say to make sure that I mean every word. "I never intended for the world to know everything about me," I admit. "Zurie's lies make everything worse, but the truth is exposed as well. There's nothing we can do about that."

"There's *plenty* we can do about that," Levi interjects.

"Not really. The damage is done." I shrug, the irritation slowly fading even as the numbing fury rages on. "The fact is the world knows about me now, and I won't hide from that. They've tried to kill me. Cage me. Control me. I'm just *done*, Levi." I pause as I look back into the sky. "I'm so fucking done. We'll find Ashgrave, but not because we're going to hide. Simply because it's home."

With an angry grunt, he jumps to his feet and paces the forest in front of me. He runs his hand through his hair, looking at the ground as he tries to find words to express his fury.

I wait. Levi speaks when he's ready to, and not a moment before.

"All I want is to protect you," he says, glaring at me. "Keep you close. Keep you safe. The world knows your secrets, and that's dangerous. That's *deadly*, Rory. You can't step into the public eye without repercussions, ones that could kill you."

"So, I'm just supposed to hide?" I counter, narrowing my eyes in defiance. "Run away?"

He stops mid-stride and studies me, his blue eyes narrowed and intense.

But he doesn't answer.

I stand, and strangely, I'm not in any way uncomfortable being stark naked in the middle of a forest, least of all in front of him. I figure this whole dragon thing is really starting to grow on me.

"I tried for ages to get the Bosses, Knights, and Spectres to just leave me alone," I say darkly, my voice tense. "It didn't work because it will never work. Levi, we're fighting. We're going to carve a place for ourselves in this world whether they like it or not. Ashgrave is that place, but I won't go there to hide from everybody. To run scared. No—I'll go there to get strong. No more hiding." I pause, watching his face as I wait for his reaction. "No more shadows."

With his shoulders squared, Levi looks intimidating in the dark night as shadows cast across his face. He glowers at me, and I see something shift in his eyes. There are cogs turning in his brain, ones I'm not following, and that concerns me a little bit.

"At least we can agree on one thing," he says calmly. "Ashgrave is more important than ever, and we're going to find it."

I nod, staring briefly at the ground as I recall my vision. "I think I may have seen it."

Levi's expression changes, and curiosity bleeds across his face as his brows tilt slightly upward. "What do you mean?"

"When I was flying through the storm earlier, I had a vision," I admit, crossing my arms as I stare into the dark forest around us. "I saw the ruins of a castle deep in a snowy mountain bank, and I heard Ashgrave speak to me." I pause, briefly grinding my teeth as I recall the memory in the hopes of finding some other clues. "It knows we're coming."

I expect Levi to say something, to ask questions or poke further, but he simply watches me. As the silence wears on, his eyes narrow ever so slightly. This is it—the moment something clicks into place for him.

As much as I love this man, whatever is going on right now is *not* good.

I wonder what plan he's concocting because those sharp, brilliant eyes have never been clearer. Usually, he shares his plans with me, and I'm a little concerned he's keeping this one to himself.

"We need to ask Drew if he has any locations matching that description," Levi says simply, looking back over my shoulder in the vague direction of the manor.

"On that, at least we can agree," I say with a tender smile.

His eyes dart toward me, and a small grin plays at the corner of his mouth. He sighs and pulls me close, wrapping his arms around my shoulders as he sets his palm against the back of my head. "Try to understand, Rory," he says calmly. Quietly. "You saved me, and it's imperative I do the same for you. I can't let anything happen to you, or my dragon and I will snap again. Both of us, instantly."

He and I are still tense from our argument, and even though I wrap my arms around his waist, I don't say anything for a while. The fact is I'll always be there for him.

I'll always love him. That will never change.

My magic, however, is evolving, morphing into something even more than I was before. That makes me more valuable to the people who are after us, but it'll also make my vengeance all the more devastating to anyone else who tries to tame me.

Because I won't just get justice. Not anymore. If someone comes after me or the people I love, I will *break* them—and burn away whatever is left until neither ash nor memory remains of them.

CHAPTER FOUR

As dawn breaks through the window in my bedroom at the southern manor, I tug on a shirt. The guys are all giving me space, and I'm grateful for the silence.

But the simmering rage within me just won't die.

I stretch out my back, the sensation of clothes against my skin unusually heightened. The cotton feels softer than it usually does, the jeans a little scratchier. A little rougher. The socks on my feet are like a cloud under my toes, and I'm not sure what to make of all these sensations.

In an attempt to distract myself, I shake out my hands.

One thing at a time.

My phone screen lights up from where it sits on

the bed, the comforter absorbing most of the quiet vibrations since I have the ringer off. I walk closer, scanning the unfamiliar number.

What fresh hell is *this* going to be?

I accept the call and press the phone to my ear, but I don't say anything. I simply wait, knowing whoever would have my number is willing to talk first.

"Well, the broadcast was certainly... *interesting*," Irena says, the line cracking briefly as she speaks.

My heart skips a beat, and I stand a little taller as gratitude floods through me.

Thank the gods, she's alive.

"Human governments will be after us now," Irena continues, her voice tense and focused. It's like she never left, as if we just talk every day. As if it hasn't been weeks since we spoke.

My grip on the phone tightens, and I have to be careful not to shatter it in my palm with my newly enhanced dragon strength. "Irena, are you—"

"Now that our former association with the Spectres is exposed, we're at risk," Irena interrupts, all business. "You're more in the public eye than me, so you need to be even more careful than usual. Human governments, private hitmen, and traffickers—they're all after you. I confirmed it this morning. As of the broadcast, you became one of the top targets in the world." She snorts derisively. "Even over the top-ten list of terrorists, Rory. It's honestly so stupid. How are you a greater threat than a *terrorist?*"

"Irena," I interject, my eye twitching slightly in annoyance.

"Of course, that doesn't change anything regarding the Bosses," she continues, plowing ahead as if I hadn't said a damn thing. "Half of them will want revenge, likely the Andusk and the Nabal—but possibly the Palarne as well. They've never been fond of Spectres, and their whole honor-bound thing might drive them to capture you for the good of all dragons or something moronic like that."

"Irena," I say again, my voice dangerously low. It's a warning—a tone she knows all too well.

One she actively ignores.

"The Darrington chatter has been minimal," she continues. "That means we're not listening to the right channels, and I really need to find them. Tell Drew to get me better access to—"

"Irena!" I snap.

"*What*, Rory?" she asks, plainly irritated as I interrupt her brain-dump of highly classified intel.

I pause for a moment to ensure she's actually listening. When she doesn't launch into another monologue, I take a deep and steadying breath.

"Are you okay?" I ask softly.

At first, she doesn't answer. In the long silence that follows, we both simply wait for the other to speak. She's hoping that I'll carry on with the conversation and take the silence as her answer.

I won't.

She's using the Spectres to escape from losing Eric. To escape from feeling. It's the Spectre way, but she's not a Spectre anymore. Suppressing her grief and pretending not to feel will only kill the dragon she probably has. If she's going to have any hope of embracing her new life and the new reality of what she most likely is, she has to face this.

Head on.

"No, Rory," she says quietly. "I'm not okay. I'm doing what I can with what I have, and I'm sorry I left."

I can't help myself. I grin, and even though it's just a small smile, it's nice to feel a bit of levity amongst all the craziness. "Did the great Irena Quinn just admit she was wrong?"

"I'm not wrong," she says with a little chuckle. "I'm just sorry I hurt you," she adds, her tone shifting.

My smile falls.

She sighs deeply, and I can imagine her rubbing her temples. "This is hard for me, Rory. Feelings have never been my thing, but I'm trying. Bringing down the organization that killed Eric is the closest thing to grieving I'm capable of right now." Her voice shakes, and even though I can't see her face, I can imagine how difficult that was for her to say. I can imagine the tears burning at the corners of her eyes, the ones she refuses to let loose. The ones she fights.

"That's fair," I admit.

"Look, Rory, this isn't all bad," Irena continues, clearing her throat. "The Spectre rebellion is happening. We're amassing. I'm finding more and more who want out, and this broadcast only *helped* me. They all knew who I was, before, but I'm notorious now."

I let out a small sigh of relief, grateful that there's at least some good in all this.

"For you, however…" Irena groans as she trails off. "This will be devastating for you if you're captured by *anyone.* You have to be careful, far more so than usual. Lie low. Hide out."

I grit my teeth at the familiar words, the same warning she gives me every time something goes wrong.

Lie low.

Hide out.

Wait for someone else to save the day—or do something so much worse that everyone forgets they want me.

It sounded so instinctive, like she didn't even think it through before she spoke.

"There aren't shadows for me to hide in anymore, Irena," I remind her.

There's an odd little choking sound, like she's at a loss for words. It's clear I caught her off guard. "I, uh—"

"I've got this," I say, not letting her continue. "*We've* got this. The five of us will be fine."

"About that," Irena says, her tone shifting, and I can tell she's grateful for the change in subject. "I've discovered something about the Knights, and it is *not* good."

"Is it ever?"

She chuckles. "Fair point. Look, Rory. They're planning joint terrorist attacks worldwide, and they're going to blame the dragons for everything that happens. Every death. The whole point is to spark anti-dragon sentiment, Rory. And…" Irena trails off as if whatever she's about to say is difficult to put into words.

"What?" I say, tense.

I'm pretty sure I don't want to hear what she's about to say.

"They're using this against you," Irena admits.

"They plan to paint you as a harbinger of a new dragon age, where humans will be slaves."

Oh, awesome.

I groan and rub my eyes. This could not get worse.

There's a muffled clatter on the other end of the line, and I impulsively tense at the familiar sound of a gun cocking.

"I've got to go," Irena says quickly. "Don't die, baby sister," she adds, and there's genuine love in her tone.

"Be safe," I reply, wondering who she's about to kill.

She hangs up, and the screen flashes in my periphery. I toss the phone on the bed, not bothering to save the number. She won't use it again.

For one, final moment, I let myself sit with the gravity of everything I've learned in the past twenty-four hours.

The Spectres. The Knights. The world, coming after me.

It sucks, yeah. But it's time to face this.

I open my bedroom door and head out into the living room, where I suspect my men are waiting—and, probably, already plotting as to what we should do next. As I take slow and silent steps down the hallway, the muffled chatter of the television floats toward me. The muffled chant of hundreds of people blend with the occasional jingle of a newscast starting. Through the chaos of overlapping conversation, I can hear the steady chant getting clearer.

"No more dragons!"

I round the corner to the living room to find my four men spread across the room. Drew and Levi stand, while Jace and Tucker sit in various sofa chairs spread across the large room. All of them are focused on the television.

Levi tilts his head toward me first, his icy blue gaze darting toward me impossibly fast before I can even step into the room. The other three seem to notice me shortly afterward, their heads slowly turning toward me as the enraged chant of anti-dragon protesters fills the otherwise silent air.

Each man looks at me with concern. Both Tucker and Jace open their mouths to speak, but I shake my head.

Lifting my hand to stop them, I shrug. "I'm fine."

They all know I'm lying, but thankfully, they let it go.

"It's time we stop these monsters!" a man shouts on the television, recapturing all of our attention. His face is red with anger as he practically screams into the microphone the reporter is holding in front of his face. "They run every government worldwide.

They own our lives. They keep us small. They keep us weak. They hold us back! They want us to be their slaves, and if we don't do something, that's exactly what's going to happen! You just wait, you idiots!"

"Thank you sir," the reporter says with an irritated tone, trying to take her microphone back.

"He's a Knight," Tucker says, crossing his arms as he nods at the television. "Head of propaganda, actually."

"Fantastic," I mutter, running a hand through my hair as a dull headache blisters through my brain.

It confirms what Irena told me—the Knights are planting dissent worldwide, stirring up trouble and doing everything they can to make the rest of the humans hate dragons as much as they do.

"We've got news from Irena." I cross my arms, squaring my shoulders and watching the television even as I speak.

"Oh?" Drew asks, quirking one eyebrow in curiosity. "Anything good?"

I laugh humorlessly. "Of course not, Drew."

Over the next few minutes, I catch them up on what Irena told me. As I share her discoveries on what the Knights are planning, Tucker goes still. His gaze darkens, and he's uncharacteristically quiet. He simply listens, his jaw tense and back straight as I share what I know.

"It's happening," he says with a groan, putting his hands on the back of his head as he jumps to his feet. "I was afraid they would do this. I was convinced— god, this blows."

"Yeah," I admit, nodding slightly as I set my hand on my hips. He mentioned this was a risk, but there wasn't much we could do about it at the time.

Hell, I'm not sure what we can do about it *now*, either.

"Rory, tell me more about your vision," Jace says from the armchair nearby, leaning his elbows on the armrests as he relaxes into the chair. His full focus and intense stormy gaze are trained on me.

I look briefly to Levi, who watches me with a stoic and dark expression that doesn't betray a hint of emotion.

I guess he told them.

"I don't remember much," I admit. "It's just flashes mostly. Snow-capped mountains. The ruins of a castle. A gate," I add, remembering the flicker of stone amongst the snow. "A door and a voice." I hesitate, a small smile playing at the edge of my mouth as I remember the feeling that burned deep within my chest at the thought of this place.

The feeling of being home.

"It called me, 'master,'" I add, tilting my head a little in confusion. "It *talked* to me. I think it's a lot more than just ruins and stone."

"That's fascinating," Jace says under his breath, his eyes glossing over slightly as he stares at me. I can see the cogs turning in his mind as he thinks deeply about everything I said, processing it all and piecing things together.

"I looked through all of the known possible locations for Ashgrave," Drew says, taking over as he walks toward me and hands me a few photos of a mountain range taken from above. "Everything I have. Every clue. Only one location checked out as matching your vision, but honestly I'd put that one at the bottom of the list."

"Why?" I ask, taking the photos.

"It's been thoroughly explored, at least the passable areas. Most of it is covered in a year-round blizzard, so much of the mountain range is inaccessible. There are rumors that it's a cursed and enchanted land, and that the unwelcome 'perish on its slopes,'" he says with a little eye roll. "So, naturally, people have been climbing the mountains like crazy for the last century. There's a multi-billion dollar tourism industry there."

"Sounds like a dead end," I admit in frustration as I sift through the photos.

Deep down, I'm hoping something in one of the pictures catches my eye. There's something about this place—something primal. Instinctive. It's not something to know, but rather simply to feel.

I think that's how my magic works, now—if I trust it, I'll know the truth.

As I scan photo after photo, nothing resonates. It's just another set of snowy mountains with white peaks that cut through the clouds. More snow. More mountains. A fog-strewn blizzard.

More dead ends.

With a deep sigh, I begin to pace and start to burn through the photos a little faster, cycling through them in the hopes that even just one stands out to me in some small way. "Maybe we should just—"

As my gaze hits one of the photos, I stop midstride and forget what I was saying. It's nothing extraordinary, and anyone else would have simply continued through the pile. But this picture speaks to me, somehow unique from the others.

This one feels oddly *familiar*.

Deep within me, my dragon flares with intuition and knowing. The slope on this mountain reminds me of something, like a childhood memory I'm trying to recall. There's a sense of nostalgia and safety, and I don't know why until I see a familiar outcropping of boulders in the corner.

I squint, tilting the photo as I narrow in on that section, and there—at the edge of the photo, and almost cut off completely—is the mountain from my vision. The cropping of snow. The hint of a gate hidden beneath the snowdrift.

It's just a clue, nothing concrete and most definitely nothing certain. But deep in my core, I know.

This is it.

This is Ashgrave.

We found it—or, at least, whatever is left.

CHAPTER FIVE

A howling gale tears past me as I stand in the snow at the base of a foggy mountain range in the middle of Nowhere, Russia. The roar of the wind screams past, chilling as it flings snow against my face, but I don't so much as bat an eye.

We're here.

Since it's hard for a diamond dragon to fly through the air unnoticed, we had to hire a series of small charter planes to get us out here. It physically hurt me to be in the sky and not flying, but we did what we had to do.

It makes me wonder why Harper takes helicopters all the time—she has gorgeous wings and a powerful body, yet she lets others fly for her.

It's strange, and I wonder if it's because, like me,

her dragon can't go anywhere unnoticed. There
haven't been too many dragons with lilac-colored
scales throughout history, and as far as I know, she's
the only one alive. She's as much of a moving target as
I am. Flying in a chopper is probably the closest thing
to anonymity she can find.

Hmm.

Truth be told, I hope that's not my future.

Now that we're here, I'm grateful the trip itself was
fairly uneventful—mostly wigs and disguises as we
took a convoluted collection of charter planes. All I
could think about was Ashgrave. All I could wonder
was if we would find anything in the misty peaks.

But now that I'm here, I can feel it.

I simply know.

Ashgrave is here—somewhere. We just have to dig
it out.

I close my eyes, feeling for it. Both my dragon and I
hear its pulse, a faint heartbeat that's almost entirely
gone. Deep down, I suspect we got here none too
soon.

I assumed I would be colder, given that we're on
snow-covered slopes and surrounded by frost that has
never melted. This is the deep sort of cold, the kind
that bites into your bones and never goes away, and I
figured that was the intention—to make life here

miserable. To scare off any who would dare venture too close. I suspected we would all be uncomfortable on this journey. Miserable, even.

But I feel completely at home, even in human form.

The blustery winds do nothing to me, and I haven't felt a single chill since we landed. Though I wear a heavy coat lined with fake fur to keep up appearances, I'm not overheating either.

It's strange. Like I've lost all sense of hot and cold.

The crunch of boots in the snow catches my attention, and seconds later, Tucker stands beside me with a pack on his shoulders as his gaze wanders over the mountains ahead of us.

"You ready, babe?" he asks.

I nod. "Are you going to be okay with Levi carrying you?"

He grins. "I'd rather you do it. A man carrying me through the mountains, even my best friend—" He feigns an exaggerated shudder. "It's emasculating, woman. Do you know what I put up with for you?"

I chuckle. "Yeah, well, I'd rather not accidentally slam into a cliff and kill you just because I'm such a noob flyer."

He laughs. "That's a fair point. I like not being dead."

I smile, briefly looking at his dashing face as my

weapons expert snares my heart. "I rather like that, too."

A low, rumbling growl catches on the wind, floating past from behind us, and I look over my shoulder as Levi stalks toward me. The ice dragon's footsteps don't make a sound, despite the deep snow around us. His blue eyes narrow as he watches the slopes, scanning every snowdrift and peak for danger, totally at home in the cold.

The growls and grumbles of two other dragons float by on the blistering wind, and I look over my shoulder as Jace shakes off a bit of snow that gathered on his forehead. He catches my eye and winks roguishly, all charm despite the clouds of breath rolling from his nose.

Drew snorts impatiently, the black smoke of his inner fire rolling through the air. The wind catches it, dispelling the dark smoke into the cold, white sky. Drew can barely hide the shivering. My poor fire dragon was not cut out for the snowy banks of an isolated mountain range, and though he towers over me in my human form, I pat his hard chest to soothe him.

The moment we touch, our connection opens, and the first thing I feel is the roar of grumpy annoyance that bleeds through our connection from him. He's irritable as hell, probably because he's so miserably cold. Or, possibly, because Tucker told all the pilots I'm his fiancée and that Jace, Levi, and Drew were our butlers.

Let's get this over with, Drew says through the connection. *I hate the cold.*

I nod and shake out my shoulders, choosing not to tell him it will probably be just as cold where we're going—if not colder.

He will be fine. He's just being a baby.

Yet again, I feel the soft pull of Ashgrave tugging on my heart, and this time I let it tempt me closer.

Tell me where you are, I ask it.

Jace growls, the low rumble from his chest almost soothing as the blustery wind whistles by. He quickly closes the gap between us and gently nuzzles my back. As his forehead brushes against my neck, I run my fingers along his face, opening the connection between us.

There's magic here, he says. But I can't tell where or what it is.

I feel it too, I tell him.

It feels familiar. His gaze wanders through the growing blizzard.

I frown with confusion. *It does?*

This is what it felt like when our mate-bond first

happened, he confesses. *I could feel you constantly, but I couldn't tell who you were, what you were doing, or where you even were.*

I smile as I look away, knowing he will be able to feel the flattered pang of butterflies that shoots through me in this moment.

Jace may not know what the magic is, but I'm sure he can guess.

It's Ashgrave. The power of the castle has seeped into the very rock of this mountain range, and it's everywhere. My guess is that's intentional, to confuse anyone who's not supposed to find it. But I can see through the façade.

As another gust cuts by, I close my eyes again and feel once more for the guiding pulse.

This time, it gives me a clear direction.

North.

As I connect with it, yet another vision flashes in front of me. My eyes snap open, and for a brief moment, I'm not on the rocky ledge eighty miles from the airport.

For that second—and that second alone—I stand at the gate to my new home.

I stand at the door that will lead me to Ashgrave, and I can feel exactly where it is. As the snow drifts past me, the wind quiet for just this second, the door glows faintly gold.

My head spins, and just as quickly as the vision hit, it's gone. I frown, my cheeks flushing slightly with nausea, and I tenderly hold my head as I reorient myself.

"Whoa, that was creepy," Tucker says.

I lower my hand and look at him to find him studying my face with a deeply concerned expression.

"Creepy?" I ask.

"Your eyes," he says, squinting as he studies me. "They went bright gold for a second."

"I had a vision," I confess. "I think I can lead us there. Get ready."

As Tucker jogs toward Levi, the other dragons step back to give me space to shift. I turn inward, giving my dragon control and bringing her forward. There are brief flickers of pain as she takes over. My clothes rip, the rags fluttering away on the wind as she takes control. I give in. I don't resist, and within seconds, I've shifted.

Same as in my human body, sensation is heightened for me now. The snow through my claws feels like powdery puffs of heaven. The wind along my scales feels like a song through my heart, and I shake out my body in impulsive joy.

A flurry of emotions burn through me, reminding me of all that's good in this world.

Love.

Home.

Belonging.

Family.

I growl happily as excitement and victory flood my chest, and I don't think I'll ever really get used to shifting. It's too fabulous. Too beautiful.

Too much fun.

My dragon is ready for this. Joy and adrenaline pump through me—through us—as she hungers for home. The snow does nothing. I feel as comfortable in the freezing tundra as Levi does, which is just odd to me. I thought I was some kind of thunderbird, but even Jace shivers a little here and there when he thinks I'm not watching.

It must be Ashgrave's magic. It's making me immune.

I beat my wings hard on the air, taking off as the strong wind cuts by. It's more powerful than I was expecting, and I waver a little as I try to balance on the cold drafts that take us skyward. I grimace and snarl as I fight the gusts cutting through the dozens of mountain peaks in the range, bending north as I follow the beacon that burns in my heart.

Lost in the white flurry of snow, passing mountain peaks that all look identical to each other, it's easy to lose track of time. At first, I count the minutes, tracing our route through the pass so that we can find our way home.

However, the world quickly blurs together, and it isn't long before I lose track of it all. Where we came from. How long we've been in the air.

All I know is where we're going.

I have no idea how the minutes—or, hell, maybe the hours—pass as we weave through the mountains. All I can do is follow the beacon.

Every now and then, I look back at Levi and Tucker. Levi shields the weapons master close to his body, protecting him from the storm as best he can while Tucker readjusts his hood and tries to brush the frost and snow from the furry lining. His cheeks are flushed red and frost covers his beard, but every time I catch his eye, he grins and flashes me a thumbs up.

He's miserable. He's just doing a really good job of hiding it.

As we bank around another mountain peak, the pulse becomes overpoweringly louder. I impulsively waver on the air, momentarily losing my balance as the beacon practically screams at me. The sensation is sudden and fierce, and with it comes another flash.

Another vision.

The gate, ever closer this time. My claws digging into the snow as the door glows gold, beckoning me closer.

A voice.

"I wait for you, Master."

As the vision clears, my head spins once again, and I teeter briefly on the wind.

Jace and Levi impulsively fly closer, hovering beneath me in case they need to snatch me out of the sky, but I recover in time. Small, glowing specks of golden light fall from my scales like dust as I shake my head, and I try to ignore it. There's too many new experiences lately for me to give each one my complete attention.

I have to stay focused.

Tell me where you are, I say into the void, hoping that Ashgrave can hear me.

It does.

Impulse and instinct take over, and I can't tell if this is my dragon or something else entirely. It's like a hand wrapping around my heart and tugging me closer, guiding me through the blizzard toward my goal.

My mind goes numb, and whatever this is takes over.

My dragon and I cut through the air like practiced

flyers, faster than I've flown before, and I can barely think. I can barely focus on anything at all except the drive to fly ever faster. To get there, and get there soon.

I duck and weave, tilting as I fly through tight gaps in the mountain and rock, the beacon leading the way.

My men are practiced flyers, far better than me, and they keep up. Through the tighter spaces, we have to file in a single line, but it never slows them down. It never stops them.

Like me, they want to see Ashgrave, and they'll do anything to get there.

The instinct leads me into a narrow passage that angles downward, toward a snowdrift covering a vast stretch of mountain slope ahead. The sun blazes through the heavy clouds, casting an eerie gray glow across everything. It's bright and blurry, overpowering and immense, but the instinct leads me into the fog. Razor-sharp outcroppings of rock whiz past, blipping into and out of existence in the blink of an eye, and with the guidance of the hand on my heart, I somehow avoid them all.

Below us, the rock opens up into a massive snow bank that disappears into the mist. The foggy blur of a blizzard clouds the air beyond it, thicker there than anywhere we've been thus far.

A flash of warning cuts through my soul, nearly stabbing me with the dread that something terrible is about to happen.

Bank upward.

It's a silent, breathless command, one rife with urgency and a hint of desperation.

I listen.

Roaring over my shoulder in warning, I obey the silent command and bank upward. The movement is sharp and almost violent, twisting me as I careen upward into the foggy sky. A flurry of snow cascades around me as the wind from my wings kicks it up.

Like the tightly knit pack of highly trained warriors they are, my men mirror my movement. They bolt after me, hot on my tail, their eyes narrowed in focus as they trust my intuitive hit.

Mere seconds later, spikes and snares go off along the entire snow bank. Traps four times larger than even Drew ignite along the mountain, their spikes like teeth as they all close in unison. Hundreds of traps go off in a second, triggered by something not even I saw. The sharp clatter of their metal snares closing on the empty air cuts through the mountain like a booming echo.

For a moment, all is still—and all we hear is the whistle of the blizzard as it nears. These traps are covered in elaborate carvings, riddled with ancient runes and symbols I've never seen. From this height, I can only make out loose detail—and I'm not about to get closer. The iron traps are coated in flakes of gold paint, all that remains of what was most certainly once a splendor to behold.

They would have impaled us. Easily. They were hidden so perfectly that no one saw them, not even Levi.

This was a trap designed to catch even the best.

A soft, distant thunder begins to roar through the mountain. Slowly, the snow at the peak of the mountain looming over the traps begins to shift, cracks tearing through the smooth white surface as an avalanche cascades across the slope. The rumble of thundering snow echoes around us, setting off other, smaller avalanches in the nearby slopes below. As the avalanche nears the traps, however, the snares slowly open once again.

They're—they're resetting.

Waiting for their next prey.

As the traps fully open and flatten along the ground, the avalanche rolls across the flecked iron. Within seconds, the slope is peaceful and serene once again, totally immaculate and utterly silent.

High above, I pause, flapping only hard enough to

hover in the air as I look at Jace, Drew, and Levi. They each watch me cautiously. Warily.

They know how close to death we just were. To die out here—forgotten in the cold—that's not how I plan to go.

Black smoke pummels out of Drew's nose as he snarls down at the traps below us. These mountains are more dangerous than we thought they'd be.

In Levi's claws, Tucker shivers, his cold breath visible on the air.

That little reminder of Tucker's humanness snaps me out of my daze. We need to get to Ashgrave as soon as possible and build him a fire before he freezes.

With a deep breath, I fly onward, leading us once more into the fog. We continue more tensely than before, waiting to see what other ways these mountains might try to kill us.

It makes me wonder, truth be told.

It makes me wonder if Ashgrave even wants me to find it—or if, like everyone else, it just wants me dead.

CHAPTER SIX

The snow is brutal as we cut through the mountains, the fog so thick we can barely see. Gales tear past us, throwing us all off balance as we struggle to stay airborne. With the blizzard this thick, I can't tell how far from the ground we even are—everything is merely various shades of murky gray, and in the surreal silver void of these oppressive clouds, it almost feels like we've flown into another dimension altogether.

But I don't *need* to see where we're going. Ashgrave's pulse leads me through the blizzard, and that little voice is all I can hear.

Every gust shakes us, and after a while, even Levi wobbles on the rough air. My muscles scream for a rest. Every fiber of my body is tense, flexed and furiously trying to keep me upright.

The angry drafts cutting by me test my limits, daring me to take it easy for even a second. I grit my teeth, my dragon and I fighting to stay airborne—to stay in control as the powerful gusts tear around us. Each blast of icy wind threatens to snare us, to knock us from the sky and send us careening deep into the cliffs and chasms below.

But we're fighters. We don't stop, and we don't give in.

The thing that unnerves me the most about these mountains is that they seem to go on forever, and though the beacon guides me forward, I don't feel like we're getting any closer. It's a strange sensation, one I don't completely understand. Still, I push through the unease, fighting the doubt, led only by instinct and intuition and knowing.

The castle is here.

It *has* to be.

Through the blizzard that gets stronger with every passing minute, there's not much to see. More than anything, the only glimpse of the world beyond the blizzard is the occasional hazy shadow of a mountain as we pass by. Every now and then, the shadowy silhouette of a cliff blocks out what little light bleeds through the fog.

Other than that, all we can see is the gloomy haze of the blizzard.

The white.

The grey.

The nothingness.

It torments me to think how long this has gone on. How long we've already flown, and yet the beacon seems ever farther away. I'm almost grateful I can't grasp the sense of time that passes.

We push onward, and every time I look over my shoulder to check on Tucker and Drew, they look a little worse for wear.

My heart pangs with cold dread, far more chilling than the snow, and I know we can't do this for much longer.

As my wings cut through the low-hanging clouds, an odd blue light pops into life below us. It flickers and shimmers, dancing like an oasis of joy and reprieve in the vast nothingness of the snow.

It's beautiful, I'll admit—tantalizing, even. Tempting. My first impulse is to fly down and check on it, to see what could be giving off such a brilliant light. The way the light glows, there's a promise of delight awaiting me if I visit it. Of peace. Of otherworldly enchantment—the sort of thing that comes along once in a lifetime.

The sort of thing only a fool would miss.

It's the sort of glimmer that holds the promise of secrets and untold magic.

As I watch it shimmer far below, the little blue light slowly wanders away. It's sluggish and steady, like it's completely unfazed by the icy gale around us.

But the path it takes trails away from the beacon.

Wherever the little blue light is going, it's not the direction we need. As tempting as it is to fly down and check on what it could be, I force myself to look away.

I force myself to soar forward.

With Drew and Tucker already pushing their limits, we can't indulge anything other than our primary focus—following the beacon and finding Ashgrave. If that light really lives in these mountains— if it's something I truly need to find—I will encounter it again.

But I absolutely *must* find Ashgrave first.

There's a voice on the wind, and for a minute, I can't recognize it or make out what it's saying. I strain to hear it over the whistle of the gusts around us. Bit by bit, I hear familiar tones and words through the gale, and it takes a moment to finally recognize who's speaking.

It's… it's *Tucker.*

My heart skips a beat with worry, and I slow down, looking over my shoulder to see what's wrong.

He points at the blue light, his eyes wide and frantic, and he's shouting at me. Through the powerful gale, I can't hear much.

"…follow it…" His words float by me on the wind. "…have to go…"

I shake my head, hoping he understands it's not going in the right direction—but it's in that moment that I notice there's something wrong with his eyes.

They're foggy, like the blizzard around us. The crisp, clear green has faded to a muddy gray, almost, and I barely recognize him.

Tucker strains against Levi's claws, grappling with the sharp talons. He wrestles against the dragon who's keeping him from falling to his death. I snap at him in frustration, my jaws clomping against the wind as I wonder what the *hell* he's doing.

It looks almost like he's trying to break free—but he would fall to his death, and that would be suicide.

And yet, as I watch him struggle, it dawns on me that is *exactly* what he's doing.

As he struggles, his eyes gloss over even more, becoming almost white. Before long, he ignores me completely, and all he can do is stare down at the little blue light.

I growl, snarling at him in an effort to get him to snap out of it, but he doesn't notice. Blips of dark red blood drip down his fingers as he cuts himself on Levi's sharp talons.

At this point, Drew and Jace swoop beside me, barely more than silhouettes in the heavy blizzard despite how close they are. They watch Tucker with the same bafflement I feel, and none of us are quite sure what to do—or what the hell is even going on.

We can't afford to stop. Not now.

Levi growls, a low and frustrated rumble in his throat as he stares down at the dazed human in his claws. None of us can figure out what the hell he's doing, and my ice dragon tilts his head toward me in concern.

As the wind howls past us, shrill and loud, Levi's deep blue eyes sweep over the ground below us—it's such a subtle movement, one he's practiced a million times. He's checking for danger, like he always does.

I missed it with Tucker, but this time, I see it—the moment the little blue light enchants Levi.

It's instantaneous. One second, his eyes are crisp

and focused; the next, they glaze over like he's not there anymore. It's like he's nothing but an empty shell of a dragon. Like his soul left, and something else entirely is now in control.

Before I can so much as breathe, he darts toward the light with Tucker still tightly clamped in his talons.

Shit.

This absolutely must be an enchantment of some sort, and it has both Tucker and Levi ensnared.

In that heart-stopping moment of icy dread, the very real fear that I'm about to lose two of the men I love most in this world floods through me.

Instinct takes over.

I roar at Jace and Drew for help and dive, doing the best that I can with what little I know of flying to catch up with the master of stealth that is Levi. He's so damn fast, and if it weren't for the raging worry in my chest, I don't think I would stand even a chance against him.

But my love for them fuels me faster than I've ever flown before.

I have to save them.

As he dives, so do I. I mirror his movements, pushing myself further than I have before. I pin my wings tightly against my body as I angle the tip of my nose toward him, hoping I can catch him before whatever this is gets so much worse.

Because it's inevitable.

I just know it.

Something tells me that if he reaches that light, I'll lose both him *and* Tucker.

As Levi plummets, he's always just out of reach. I slowly catch up to him as we careen through the icy sky, his tail passing briefly in front of my face. I'm so tempted to chomp on it, to bite him in the hopes that a quick burst of pain might snap him from this daze. Against my better judgment, I try it—but my jaws clomp against nothing but the air with every bite.

The light's getting closer.

We're almost out of time.

With no other plan and no idea of how to stop this, I dig deep into my soul. The frustration burns in me like fire. The worry. The doubt. The dread. It all surges within me, taking over and begging for release.

So I release it.

And I *roar*.

My dragon's powerful scream echoes through the mountains, far louder than it should be, the shrill sound a demand for him to stop. To listen. The sound carries weight with it—a ferocity that digs deep into my bones and demands obedience.

With a roar like that, there is no disagreement.

To my utter relief, it works.

He slows almost instantly, and we nearly crash into each other. Running on mostly instinct, I twist at the last minute and roll around him, my wings brushing his as I hover just below him. The movement felt so graceful—so natural—that I almost feel as though my dragon simply took over for a second.

Thanks, I tell her.

After all, I truly like not falling to my death. I suspect she's none too fond of that, either.

With my body between Levi and the little blue light, I can finally look him in the eye again. He shakes his head violently, snarling as if he's trying to cast something out of his mind. His eyes dip in and out of focus as he stares at me, and he looks utterly dazed. The expression reminds me of someone who just hit his head against a rock, even though he and I have simply been flying through the air.

That must have been one hell of an enchantment. My poor ice dragon almost looks hungover.

Levi watches me with confusion, his eyes a little wounded and very much concerned, and it's clear he has no idea what just happened.

In his claws, Tucker shivers violently. Frost clings to his beard, and his skin is quickly losing its color.

Damn it all.

If I ever find those little blue lights, I'm going to *destroy* them.

As the gusts tear around us, I can't pause long enough to touch him and open a connection. I want to understand this—I want to dissect everything that just happened so that it *never* happens again—but we can't. Instead, I try to lead him back up to the air, away from the light. Away from whatever it is that just tried to snare him.

He looks over my shoulder, and his eyes gloss instantly over.

Shit. Not *again*.

I snap impatiently at the air in front of his face, my jaws clamping shut with an audible clomp. A huff of hot air blows through my nose and over his face, white sparks crackling on my breath.

It works.

He shakes his head again, growling in frustration as he tries to figure out what's going on, but I already know.

Those little blue lights must be wisps of some kind, little enchantments designed to misdirect and mislead, to ensnare and take over. I've heard of the myths, the little blue lights that lead you to your death in a swamp, or through a dark wood. All my life, I figured they were nothing more than a scary story or a moral to stay focused on your goal, but apparently, they're real—and they're far more deadly than I ever thought.

Two silhouettes appear in the mist above us as Jace and Drew fly closer. Jace lets out an audible sigh, and Drew snarls with anticipation, like he's wondering who he has to kill—who would dare try to harm his woman or his brothers.

Both of them watch us with concern, but we can't stop to talk about this.

We have to fly.

Now.

I beat my wings against the air, lifting myself once again into the sky as I listen in my heart for the beacon, and Jace briefly looks down at the blue light.

His eyes begin to gloss over, same as Levi's did.

Damn it all.

I snarl, frustrated. We can't keep fighting this. I need them to stay focused, but it seems like I'm the only one who's not ensnared by the little blue lights. I'm the only one immune to their enchantments, and if this keeps up, I'm going to lose them all.

At a bit of a loss as to what we can do about this, I look down to find a half dozen more. Each wisp wanders in a different direction. Through gaps in the blizzard, I see one leading the way down along the edge of a cliff, down into a dark abyss with spikes steep at the bottom. Another shivers beside a wall, and at the speed Levi was flying, crashing into the rock would have killed him instantly.

These little blue bastards are trying to kill my men.

The fury and rage build in my chest, stronger even than I can manage or contain. I don't know what to do, and I'm not used to that. I'm not used to the not knowing. To feeling out of control.

The unknown only makes me angrier.

I snarl into the sky, magic brewing in my chest. It bleeds into my mouth, crackling and overwhelming as it threatens to escape. In the past, I would have tried to rein this in.

This time, however, I don't hold it back.

I roar into the sky, into the mountain, furious and angry as hell. Even though I can't speak to them, I let every wisp out there know exactly what I think of it. *Exactly* what I want it to do.

Go to *hell*.

The clouds around me swirl harder, the wind more fierce than before. Lightning crashes through the blizzard as storm clouds brew above me.

The whole mountain range feels my fury, and the slopes tremble beneath my voice.

Deep below, the blue lights shiver under my roar,

freezing with fear. My breath lasts longer than it should, and as I pour my rage into the sky, they shatter —one by one.

When the last one dies, my roar fades. The fire in my chest still burns, and my roar echoes through the mountains even as I suck in deep breaths of icy air.

I snarl, white sparks shooting across my scales as I dare another of those damned blue lights to reappear. Scanning the mountains, I look for other wisps—for any foolish enough to ignore my warning—but they're gone.

For now.

Despite my still-bubbling rage, I give myself the moment to enjoy my victory—in this new dragonish life of mine, my mere voice can scare off dark magic.

I won't lie. That's pretty damn cool.

However, I have no idea why the wisps left or if they'll stay away, and we don't have time to figure any of that out right now. We need to get to Ashgrave soon, or we're all going to die. This mountain range is a deadly place.

It makes me question what other magic is here. If this is Ashgrave's defenses, or if perhaps another thread of the gods' magic survived in this frozen wasteland and wants its competition—*me*—dead.

Deep in my chest, the beacon flashes stronger than ever.

Finally. I can tell we're close.

Whatever its motivations, the castle wants me to find it.

And I *plan* to.

CHAPTER SEVEN

After a tense scan of the blizzard around us, I check on my men.

With the wisps finally gone, they all grit their teeth through the raging tempest of snow and fog. Jace, Drew, and Levi hover nearby, ready to carry on, with their full focus on me.

But Tucker's skin is almost blue. His eyes drift shut even as he fights to stay awake, and he shivers in the icy gale. Frost coats the entirety of his coat, right down to his beard and the tip of his nose.

We have to get him out of the sky.

I snarl, trying to fight the cold dread that sinks into my veins. With no time to lose, I once again lead the way through the storm.

We're so close, and the closer I get, the more overpowering the call is for me to come. Every wing beat, every thump of the distant pulse—it beckons me, nearly taking me over.

At this point, I couldn't ignore it if I wanted to.

So close.

We tear through the sky, weaving around mountain peaks faster than ever as the countdown approaches zero.

No time to waste.

Another gust blasts us from below, tearing past with chilly ferocity and such a biting cold that even I feel it this time.

Any second now.

I can feel it.

As we round another mountain peak, I see a familiar snowy bank down below. The rocky outcrop. The sharp cliff face on the far edge of the bank.

It's all there. Everything from my vision.

I angle toward it, dropping abruptly in altitude to land. My claws dig into the snow, kicking up a flurry of white powder as I awkwardly land, and I scan the world around us for any signs of Ashgrave.

For the gate. For the tower. For the ruins.

For anything at all from my vision besides the rock and snow.

But there's nothing.

No glowing. No voice.

Just the biting cold of the wind.

Jace snarls as he lands, pacing as he examines the foggy white world around us. Blue sparks dance over his skin as he no doubt tries to figure out what we did wrong.

Drew steams with annoyance, his inner fire burning brighter than ever as black coils of smoke spiral from his nose. A deep and growly rumble in his chest echoes through the mountains, and part of me is worried he will set off another avalanche if he doesn't stop.

Once they land, Levi gently releases Tucker. My weapons expert falls to his knees as the wind ruffles the lining of his hood. Levi stands guard, trying to block as much of the wind as he can, to protect his best friend, even as Tucker's teeth chatter.

"M-maybe your roar scared t-the door away," Tucker snarks, stuttering a little as he shivers. He's trying to downplay how close to death he is, but I don't laugh.

I can't. I'm too focused.

Because he's wrong. Ashgrave is here.

I can feel it.

A soft and curious growl rumbles in my throat, and I once more scan the far cliff. Instinct tells me to shift, and since intuition alone got us this far, I listen. My dragon surrenders control as I return to my human form, teetering slightly as I fall to my hands and knees.

After so long as a dragon, I have no clothes at all, but I can't bring myself to care. I feel utterly ensnared by the magic of Ashgrave. By how close it is.

I push myself to my feet and stand in the snow, stark-naked as my hair dances in the wind. The blizzard pelts against me, but it feels almost soothing. Soft. Gentle.

Like a caress.

That seems to catch the others off-guard, and my men watch me curiously. In my periphery, I notice Tucker's eyes drift over my body. It's comforting to know that even in the miserably biting cold and so close to death, he's still his normal horn-dog self.

In my chest, the beacon pulses louder, practically screaming at me that it's near.

Led by something strangely *other*—something I don't entirely understand—I walk toward the snow-covered cliff at the edge of the snow bank. The rock rises above me, jutting from the ground.

It's like I'm trapped in a dream, listening to directions from a voice I can't hear, merely moving through the motions of something significant without understanding any of them.

Tenderly, I brush aside some of the white powder clinging to the cliff to reveal the rock beneath.

In my vision, the door was hidden here. It was cloaked somewhere in the rock under the eons of snow piled above it.

All we have to do is find it.

At first, there's nothing but grey stone. As I continue to brush aside the snow, I start to wonder if I'm wrong. If there really is nothing here. If that voice was just a misdirection to lead us to our deaths.

So far, given our experience in this mountain range, that seems like an Ashgrave-ish thing to do.

But then I see it.

And I smirk in triumph.

One little symbol, carved deep into the stone—an intricate weaving of circles that look something like a flower.

As I continue to brush away the snow, more urgently this time, I see more. Carvings. Etchings. Lines. Everything I saw in my vision—and *more*.

My fingertip brushes along one of the symbols, and it glows gold beneath my skin. That simple, soft motion sets off a flurry of light that traces across the stone, melting away the snow to reveal an intricate tangle of magical light and symbols I don't recognize.

There's a gentle hum, just a quiet rumble, nothing

much at all. A sharp pop follows the strange thunder, and a tall rectangle in the vague shape of a door appears within the symbols.

My breath catches in my throat as I recognize the door from my vision.

The gate.

The only problem is there are no hinges. Nothing at all that could allow the door to swing open for us.

I frown, setting my palms against the rock as I study the unfamiliar symbols for clues. As I watch, however, the stone shifts and changes. Within moments, a door appears where there was nothing but mountain and golden light before, and it creaks open on hinges I can't even see. It's sluggish, like there's not much energy left to open it, but the entrance invites me inward.

And there, deep in my chest, I feel the surge of knowing.

I found my home.

I found Ashgrave.

And now, the moment of truth—finding out if it truly wants me here, or if following my intuition will ultimately kill me.

CHAPTER EIGHT

As the door stands open before me where there was nothing but a rocky cliff before, the blizzard slows to almost a whisper. It's as if reaching Ashgrave tamed the gale.

Snow drifts gently around me, now, sticking to my hair and eyelashes as I peek into the dark stairwell that cuts deep into the mountain. It angles downward, deep into the abyss and seemingly endless as it winds into the mountain. The steps disappear into the shadows.

The sun slowly peeks through the dispersing fog, casting a thin trail of cold light into the stairwell. My shadow stretches across the first dozen steps, but nothing is visible beyond that.

If we go down there, I have no idea what we'll find, and the thought sets my nerves on fire.

A quick gust of wind blows past me, and I glance over my shoulder as Drew kneels in the snow in his human form. The edges of his body still shimmer slightly from his shift, and he squares his shoulders as he stands—delightfully naked.

It takes everything in me to fight the urge to let my eyes trail downward to his gorgeous cock.

"Stay here," Drew demands, his intense gaze trained on the open door. With a few powerful strides, he walks around me as he heads toward the doorframe. "I'll check it out and let you all know if it's safe."

As he nears the open door, the air around me shifts. It's sudden and violent, almost heavy, like the threat of an incoming bullet.

I throw my arm out to stop him, my hand hitting his chest just before his foot can touch the first step.

He hesitates, lifting one eyebrow curiously as he turns his attention toward me.

Down below, deep in the darkness, something stirs. Just a glint in the low light, but movement all the same.

Everything in my body says that if any of my men go down there, they'll die. That I won't be able to save them. That even with all of my magic, I won't be able to stop whatever comes for us.

After all, this is the heart of Ashgrave—the home of the gods' power. As we've already seen, this enchanted place is protected by dangers and terrors we can only dream of.

Only I can go.

"You all need to stay here," I say, casting my gaze across all of them, pausing as I meet each man's eye. I need them to understand how serious this is. That I mean it.

Suffice to say, they're not fond of my decision.

Almost in unison, they frown and glare at me. Drew and Tucker talk over each other as they disagree, and even Levi growls in frustration.

Drew snorts impatiently. "Absolutely not—"

"Are you crazy?" Tucker adds, his teeth still chattering. It comes out more like, *"Ahr ooh gravy,"* but I know what he's trying to say.

I need to get that man some shelter and a fireplace, and *soon*.

The air around me buzzes with magic as Jace and Levi shift into their human forms to join the conversation. Well, *argument* is probably a more accurate term, but I'm not budging on this.

I won't let these men die. Not for me. Not at all.

"You're not going." Levi's form shimmers as he finishes his shift, standing tall as he stares at me in defiance. His intense blue eyes narrow as he dares me to disagree.

I frown, entirely unhappy with this new evolution in his protectiveness. Zurie's broadcast changed him, but we don't have time to discuss it right now.

The men continue to yell over each other. Of the four of them, only Jace watches me quietly. The former dojo master is tense and still, his mouth a grim line as he studies my face. Arms crossed, he looks me over, as if he's reading my thoughts and piecing something together.

He understands.

"Shut up, all of you!" Jace snaps.

Tucker, Levi, and Drew pause in their ranting to glare at the thunderbird, but Jace just watches me in silence once again. It's a silent shift of power as he gives me control of the conversation, and I appreciate the assist.

I give him a subtle nod in thanks before I turn my attention toward the others. "This place is going to kill you if you try to go in. *Especially* if you try to go in without me."

"It's just as dangerous for you," Levi snaps.

"It's not," I correct, frowning. "I'm the only one

who was immune to the wisps, remember? I think this place is trying to protect me, even from you. I believe it thinks you're intruders."

That's my theory, anyway. Only time will tell if it's true.

For a moment, no one speaks, and the only sound is the howling whistle of the wind as it carries flurries of snow past us. The chatter of Tucker's teeth catches my attention, and my throat tightens as I watch the color slowly drain from his face. He can't handle this cold any longer.

"Drew, keep Tucker warm," I order, knowing the fire dragon still has some smoke left.

With that, I turn my back on them, square my shoulders, and head for the stairwell.

Wordlessly, Drew grabs my arm. His grip is strong and tight, and his powerful fingers curl around my bicep, stopping me in my tracks. With a gentle tug, he twists me around to face him.

I stiffen impulsively, all but daring him to try to stop me. Eyes trained on him, I stare him down, silently demanding he let go.

For a moment, the two of us simply watch each other. Even if I tried to break free of his grip, I couldn't.

Not Drew. He's too damn strong.

His eyes dart between mine like he's looking for something, and in the screeching whistle of the wind, I can't help but wonder what he's searching for.

After a moment, he simply smirks, and his grip on my bicep loosens.

"What was that?" I ask, admittedly confused as he lets me go.

He shakes his head, chuckling to himself. "I'll tell you later."

I want to press this, to figure out what the hell he's getting at, but just one more glance at a shivering, miserable Tucker urges me forward.

Ready for anything, I hesitate at the top of the stairs, looking down into the darkness. The Spectre in me screams at all the unknowns, all the ways this could go south quick—but my dragon urges me forward.

I may be at a loss for what to do, but my dragon knows there are answers down there. This is a place of secrets, with infinite long-buried truths just waiting to be unearthed. Ashgrave can give me everything I've been hunting for since all of this began, and if we're going to make it, I have to trust her.

In this life, before Tucker, before my men, I was never one to trust. But this is a new world, and my dragon and I need each other.

I set my foot on the first step, half-expecting a volley of booby traps to go off with the simple shift in my weight.

Nothing happens.

More for my peace of mind than anything else, I summon my magic into my hands. The white sparks shimmy along my skin, and delicate ribbons of light snake up and down my arms.

I have no idea if my magic will work on whatever is down here, but I do know one thing for certain.

This is *not* where I die.

With each step, I'm carried deeper into the shadows, into the abyss carved deep into the mountain. The impatient part of me wants to charge down the steps, to do whatever it takes to make sure this is safe so that I can go back and get Tucker. He's so close to frostbite. To death. Knowing how near he is to becoming a frozen corpse terrifies me, but I grit my teeth and force myself to take steady steps instead.

Rushing won't do anyone any favors, and that's how deadly mistakes happen.

Zurie screwed me over, but she did one thing right —she taught me that I cannot fail, and I won't. I refuse to make mistakes, especially not when my men's lives are on the line.

As my bare foot rests against the next step, the

sconce above me flares to life. I jump, reflexively lifting my hands as I prepare to blow something to smithereens, but I manage to pause and contain the magic as familiar blue fire crackles in the sconce above me. It casts a soft glow across the stairwell, illuminating the next dozen steps, and I wonder what set that off.

It sure wasn't me. At least—I didn't do it on purpose.

I can feel my dragon pushing at me, urging me downward, willing me to go faster. Yet again, I listen.

Because I trust her.

My shoulders tense, ribbons of pain shooting down my spine as I flex the fingers on my left hand to relieve some of the apprehension. My foot brushes against another cool stone step, and I scan the walls, waiting for something to spring to life as the next sconce flares into existence.

This sconce casts a blue glow across the far wall. I pause, surveying the world around me, looking for dangers as I was always trained to do.

To my dismay, I find some.

There, embedded deep in the stone, are tiny holes —each just large enough for an arrow. Four dozen of the holes cluster close together, and I freeze.

A trap.

I grimace, wondering what to do—if I'll set it off, or if I'm immune. I figure Ashgrave thinks my men are intruders, but given how dangerous the trip has been thus far, I can't be sure I'm entirely safe.

The arrow holes are so subtle that most people wouldn't even notice them. Most people wouldn't even know what had hit them until they were pinned against the wall, dying.

The holes cover the stairwell from floor to ceiling, creating an impenetrable line, something no one can avoid.

Not even me.

No one is getting past this trap unless the castle allows it.

I square my shoulders, sucking in a deep breath and reaching for my dragon. All of my training screams that I should find another way in, but she urges me onward.

Through the trap.

I close my eyes and frown, almost not quite believing what I'm about to do. A Spectre—even a former one—simply walking into a trap.

It's unheard of.

I set my foot tenderly on the next step and let out a slow breath as I expect the volley to sail through the air. I listen for the whistle of air over a feather, for the sound of metal screaming toward me.

But there's only silence.

I peek through one eye to find myself staring at the wall of arrow holes. In the low blue light, I can see the glint of the deadly metal on the other side, cocked and waiting to kill.

It has simply chosen to not kill *me*.

I take a shaky breath and continue into the darkness, the air still and eerily quiet.

Time seems to move differently down here. Just as with the blizzard, there's very little sense of the minutes or hours that go by. All I can think of is Tucker's shivering body, the clatter of his teeth as he tried so hard not to show his misery.

Yet, somehow, the stairs never seem to end.

The stairs go on forever, and I grit my teeth with anxiety each time another sconce flares to life.

Every dozen steps. Like clockwork.

As the stairwell continues into the abyss, I can't help but wonder if this is some kind of enchantment. I mean, there are wisps that can dazzle a brilliant man and send him careening to his death. A blizzard that blocks out all light, and all hope of escaping it.

Why *wouldn't* there be some sort of stairwell that goes on forever?

One that has no end to it.

No answers.

Even as I fight the doubt, my dragon coils with delight. With knowing. She can feel something I can't, and I try to suppress my impatience.

As the next sconce flares to life, I squint into the darkness, trying to see what's beyond it.

A dim light pulses across the floor.

Across the last step.

Finally.

I hurry, moving just a hair faster at the promise of finally being done with the stairwell, and an archway appears from the darkness. It leads to a vast stretch of shadows, and I hesitate on the bottom step as I stare into the gloom.

Once again, a dim blue light pulses briefly to life, like a fading heartbeat. It casts shadows across the floor—across my feet—and I wonder what they could possibly be from.

I wonder what impossibilities made real lie ahead of me.

Even without any more stairs to contend with, I hesitate at the open archway and peek into the next room as the dim light pulses once again.

The brief glow casts eerie blue shadows onto an expansive underground chamber that goes on above me farther than I can see. The darkness is like a black fog high above me, impenetrable and eternal.

The room itself seems to be filled with some sort of strange and ancient machinery comprised primarily of cogs. Sputtering gears line the walls, half of them completely still while the other half creak and grumble, trying to complete their tasks without the energy to do so. It's as if I'm stepping into a clock, and the giant machine rises into the gloomy black smog above me.

Clusters of mechanical gears and metal boxes clutter the room with no rhyme or reason that I can find, while dark archways like the one I'm standing in now line the walls, leading in a dozen directions.

A Spectre nightmare.

That many entrances poses a major security threat. In a moment, I could be completely surrounded—or, if I were to go down any of them, I could be lost forever in a labyrinth of gods-know how many hallways and rooms.

The grating whine of ancient metal screeches once again through the air, and I grimace. Yet again, the pulsing blue light fades.

I wait a moment, trying to see where the light came from, and I don't have to wait long. Barely a second later, the dim pulse flares to life from a pedestal in the center of the room. The blue glow radiates from the base of what looks like a giant keyboard made from stone, covered in markings I don't understand.

It calls to me.

There's a tug on my heart, the sort of wistful urging that feels like nostalgia and home. But this is a place of enchantments, and I have to be careful.

My magic still burning in my palm, I carefully walk toward the pedestal, prepared for just about anything. With so much at stake, I'm more than willing to blow it all to hell should the need arise.

"MY QUEEN," a wheezing voice cuts through the air, echoing through the room like death itself.

The voice booms, somehow frail and overpoweringly loud all at once, and I have never in my life heard anything even remotely like it.

Caught off guard, I drop into a fighting stance and lift my hand. It's an impulsive motion, and even though I thought I was ready for anything, I'm still caught off guard.

"YOU HAVE COME FOR ME," the voice says again, a hint of joy cutting through the wheezing breathiness. "I NEVER DOUBTED YOU. NOT ONCE."

I hesitate, not entirely sure what to make of this.

My castle... talks?

I had expected perhaps a mental connection, or some sort of intuitive knowing when I touched the walls.

But *talking*…

"YOU ARE NOT THE QUEEN I REMEMBER," he continues, his voice almost ear-shattering as the cogs whirl and whine through the air. "YOU ARE NEW TO ME, BUT YOUR MAGIC IS NOT. YOU ARE THEREFORE MY QUEEN. THE GODDESS OF CHAOS. THE MISTRESS OF THIS REALM AND MASTER OF ALL WHO DARE TREAD HERE."

I furrow my brow in confusion, wondering how many bolts are missing from this thing's brain.

The Goddess of Chaos? What even—

With a quick breath to steady my racing heartbeat, I close my eyes and try to calm my nerves. Ultimately, I bite my tongue. Though I debate telling him what happened in the pit—that I'm *not* a goddess at all, least of all some Lady of Chaos—but I figure it's better to have a vengeful castle on my side.

He does, however, already know I'm not any of the original gods, and that freaks me out. He knows so much about me, and all I did was step into his domain.

Shaking out my shoulders to ease some of the tension, I try to figure out how I want to play this.

After all, he's an ancient castle with enough

lingering magic to enchant the mountains, so I'm not through the woods yet.

"You're Ashgrave," I say a little more wistfully than I intended, admittedly in awe of my new, talking castle.

"I AM. YOU CANNOT FATHOM HOW GRATEFUL I AM YOU FOUND ME, MY QUEEN. I HAVE BEEN WITHOUT A MISTRESS FOR FAR TOO LONG."

"I saw you," I confess, pausing as I reach the glowing pedestal in the center of the room. "I had a vision."

"YES," he answers, unsurprised. "I HAVE BEEN CALLING FOR YOU SINCE I FIRST FELT YOUR MAGIC, BUT IT HAS BEEN SO DIFFICULT TO SPEAK. THERE'S NOT MUCH OF ME LEFT. ONLY RECENTLY WAS YOUR MAGIC STRONG ENOUGH TO HEAR ME. YOU HAVE GROWN QUITE QUICKLY."

"Flatterer." I chuckle and set my hands on my naked hips, my magic extinguishing with a small hiss.

"YOUR GRACE, FORGIVE ME. IN MY JOY AT FINDING YOU AGAIN, I FORGOT THE CUSTOMS. I'M AFRAID MY POWER IS WEAK, BUT WHAT I HAVE IS OF COURSE YOURS TO USE IN WHATEVER WAY PLEASES YOU."

"Thanks," I mutter a bit absently, admittedly not really sure what the hell that even means.

The fading heartbeat stops, and though the azure silence stretches on, the brilliant blue glow grows stronger. It fills the room with soft light, cutting into the shadows above me to illuminate ever more cogs and gears as they whir and sputter across the walls.

Light blips through the cobblestone floor, weaving in a thin line toward me from all directions. I tense, not sure of what this is, but it reaches me too quickly for me to do anything.

A soft glow seeps from the floors, and ribbons of light curl around me. They twitch and dance, curling over my skin and legs one by one. Each touch is soft as silk, the sensation more like an embrace than anything else—like they've somehow missed me.

The ribbons fuse together, and in mere moments, what were once glowing threads of light becomes an elegant blue gown. It drapes over me like it was made for only my body, designed eons ago by someone who already knew every inch of my skin.

I lift my hands, studying the soft blue fabric as it trails up my arms, the gentle glow of the dress the perfect contrast to the warm glow of my skin.

Soft tugs on my hair catch my attention, and more ribbons of light filter along my neck. My hair lifts, twisting and curling, and I absently press my fingertips along my scalp as the castle works its magic.

"IN MY WEAKENED STATE, I CANNOT FIND YOUR CROWN, MY QUEEN," the castle practically roars around me. "IT IS UNFORGIVEABLE, AND I CANNOT EXPRESS THE WAYS I HAVE FAILED YOU. I PRAY ONLY THAT YOU FIND GRACE TO FORGIVE ME."

"I'll live," I say with a small chuckle, still dazzled and a bit confused as I study the fabric along my body. "I'm fine with the magic dress for now, Ashgrave."

"YOU… YOU ARE NOT UPSET?"

I huff in surprise. Upset? What kind of master did he have before that would think he had failed her in a situation like this?

Probably someone like Zurie.

My jaw impulsively tenses, my throat tightening as I remember my former mentor, and I stand a little taller.

"Uh, no," I say calmly. "I'm not upset." As I speak, I gaze up into the abyss above me as I search for a face —something more concrete to speak to than a disembodied voice.

"THAT IS KIND OF YOU," he says, genuine confusion in his voice. "KINDNESS IS NOT COMMON HERE."

I nod, not thinking much of it. Deep down, I want to give the order for my men to join me, but I'm still not sure this is safe.

Before I put their lives on the line any more than I already have, I need to be absolutely certain.

"You said you can feel my magic," I point out, turning on my heel as I study the walls around me. "What do you sense?"

"YOU ARE SOMETHING NEW," he answers, a twinge of curiosity in his voice. "SOMETHING INCREDIBLE, EVEN BETTER THAN BEFORE. GOD MAGIC IS NEVER STAGNANT, BUT GROWS AND ADAPTS WITH TIME. YOU ARE THE NEXT GENERATION OF GREATNESS, AND IT IS MY SOLE DUTY TO SERVE YOU IN WHATEVER WAY YOU DEEM FIT."

I smirk. Talk about flattery.

"I SENSE FOUR INTRUDERS AT THE GATE," the castle booms. "SHALL I KILL THEM, MISTRESS?"

He asks the question with all the casual boredom of a butler asking someone if they'd like some tea.

"No," I say curtly. "Those men are allies. Protect them at all costs."

"OF COURSE, MY QUEEN," he replies. "ARE THEY YOUR SERVANTS?"

I laugh, and it comes out as a weird little snort through my nose. I can't help it. I want to say yes just to mess with them, but I rein in the impulse in case it's something I can't change later. "They're my…" I trail off, searching for the right word.

Lovers.

Family.

The source of my hope.

"Protectors," I finally answer.

"AH, YOUR LORDS," the castle says, as if it were obvious. "VERY GOOD. A QUEEN MUST HAVE HER LORDS."

"Yeah, I guess," I say with a shrug, wishing he would stop this queen-nonsense. "Bring them down here, Ashgrave. They need shelter immediately."

"AT ONCE, MY QUEEN."

My heart flutters with relief, and I let out a slow breath as I set my hands on my hips and scan what remains of him. "What happened to you?"

In the short silence that follows, a soft sigh escapes him, the sound echoing through the vast chamber as the dim blue light once again pulses in the pedestal nearby.

"SOMETHING I HAD HOPED WOULD NEVER HAPPEN," he confesses. "WHEN THE GODS WERE DRIVEN UNDERGROUND, THEY ORDERED ME

REMOVED OF MY POWER. DOING SO WAS MERELY A DEFENSE MECHANISM THE FIRST QUEEN DESIGNED TO PROTECT ME IN THEIR ABSENCE, AS I AM THE TREASURE TROVE OF THEIR POWER AND WEALTH. IT WAS ONLY TO BE DONE WHEN THEY PLANNED TO BE GONE FOR EONS."

Even though he only spoke for a few moments, I balk at the sheer amount of information there is to unpack from what he said.

The implication of immortality.

The vast trove of wealth and magic likely hidden here.

The fact that the gods did not leave, but were driven away.

The implication that they're not gone, but merely underground.

Overwhelmed and a little flooded, I try to focus on what stuck out the most to me. "How could they remove your power?"

"THERE ARE ORBS MADE FROM THE GODS' MAGIC. THESE ARE UNIQUE AND IRREPLACE-ABLE, EACH DIFFERENT FROM THE LAST. THE FIRST QUEEN FUSED HER MAGIC WITH STAR-DUST AND CRYSTALS FROM DEEP IN THE EARTH TO CREATE THESE ORBS, AND THEIR

POWER NEVER DIES. I NEED THESE ORBS TO REGAIN MY ABILITY AND MIGHT SO THAT I CAN PROPERLY SMITE PEOPLE FOR YOU, AS ALL GOOD CASTLES DO."

I chuckle. I like the way this castle thinks.

However, I get a flare of warning, deep in my chest. It comes from my Spectre training, and the initial hit is a caution to be careful—this is a magical entity long stripped of its power. I can't take what he says at face value, not really. Not until I figure out if I can trust him.

After all, he could just be manipulating me into retrieving these orbs for him. All of this flattery and obedience could just be a ruse.

In my core, my dragon twists in irritation that I would dare think such a thing. She knows this castle, and based on what I'm getting from her, there's nothing for me to fear.

I frown, not entirely convinced.

"Where are the orbs?" I ask.

"THEY WILL CALL TO YOU," Ashgrave says. "THEY ALL WILL, AS YOU NEAR."

"How many are there?"

He sighs, the sound deep and sad. "AS WITH SO MUCH OF MY MEMORY, I HAVE FORGOTTEN. I REMEMBER ONLY THAT THERE WERE MANY,

AND EACH SERVED A UNIQUE PURPOSE. THE POWER RESERVES I HAVE LEFT ARE FAILING. IT WON'T BE LONG BEFORE I CAN'T BE BROUGHT BACK, AND I WOULD HATE TO FAIL YOU, MY QUEEN. IF I WERE TO DIE, THERE WOULD BE NO CASTLE TO SMITE YOUR ENEMIES FOR YOU."

"That would be a shame," I admit with a smirk.

"I HATE TO ASK ANYTHING OF MY QUEEN," he continues. "IT IS MY DUTY TO SERVE YOU, AND NOT THE OTHER WAY AROUND. HOWEVER, IF YOU DO FIND THE TIME, I WOULD BE EVER MORE ETERNALLY GRATEFUL TO HAVE THE ORBS RETURNED TO ME. EVERY OUNCE OF MY MAGIC, EVERY MOMENT OF MY POWER, IS AND ALWAYS WILL BE DEDICATED TO SERVING YOU."

"We'll figure this out," I promise. "I won't let you die, Ashgrave."

There's an odd sort of silence, just a brief pause, and I can almost feel the confusion dripping from the machine around me.

"YOU ARE DIFFERENT," he says simply.

"What do you mean?"

"YOU ARE ODDLY... NICER," he confesses, his tone dripping with curiosity. "I FEAR THE KIND-

NESS WILL BE THE DEATH OF YOU, MY QUEEN. THIS WORLD DESTROYS THE KIND, AND I WILL NOT LET IT HARM YOU."

I laugh. He has no idea what I'm capable of. With time, he and I will figure each other out.

"You can't think like that, Ashgrave," I say quietly. "Kindness is sometimes the only thing that makes this world worth being in."

"INTERESTING," the castle says wistfully. "I LOOK FORWARD TO GETTING TO KNOW YOU, MY QUEEN."

"The feeling is mutual," I admit with a small smile. "Now, my men—are they on their way?"

"YES, THEY ARE IN THE STAIRWELL. I SHALL REDIRECT THEM TO THE MEETING ROOM, AS THE FIRST QUEEN DEEMED THIS ROOM TO BE A HOLY SPACE, WHERE ONLY THE GODS MAY ENTER. WOULD YOU LIKE ME TO TAKE YOU TO THEM?"

I hesitate briefly, wondering yet again if I should tell him I'm not a god. That, by his own rules, I shouldn't even be in this room. I know what Levi implied, and I realize that being a diamond dragon is rare. But everything *about* me and this situation—this new life—is rare.

That doesn't make me a god.

At least—I don't think I could be one.

This whole diamond-dragon thing, well, I figure it can only be yet another oddity in a long string of amazing happenings and incredible luck.

After all, I'm just a human who was in the wrong place at the wrong time and made the best of her situation. I'm the only human to become a dragon, with the possible exception of Irena—as long as she doesn't kill her dragon in all of her grief.

For the moment, I keep my mouth shut, as I don't want to say the wrong thing to a wrathful castle. "No, Ashgrave. Bring them here. To me. Now. My men are allowed anywhere I go. Nothing is off-limits to them."

There's the briefest hesitation, as if Ashgrave is both morbidly curious and utterly confused, but that doesn't slow him down. "OF COURSE, MY QUEEN."

"And build a fire," I add. "They all need to get warm. There's a human amongst them who's close to death, and I need you to help him recover."

"A HUMAN?"

"Yes," I say, an edge of warning to my voice. "Is that a problem?"

"NO! NO, OF COURSE NOT, MY QUEEN. I JUST…" he trails off, and it's almost entertaining to hear his constant string of confusion.

He's been isolated for a long time, and it seems as though this "first queen" of his was a real charmer.

The moment of tension passes almost instantly. "I AM AT YOUR COMMAND, MY QUEEN. THIS IS YOUR DOMAIN, AND I AM YOUR SERVANT."

Deep in the shadows of the massive room, a fireplace I hadn't seen before erupts with blue flame. Almost instantly, a soothing heat snakes through the air.

I wonder if Ashgrave truly has the magic to use on things like this—on anything other than the essentials —but he said it himself. His purpose is to serve his Queen at all costs, even to himself.

His purpose is to serve *me*, even to his own demise. It's a purpose he fills almost gleefully.

I still can't quite fathom such a thing.

CHAPTER NINE

I lean my arm against the mantle, resting my forehead against the back of my hand as the heat from the crackling fire rolls over my face. I close my eyes, savoring the warmth after all the cold. Even though the snow didn't bite into my bones like I expected, I still prefer the heat.

That might be a problem, since I'll be living all the way out here once we get Ashgrave operational.

Damn.

The soft tap of footsteps down the stairs catches my attention, and I crane my ear to detect the nuance of each person's gait—even though I already know who it is.

The quick and stealthy pace of my mate.

The slow and steady footsteps that can only belong to Drew.

The shuffle of someone who's not quite steady on his feet, who stumbles and catches himself quite often. That must be Tucker, delirious from the cold. He's usually so quick-footed, and he does an endearing little shuffle every twelfth step. I'm pretty sure he doesn't even realize he does it, but I love hearing him walk. I always know it's him.

And of course, the silence.

Levi—my cunning ice dragon, undetectable even to me.

My chest pangs at the thought of the booby traps I passed on the way down here. At the thought of the men I love walking past those same arrow holes and coming that close to death.

"Ashgrave," I say, catching the castle's attention.

"YES, MY QUEEN."

"You are not to kill these men. Do you understand?" I ask, my grip tightening on the mantle as I swallow hard. "Ever. For any reason."

"OF COURSE, MY QUEEN," the castle answers immediately.

Behind me, sconces by the doorway I originally walked through flare to life with blue flame. The flickering sapphire blazes cast soft silhouettes against the wall, and before long, four familiar shadows stretch onto the floor as my men hurry down the stairs.

In mere moments, Levi rounds the corner first. His expression grim and eyes narrowed, he scopes the room with a gun in his hand, wearing nothing but cargo shorts. His icy gaze immediately lands on me, and his shoulders relax slightly when he sees that I'm okay. He does another visual sweep of the room, apparently unfazed by the massive cogs and enchanted machinery covering the walls around us.

As always, Levi is looking for threats and making sure that this is safe. I sigh and cross my arms, watching him carefully as he secures the room, and I can't help but understand where he's coming from.

He wants me to be safe. We need each other. If anything happens to me, his fragile relationship with his dragon will fracture yet again, and he may never be able to heal it. Add Zurie's revenge into the mix, and we've just lost the one thing that kept us both alive for so long—our shadows. Our secrets. There's a new tsunami of danger rolling over us, and he's just doing his best.

Still, I wish his best wasn't so damn *controlling*.

Drew follows shortly after, a gun in his right hand and his left arm around Tucker as the weapons expert leans against him for support. My weapons expert holds a gun in his hand, lifting it slightly as he scans the world around him with a dazed expression.

"Do I need to kill anybody?" he asks, slurring, waving the gun as if he's trying to do a full sweep.

"Get that out of his hand, damn it," I snap.

"We tried," Drew mutters, his eyes still on Tucker. "He's so damn stubborn."

"Gotta kill the bad guys," Tucker mutters, his skin is starkly white compared to Drew's as he waves his gun. "Boom, boom."

My heart pangs with dread. "Get him by the fire!" I demand, ushering Drew over to me.

The fire dragon hesitates, if only briefly, when his eyes finally land on me. His gaze wanders over my dress. My hair. My face. It's as if he's snared by something, and I briefly glance down at myself in confusion.

Oh, the dress. Somehow, amidst all the craziness of talking to an ancient castle, I'd almost forgotten the magic gown. Hell, I still don't know what Ashgrave did to my hair. I didn't even think to check.

"Drew," I say firmly, trying to snap him out of it. "Tucker needs to get to the fire."

"Right," the Darrington says, clearing his throat as if he were caught in the act of doing something he shouldn't. "We tried to keep a fire going, but the blizzard picked up again almost as soon as you went down the stairs."

Delirious and staggering, Tucker drops his hold on Drew and makes his way over to me and the fire. Levi and Drew both follow, spotting Tucker to make sure he doesn't fall, and Levi deftly grabs the gun from Tucker's hand before he can accidentally fire.

Even so close to death, Tucker would go down fighting.

Gods above, I love this man.

When Tucker reaches me, he collapses into my arms. He's shivering from head to toe, and there's almost no color in his face. He feels like ice, and every breath is too short. Too quick. It's like his lungs won't work properly.

Everything about him is ice cold—his clothes, his skin, his nose, even his hair. As he leans into me, I fall to my knees beside the fire, positioning him so that he can get most of the heat. He's slurring under his breath, and though I think it's a string of cuss words, I can't really tell.

I grimace as I survey the former Knight. "Drew, didn't you—"

"We did everything we could, Rory," Drew interrupts, kneeling beside us he holsters his gun. "He's going to be okay. He just needs the warmth and some time by the fire. That's all."

"Everything's great," Tucker says through chattering teeth, his lips a little blue. "I feel awesome."

"Shut up, you idiot," I say, laughing. "Be serious for two seconds."

"Nah," Tucker says, chuckling. He coughs, his eyes scanning my face as they slip in and out of focus. "You do somthin' to y'hair?" he adds, slurring his words a bit as he struggles to get warm.

I chuckle. "Oh, good. I was afraid you wouldn't notice."

"I pay 'tention," he stutters, his teeth still chattering.

"Ashgrave, get him some blankets and pillows," I demand, not even sure if the castle is capable of such a thing. "Do you have any—"

Before I can even finish the thought, a sconce roars to life in the shadows nearby, illuminating an elaborate chest pressed against the wall. The lid of the trunk pops open, and from this angle, I can see the top layer of blankets.

"Magic castle for the win," Tucker mutters, shivering.

Drew and Levi rush to the trunk before I can so much as stand, and the two of them pull out piles of pillows and blankets. Between the three of us, we set up a small infirmary by the fire, giving Tucker something to lay on and cover himself with. In a matter of a few minutes, he's curled up by the fire, the color slowly returning to his skin.

I let out a slow sigh of relief, grateful that Tucker's going to be okay and even more thankful that my men are like brothers. That they look out for each other just as much as they look out for me.

But one's missing.

As if on cue, my dragon stirs as she feels our mate getting close.

Moments later, Jace jogs down the last few steps. His tall frame fills the archway as he stands with broad shoulders at the entrance, his eyes narrowing as he scans the strange room. He takes a quick inventory of his surroundings before his gaze lands on me, and he lets out an audible sigh of relief. Instantly, his demeanor shifts, and his whole body relaxes.

"The stairs and skies are clear. I was making sure no one followed us," he says as he walks toward me. He hesitates as he nears, his eyes scanning my hair and the flowing blue silk that now drapes across my body. A small grin plays at the corner of his mouth as he holsters his gun. "You going for a new look, Rory?

Personally, I'm a bit more fond of the whole rogue badass vibe."

I chuckle and flip him the bird.

"You look regal," Drew adds, standing as Tucker starts to softly snore by the fire. My fire dragon flashes his trademark devilish smirk as his gaze also briefly roams over my body.

His eyes land on mine, ensnared and enraptured by something I don't quite see, and I get the feeling that his words have deeper meaning.

Like he's hiding something from me—but, then again, that's just his way. I'll never unravel all of Drew's secrets, no matter how hard I try.

"Yeah, well, I guess that's the castle's style," I add with a shrug. "I didn't exactly get to pick from a wardrobe."

"The castle's style?" Jace asks, quirking an eyebrow in confusion.

Before I can answer, I feel a hand on my waist. In the blink of an eye and with no warning, Levi is suddenly beside me, silent as ever. His arm wraps possessively around my back as he pulls me close, scanning the castle walls around us.

Drew rubs his eyes, leaning his elbow against the mantle as he sets his other hand on his waist. "Rory, do you feel like explaining what the hell is going on? We just saw the stairs glow and heard a voice telling us to come down. We had no idea what happened to you. We were ready to massacre anything that moved, so I'm grateful Tucker thought to pack us clothes and weapons in his bag."

Jace nods, crossing his arms as he leans against the wall nearby. "The only reason we knew you weren't dead was because I hadn't gone crazy and tried to kill them," he adds with a nod toward the others.

Even though the thought is grim as hell, a small smile pulls at the corner of my mouth as I look at the former dojo master. My heart flutters as our connection sparks a flurry of delight through me.

"I officially have a castle, guys," I say, gesturing toward the vast darkness above us. "Ashgrave, say hello."

"I AM ASHGRAVE, WRATHFUL SERVANT OF THE QUEEN OF CHAOS, GODDESS OF THESE MOUNTAINS. IT IS MY DUTY AND HONOR TO DEFEND THE QUEEN AT ALL COSTS, AGAINST ALL OPPONENTS, AT ANY TIME. SHE HAS BUT TO ASK, AND I WILL SMITE WHOMEVER IS FOOLISH ENOUGH TO DEFY HER."

In unison, all three men currently on their feet tense and draw their weapons, aiming the barrels of their guns instinctively into the darkness above us all.

Their intense gazes scan the murky black smog above us, as if expecting to see a face pop out of it at any moment.

From the pile of blankets by the fire, Tucker laughs and rolls over so that he can look me in the eye. "Aw, babe," he says, still a bit delirious. "You have an evil butler, now? I'm jealous."

In the silence that follows, Jace and Drew simply stare into the darkness above us, their lips parted in shock and surprise.

Jace quirks an eyebrow, his gaze finally landing on me as the spell of shock and awe slowly fades. "Your castle talks."

"That it does," I say quietly. "Color me surprised."

"This is amazing." Drew takes a few steps into the center of the room, muttering under his breath as he scans the ruins.

I only catch words here and there, not totally following what he's saying to himself. I have to confess, this isn't the reaction I expected from him.

"Excellent," he adds. "Remarkable, really. Better than I imagined."

Irritated, I pinch the bridge of my nose and shake my head. "You knew he talks, didn't you, Drew?"

"I had a hunch," my fire dragon admits with a shrug. "I didn't want you to get your hopes up."

I balk, utterly confused as to how that's supposed to be appealing. "Get my hopes—*what?* Did you think I would be disappointed if my *magic castle* didn't *talk?!*"

"Now that you're back, is he returning to full power?" Levi interjects, frowning as his icy gaze darts toward me. "If he's capable of enchanting us and trying to lead us to our deaths, he must have power reserves. Is this place secure enough for you to stay?"

I see what he's really doing—it's as if he can't think of anything but finding me a secured home base from which to operate. I debate calling him out on it, reminding him of who he's dealing with and what I'm capable of doing, but I decide not to start anything. Not now.

Not yet.

"Not much is left," I admit. "Apparently, he relies on power orbs infused by the gods' magic, and those were removed long ago. He doesn't know where they are, and he can't be fully operational until he gets them back."

"TO BEGIN, I NEED ONLY ONE," interjects the castle. "THERE ARE THREE TYPES OF ORBS, EACH WITH VARIOUS LEVELS OF POWER, AND TO BEGIN, I NEED ONLY THE STRONGEST."

"Oh, *only*," Tucker adds from his place by the fire, giving off a little sarcastic snort. "Glad it's simple."

"How many orbs are there?" Jace asks.

"He can't remember," I answer for the castle. "A lot of his memory is corrupted."

Jace grumbles in frustration, rubbing his temples as we all simultaneously realize the mammoth task ahead of us.

"BUT I WILL REMEMBER," the castle promises. "ONCE YOU FIND THE FIRST, THE OTHERS WILL BE EASIER. I PROMISE, MY QUEEN, I WILL NOT DISAPPOINT YOU."

"I know, Ashgrave," I say comfortingly. I scan the walls, studying the ruins as I try to think of where these orbs could be or if they even still exist. If any of them—or all of them—were destroyed.

I really, *really* need a clue.

"What happened, Ashgrave?" I ask, taking slow and steady steps away from the fire as I near the glowing blue pedestal. "To you? To the gods? How did all of this start?"

"I WISH I HAD MORE ANSWERS FOR YOU, MY QUEEN," the castle says. "I DO NOT KNOW WHERE THE GODS CAME FROM, AS THEY NEVER SHARED THAT KNOWLEDGE WITH ANYONE. NOT EVEN ME. I KNOW ONLY WHAT HAS HAPPENED SINCE MY INCEPTION."

"Tell me," I demand.

"THERE WERE THREE GODS: CAELAN, MORGANA, AND RAZORUS. MORGANA CREATED ME, BUILT ME FROM THE SNOW AND ROCK WITH HER OWN MAGIC. EVERY LABYRINTH, EVERY WALL, EVERY VANTAGE POINT, EVERY ENCHANTMENT—SHE DESIGNED IT ALL. SHE INFUSED HER MAGIC IN THE ORBS, GIVING ME ACCESS TO HER POWER IN ITS RAWEST FORM. I AM HER CREATION AND THEREFORE, BOUND TO SERVE HER AND HER SUCCESSORS. NOW THAT YOU ARE HERE, MY QUEEN, THERE IS MUCH TO TELL AND SHOW YOU. BUT FOR NOW, LET US BEGIN AS YOU WISH—AT THE END."

On the far wall, two sconces roar to life and illuminate a door as it opens to reveal another stairwell. More soft, blue lights blink into existence, leading down into the darkness and cutting through the gloom.

"I'll stay with Tucker," Levi says, his grip tightening around my waist. "You go."

I tenderly run my fingers along his jawline in gratitude, the sensation of his skin against my fingertips almost intoxicating.

Thanks, I say through the silent connection he and I share, even in human form.

He nods, his face still grim and fraught with concern. *Be safe.*

I just smile, tilting my head slightly as if to say *Come on, man. You know me better than that.*

Without a word, I walk toward the steps with Drew and Jace in tow. Though I know they're curious to find answers, I suspect they're merely coming with me to make sure the castle doesn't try anything.

I don't think it will. It already had too many chances to kill us. If it wanted me dead, I would probably be impaled on something and long-buried beneath the snow.

Perhaps not the most comforting of thoughts, sure —but at least the castle is on our side.

Probably.

CHAPTER TEN

Drew, Jace, and I trot down the stairs for what feels like an eternity, but that's mostly because of my heart hammering in my chest.

After all, I'm walking through the halls of an enchanted castle older than most of recorded history, and it's about to reveal secrets to me that most of the world will never know.

Despite everything I've seen in my life, despite everything I've endured, I'm practically giddy with anticipation.

This is just too damn *cool.*

The stairwell ends at another arched doorway that leads into a massive room. Though it's not very wide or deep, the ceiling goes on forever, stretching above us into the darkened shadows.

As I stare overhead, a dim glow radiates through the gloom. It churns and rolls like thunder through the clouds. The enchanted ceiling above us boils and brews, and a single bolt of lightning briefly casts a white glow across everything.

The wall across from us shimmers with gold light, almost like a vertical pool of golden water. It ripples and moves, captivating and entirely charming, and I'm not quite sure what I'm even looking at.

"What is this place?" I ask.

"THE MURAL ROOM," Ashgrave answers. "I RETAIN MY MEMORY THROUGH MURALS, AND IN THIS ROOM YOU CAN ACCESS THE COMPLETE HISTORY OF THE GODS. THIS ROOM TELLS ALL OF THEIR STORIES, BUT THERE ARE SO MANY. SINCE YOU WANT TO KNOW WHAT HAPPENED TO THEM AND TO ME, I SUGGEST THAT WE SEE THE OTHER STORIES ANOTHER TIME. YOU COULD SPEND MONTHS DOWN HERE, SIMPLY WATCHING AND LISTENING. BUT FOR NOW, I WILL TELL YOU OF THE END."

The wall springs to life, elaborate gold swirls cutting through the rippling shimmer as Ashgrave speaks.

"THERE WAS A TIME LONG AGO WHEN

DRAGONS RIGHTFULLY RULED THIS EARTH," Ashgrave says.

As he speaks, images appear in the golden swirls of dragons flying high over the mountains. Humans toil in a field below, farming wheat and harvesting the stalks.

The pictures slowly move, like snapshots in time, as the farmers carry their wagon toward a castle and bow before three gods sitting on thrones. The farmers lift the wheat in offering, and the gods raise their chins slightly as if debating whether or not to accept this tribute.

"THOUGH DRAGONS RULED THIS EARTH," Ashgrave continues, "THE GODS RULED THE DRAGONS. MY REALM WAS A THRIVING CAPITAL TO THE ENTIRE WORLD, WITH UNPARALLELED LUXURIES, TRADE, AND CULTURE."

The images on the wall shift, showing a mighty castle carved into the mountain. There isn't so much as a hint of snow—instead, green grass covers the slopes, and ornate roads covered in stunning pavers twist through the mountains in all directions.

"BUT HUMAN DISSENT SLOWLY CORRODED EVEN DRAGON MAGIC, AND IT BECAME CLEAR THE HUMANS' SHEER NUMBERS COULD

THREATEN THE HAVEN DRAGONS HAD BUILT," Ashgrave says, a red tint rolling over the image of the Capital.

I'm a little hesitant to believe dragon rule was some sort of blissful utopia. Ashgrave's bias is almost painfully clear, and if my intuitive hits on the First Queen are right, Morgana wasn't exactly some benign ruler who presided with grace and compassion.

However, I stiffen impulsively at how familiar this story already feels. After watching the newscast that exposed me, the world shifted, too. The riots. The boycotts. The anti-dragon sentiment. The people who hate me, even though all they know are lies told by a woman who wanted me dead.

Funny how history tends to repeat itself.

"THE GODS, OF COURSE, HAD DEVOUT FOLLOWERS—THE ANCIENT ORACLES. THE ORACLES' SOLE DUTY WAS TO PROTECT AND SERVE THEIR MASTERS."

As Ashgrave speaks, the image of a woman wrapped in a white robe appears. Her eyes closed and peaceful, the woman's long blonde hair flows around her beautiful face like water as she fills the entire mural wall.

"THE ORACLES EXISTED TO SERVE AND PROTECT THE GODS, BUT OVER TIME EVEN

THEY FAILED. THEY WERE INFILTRATED BY AN
EMERGING ORDER CALLED THE KNIGHTS—
HUMANS WHO WERE UNITED AGAINST DRAG-
ONS. THEY BELIEVED THEY HAD TO DO WHAT
MAN HAD DONE FROM THE BEGINNING—TO
OVERCOME AND CONQUER."

I grit my teeth, wondering if the Knights could
truly be that old. For them to have roots in the original
destruction of the gods seems almost impossible.

But after all I've been through, I'm quickly learning
not to use that word.

Not anymore.

"THE GODS WERE TRICKED BY THOSE THEY
TRUSTED INTO PERFORMING A RITUAL THAT
WAS SUPPOSED TO STRENGTHEN THEIR
MAGIC. INSTEAD, THE RITUAL STOLE IT,"
Ashgrave says, fury dripping from his voice as the
image of the woman fades away to dust.

"THE GODS WERE BETRAYED BY THE VERY
PRIESTS WHO ONCE SERVED THEM. WITH
THEIR POWER DRAINED AND LOCKED AWAY,
THE GODS WITHERED. THEY WERE CLOSE TO
DEATH, AND THE TRAITORS ATTEMPTED TO
KILL ALL THREE. BUT GODS ARE HARD TO
KILL, AND THEY FAILED. WITH NO IDEA HOW
TO FINISH THEIR PLAN, THE KNIGHTS SEALED

THE GODS AWAY UNTIL THEY COULD FINISH WHAT THEY HAD BEGUN."

The mural cuts once again to the view of the capital, only this time, it's ablaze. Flames burn away the fields, slowly flickering as the mural's magic paints a surreal and barely-moving picture. Fire billows from the castle windows, scorching the stone and leaving black scars across the beautiful fortress.

"WITH THE GODS WEAKENED AND GONE, MY MAGIC WAS LIMITED," Ashgrave continues. "THE KNIGHTS STORMED MY WALLS TO TAKE THE TREASURES HIDDEN HERE, AND I HELD THEM OFF FOR MONTHS. THE FEW REMAINING ORACLES AND I KNEW THAT I COULD NOT KEEP THE KNIGHTS AT BAY FOREVER, HOWEVER, AND THEY REMOVED THE ORBS THAT POWERED ME. THEY SPIRITED THESE AWAY TO LOCATIONS THE GODS HAD GIVEN THEM, KEPT SECRET IN CASE I WAS EVER COMPROMISED."

The mural fades into the golden shimmer once again as the last image of fire disappears.

"AND THUS I HAVE WAITED, MY QUEEN," Ashgrave finishes. "I HAVE WAITED FOR THE GODS' MAGIC TO RETURN IN WHATEVER FORM IT MIGHT TAKE. I'VE BEEN WAITING FOR

YOU FOR EONS, FOR FAR LONGER THAN I CAN EVEN REMEMBER. I AM HERE TO DO YOUR BIDDING, WHETHER THAT INVOLVES RETURNING ME TO MY FORMER POWER OR NOT. WHATEVER YOU DESIRE, WHATEVER YOU NEED, I AM AT YOUR SERVICE."

In the silence that follows his declaration, I simply stand there with my arms crossed as my eyes slip out of focus. I think through everything he just told me, briefly wondering if he might be lying.

It's strange to speak to a sentient being with no face, of course, but what irks me the most is I can't check for tells of a lie. If he's playing me, I may not be able to tell until it's too late.

So far, I don't see many reasons why he would— and my dragon trusts him implicitly.

He needs to return to full power, and as far as I can tell, I seem to be one of the few people who can help him achieve that. However, if that was truly all he cared about, he could have had anyone enter and given them the mission. He wouldn't have tried to kill my men—hell, the more who visit him, the better his chances of retrieving all of his power.

Instead, he waited only for me. If he was truly on death's door and just hungry for his power to return, he wouldn't have taken that risk.

Morgana made him, and I have her magic. Therefore, he is loyal to me.

I stew on that thought—on how I intercepted the gods' magic when I was thrown into that pit. It seems as though they were supposed to be down there, not me.

The thought just seems odd. Strange, even. The idea of tossing gods into a pit just seems laughable, and though I can't put my finger on what it is, something about this whole situation seems off.

As my mind wanders over the moment I absorbed the gods' magic, I'm forced to relive the agony that tore through me—the way I was sucked into that surreal, *other* world. It was some kind of in-between, neither death nor life, and I once again remember the voices in the mist. I can't recall much of what they said, but I know they wanted me to come to them.

And if I'm not mistaken, there were three voices.

Including one woman.

My jaw tenses, and my whole body stiffens at the thought. Though I've been trying to figure out this whole time what those voices and the mist even were, I have to wonder if those were the gods.

I almost can't fathom the idea.

If I'm right—if those truly were the gods—it would

seem they're not quite dead, even after all this time. I have to confess that's deeply troubling.

After all, I have their magic, and I doubt they'll be content to sleep forever.

Worse even than that is how the gods were destroyed by mortals. By *traitors*.

By trusting.

The realization cuts deep into me, igniting old insecurities the Spectres beat into me throughout my life.

Rule 12 of the Spectres—trust no one.

I take a deep and steadying breath, rubbing my eyes as I force myself back into the moment. Jace sets a comforting hand on the small of my back—just a gentle reminder that he's here, and he always will be. Drew wraps his massive hand around the back of my neck, his warm touch soothing in the silence as it stretches on.

I refuse to live by the Spectres' rules anymore. It's not who I am.

Trust is what allowed me to survive thus far. I'm not like the old gods. This is a new world, and I'm a new woman.

And, apparently, I have a glowing magical orb to find.

CHAPTER ELEVEN

Wrapped in my new flowing blue gown, I sit on a snowy mountain peak as I watch the sun set across the mountain range. Wind howls past me, ruffling my hair. For a brief and blissful moment, it feels almost like sitting on the roof of my old tower at the dojo.

Up here in the snow, I *should* be shivering. I've been sitting out here so long that my skin should be blue, but I feel fine. The white powder beneath my toes feels more like sand than snow. The howling wind feels more like a caress than a tempest.

Up here, alone and at peace, I lose myself in thought.

Since the shift, everything is different. Though I love all of these changes—most of all my dragon—I simply wish I understood it better. It's the little things that somehow bug me most. Not knowing why I feel so at home in the frigid snow. Not knowing why my magic is surging again. Not knowing what I even am anymore.

The unknown is foreign to me—as a Spectre, I simply hunted down whatever information I needed. It was always in a database *somewhere*, and the key to unraveling secrets was simply to find it.

There's no database on harboring god magic, though, much less what happens when you fuse with it.

I suppose I should feel anxious, but if anything, I'm starting to adore the weirdness of my new life. The way a new crazy curveball seems to come at me out of the blue at any given moment. How predictably unpredictable my life is now.

It's kind of fun—in an insane, talking-castles sort of way.

With a soft little sigh, I lean back on my palms. Try as I might, this mountain peak just isn't the same as my tower. There was something so therapeutic about sitting up there, about having a bird's-eye view of the forests and dojo around me. But all I can see from up here is snow and sky.

I can feel Ashgrave's pulse in the distance—still

calling to me, just in case I need a reminder of how to get home. I didn't really want to leave at all, but we needed to. There's no cell connection out there and no way to connect to the world outside, which means we have to find another place to stay so that we can coordinate our next move.

Truth be told, I feel sort of stuck, and that annoys the living *hell* out of me. I have no idea where to start with finding the power orb.

It's not like I can just trot around the world yelling, *"Here orb! Come!"*

I groan and rub my eyes, wondering what on earth we're going to do. We're clever, and between the five of us, I know we'll come up with something. It's just frustrating to not have any leads.

The last time I was out of options, I went to the dojo. I drove into the dragon's den, and I broke nearly every rule I used to live by in order to get the intel I needed.

The answer's here, right in front of me. *Somewhere.* I just know it.

I bite my lip, wondering what I could be overlooking. What I might be missing.

Now that Tucker has his energy back, the guys are in a cabin about six hundred feet down the mountain. Ashgrave doesn't have control over all of the enchantments around the mountain range, unfortunately, but he *was* kind enough not to kill us on the way out. With a few tweaks, he toned down the power on the blizzard surrounding the castle—but only just enough so that we could fly out unnoticed by satellites.

The concept of satellites enchanted my castle almost as much as the wisps enchanted my men. Ashgrave simply *loves* the concept of "spying on people from the stars," as he put it. He begged me to get him one or two satellites of his own.

I chuckle, rubbing my jaw as I remember wandering a few of Ashgrave's halls on the way out. I think that castle and I are going to get along just fine.

With my men coordinating where we're going to go next and what our new base of operations is going to be, I took the chance to get some much-needed time to myself. However, it's probably best that I head down, soon. Now that we're out of the mountains, we don't have the cover of the blizzard anymore. We can't stay in one place too long.

I groan in disappointment. We're on the run, yet again.

Yay.

Through the billowing wind, I hear wings on the air. I tense, my fists impulsively closing as I summon my magic without even thinking. White sparks and ribbons of brilliant light race through my fingers with ease, and I marvel briefly at my vast new power. What was once so difficult now comes effortlessly and far more powerfully than before.

A familiar red dragon rounds the bend of the mountain, black smoke barreling out of his nose as his eye catches mine. My shoulders relax as Drew gets closer, and only then do I notice a blanket shivering in the wind like a banner from his claws. As he nears, he tosses it at me, the blanket hitting my face and virtually drowning me in cotton.

I can't help myself. I laugh despite everything we're going through and everything on my mind.

Ass.

He lands, the ground trembling slightly beneath his claws as the snow sizzles wherever it touches his scales.

I fight with the blanket, trying to untangle myself from it as he shifts down to his human form. In moments, a very handsome and *very* naked Drew Darrington jogs over to me, shivering as his breath freezes on the air.

He sits beside me and, in a matter of seconds, wraps us both in the blanket like we're the center of a cotton-based burrito.

His arm weaves around my waist, tugging me

closer to him as my butt slides over the blanket beneath us, and his warm skin presses against mine. His touch is like fire and sunlight, and even though the snow doesn't get to me like it used to back when I was human, I lean into him with a small sigh of relief that he's so delightfully warm. I set my cheek on his shoulder and let him hold me.

Together, we sit in silence, simply watching the horizon. I have to confess, it's nice to have a small amount of peace through all the craziness. As the wind howls around us, Drew wraps the blanket ever tighter, pulling me even closer, and I can't help but wonder if he has an ulterior motive.

I don't think I'd mind a romp through the snow, but I can't imagine a fire dragon would enjoy sex in such an icy place.

Warm and comfortable, with my ear pressed against his body, my eyes slowly begin to close as I listen to his pulse. It's soothing and rhythmic, steady and calming, and it's such a relief to know he's here.

That he will always be here.

Even if he doesn't always tell me everything.

I frown a little, remembering the way he looked at me when he walked down the steps. When he saw me in that gown. Something shifted for him, like seeing me in this dress confirmed something that had been on his mind for a while, but he wouldn't tell me what it was.

"Why did you smirk at me?" I ask softly. "When you walked down the stairs and saw me in Ashgrave—what was that look?"

With my eyes still closed, I can't see his face, but I know him well enough that I can imagine. He probably has that stoic frown on his lips, his mouth a grim line as he stares off into the horizon and refuses to answer.

The silence stretches on for minutes, and it seems like I really might not get a reply. But this is Drew, and I'm used to him hiding things.

I groan in mild irritation, wondering if I should press this, when he sighs.

"I've been noticing things," he finally confesses. "Just little things here and there, but it's becoming more pronounced. The more I discover about you and this new magic of yours, the more significant these little things become."

"You're being vague," I point out. "It's annoying."

He chuckles, his arm sliding up my torso as he holds me tightly. "We all knew you were meant for more than the dojo, Rory. But I see something more than even a new home or public persona. What I see—what I've seen since you shifted, especially—is the beginnings of a world leader. Of a powerhouse." He pauses, and I feel his lips brush against the top of my head as he kisses me. "A queen."

I snort derisively. "No thanks."

Tenderly, he grabs my shoulders and adjusts me so that I have to look at him. When I finally indulge this domineering shifter and begrudgingly open my eyes, he's grinning.

"Rory, the fact that you don't want it just makes you more qualified to have it."

I roll my eyes and gesture around us. "Who am I going to rule, Drew? The snow bunnies?"

He shrugs. "People are attracted to power. You'll see. As time goes on, this place will grow. I don't know what it'll look like yet, but I know that with you at the helm, it will be breathtaking."

Despite the heaviness of what we're talking about, I can't help but smile. He's such a smooth talker.

"You're a queen," he says again, his hands sliding from my shoulders as his fingers trail down the sides of my body.

The slow, sensual movement stirs ribbons of lust deep within me, and my traitorous body aches for him even as I'm trying to simply listen.

He only pauses to rest his powerful hands on my hips as he leans in toward me. "You are a Boss, and I want to see you take your place among the seven dragon families as number eight."

I quirk an eyebrow, not entirely sure where this is coming from. "That seems a little ambitious for my tastes, Drew. I'm just trying not to die right now."

He shrugs again, his warm touch leaving my skin as he rests his elbow on his knee beneath the blanket. "You'll come around to this one way or another, Rory. It's inevitable. I'm just planting the seed."

My smile falls. Not entirely fond of the way he worded that, I wrap my arms around my leg and lean my cheek on one knee as I stare out at the mountain range again.

The whole idea of ruling—of being a leader and carving a seat for myself at the table of the Bosses—I mean none of it even remotely interests me. I've dealt with them all, and the only one I like is Harper.

I'm not interested in politics, nor am I interested in their games.

To keep from getting into an argument with Drew, I simply don't answer. It's our unspoken agreement when we want a conversation to just stop, and it means we can perhaps come back to it later.

Luckily, he takes the hint.

I busy myself with the horizon to distract my thoughts from going too far down the rabbit hole of the seed he planted. His little plan worked, and now it's all I can think about. But it just doesn't seem like me. What's a queen without subjects? What's a Boss without those who follow? Out here in Ashgrave, I have my men, and that's everything I need.

Why make it more complicated by needing to rule anyone at all?

Something darts along the horizon, small and blurry at first, and it's so subtle I almost ignore it. My instinct flares, however, and I stand to get a better look. The blanket slides over my shoulders as I brace myself against the wind.

"What do you see?" Drew asks, squinting at the horizon.

I narrow my eyes, and instead of answering, I merely watch. I wait. There's something out there, and my dragon doesn't like it.

It takes a few moments, but as the seconds pass, the glimmering shadow in the distance becomes clearer and begins to sharpen into a silhouette.

A dragon.

Damn it to hell—we've been found.

Before I can speak, Drew curses under his breath and jumps to his feet. His hands ball into fists as he squares his shoulders and stares off in the same direction as me.

I guess he sees it, too.

"Who could have found us?" I demand, looking at him. "And *how*, Drew?"

"I don't know," he confesses. "Even my network has limits and, possibly, moles." He pauses, casting an ominous glance toward me as we both tense. "If someone ratted me out, Rory, I'm going to burn them alive."

"You and me both," I quip, returning my attention to the horizon while I prepare for war.

As the dragon nears, he begins to look strangely familiar even though I'm not entirely sure why. Something about the red of his scales and the shape of his mouth. Even though I've never seen this dragon before, I feel like I know him.

"Milo," Drew growls under his breath.

"Oh, great." I rub my temples, wondering how this could get any worse.

"What's odd is that it's *just* Milo," Drew adds with a wary frown. "There's no security detail, and he *never* leaves home without one. They're probably nearby."

"We need to go get the others," I say, beginning to slide the dress off my shoulders so that I can shift.

I'm not usually a *dresses* kind of girl, but I *really* like this gown. I'm not about to tear my only memento from the castle to shreds.

"No, Rory. Wait," Drew says, grabbing my arm. His grip is rough and strong, and he tugs me toward him. I can't help but fall onto the balls of my feet as I lean into him, my forearm resting against his chest as he holds me close. "You can't shift."

"Why the hell not?" I frown, furrowing my brow in confusion.

"We have to keep your dragon a secret as long as possible," he answers. "The Fairfax dragons won't talk, and everyone else who witnessed your shift in the battle for the dojo is either dead or a prisoner. The world doesn't know yet, and we need to keep it that way."

Instead of answering, I turn my attention back toward Milo as he gets nearer and nearer. Damn, that dragon's fast. It won't be long before he reaches us.

But I have to admit, Drew's right.

Drew lets out a slow breath as he realizes I'm giving in, and he steps back to give me space as his body begins to shimmer and change form. In mere moments, his magnificent fire dragon takes over, and he shifts. My Darrington dragon snarls, stretching his wings as he glares at his brother and prepares to draw blood, should the need arise.

And it will most likely arise.

With nothing else to do, I cross my arms and glare

at the dragon as he nears. He's too close for me to go get the others on foot, but I hate the idea of not letting them know trouble is on its way.

Milo lands about fifty feet off, shaking the mountains as his claws dig into the rock. His gaze sweeps between us, and his eye lingers a little too long on me.

Drew bares his teeth, lifting his neck and spreading his wings in warning, but it's no contest. Of the two of them, Drew is far superior. Stronger. A better fighter.

Milo knows that.

This feels like a trap, and I don't like it one bit.

Milo lowers his head and extends his wing toward Drew, silently asking if they can talk.

I look briefly at my fire dragon, who stiffens. His glare never leaves Milo's face, and for a moment, he doesn't move. It's like he wants to make Milo uneasy—like he wants Milo to prove he even deserves an audience.

After a moment or two of breathless silence, Drew brushes the tip of his wing against his brother's, and their connection opens. Subtly, I set my palm on Drew's leg so that I, too, can join the conversation.

What are you doing, baby brother? Milo asks, his voice echoing through my head as the connection resonates between the three of us. *Why do you keep playing this game with this girl? It's getting out of hand.*

I wrinkle my nose in disgust, but I try not to make it obvious that I'm listening in.

What's your game, Milo? Drew asks. *If I come home, Father gives me control of the family. You'll lose all your power. You don't want me to come back, so why are you really here?*

Milo chuckles, the soft puffs of air rolling through his nose as he shakes his head a little, like Drew is a sweet, stupid little child who simply hasn't figured it out yet. *You're going to give her to me, and I'm going to turn her over to Father to cement my rule. If I allow you to come home, you will first bow to me and declare your loyalty. Do you understand?*

Drew sets one wing around me possessively. *And why would I do that?*

Because I found your network, little brother, Milo says, tilting his head as his eyes narrow. *I know your movements. I can take all of your money. Everything you've built will disappear overnight unless you hand her over to me right now. You'll be left penniless, and let's be real—once you're useless, she will leave you anyway.*

My grip tightens on Drew's leg, my fingers digging into his scales as I grit my teeth at Milo's audacity. Ribbons of white light burn over my skin as a surge of anger fuels a hot wave of magic.

I'm about to blast Milo's ass into last week.

I dare you to try, Drew says, growling.

This isn't a bluff, Drew, Milo says, tensing. *If you don't do what I say, you'll lose everything. Is that really something you're prepared to live with?*

Drew snaps his wing away, breaking the connection. A low and brutal growl builds in his chest as he prepares for battle. Milo snarls, his head low as he bares his teeth.

Tension bubbles through the air, and it's clear this isn't going to end well. This is going to end in blood and, if we're not careful, maybe even something we regret.

This could get ugly, and the Darringtons have already proven they have an incredible resilience to my magic. Drew can resist a full blast to his body at point-blank range, even in human form. Even though I managed to scar Jett, the attack I made against him *should* have killed him. I have no idea if Milo is as strong as those two, and I might need another plan of attack if this goes south.

I sure wish I had a sword—or even just a dagger.

Something.

A little light goes off in the back of my mind as I remember the dagger I briefly held in my palm back on the stormy cliffs of that island in the middle of nowhere—the little Spectre blade made purely of magic.

It makes me wonder.

Perhaps—just *maybe*—the weapons I can sometimes summon from my powers are enhanced. There's a chance they can do what a blast of magic never could, since it's a focused application of magic that I can use more strategically than a raw and raging blast.

Silently, I debate my options, and I wonder if I can summon that little dagger again.

I have to try.

As the two of them snarl and circle each other, I step back to give them space. With one hand hidden behind me, I try to summon the dagger again.

The problem is I have no idea how I did it in the first place—but what else is new? That's how all my powers seem to start. There's no instruction manual for god magic.

Carefully, my eyes still trained on the snarling dragons in front of me, I summon my magic into my palm. At first, all I feel between my fingers is the familiar heat as it shimmers and flows over my skin, and I try yet again to remember how I summoned it the first time.

It was reactive. Uncontrolled. In the moment, the blade was what I needed—what felt right. Lost in the flood of my magic, I simply thought of what I wanted, envisioning it, and the dagger came on its own.

I lick my lips as the two dragons growl, far too close for comfort given that I'm standing on a mountain peak and not supposed to shift. If their tails hit me, I'll fly off the edge of the mountain and have no choice but to let my dragon take over—unless I get lucky and catch a snow bank.

Even then, this place is prone to avalanches.

This is just *not* good.

My chest tight and panging with dread, I try again to imagine the dagger in my palm. For a fleeting second, it flickers into existence, and I can feel the weight of something heavy in my hand. My fingers tighten around it, and there it is—a dagger made purely of light. Purely of my magic.

Before I can so much as grin in victory, Milo launches at his brother's throat, and the duel begins.

The two of them roar, the mountains shaking under their might, and Milo's tail swings through the air. His head tilts toward me ever so slightly, and I figure he's keeping tabs on me in his periphery. I try to dart out of the way, but he corrects his blow.

That jackass.

He's *trying* to hit me.

Before I know it, Milo's tail hits me hard in the gut.

I'm thrown backward, tumbling down the mountain to a small snow bank not far below, and the dagger dissolves into glimmering dust.

Damn it.

I cough and sputter, trying to catch my breath after he knocked the wind out of me. With my hand on my stomach, my world spins. For several minutes, all I can see are stars, and I try desperately to get to my feet again.

There's a pained roar and the shuffle of scales across snow before something is thrown into the air over me. I look up as Milo careens down the mountain, kicking up heaps of white powder as he falls. Drew stands over us on his hind legs, his wings stretched wide as he debates going after his brother.

I know the look on his face—that deadly glint to his eye, the way his lip curls in a vengeful snarl.

Drew is debating *ending* this.

For good.

I wonder if he could do it. If he could really kill Milo. He already gave up protecting him from the Fairfax dragons, and I wonder how much of his love for his brother died when he did that. After everything he's endured in Milo's name, I wonder how much bad blood has corroded what was left of their relationship.

Not far below me and much too close for comfort,

Milo recovers. His claws dig effortlessly into the cliff face, sending rocks tumbling along the snowy slopes below him. Like a bullet from a gun, he launches into the sky and shoots back up the mountain.

He is *blindingly* fast.

His wings cut hard through the air, and at first, I think he's careening toward Drew to finish this fight he knows he will lose. It's a fool's game, really, and I don't know what he's trying to do.

At the last second, he banks toward me.

Very suddenly, his plan becomes painfully clear. This whole fight was a diversion, and neither Drew nor I saw the truth until it was too late.

He just wanted to put space between me and Drew, and this was his ploy all along.

Shit.

With little in the way of options, I summon my magic and fire a furious blast right at his stupid face.

The beam of white light hits a brutal blow, and I don't even try to hold back. This is new magic, powerful and unwieldy, and it has obliterated fully grown dragons to dust. I don't even think before I fire —I simply give Milo everything I have because I refuse to let him take me.

I simply *refuse,* and damn the consequences.

Tapping into my reserves and the full weight of my

bubbling fury, I lean into the blast of powerful white light. It blisters through the air, crackling as it hits him hard in the face.

He screams in agony, the sound shrill and grating. In the distance, the roar of an avalanche thunders through the mountains as his voice cuts through the clouds.

For a moment, the whole world burns white. The pained roar of a dragon in utter agony lingers on the air, and I wonder if I just killed Drew's big brother.

Gods above, I hope Drew can forgive me.

As the white light slowly fades, a second roar rumbles across the mountain range, and black smoke breaks through the middle of my magic. Milo barrels through my powerful beam, his scales smoking and smoldering as he roars at me.

White sparks burn along his body like a shorting circuit, but he doesn't stop. He doesn't slow. He's furious, clearly hurting, and far more determined than ever to snatch me from the ground.

My chest pangs with dread.

These stupid Darringtons just won't *die*.

I summon another blast, but I'm not fast enough. Milo is a lot of things—weak, sleazy, even manipulative. But he's also fast as hell.

Faster, even, than Drew.

His claws wrap around my waist, the sharp talons digging into my skin and ripping my beautiful dress as they draw blood. Within moments, he darts into the air, barreling off the cliff with his wings pinned to his side to give himself more speed.

What an *asshole*.

Trapped in Milo's claws, I can't see much but the blurry white of a snowy world passing quickly by. Mostly, it's just the flurry of red scales and white powder as he cuts through the mountainside in an attempt to shake Drew. Every now and then, the sky behind us comes into view, and I see my furious fire dragon giving chase. Black smoke barrels out of Drew's nose as he gets ever closer, the muscles in his back and wings pumping as he furiously tries to catch up.

Milo occasionally glances over his shoulder, a rumbling growl building in his chest as he fails to shake his brother. It's clear he didn't expect Drew to keep up, and I suspect he's frustrated he hasn't out-flown my fire dragon yet.

Being carried off in a dragon's claws wasn't exactly on my agenda for today, and I'm about fed up with this whole damn thing.

Sure, Drew had a point about hiding my dragon,

but I'm not going to do it at the expense of my safety—or Drew's.

And I'm *certainly* not going to let Milo carry me away in his claws, least of all to just dump me at Jett's feet.

Screw this.

My dragon stirs with anger, ready to rip out Milo's spine, and it's all I can do to keep her at bay. Before we shift, I want to at least try one more thing.

Even though I'm being shaken like a rag doll in his claws, I manage to twist in his grip to get a better vantage to attack him. One of his talons gouges my stomach as I wriggle in his grip, the movement ripping my dress open in the middle, and I suck in air through my teeth as I fight through the pain.

I'm going to beat this man senseless.

I swear to the *gods.*

Seething, I unleash a furious blast of my magic at his underbelly—a dragon weak spot, one he all but handed to me on a silver platter by carrying me off in his claws.

Idiot.

Milo roars in anguish, and for a moment, the two of us simply fall as he loses his altitude. Though I kind of hoped to at least knock him unconscious, he recovers. His wings pop sharply outward, wobbling as they shake violently on the wind, and he glares down at me with black smoke barreling out of his nose.

But he keeps flying.

He's not as resilient to my magic as Drew or even Jett, but he can hold his own. And, considering that he has now survived two consecutive blasts, I don't want to take any more chances.

I could end this, after all.

All I have to do is shift.

My magic swells again at the idea, my dragon aching to rip this shifter a new asshole, and I feel her pushing past the limits of what I can control.

It's like a hand against a balloon, changing the shape, trying to pop it with nothing but force.

I grit my teeth as the surge burns within me, and I hate feeling so out of control—especially after everything I've done to rein this in. After everything I've endured.

Right now, I just don't see any reason to hold back anymore.

I'm so freaking *done*.

Instead of fighting the surge—instead of fighting the swell of magic this time and trying to zen myself into oblivion—I give in. I let my dragon take over, and through all of the wrath and rage, I feel a flicker of gratitude from her.

Thank you for letting me do this.

Thank you for not fighting me anymore.

All I can do is nod as the magic takes over completely.

Familiar ripples of pain cut through my body, consuming me as my figure morphs into my beautiful dragon. The pain sears through me, but it's quickly replaced by relief as my body stretches and reshapes.

As I become a diamond dragon.

It all happens so quickly that Milo doesn't even have a chance to process what I'm doing.

Milo's claws stretch open as my body grows, and even as he loses his grip on me, I dig my talons into him so that I can hold tight.

He won't get away from *me.*

I snarl, the broiling thunder in my chest strong enough to carry through the mountains. My full rage takes over as he gapes down at me in shock, but I don't give him time to recover.

My claws rip into his body, drawing torrents of blood that stream from each wound. Teeth bared, I dig my razor-sharp talons into him as deep as they can go.

After all, I want to make sure I have a good grip for what I'm about to do to this asshole.

With my wings still tucked tight to my body, we fall through the air, careening like missiles through the sky toward the snow below. It's intentional, of course. Though my stomach churns as we lose altitude, I wait for the perfect moment and use the momentum against him even as he tries to recover.

The poor fool beats his wings hard against the air, trying to shake me, trying to wriggle from my grip, but he can't.

He won't be free until I *let* him go.

My powerful body tenses as I twist mid-air, throwing him at the nearest mountain. With perfect timing, I release my claws. He sails through the air like a ragdoll, dazed and caught off guard by the sudden and powerful blow. Ribbons of red blood streak from his gaping wounds, falling through the air.

As I expected, he's too stunned to recover. He just falls, and with a few powerful strokes of my shimmering wings, I fly after him. Fueled by my ire, I keep up with him as he tries to right himself.

Unrelenting and unwilling to give him even an inch, I slash at his wings every time he starts to recover. Maybe it's a little cruel, but he needs to learn his lesson—and this is the only way assholes learn.

Besides, his body will heal—even if his ego doesn't.

As he reaches the cliff, I grab his neck and slam him *hard* into the wall. The rock cracks underneath him as we form a small crater in the vertical cliff. Flurries of white powder float by us, kicked up by our one-sided duel, and I dig my claws into the stone to keep him pinned.

Taking a page out of Drew's intimidation play-book, I stretch my wings out as far as they'll go to show him my true size and strength. The sun shines across my scales as my body glimmers like diamonds.

I growl, and the mountain rumbles around me. Snow breaks off below us, and yet another avalanche crashes down the mountainside—but this time, it was *mine*.

That feels pretty damn good.

Milo's eyes widen, and though he claws at my arm, trying to break free, I don't so much as flinch. His talons scrape across my skin, and I snarl at his audacity to so much as *dare* touch my dragon's beautiful scales, let alone damage them.

He looks absolutely terrified, and his sharp, wary eyes make it clear that he knows exactly what I am.

With my claw on his throat, mere inches from his jugular, the connection between us opens. For a moment, I don't say a thing.

I simply permit him a glimpse into my mind—so that he can fully feel my absolute *fury*.

Seething, snarling, I allow my anger to pour through. My hatred. My resentment. I let him feel it all. I don't hold back even an ounce of my rage because I want him to know that everything I'm about to say is said with absolute certainty.

I'm dead serious.

I am not a toy, I tell him, leaning toward him ever so slightly to drive home my point. *I am not something to claim, and I am so fucking done with the lot of you. With all of the Bosses. With you all and your conniving attempts to chain me. With your attempts to manipulate and control the people around me.*

White sparks dance on my breath, and for the first time, I wish I could blow smoke because I would blow it right into his face right now.

I think you're bluffing, personally, I say, leaning toward him as I refer to his threat against Drew's network. *But even if you aren't, I want to make something abundantly clear to you, Milo Darrington. You are not allowed to so much as look at Drew's network again. You aren't to touch Drew's money, his resources, or anything he owns. In fact, you're going to double Drew's total net worth within twenty-four hours, or I'm coming for your head. If I catch you again, Milo, I won't be so generous as to let you go next time.*

I pause, trying to tune into what he's feeling and searching through our connection for what's going on in his head. For the most part, all I feel is a flurry of panic and shock, and it's clear he hasn't quite processed what he's seeing or much of what I've said.

How disappointing. I expected a Darrington to be a little quicker than that.

Milo, listen to me, I snap, snarling as I try to make one last thing abundantly clear to him.

Listening, he says simply, his eyes darting between mine as he stills.

Agree to my terms, I demand. *Immediately.*

He hesitates, and though I expect him to growl in defiance, he simply nods. *Done.*

Good boy. I don't bother to mask my condescending tone. *Now, if I hear so much as a whisper about the fact that I can shift—if I hear so much as a rumor that I'm a dragon—I will come for you, Milo Darrington, and I will kill you myself. Drew can't stop me. Jett can't stop me. No amount of security detail will get in my way. I will gut you like an animal, and you will die a slow death.*

For a moment, I let him sit there, and I'm careful to guard my thoughts so that he doesn't sense anything else from me because those words didn't even feel like they were entirely mine. It was a little too much, even for me, but the anger—that's absolutely mine. I figure my dragon is going medieval on this asshole, and given everything he's tried to do to us, I'm not about to hold her back.

Without another word, I let him go, and he careens down the cliff. His body bounces across the rock several times, kicking up pebbles and snow as he tries to recover. It takes a little while, but he eventually rights himself on the long tumble down the mountain and flies off, keeping low through the slopes.

Every now and then, he looks over his shoulder at me with a terrified expression until he gets too far away for me to see clearly.

I snort in annoyance. Good riddance.

Movement in my periphery catches my attention, and I impulsively tense, ready to rip apart whoever else is foolish enough to attack me right now.

But it's Drew.

He soars toward me and digs his claws into the rock as he lands beside me, dark smoke coils from his nose as he watches his brother retreat.

After Milo finally disappears, Drew turns his full attention toward me. Tenderly, he sets one wing around me and presses his forehead against mine, our connection opening as our scales touch.

You shouldn't have shifted, he says almost instantly, like he didn't even want to wait for the connection to open before speaking.

Even though he's chiding me, I can feel the intention behind his words. He's too proud of me to actually be angry, and through the pride, I also feel a thick ribbon of lust snake through.

I think a thank you is in order, I tell him. *Seeing as Milo's going to double your net worth by tomorrow.*

Drew snorts, and for a moment, all he can do is laugh. He throws his head up into the air as huffs of hot air roll through his nose. *I can't believe you did that. He's actually going to double my account balance?*

I made him swear, I say, beaming with pride. *I even called him a 'good boy' when he agreed.*

Oh gods above, are you serious? Drew practically howls with laughter. *The only thing he loves more than power is money—and you called him a 'boy' after taking it?*

You're welcome, I reply, and I wish dragons could grin because I would be beaming right now.

That was hot as hell, Drew says as he once again presses his forehead against mine. His wing tightens around me, pulling me closer. *I'm taking you, Rory Quinn. Right now. If you don't want to fuck as dragons, I need you to find a place to shift back immediately.*

I laugh, sparks shooting from my nose as I growl with lust and triumph.

Kinky.

CHAPTER TWELVE

Thanks to Milo's stupid little abduction, my beautiful new dress had a life of roughly six hours before it was torn to shreds.

Damn it.

Wearing jeans and a hoodie that make me feel a bit underdressed, I lean my head back against the wall and close my eyes as I blow a raspberry at the ceiling.

In the tiny dining room of yet another small cabin far from Ashgrave—and even farther from the place where I whooped Milo's ass—my men and I stand around the table in silence. Levi leans against the doorframe while the rest of us frown, staring at the surface of the empty table while we all lose ourselves in thought.

Since Milo found us, we had to move.

Again.

Faced with an impossible task and the world breathing down our necks, we absolutely *must* come up with a plan.

In the quiet, we're all lost in thought. Each of us is internally debating and trying to come up with a plan to find these orbs.

And we're *all* stuck.

We weren't expecting to run into this roadblock, and these ancient orbs could be anywhere. It's frustrating to think that I still have no leads. Nothing at all to go on except the fact that I need them and the hope that they even exist anymore.

I rub my eyes in frustration, wondering where we should even start.

"So, what's the plan?" Tucker yanks a chair out from the table and sits, leaning his elbows against the wooden surface as he runs his hand through his hair in aggravation. "Where do we look for these orbs? Do they even exist? It's been eons, right?"

"They exist," I say without really thinking about it. It's like my dragon reached up through me to speak, and I somehow know that even with no proof, I'm right.

In that moment, I just know.

I scan the room as each of my men turn to look at

me. They're quiet, simply watching me and probably equally as confused about these new powers as I am.

"So…" Tucker asks, trailing off momentarily as he shrugs. "Do we have a magical GPS or something? Some kind of glowy orb tracker?"

I chuckle, shaking my head. "I wish."

"Let's look at the facts," Jace interjects, and for a minute, he looks once again like a dojo master taking control of a situation. Shoulders squared. Back straight. One arm is crossed over his chest, his elbow resting in the palm of his other hand as he rubs his jaw.

Deep within me, my dragon leans toward him, turned on by the simple fact that he exists.

Whoa there, girl, I chide her. *Let's focus on the matter at hand, at least for the moment. Rein in your lust for, like, two seconds.*

She snorts at me in irritation, and I can feel her bubbling impatience stirring deep within me.

"We have one lead," I say with a little shrug. "Well, sort of. The Knights destroyed the gods, and even though Ashgrave said it was the Oracles who removed the orbs, the loyalists were infiltrated. It's possible the Knights took Ashgrave's magic, not the Oracles."

"But that was ages ago," Drew points out. "That magic could be anywhere by now."

"I know," I admit, crossing my arms as I lean back in my chair. "I mean, think about the ritual pit, right? That was on Vaer property. How could dragons have acquired such important property if it belonged to the Knights? Would the Knights have protected that at all costs?"

"Ah, well…" Tucker says, stumbling a little over his words. "That actually wasn't Vaer territory."

"What?" Drew, Jace, and I ask in unison.

"Yeah," Tucker says with a little chuckle. "That was a carefully orchestrated coup. The Knights wanted to monitor that land even though the Vaer were trying—very successfully, I might add—to take it. So, it was strategically *allowed* to be taken. The Knights had everything in that area recorded twenty-four-seven. It was always important, but no one knew why." Tucker hesitates, his gaze falling briefly to the floor. "Well, my father knew why, but he didn't tell anyone. Not even me."

I study Tucker for a moment, yet again wondering if he's okay. The feud between him and his father is coming to a head, and when it ends, it won't be pretty. With the General's sheer determination and hatred for those who defy him, I suspect there will be a *lot* of blood.

After all, the General isn't the sort of man to be redeemed. He's done too much. Hurt too many.

And Tucker will have to pull the trigger.

It's a difficult concept to focus on right now, especially with so much else on our plate. With a deep and steadying breath, I close my eyes to clear my head.

When a Spectre is stuck, there's a short list of options for her to run through. I may not be a Spectre anymore, but there's a few useful bits of my past left, and this is one of them.

Item one—run through your allies.

There aren't many.

Irena. Russell. Harper. I briefly wonder if Jade Nabal might be helpful—after all, she seemed kind when I met her back at the neutral zone. However, she *is* a Nabal. For all I know, the kindness is just a front.

Okay, so—three. Three allies.

I groan in irritation.

Irena is still missing, but she might know something about the orbs since she had access to the Spectre files.

As Drew and Jace launch into a discussion about where the orbs could be, I slip my phone out of my pocket and pull up the last number I remember her having. My thumb hovers over the keypad as I debate what I should even say.

Briefly, I consider just putting my phone away, but this is simply too important.

Mom's sick, I text her in our little code from way back. *Call when you can.*

In reality, it means *I really freaking need your help, so call me the moment you're not actively slitting someone's throat, please.*

As I slide my phone back into my pocket, I ruminate over our other two options.

Russell has all the same intel that Jace had when he was dojo master, so there's probably nothing new to follow up with there.

But Harper...

"What about Harper?" I ask Jace. "Does she know anything about this?"

Jace rolls his eyes and shakes his head impatiently. "I've been trying to reach her, but so far I haven't had any luck. It seems like she's in a place with no reception right now, which means she's off trying to recruit allies for her war against Kinsley. When she's back in contact, I'll ask."

"Thanks," I say with a nod, figuring I could probably ask her myself. "We can't just sit around waiting for her to get back, though. It could be days or weeks." I hesitate, briefly wondering if it might take even longer.

After all, she *is* in Boss Mode. That means everything else just kind of disappears until the crisis is averted and all fires extinguished.

"Well, if we were gods, where would we hide shiny magic orbs?" Tucker asks, gesturing toward the window. "Did they have holy sites? Places of power? Anything?"

"Most were kept secret," Jace admits. "What the world did know has been lost to time. There's just not much to go on."

"Damn it," I mutter, smacking my palm against the table. "We need intel." I frown, running through our list of allies again—but there's one I didn't consider, one man who's not really an ally at all.

Brett.

"Have the Fairfax dragons questioned Brett?" I ask, my tone a little wistful as the idea slowly dawns on me. "If the Knights really did have anything to do with the orbs, maybe he knows."

The room is eerily silent for a moment, and I look up to find everyone watching me with a hint of disbelief—even as, one by one, a strange sense of knowing washes over their faces.

"He might," Tucker admits.

"They have to be careful," Jace says with a small shake of his head. "They can't give him much to go on, or he might lie and pretend to know about the orbs to weasel his way out of prison."

"Russell will know what to do." I rub my jaw, wondering how he's going to play this.

Carefully, I hope.

It's one of the few ideas we even have.

"I don't like it," Drew admits. "We shouldn't rely on that man."

"We have nothing else to go on," I point out with a frustrated shrug. "What else can we even do, Drew?"

"Well, there is *one* option," the Darrington dragon admits, leaning back in his chair as he slumps against the hard seat.

I frown, furrowing my eyebrows as I watch him and wait for him to explain what the hell that means.

"You have a lead?" Jace asks, surprised.

Drew groans, hesitating as he rubs the back of his neck. It's like he's searching for the right words and having a hell of a time with it. "Calling it a lead is generous," my fire dragon admits after a while. "I really don't like it, and I haven't wanted to say anything because this is the furthest thing from a safe bet that we could possibly find right now. But it seems like we have very little in the way of options at the moment."

"Spit it out, man," Jace snaps, sounding about as

irritated as I feel.

"There's a guy in Vietnam that claims to have access to an ancient tome of dragon god lore that has never been revealed to the world," Drew answers with a small flourish of his hand, like he doesn't quite believe it.

I snort derisively. "That sounds too good to be true."

"Exactly," Drew says with a small nod as he looks at me. "That's why I hate this lead. It feels more like a trap than the truth. The world knows all about the dragon vessel, so they know you probably need information. The description of what he's got is just plain vague, and he doesn't have anything to prove what he's claiming. Hell, he can't even open the book. It could just be a trap to get you in close to him."

I laugh in disbelief. "He can't even open the book?"

"What kind of proof does this guy even have?" Jace interjects.

"Pictures of the locked book," Drew says with a shrug. "He says no locksmith can open it. That it's magical. I've had trouble verifying the authenticity, and without being able to study the bindings and do a carbon test on the paper, we don't know how old it really is. And even if it *is* old, it could be a carefully preserved collection of horseshit for all we know."

"Then how do we know this is any good?" I ask, frowning.

"Apparently there's a note that came with it," Drew says, his body stiffening as he answers. "And this is the part he's shown the world. It's a simple letter, very short, and the last third of the letter—including the signature—has been torn off. It's a request to keep the book safe and hidden, as it tells the truth of the gods no one is supposed to know, and that letter, well," Drew adds as his gaze lands on me. "It *has* been authenticated. It's almost three thousand years old."

"Wow," Tucker says with a small whistle. "How has that paper not faded away to dust?"

"Care," Jace answers. "But it doesn't *mean* anything. He could put that note with any book and say it's authentic. We have no proof that the book the note's talking about is the one he's trying to sell."

"Exactly," Drew says, nodding to the former dojo master as they agree on that point, at least. "This guy says he's had assassins come after him for possessing this book, and he keeps both it and himself locked safely away under heavy security."

"Oh, good." I don't bother masking my sarcasm as I shake my head. "So we'll be walking into a heavily armed den filled with security detail and dragon killers."

"Yeah," Drew says, rubbing his neck.

As the guys continue to debate and discuss, my mind wanders. If this is true—if this is real—then it might have information on where the orbs were taken. Someone who claims to know the truth of the gods would know the inner workings and possibly even know where the orbs were supposed to go, if not exactly where they are.

Deep within me, my dragon coils with curiosity at the thought. It's a sense of anticipation. Of excitement. Of hope.

But *not* of knowing. This is new to her, too.

One thing is for certain—she and I will know if this book is real. All we have to do is touch it.

"I need to see this book," I finally say.

"But who knows if the book truly has accurate information?" Jace asks with a shrug. "It's not worth the risk. Even if we get it and you somehow open it, everything in it could be false for all we know."

"Then we cross-reference it to Ashgrave's mural room for verification," I say with a shrug. "If it's full of horseshit or if it's wrong, we throw it away. At least we *tried.*"

Drew hesitates a moment, his brow furrowing as if he hadn't thought of that. "True. We can."

"How much does he want for it?" I ask my fire

dragon.

"Seventeen million in American dollars."

Tucker laughs. "Holy shit!"

"Yeah, I know," Drew says. "But that's ancient artifacts dealing for you."

"Well, who cares?" Tucker asks with a shrug. "That's pocket change for you, right moneybags?"

Drew smirks. "It is now, especially after Milo's very generous donation." Drew's gaze darts toward me, and his smirk broadens.

I grin. It serves that asshole right, and I can't help but wonder how much money he had to give Drew. "He complied?"

"Oh yeah," Drew says, laughing as he slowly nods his head. "He doubled everything to the *dime.*"

My smile falls. "Did you find out how he got access?"

Drew chews the inside of his cheek as his grin fades, and he crosses his arms while he looks away. "Yeah."

"Who do we need to kill?"

My fire dragon sighs and shakes his head. "I'll handle it, Rory."

"Drew, I—"

"I'll handle it," Drew repeats, his tone dangerously tense as his dark gaze narrows in warning.

I frown, studying his face for the deeper meaning, and it takes a moment for it to click. He knows about *one* mole, but I think he suspects there might be more —and he intends to torture the one responsible until he works the kinks out of his network. Knowing Drew, he will be brutal. Efficient. He will break the one responsible for me nearly being captured until there's nothing left but a husk of a shifter, and then he will burn the man to ash.

Drew just doesn't want me to watch that, and he probably hopes I don't figure out what he's up to.

My jaw tenses, and I silently nod, giving him space on this one.

"So, where is this guy?" Levi interjects, his intense gaze trained on Drew as he leans against the wall by the door.

We all pause and turn toward him as he breaks his silence for the first time tonight. It always feels like there's a shift in the conversation when Levi talks because he only speaks when he has something truly important to say.

"Ho Chi Minh City," Drew answers.

"Oh, good," Tucker says sarcastically, throwing his hands in the air. "So, it's only one of the most heavily populated places in all of Vietnam. Great."

"This is dangerous," Levi says with a frown as his

gaze drifts toward me. "I don't want you to go, Rory."

At least he didn't *demand* I stay back this time, but his lack of confidence in me is starting to grate on my patience.

I impulsively stiffen at the comment, and it reminds me too much of all the times people have tried to control me throughout my life. I wonder if he's changing—if me being forced into the global spotlight and losing my shadows is changing the way he thinks of me. I grimace, but as we watch each other, his scowl shifts into gentle concern.

I sigh, rubbing my temples, and decide to give him the benefit of the doubt. All of this is new to him, and he still very much likes going unseen.

We simply *can't* anymore.

"I'm the only one who can tell for sure if it's real, Levi," I point out. "I need to hold it to know."

My ice dragon shakes his head, angry, and simply looks away with his arms crossed.

"Are you sure about this, Rory?" Jace asks, leaning his fists on the table as he watches me with wary caution.

I laugh. "Hell, no. I'm not even *remotely* sure about this. For all we know, this book could be a fake, but we need a lead. We need *something*, Jace. We can't just keep going from cabin to cabin, waiting for our luck to kick in. The longer we do this, the longer we stay in hiding, the higher our risk of getting caught."

I pause, and the silence stretches on far longer than I would like. Each of my men watches me warily, as if waiting for me to continue even though I was done.

With a small sigh, I gesture toward the window. "If anyone has a better idea, I would really love to hear it because I do *not* want to do this. But as far as I can tell, this is our only choice."

Though I hope for a response—to kick start another discussion filled with options—the silence stretches on.

This time, I wait. I really want an alternative. I really want someone to come up with something better. Something that doesn't take us into the heart of a populated city in a world that knows not only *my* face, but also my *men's.* My *allies.*

We're exposed, and I hate it.

When no one says anything, I kick off the wall and lean my palms against the back of the nearest chair. I have to confess I'm a little disappointed, but now I'm more certain than ever this is what we need to do. "Drew, let's set up a meeting with this guy. Don't let him know I'm coming or who any of you are."

Drew nods. "He won't have a clue, Rory," my fire dragon says. "I promise."

CHAPTER THIRTEEN

The buzzing streets of Ho Chi Minh City whiz by us through tinted windows as our driver takes me, Jace, and Levi through the tangled web of storefronts and scooters.

Our contact, Mr. Viet, insisted he wanted to send us a limo to pick us up from the airport—after all, he thinks we're about to drop seventeen million on an ancient artifact, and any smart seller would treat us like royalty to make sure the purchase goes through.

Personally, I don't care about limos, but the guy's kind of pushy.

It's next to impossible to drive a stretch limo through these chaotic streets, however, so after a thousand apologies from this man over something I care absolutely nothing about, we now sit in a modified sedan with windows tinted so heavily that they might as well be fully black. The bright and sunny world outside looks muted and muffled through the windows, and with the sunglasses I'm also wearing, it's almost impossible to see out of them at all.

But the sunglasses are important. They're part of my disguise.

It takes everything in me not to scratch at the jet-black wig I'm wearing, but it's an integral part of the role I'm playing: American Heiress.

A short black dress clings to my body and ends halfway up my thigh, and though I have to actively fight the impulse to continue tugging it down my legs, I manage to keep still. It's been ages since I wore heels, but Zurie made me learn how to fight in them, just in case I ever needed to disguise myself on a mission.

At least that horrible woman was good for a few things.

"Comm check, two," Tucker says through the comm in my ear.

I subtly brush my hand through the wig's dark curls, making sure the comm is hidden. It makes sense for my bodyguards to have them, but not me.

No one can see mine.

"Comm check, one," Drew says in response. "In position."

"Good," I say under my breath, too quietly for the driver to hear. "Get ready."

Levi and Jace sit on either side of me, dressed in suits and also wearing dark glasses that block out most of the light. As the least recognizable of my men, we decided Levi would pose as my security detail—and, shockingly, with a bit of hair gel, sunglasses, and a change to the way he walks, Jace does a convincing job of blending into the background.

I'm starting to think he would've made a good Spectre in another life.

A few bodyguards patted us down in a private room at the airport, to my surprise. I figured they would wait until we arrived at the hotel to check for guns—which of course, we left with Tucker—but I think this is all part of the game.

They didn't wait to pat us down at the hotel because they didn't *need* to. From here on out, we're being watched.

And they wanted us to *know* it.

Though I wish we could have found wigs for both of them as well, it just wasn't possible on such short notice. We will simply have to make do with what we have.

The driver that was sent for us keeps looking in the rearview mirror through the small divider that separates him from the backseat. I frown as his gaze wanders over me yet again, and I've had about enough of his curiosity.

Without a word, I reach forward and slide the small metal divider closed so that he can't look back at us anymore.

Jace tilts his head slightly toward me, and though I can't see his beautiful eyes from behind the sunglasses, I can imagine what he's thinking.

Good move.

I nod. From here on out, I have to assume everyone we interact with works for the man we're going to see. We need to remain undetected, and that's incredibly difficult in a world that knows my face.

I adjust in my seat again, hating the uncomfortable dress as it slides up my legs, and my bare thigh brushes the back of Levi's hand. The subtle motion opens our unique connection, and a surge of humming anxiety bleeds through from him. Silent as ever, he scans the world around us, his shoulders tense and his back arched, as if he's waiting for something to happen.

As if he's waiting for something to go wrong.

I don't know what to say to comfort him. So, instead, I simply let my soothing love for him seep through our connection, trying my best to overpower his buzzing dread. He stills for a moment, tilting his head toward me, and though I can't see his icy blue eyes from behind the sunglasses, a small smile plays at the edge of his mouth.

Thanks, he says through our connection.

I nod and wrap my hand around his. *We're going to get through this. We always do.*

His smile fades, and he lets out a little sigh. *I know I've been tenser than usual lately, and I'm not trying to control you, Rory. It's just that everything is changing, and I don't want something to catch us off-guard.*

That's fair, I admit with a slight frown.

It's just... He groans, lifting his glasses slightly as he rubs his eyes in exhausted frustration. *This feels too familiar.*

How so?

This—all of this. He gestures with his other hand at the car, the street, the driver.

Jace frowns, glancing between us as Levi and I have a silent conversation, one he can't join in on.

I need you to be a bit more specific, I say with a chuckle.

Levi, however, doesn't laugh. *It all reminds me of my time in the forest, when the only way I could eat was to hunt. The moment the animals knew I was there, they ran off. Have you seen a dragon chase down a rabbit? It doesn't go well. Those little bastards are fast.*

Before I can help myself, I snort with laughter.

Levi pokes me in the side. *You laugh now, but wait until you're starving and that's the only animal you've seen for days.*

My smile falls.

Levi sighs, running a hand through his gelled hair. *If you want to be a hunter, you have to go unseen. If you want to go unseen, you have to stay in the shadows. You have to be quiet until it's too late for your prey to run. And, Rory, we don't have any shadows left. Do you know what that makes us?*

I frown, my fingers tightening slightly around his hand. *This isn't the same thing, Levi.*

It's exactly the same thing, he answers, lifting his chin slightly as he disagrees. *And, to answer the question you ignored, all of this makes us prey. No matter how good you are, there's always a bigger animal out there that wants you dead. That wants to eat you alive. The way you become the hunter is by sticking to the shadows and staying silent. It's by going unseen. The moment you step into the field, the moment anyone can see you, that's when you become the prey.*

I honestly don't know what to say. I bite my lip absently, briefly forgetting about the hot red lipstick and layers of makeup I put on for this stupid meeting.

Levi can be dark sometimes, but he's not usually wrong.

I've never let anyone treat me like prey. Not really. People hunt me perhaps, but they know they're dealing with a fellow hunter.

However, Levi has a point. In this new world with all sorts of new enemies, I have to be smart. Plenty of them actually *do* see me as nothing but prey.

And even the most skilled hunter can get caught.

"We're all clear," Tucker says through the comm in my ear. "I see you guys driving below. You're almost to the hotel."

"Thanks," I say quietly, wondering which of the tall hotels around us he picked to camp out in. All he told me was that he needed a good vantage—and there aren't many rooftops with a clear shot into the penthouse of Mr. Viet's elaborate hotel.

"I don't suppose anyone came up with a magical last-minute plan to avoid this entire situation?" I say quietly into the comm.

"Afraid not," Drew says.

Beside me, Levi frowns. "I don't like this."

"None of us do," Jace answers quietly, his hand over his mouth as the conversation continues. "We need Ashgrave back online, and to do that, we need the orb. This guy is all we've got."

"All right, guys. I'm finally into the security footage," Drew interrupts. "It won't be long before they detect the hack and boot me out, but I can see you driving up. You're here."

As he speaks, the car rolls to a stop in front of a tall building with two bellhops in white gloves manning the front doors. The chauffeur jumps out and opens the car door beside Jace, and the three of us file out onto the sidewalk.

The hotel towers over us, stretching into the sky above, and I try my best to mask my tense wariness with a bored frown as I scope the place.

To my dismay, there's not much in the way of exits. It's a vertical building made almost entirely of glass that reflects the sun. The cool September weather is a relief, much more comfortable than I was expecting, and I can almost taste the coming autumn in the air.

Behind me, a horn blares as several cars race down the street, weaving between scooters at a breakneck speed that makes me wonder how many casualties the city experiences on a regular basis. The scooters don't seem to care or honestly even notice the aggressive drivers soaring past them. They file through the streets in clumps, sometimes one or two breaking off to inch around a car that's just trying to turn.

"Damn, babe," Tucker says in my ear. "You look

hot. Your ass always looks great, but that dress does it wonders."

"Tucker, focus," Drew chides.

"Don't lie to me and say looking at her doesn't turn you on," Tucker counters, the dull click of a rifle cocking rolling through the comm link as he speaks.

"Of course she's hot," Drew says, and I can practically hear the smirk in his voice. "She's my woman. You think I'd settle for less than the best?"

"Thanks, guys." Doing my best to keep my voice low, I try to hide the smirk pulling on the edge of my lips as they banter. "Let's stay focused."

The bellhops bow to us as they open the grand double doors. A blast of cool air sails over my face like a soft breath, and I square my shoulders as I prepare for whatever awaits us.

"You should have worn the red dress though," Tucker continues, ignoring me.

I chuckle as my heels clack across the tile floor. "I'm not trying to stand out here."

"You can't really help that," Jace quips, leaning toward me as he speaks in a hushed tone.

"Yeah, you're way too hot," Tucker agrees.

Oh, Tucker.

Never change.

I need to focus, so I simply stop answering as I

head into the extravagant hotel. The lobby roof arches above me, murals painted in gold and red along the ceiling, but I only give the beautiful artwork a passing glance.

After all, this is a mission, not a vacation.

Jace and Levi walk slightly behind me, their chins lifted as they brazenly survey the area around them. After all, if they're posing a security detail, they need to be aware of their environment. It is the perfect cover.

It's also, of course, a risk. I'm not the only one of my team who has a recognizable face, and no amount of makeup or lipstick can actually mask what I look like to someone who takes a moment to scrutinize us. There's a very real chance that this could all go south, and I'm basically just preparing myself for the worst.

At least then I can be pleasantly surprised if it all doesn't blow up in my face.

One of the bellhops leads us through the massive atrium carved into the middle of the hotel. Seven golden elevators line the far wall as the bellhop takes us past a long stretch of gilded desks with beautiful women ready and waiting to check in new guests. They all smile as we pass by, their eyes locked on us in the otherwise empty atrium, and I silently wish we could just blend into a crowd.

But that's not how rich men work, and the guy we're meeting is definitely loaded.

If we're about to drop seventeen million on a book, we have to play the part, and that means looking like the kind of people who have that much money just laying around.

And, unfortunately, that means attracting attention—even if I *do* hate the idea.

I scan the atrium, craning my neck as I look all the way to the top. If I have to guess, I'd say the atrium goes about ten floors—an engineering feat to be sure. Real trees fill the space, and windows along the sides of the atrium let in the cool light from above.

"Tell me about the layout," I whisper into the comm, my lips barely moving. "What does this hotel look like?"

"Seventy floors," Drew answers. "Six atriums. Each atrium has a few floors of solid rooms in between. It looks like our penthouse is right above the last atrium. Stairwells in every corner in case of an evacuation, but the elevators also work in a fire."

"Are you telling us we should be ready to blow something up?" Jace says quietly into the comm.

"I'm just saying," Drew answers, and I can hear the smirk in his voice. "If the situation calls for it, maybe don't hold back."

I chuckle.

The elevator doors open as we near, and we don't even have to wait a second before walking into the empty elevator. The bellhop once again bows his head as the doors close, and we're finally alone.

I eye the camera in the corner. Well, we're *kind* of alone. As long as we're in this building, we should assume someone's at least watching.

"Tell me more about this guy," I say, mostly to calm my nerves. "What else should I know?"

"He's a conman," Drew answers. "Bubbly, gregarious, and dark as hell."

"I think we're going to need a bit more than that," I say with a frown.

"He'll sell anything," Drew answers. "Even people. He has no problem killing to get what he wants."

"That's hearsay," Jace counters quietly. "We have no proof."

"You think a guy who got to this level of success through illicit dealings would leave proof?" Drew asks.

Fair point.

"He's incredibly rich and influential," Drew continues. "Friends with everyone who has any sort of importance or significance in the city. He owns this place."

"Awesome," I mutter.

"And, may I add, this guy's security system is even tighter than expected," Drew says with a frustrated grunt. "There are cameras everywhere. From what I can tell, there are about fifty security guys here, and there might be a few more that I'm not seeing."

"Jesus, this guy's paranoid," Tucker says.

"Or just trying to protect a valuable treasure," I counter.

"You have a plan?" Levi asks, and I catch his eyes darting briefly toward me from behind his sunglasses as I stand beside him.

"Of course she does," Jace answers for me. "Levi, she's got this."

"I know," my ice dragon answers, rolling out his shoulders as he looks away. "But the world is changing. Are we really ready for it?"

Jace and I hesitate, both of us frowning as we briefly look at each other and not entirely sure how to answer.

"Get ready, guys," Drew interrupts. "The doors are about to open."

Almost instantly, the elevator slows down, my stomach churning with the motion. Seconds later, the doors open onto another beautiful stretch of the hotel. A gorgeous woman in a bright green dress smiles broadly as we walk in, her dark hair and warm skin a beautiful contrast to the gown she's wearing.

As her eyes land on my face, they flair briefly in recognition even with my sunglasses still on, and I worry that she suddenly figured out who I am.

After all, there's only so much good sunglasses, a wig, and some lipstick can do.

Her smile briefly falters as we walk into a gorgeous room filled mostly with water. I do a quick scan, mostly looking for security detail, cameras, or weapons—but, thankfully, there's nothing to be concerned with.

Black slabs of stone cut through the shallow pool, offering a makeshift pathway through the serene garden, and bamboo lines the walls. The leaves of the natural plants tremble slightly in the air-conditioning, and the soothing trickle of water fills the space.

But even as I scope the area around us, my full attention is on her.

I would hate for our cover to be blown when we're so close to the end.

"Welcome," she says with a slight Vietnamese accent to her voice. "Please come this way." She gestures down the path of stones through the water, and without waiting for us to say anything, she leads the way.

I hesitate. I'm torn between listening to my intuitive hit to leave, and getting this book that may be our only answer.

But we've come this far.

Begrudgingly, I take a few steps onto the stone, my heels clacking with each step. Levi and Jace follow behind me, their hands clasped behind their backs as they scope the space.

At the far end of the path, two butlers reach toward the handles of a set of wooden double doors as tall as the ceiling. With a grand flourish, they open the entrance and gesture for us into another massive room.

Either this guy is trying to wow us with his money, or he's compensating for something.

In this new space, windows line the far wall, letting in cool light that casts its beams across a broad executive's desk. Four cameras sit lodged in the corners of the room, and I frown at the excess. Ten guards dip in and out of the various hallways branching off from the office, passing the priceless art covering the walls as they run their patrols. Most of the art isn't even recognizable, at least not to me, but the way it's hung and lighted makes me assume it's expensive.

At least, Zurie would've marked it as a potential theft target based on that alone.

A man dressed in a pinstripe suit sits on the surface of the desk beside the wall of glass, looking out into the open sky with both hands resting on one of his knees. It's as if we caught him in mid-thought, but I assume this is all part of the ruse.

After all, he knows we are coming.

His head snaps toward us like we caught him off guard, and a broad smile stretches across his face as he sees us. He jumps to his feet and jogs over to me, taking my hand in his and shaking it gently. "It's so nice to finally meet you, my darling! Welcome, welcome. Can I get you champagne?"

I simply shake my head. It's best not to speak too much, at least not with everything at stake.

Can't let myself be recognized, after all.

"Oh, don't be ridiculous," he says with a small laugh, waving away my refusal as if it were a joke. "I promise you'll get only the best. That's all I ever give my clients, dear Melissa, and I can't wait to see what our new friendship holds."

Melissa—my cover name for at least as long as we're here. He doesn't even acknowledge my men, even though he greets me like an old friend, and I'm thankful that at least for now he seems to be buying the ruse.

After all, my men are supposed to be my security,

and to art dealers like this, I suspect a security detail is often simply overlooked.

All he cares about is the person paying him.

"How was your trip?" the gentleman asks as he snaps his fingers.

The woman who initially led us in jogs toward him out of a side hallway with two champagne glasses and an ornate golden bottle with the foil still wrapped over the cork. She bows as she hands it to him, and he takes it without so much as looking her way.

In a subtle movement, so smooth I almost don't notice it, she hands him a small note. His eyes dart briefly toward her before he turns his back on me, and the rustle of paper catches my attention.

My heart pangs in warning, and my dragon wants out.

I don't blame her. I do, too.

"He'll talk you to death if you let him," Drew interjects through the comm in my ear. "Classic sales guy, loves the old cognitive overload method."

Oh, gods. Just what I need today.

"Do you have the book with you?" I ask, intentionally deepening my voice lightly just in case any recordings of me speaking have been leaked recently.

It's better to be safe than sorry after all.

"Of course, of course," Viet says as he raises a champagne glass toward me.

Not one for games, I frown and simply look at it. I don't try to take it, and I don't say no. I simply wait for him to get the hint.

His smile briefly fades, and his gaze drifts between me and the champagne glass he's extending toward me. To his credit, he seems to get the gist fairly quickly.

Clearing his throat, he nods and hands both glasses to his assistant, waving her off as he gestures for me to join him by the desk. As I oblige him by taking a few steps closer, he lifts his phone out of his pocket and scans the surface. He's reading something, and his eyes start briefly toward me before he clears his throat and shoves the phone away.

"You're a woman after my own heart, you know that?" Viet says, grinning again. "You're just like me. Right down to business."

I suppress a groan of irritation and manage to simply force a brief smile. This is a classic sales technique to build empathy, and I'm just not buying it right now.

I want that book, and I want to get the hell out of here.

"Shit," Drew says in my ear.

My heart sinks, and dread floods through me. I desperately want to respond, to figure out what's going on. But I can't.

Not now.

"What is it?" Jace asks, his voice tense and quiet. Out of the corner of my eye, I see him tilt his head away as he talks into the comm. Behind him, the girl in the green dress hesitates at the door, briefly looking back at me before she trots out into the main entry and the doors close behind her again.

"A worldwide alert just went out from an agent working for Viet," Drew answers. "He's holding an auction. Tonight."

"An auction for what?" Tucker asks, and I hear a gun cock beside his comm.

"For Rory," Drew answers.

There's a moment of tense silence that follows through the calm, and in my periphery, both Jace and Levi instantly stiffen.

Just *great.*

"Here it is," Viet says with a broad smile, opening up the drawer in his desk. He grabs something out of it and lifts a book into the air. The sun glints off the metallic threads woven into the binding, and he simply studies it for a moment as he holds it aloft, tilting it from side to side as if he's never seen it before.

He's just milking this.

"You need to get out of there *now*," Drew says into the comm, his voice dripping with dread.

With that warning, I have a choice to make.

The book is mere inches from me, and if I want to, I could probably just take it. Just steal it just like Zurie taught me. After all, if this guy put out an alert and wants to auction me off, he's clearly not a good person —and I've never much minded stealing from assholes.

I reach my palm toward him in a silent request that he hand it to me, doing everything I can to remain relaxed as I gently spread my fingers and wait for him to obey.

As he surveys the tome in the sunlight, I have to admit it does look ancient. The faded binding, the scuffs along what little of the pages are exposed.

And a tarnished silver lock stitched right into the binding itself.

"Well?" I ask, my hand still outstretched as I wait for him to give it to me.

He finally looks at me, a small grin on his face. "Well, that's not quite how this works," he says with a hint of sarcasm to his tone.

"I need to hold it before I'll pay you a dime."

There's a moment of silent standoff, but I don't give an inch. We simply watch each other, each daring the other to break first, and I can't help but wonder if this is truly a sales negotiation or simply his way of stalling.

Probably both.

Finally, his small grin breaks into a full smile, and he hands me the book as he concedes.

The moment the ancient tome touches my fingers, I have to admit that my hopes are high. I want this to be the answer to all of our problems.

But nothing happens.

I'm expecting some kind of spontaneous hit. Some sort of intuitive knowing that this is right, that this is magic, that this really *does* have to do with the gods.

Instead, the dull tome sits lifelessly in my hands, heavy as it weighs against my palm.

"What interests you about this book?" Viet asks as he leans one hand against his massive desk.

I simply ignore him.

I'm too consumed with the artifact, with trying to figure out if there's just something I need to do to activate it. To make it wake up.

But my dragon doesn't so much as stir as I turn and tilt the tome in my fingers. There's no connection to it at all, as if she can't even see it or sense it.

It's a fake.

With my eyes still hidden behind the sunglasses, I allow myself one moment to squeeze them shut in frustration. A small frown breaks through my mask of stoic boredom, and I simply hand it back. "It's not what I'm looking for."

Even though my tone is even, I can't fight the surge of frustration that burns deep within me.

Instead of taking the book back, he sighs and sits on the desk, draping his arms over his knee as he studies me.

I frown, absolutely done with his games. I'm about to hurl the damn thing at his stupid face if he doesn't take it from me, *right now.*

"You don't want it?" he asks, his brows twisting in confusion.

I have to admit, he's an excellent liar. If I didn't know that he'd already put out a hit on me, I would actually assume he was just some salesman trying to peddle a fake. As far as I can see, he doesn't even have any tells. There are no signs of a lie on his face, and I have to admit I'm impressed.

There aren't many people in this world who can convincingly lie, and he's one of the few.

"Is it a fake?" He quirks one eyebrow, watching me and waiting in silence for me to answer.

Yep.

I'm done.

"Have a good day, Mr. Viet." With a bored sigh, I toss the book on the desk and turn on my heel. With a simple shrug, I actively scan the room for a way out. Six of his security detail peek their heads out from the various hallways branching off from his office, all of their eyes trained on me.

There might be a way out of this.

Maybe.

But we need to go. Now.

"It's frustrating, isn't it?" Viet calls after me as I put distance between us. "When you think something's real, only to find out it's fake. Like a woman wearing a wig."

The massive double doors to the elevator open, and instead of a secretary, this time twenty men funnel in. Each wears a suit and a comm in one ear, the wires coiling down their necks to the battery packs hidden in their shirts.

I quickly scan each man, noticing a small bulge on the right thigh on all of them.

Handguns.

I can't believe that I'm about to fight my way out of all of this mess over a *fake*.

We really have hit a dead end, and that usually

means I'll have to do something desperate to make any progress.

But first, I need to not die.

"I'm working on a way out for you, Rory," Drew says in my ear, a breathless hint to his voice. "You guys hang on. Just buy me some time."

"Is this about money?" I ask, tilting my head so that I can see him in my periphery.

"Of course, it's about money," he says with a laugh, rubbing the back of his neck as he stands. "It's always about money, at least with me."

I roll my eyes. Greedy asshole. "Do you just want me to buy your stupid fake?"

Yeah, I'm playing dumb. I know what he really wants, but now it's my turn to stall. I just need enough time to come up with a plan—or, maybe Drew will beat me to it.

Right now, it's a race to see who gets us out of here first.

To his credit, Viet laughs. "No, I don't want you to buy my fake. I actually figured that the Palarnes would buy it," he admits, chuckling. "I just want to capitalize on the popularity of the *dragon vessel*," he says exaggerating my title. "Everybody wants a bit of dragon lore now, and I figured sure, I can make a few million off of it." He shrugs. "I never expected to catch you. So, no, I don't want money from *you*. I want money from the people *chasing* you."

"How'd you figure out who I am?" I ask, already suspecting I know the answer.

"My assistant," he admits, slowly wandering toward me with his hands in his pockets as if all of this is kind of boring. "She's a fanatic, you know? Loves all things dragons. It's her guilty pleasure, I think. Without her, honestly, I never would have known who you are. It's a good wig."

I sigh impatiently, wondering how I really want to play this.

Wondering what it's going to take to get me, Jace, and Levi out of here alive.

Briefly, my eyes scan the man's body as I think through what weaknesses I know he has. But in the end, I only know one.

His greed.

"You don't want to do this," I tell him, turning to fully face him as I square my shoulders. Beside me, Jace and Levi do the same, each keeping careful watch on half the room. The elevator dings, and ten more men file into the watery atrium, stalking toward us as they splash through the shallow pool.

His plan is to outnumber us, but he forgets what

he's messing with—or, possibly, he never knew from the beginning.

"I *really* want to do this," Viet corrects, nodding slightly to emphasize his words.

"I can withdraw all of your assets, Viet," I lie. "I can leave you penniless."

Through the comm in my ear, Drew snorts derisively. "Dear, not even I can do that."

I don't care. It's just a bluff to see what his priorities really are, and if I can manipulate his greed.

"Maybe," Viet says with a nod, licking his lips as he considers the option. "But it would be easy for me to recover, especially if I capture you."

So, that's it then.

I simply look at the poor fool for a moment, and it's suddenly clear to me that he has no idea the hell he just unleashed on himself. "Do you think this will be easy?" I ask. "That a valuable asset like me—one even the other Bosses couldn't capture—did you think this would be simple?"

"No," he says calmly, pausing mid-stride. "Of course not."

With that, he snaps his fingers, and all thirty of his soldiers draw their guns.

A power play.

Classic.

"I know your men won't shift," Viet says, tilting his head and raising his brows as if he's chiding a child. "Not in a human zone, and that works in my favor."

Good. He has no idea I can shift, and that means Milo has kept his word.

War it is then.

So be it.

Poor fool.

CHAPTER FOURTEEN

Viet has made one incredible mistake.

He assumes we give a shit about the law.

As his guards aim their weapons at us, I scan the handguns to detect how real the threat is. Sure, it's going to hurt if we get shot by a low caliber bullet, and hell, they could even kill us if they shoot the right spot. But dragons are notoriously difficult to kill, and we need a high caliber bullet to take us out.

If they're using low caliber bullets, it means they have absolutely no idea what they're doing, and that could work in our favor.

It takes me just a few moments to recognize the handguns, however, and they are in fact dragon-killers.

Damn.

"I'm switching gears," Drew says through the comm in my ear. "I'm going to try to get control of their security system and see if I can force a way out."

"And I have enough weapons to kill a herd of buffalo," Tucker adds. "I'm just waiting for a good shot."

All right then. I guess I need to stall some more.

"What's your plan exactly?" I ask, taking off my sunglasses and tossing them aside since there's no longer any need to play this little game. "How do you think this is going to go?" My glasses slide across the floor as I tug off the wig, shaking out my hair as I breathe a sigh of relief.

Gods above, I *hate* wigs.

"The plan," he says, squaring his shoulders as his hands remain in his pockets, "is that you're going to come quietly, and I won't kill anyone. The moment you put up a fight, I'll kill your men." He nods to Jace and Levi, making the threat as casually as if he's throwing poker chips on a table.

All around the room, guns instantly cock, and the barrels are all aimed at either Levi or Jace.

"That was a poor choice," I tell him, and despite the fact that live guns are aimed at us, ones that could actually kill us, all I feel is anger.

No one threatens my men and lives.

With a hot and angry flash of white light, I summon my magic, and everyone in the room except for Levi and Jace flinches. These are humans, not dragons, and every one of them is in over their heads.

They're not just playing with fire anymore. They're playing with lightning. They don't realize the raw power I possess, nor do they realize how deep the quicksand they just stepped in really is.

Their loss, not mine.

As Viet and I stare each other down, I come up with a hasty plan—blind them and destroy the ground at the same time. The goal, as long as everything goes right, is to create chaos and evacuate the building. With a bunch of panicked crowds, it'll be easier for us to escape and blend in.

Yet another reason I'm glad I didn't wear the red dress.

I quickly scan the floor, guessing at where the support beams might be. If I can angle us in the right way, we won't fall with the rest of them into the atrium below us.

But that's a big if.

I don't really want to fall ten stories today. Even for me, that would *really* hurt.

"This is your last chance," I say, quirking one eyebrow as I stare down Viet. "You have guns, sure.

But don't for one second think you can win this. There's a reason the Bosses haven't been able to capture me, Viet. Why do you think that is?"

To drive home my point, I slowly lift my hand as white sparks fizzle in my palm, hovering just above my fingers. Ribbons of white light cascade down my arm, shimmering across my body almost like my dragon's scales in the sun.

I'm sure it's one thing to hear about my magic, but it's an entirely different beast to see it. To realize, in the moment, exactly what it can do.

To see it so close to you.

At least, that's what I'm hoping is going through his head.

Viet hesitates, his gaze locked on my hand, and I can see his sense of self-preservation battling his greed.

The question is simply which will win.

Probably greed. It almost always wins, especially with men like this. I've seen it time and time again in the Spectres when someone thinks he doesn't have to pay for a service he ordered from the Ghost.

Zurie always got her payment one way or another.

Viet nervously licks his lips and adjusts his tie, all while staring at the sparks in my fingers. I can practically see the fear bubbling through him as he no doubt wonders just what I can do. Just how far my limits go.

"Do you really want to die today?" I ask him, giving him one last chance to back down.

His gaze shifts toward me, and for a moment, I think he might actually give in. His hands drift to his lapel, and for a moment, he aimlessly fidgets with his suit coat.

And that's when I notice the small bulge by his breast pocket. It's subtle, hidden so well I almost didn't notice it at all. But it's there.

A gun.

He reaches into his suit coat and whips out the weapon. His gaze drifts to my legs, and I figure he's going to try to shoot my knees so that I can't walk. He doesn't want me dead, but he doesn't want me getting away, either.

I don't give him the chance to pull the trigger.

With my magic already in my hands, I drop to my knees and slam my palms against the floor. Impulsively, Jace and Levi grab my shoulders and kneel just as a couple of gunshots scream through the air.

But we're dragons.

We're faster.

As my magic hits the ground, a blinding burst of white light fills the room. As I focus my power into the tile, it takes everything in me to keep the blast from going wild, from arcing and hitting everything around me.

I refuse to let it hurt my men.

A blast of air pulses from me, knocking several men on their asses before the entire world goes white. In the blinding light, glass shatters. Men scream. Wind kicks through the room as the wall of windows is broken open, and I wonder how many security guards just fell to their deaths.

Part of me wants to feel bad, but after all, they *did* just try to kill Jace and Levi.

No one gets to live after *that.*

Beneath us, the floor trembles as the building takes the full brunt of my blow.

When the blinding white light slowly begins to fade, there's utter chaos. A huge crack snaps through the middle of the room as the tile begins to break and fall to the floors below. Men lay on their sides, on their backs, some unconscious and some not breathing at all. Several of the beautiful pieces of art around the room now lay on the floor, broken in half.

Barely twenty feet from me, Viet lays on the ground, his gun on the floor five feet to his left. He slowly sits up, his eyes slipping in and out of focus as he blinks rapidly, trying to get his bearings. Our eyes meet, and even though he's clearly dazed, he instantly bolts for the gun.

I don't think so.

Still boiling at this man's audacity, I fire again into the ground, and the tile gives out completely. Bit by bit, holes appear in the floor as the penthouse slowly corrodes and breaks apart. Water cascades like a waterfall from the room behind us, dropping like rain into the atrium below as the greenery of thick trees fully comes into focus through the holes in the floor.

This is the part I'm not looking forward to.

"Look for the support beams," I tell Jace and Levi as the building trembles. "We have to get to—"

Before I can even finish my thought, the ground beneath me gives out. My stomach launches into my throat as I fall, and the once-stable ground beneath me opens up to a ten-story drop over a pool of bright blue water. I figure it's probably not deep enough for a ten-story fall, and if I hit that, it's going to *hurt*.

Even as a dragon, I'll probably break things in a fall like that.

My world tumbles. Disoriented, I lose track of what's up and what's down as brown and white blurs race past me.

A hand grabs my wrist, stopping me as I fall, and my legs stretch out beneath me as I try to regain my balance and get my bearings. I look up to find Levi gritting his teeth as his fingers tighten around my arm.

With his fingers brushing my skin, our connection opens, and I feel a flood of adrenaline seep through from him. The need to protect. The need to provide.

And, most of all, love.

Above him, Jace grimaces, one hand on Levi's forearm and the other clutching an exposed beam as we dangle ten stories from the ground.

We could shift, yes, and while the law means very little to us, at least right now, it's something I only want to do if absolutely necessary. If we shift within even this giant atrium, there will be witnesses, and where there are witnesses, the people hunting me will follow.

Shifting has to be a last-ditch effort, at least whenever we're in human-run areas. Besides, the world will just use it as more fodder that I need to be taken out. Media outlets everywhere will spin it like I'm some danger to the population, like I'm out to start a war.

It'll only fuel the Knights and their vendetta against me, making it easier for them to take me out.

But *hell* yes, I'll shift before I die or before someone captures me. That's my line.

Far below, people scream as they run for cover.

More bits of tile and exposed ductwork fall to the atrium floor like a rocky avalanche of debris.

"I lost sight of you guys," Tucker says through the comm. "Are you—"

"We're fine," Jace says through gritted teeth, grimacing as he tries to lift us onto the ledge. We slowly rise into the air as Jace's incredible strength takes over, but it's slow-going.

Above us, Viet peers over the edge. He seethes, glaring down at me as blood drips from a gash in his forehead. Dirt smudges his cheeks, and tears in his beautiful suit expose blood-stained skin.

"You should have made this easy." The businessman loads two bullets into his handgun and cocks it. "Now I have to hurt the people you care about. This is your fault, little girl, and I want you to remember that every time you think about how they died. You hear me?"

I wrinkle my nose in disgust, summoning my magic as I prepare to rip a new hole in this guy's face.

With Levi and Jace between me and him, however, I would put them at risk. Either way—a gun or my wild magic—the men I love are in grave danger.

Before I can so much as aim, however, a red dot appears on his forehead. I briefly frown in confusion, trying to figure out where it came from.

"Give the word, babe," Tucker says in my ear.

I smirk, looking up at Viet as he takes aim at my mate.

"Bye, Viet," I say.

The salesman tilts his head in confusion, opening his mouth to ask me what the hell I'm talking about, when a gunshot cuts through the air. He grunts and falls back, the gun falling past us toward the ground below.

"Thanks, babe," I say into the comm.

"I've always got your back, honey," Tucker says casually. Through the comm link, the various attachments on his gun clatter and clink as he disassembles it.

"The police are being dispatched," Drew says into the comm. "I'm disabling the security system that was locking you all upstairs, so you can escape through the stairwells. I'll initiate an evacuation of the building to give you cover on the way out."

Almost instantly, the fire alarms scream through the air. White lights along the ceiling blip and flash, warning people to take cover and escape.

"Now get the hell out of there!" Drew orders.

"You don't have to tell me twice," I say as Jace hoists Levi onto the beam. Between the two of them, they pull me up, and we carefully crawl onto what's left of the penthouse floor.

Viet's corpse lays beside the hole we nearly fell through, his eyes closed and a small bullet hole in his forehead. I shake my head in disappointment. It didn't have to be this way, but he let his greed kill him.

That blood is not on my hands, nor is it on Tucker's. That's all on Viet.

A few lingering security guards scramble to run away as I climb through the hole, dropping weapons and wallets in their panic. Since their boss isn't paying the checks anymore, I figure they're not about to put their lives on the line to capture me now.

A few men in suits disappear through the various doors in the massive office, and over by the elevator, a door to the stairwell slowly closes as a man in a suit runs downstairs as quickly as he can.

Time for our exit, then.

I bolt toward the stairwell, grabbing a few loose handguns off the floor as I go. As I shove my shoulder against the door, I quickly check the ammunition in each of the weapons I found.

Forty bullets.

I can work with that.

Jace and Levi grab a few of the lingering weapons as well, and between us it seems as though we managed to get roughly seven. The three of us jog after the security guard, each of us checking and cocking our weapons as we go. I don't exactly have much in the way of pockets, so I keep two guns and store the third in Jace's pocket. As my hand slides into his suit coat, he grins and kisses my cheek.

Before long, we blend in with the crowds as the building groans and creaks around us. We have to be careful to hide the handguns, but thankfully most people are too panicked to care about us or our disheveled appearances. My attacks did more damage than I realized, and it almost feels like the building could come down on us all at any minute.

"Drew, get us a way out of here," I mutter into the comm under the panicked murmur of the quickly filling stairwell. "A car or something."

"Top level of the garage," Drew answers instantly, like he was already searching for it.

Probably because he already was.

"You've got one floor to go," Drew adds. "Who's the better driver?"

"Me." Jace and I say in unison.

We look at each other and smirk, each accepting the challenge.

"Race you," Jace says, grinning wider.

"That's cute," Levi says with a small smile on his face as we reach the door to the garage. "But I'm driving." He pushes open the door and jogs through.

I quirk an eyebrow. "Oh, you are, are you?"

Instead of answering, he simply looks over his shoulder and smirks, lifting one eyebrow as he dares me to argue.

"What are our options, Drew?" I ask. "Do I need to hotwire something?"

Drew snorts derisively through the comm. "Don't be ridiculous."

"Then what—"

Before I can finish the thought, a gorgeous black Maserati ten feet away roars to life. The headlights come on, and there's an audible click as the doors unlock.

"Get in," Drew says.

I grin. "Oh, you shouldn't have. It's not even my birthday."

"Get the hell out of there, Rory," Drew says, but I can hear the smile in his voice.

The three of us bolt toward the sports car, each of us vying for the driver's seat, but Levi is just a hair faster. He reaches it first and jumps behind the wheel, not even giving us a chance to argue.

Ugh.

Fine.

Since I figure Jace and I will probably need to shoot someone, I hold open the backseat and gesture for him to hop in. He grins, bowing sarcastically in thanks, and dives in.

"You have any water in this taxi?" Jace asks sarcastically as I settle in and slam the door shut behind me.

"Nope," Levi says simply, throwing the car into reverse and punching it. The tires screech as he backs out of the space and takes off through the garage, effortlessly floating over the concrete as he practically floors it through the structure.

Jace and I take a quick inventory of the weapons sitting between us. There's enough for an emergency, but not much else. We need to meet up with everyone at the rendezvous point and plan our next move.

If we survive that long, of course.

The car screeches around a bend. The violent motion throws me and the guns off balance, and I slide over the seat toward Jace as one of the handguns hits the floor.

Levi doesn't stop for anything, even as cars begin to back up and make their way out of the garage. He effortlessly weaves around them, shifting gears as the Maserati obeys his every whim. Tires screech and people gesture wildly at us as we pass, but he miraculously doesn't hit anyone.

"When did you learn how to drive so well?" I ask,

sliding over the back seat toward Jace as Levi takes another corner too fast.

Levi floors it down the last exit ramp and onto the street, tires screeching as he drifts onto the asphalt and barely misses three scooters and a truck. Horns blare, but that's just the sweet symphony of Ho Chi Minh City driving.

"I'm trying to focus, honey," Levi says with a small smirk.

"Uh-huh," I say, sliding across the seat again as he takes the corner.

He zips effortlessly around scooters and cars, driving like a local as he races toward the rendezvous point.

"I have access to a few of the traffic cams," Drew says through the comm. "I'll make sure you're out of trouble before I head out."

"Forget pursuers," Jace mutters. "With Levi driving, we might hit a brick wall."

"I'm a fabulous driver," Levi says calmly, shifting gears as he drifts around a bend. The car darts perfectly through a gap in the traffic, barely missing two bumpers and a cluster of scooters as he rights the wheels and floors it. "Has anyone died?"

"That's not really a metric for success," I admit, laughing as the car roars.

Jace wraps his arm around me, keeping me in place as we drift around yet another corner. "Seriously, Levi, do we need to have a talk about how you learned how to drive like this?"

"Vaer don't like rules, okay?" Levi says, shifting gears as he barrels down the road. "Honestly, this is just like the capital. It's not much different."

"Uh-huh," Jace and I say in unison, briefly looking at each other with skepticism.

Two black cars race out onto the street behind us from a side road, quickly gaining as they weave through the thick traffic. In the rearview mirror, Levi glances back at them, already on it and ready to dodge them if need be. I grab and cock a gun, ready to fire.

The cars behind us beat me to it.

A hail of bullets opens on us, but nothing hits the windows. It seems like they're trying to hit the tires, and small sparks erupt across the street as the bullets ricochet across the asphalt.

Levi curses under his breath and swerves, trying not to give them a target as we race ahead.

"Viet's guys?" I ask.

"Looks like it," Drew answers. "Seems as though his nephew is taking control now, and they still want you."

"Fantastic," I mutter, grabbing the nearest handgun and cocking it.

Time to fight back.

I slam my fist against the back windshield, breaking open a small hole through which I can take aim. After a brief second of eyeing the silhouettes in the cars behind us, I unload four bullets into the driver's side of the closest car.

It's a little wasteful, since there's only one silhouette, but with the weaving cars and active shooter situation, I'm trying to give myself some grace.

Their windshield shatters, cracks splintering across the glass. The car swerves and hits the other one before driving onto the sidewalk and crashing into a brick wall. The airbags deploy.

For a moment, it looks like both cars are out—until the second one recovers and weaves around the first. After a few shaky moments, the black sedan floors it after us.

A thick group of scooters joins the main road, and to my horror, the pursuing car only drives faster. It clips the back tire of one of the scooters, sending it into a tailspin as the driver falls to the ground. The others all swerve away, astounded by this driver, and he plows through them. They manage to avoid him, some by mere inches, and several of them smack their palms against the car, yelling at him as he passes.

He doesn't slow or swerve. Though I can't see anything but silhouettes through the tinted windows, the driver doesn't seem to care that he nearly killed ten locals.

The passenger-side window on the sedan rolls down, and I catch sight of the barrel of a handgun before another hail of gunfire rattles the back of the car.

They really want to take out our tires.

Levi careens around another bend, only to cuss under his breath.

"What is it?" I ask, staying low as I look over my shoulder out the front window.

Five SUVs race toward us, and as we head directly toward them, they only speed *up*.

"Those aren't Viet's guys," Drew says through the comm in my ear.

"What? Then who are they?"

"They look foreign," Drew says, his keyboard clacking. "This is someone else. I can't figure out who yet."

Jace and I look at each other as the reality of this situation finally hits us. It looks like new players just entered the game.

The tinted windows on the five SUVs roll down, and this time several handguns emerge.

"Screw that," Levi mutters, drifting around a corner as a hail of gunfire rattles after us.

This is surreal. Gunfire through a major city, all to capture me. Screw dragon and human relations—this comes right down to violating local laws, all to capture somebody who hasn't actually posed any real threat.

They all just want my power, and it seems like they are truly willing to do anything to get it.

Sirens blare in the background, and I wonder just how many people are coming after us, from how many different organizations, with how many different motives.

Bullets shatter the whole back window, and all of us duck as the five SUVs gain ground on us. To hell with the tires—it seems like these guys are going in for the kill.

"Who *are* these guys?" I snap, trying to get a glimpse at them in a rare moment when they aren't shooting at us.

Keeping low and doing his best to keep cover, Jace holds two handguns and unloads the bullets into the front windshield of the nearest vehicle. Two of the four silhouettes go limp in the passenger and back seats as bullet holes tear through the windshield, and I smirk with pride.

My mate—the killer marksman.

"Nice shots, dear," I say, cocking my gun as I take aim on the driver.

In my pocket, my phone vibrates.

A call.

Now?

Of all the—

Fine.

Without so much as looking at the number, I raise the phone to my ear. "What?" I ask tersely.

"You're just so popular," Irena says calmly, the hint of a smile in her voice.

"I'm a little busy to chat, Irena," I say as gunfire erupts on our car again.

"I know," Irena says calmly. "MI6 and the CIA are joined in a combined attempt to take you out, baby sister. That's pretty impressive. I have to admit I'm a little jealous of all the fun you're having."

"Damn it," I mutter, looking at Jace. "Human governments found me already? How?"

"They've been watching the worldwide alerts," Irena answers. "Absolutely anything that has your name or a reference to you, and that Viet character is asking for the highest bidders to fight for you."

"Yeah, I know about that," I admit. "He's dead."

"I figured," Irena says calmly.

"How did MI6 and CIA converge so quickly?"

"Satellite agents I assume," she says, and I can practically imagine her shrugging. "They have people posted everywhere just waiting for you to show up. But don't worry, Rory. I'm sending in support."

"What kind of support?" I ask, furrowing my brow in confusion.

There's a whistle through the air. It's a familiar sound, one that gives me flashbacks of falling through the sky. Of the earth-shattering agony of a missile exploding against my back.

My heart clenches.

I look out the shattered back window just as the missile streaks through the air, aiming for the sedans behind us. They swerve at the last second but they can't avoid it, and in mere moments, the first three sedans catch fire. They launch into the air and roll, each of them ablaze as they block the entirety of the road.

"That kind of support," Irena says.

I grin, letting out a small sigh of relief. "Thanks, big sister."

The two SUVs in the back of the line careen

around the charred remains of the others, flooring it as they catch up to us.

Man, these guys just won't die.

"Huh," Irena says absently. "I guess our aim was a little off. No worries, Rory. We'll load another."

Gunfire blisters across the back bumper.

"Might want to hurry," I say through gritted teeth, returning fire through the open hole that was once the back windshield.

"Hang on," Drew says in my ear. "I'm coming with backup."

Before I can so much as ask a question, a red car speeds after the remaining SUVs from behind. The sleek sports car is low to the ground and faster even than our Maserati.

Much to my delight, the window rolls down, and Tucker leans out the window with a bazooka over his shoulder.

I groan, smiling even as I shake my head.

Subtle.

Tucker fires the bazooka, aiming for the two remaining SUVs, and they meet the same fate as the others. Drew effortlessly swerves around the blazing remains of the cars, racing after us like a red streak along the road.

"Where'd you borrow that one?" I ask into the comm.

"The rich guy wasn't using it," Drew says, smirking through the windshield.

We speed off down the road, going faster and faster as I hope no one else interrupts our route. We're not out of the woods yet, but I let myself breathe a small sigh of relief.

My men are truly amazing.

Even though the book was a fake, it wasn't a waste of time. The letter proves that this book existed at some point in the past, and now all I have to do is find it.

I take one last glance at the flaming wreckage of the people who were after us, and it irks me that even though we were absolutely careful, even though we did everything we could to cover our asses, we were still found out.

All because I was recognized.

I frown, sinking in the seat as I rub my temples. I knew I didn't have my shadows anymore, and I'm trying my best to embrace this. But being in the spotlight nearly killed me.

It nearly killed us all.

CHAPTER FIFTEEN

After ditching the cars at the rendezvous point and getting a charter plane out of Ho Chi Minh City, we have only one option.

Come up with a plan B.

We sit in silence in the small cabin of a sixteen-person charter plane. It's just tall enough for Jace to stand, provided he tilts his head forward to keep from banging it on the ceiling, but we're all strapped into our seats as we wonder what the hell we're going to do. The pilot's door is shut and locked, and the *Fasten Seatbelts* light pops on as we hit some turbulence.

I chuckle under my breath. Like any of us need a seatbelt.

No one wants to break the silence, but we really need to talk about what happened. Since the escape from Viet's penthouse, it's been non-stop movement with only one focus—getting the hell out of the city.

Now that we have a moment to breathe, we have to go through our quickly disappearing options for what on earth we can do next. For the moment, the plane is headed to Dubai, but that's just because it's the first city Drew could think of where he has a safehouse.

"That was too close," Jace says, standing as he leans his arm against the overhead bin of the small plane.

My eyes rove the otherwise empty seats, grateful we found a private way out of the city so quickly. Milo's *generous* donation makes it easier to pay for what we need.

If we had stayed behind, it would have been a disaster with everyone moving in. CIA, MI6, Viet's guys, and who knows who else. Probably the Bosses as well.

I groan and rub my temples.

"It was kind of fun though," Tucker says with a grin. "I've never blown up two SUVs at once before."

"Is this a joke to you?" Levi asks, his voice dark and dangerous.

In unison, the rest of us turn our heads to look at him only to find the ice dragon fuming. He stands at the far end of the plane, his hair brushing the ceiling as he glares at Tucker with those icy blue eyes. His cold gaze sweeps across the others before landing on me.

Tucker frowns. "What crawled up *your* ass?"

"She nearly died!" Levi snaps, pointing at me.

"*She* is right here, Levi," I say, crossing my arms as I lift one eyebrow skeptically.

He grimaces and gestures at all of us. "How can we keep you safe, Rory, if the world can recognize you at a glance?"

He stares me down and pauses as if waiting for me to answer his clearly rhetorical question.

I don't take the bait.

He takes two menacing steps toward me as he fumes. "All it takes now is one person who happens to like dragons, and then we're exposed. No stealth. No secrets. We have *nothing* left."

"That's enough!" Drew smacks his hand against the side of the plane, and the lights flicker.

The plane briefly trembles, losing a hair of altitude as the pilot flashes the seatbelts sign once again.

We all pause and watch the fire dragon as he glares daggers at Levi. "Rein it in."

It clicks for me then.

Levi's anger. His tension. The way he's been on edge ever since Zurie's announcement. The way he's begun to change. All of the little things I've noticed that have been adding up.

In that instance, it all makes sense.

The stealth and shadows are all Levi has ever known. He has always been the hunter, but he has never been the prey. He has always been the one hiding in the brush, invisible until it's too late to run. He and I share that past, and now we have to face a new future together that's daunting as hell because it's unlike anything we've ever experienced before.

This isn't just about the world knowing I exist. This is about Levi losing the one way of life he knew could keep me safe.

More than even that is everything at stake if I die. He said it himself—he and his dragon have rekindled their relationship, but only barely. Only mostly. It's still rocky. It could still fracture, and if anything happens to me, he'll lose everything. Not just our love, not just me, but his dragon and sanity, too.

For him, absolutely everything he has ever known is at stake.

I lean forward, setting my elbows on my knees as I adjust in my seat, pressing my fingertips together as I search for the words to express what he needs to hear. "We're walking into the unknown, Levi," I say quietly. "But we're doing it together."

With that, I lift my gaze to find him already staring down at me, and as our eyes connect, his expression softens.

Only slightly, but still—I see a shift in him, however small, and I know he understands.

Or, at least, he's starting to.

"This is what the world is now," Drew says, taking several steps toward us as he looks Levi dead in the eye. "This is what we have to work with. Any chance of us going unnoticed is gone, and we can't fight that anymore. We can only adapt and overcome."

The broad-shouldered fire dragon squares off against Levi, and the two lift their chins as they face off in a silent glower. It's almost a challenge like he's daring Levi to disagree and demanding that he step down.

There's a tense silence as they stare each other down, neither agreeing with the other, and the brief moment of understanding I shared with Levi seems to flit by.

I need to change the topic before this devolves into something I can't repair.

"The book was a fake," I tell them.

That seems to break the spell, and both Drew and Levi look down at me. Drew relaxes somewhat and takes a few steps back. "I know," he says, his tone dripping with disappointment. "I overheard it on the comm. Not only did he have a fake, he *knew* it wasn't real. He made it himself."

"Yeah," I agree, letting out a small sigh as the two of them step away from each other. "He was just trying to squeeze money out of rich people and capitalize on the fact that I even exist."

"What a waste," Drew says with a groan, rubbing his eyes.

I shake my head. "Not a waste, Drew. It means the real one could still be out there."

"We still don't have a lead though," Jace points out. "It's back to square one."

I groan and rub the back of my neck, frustrated as hell and not sure what to do next. The plane begins to descend as we reach Dubai, and my phone buzzes in my pocket as I once more get connection.

I fish it out to find a text from an unknown number.

I went to visit Mom, but you weren't there.

It's Irena, writing to me in our code.

It means *call me back.*

Without hesitating, I dial the number, and she answers on the first ring.

"Did you have fun?" she asks, a bit of levity and joy to her voice that I wasn't quite expecting.

"Oh, yeah. Loads," I say dryly. "Thanks for the assist. When did you get a rocket launcher?"

"That was actually one of my Spectres," she says absently, almost like she's examining her nails with a hint of boredom. "He was nearby, and he mobilized before I could get there."

I hesitate, and it's surreal to think she has a growing network of former Spectres.

More than that, however, is the fact that she *trusted* someone.

There's so much going on in her world, and I don't get to see any of it. I'm not used to being away from her for so long, or to us having such different missions. I grip the phone a little tighter, wondering what to say, or if I should even approach this.

If maybe I should just let it go.

"I, uh…" I pause, pinching the bridge of my nose as I try to regain my thoughts. I still need to ask her about the orb. In all the chaos, we haven't had a moment to catch up since I visited Ashgrave. "Have you heard anything about an orb? It has to do with the dragon gods."

"An orb?" I can almost hear the frown in Irena's face as she pauses briefly to rack her brain. "No, I don't think I have. I never saw any mention of that in any of Zurie's files, and there was a lot in there. I'll keep an ear to the ground for it. Can you send me some specs?"

"Not really," I admit. "We'll send you whatever we have though."

"Are you going to lie low, now?" she asks, and though she's feigning boredom, I can hear the slight twinge of hope in her tone.

As Dubai looms closer out the window, I don't answer. Truth be told, I don't really think I even can anymore.

"Bye, Irena," I say instead. "Don't die, okay?"

CHAPTER SIXTEEN

I sit on the balcony of our safehouse as the hot desert night bakes me. I take a deep breath in the heavy heat, straightening my back as I sit cross-legged on a plush white towel I got from the bathroom of Drew's condo.

I'm so tempted to open my eyes. To stare out at Dubai from this excellent vantage point. Instead, I force myself to focus on clearing my thoughts and reaching inward, toward my dragon.

Apparently, a lot of celebrities own condos in this tower, so it's far easier to go undetected through the halls than it usually would be in a hotel. There are private walkways weaving through the building like a labyrinth. Room service simply leaves whatever you need at the door, all in the name of room service.

We've been left completely alone the entire time we've been here, and it has been absolutely amazing.

The only problem is we're at a dead end with no leads, and I feel absolutely stuck.

I *hate* feeling stuck.

As I suck in another deep breath, I try to summon a vision. Both times it happened so far, they just came on their own, and I wonder if that's simply how this magic works. Visions don't really seem like the sort of thing that can be controlled, but I'm trying anyway.

Because of course I am.

The sliding glass door opens behind me, and Tucker's footsteps trot across the concrete, lighter and stealthier now we've been training together for a while.

He sits beside me and sighs loudly as I continue to meditate, his knee bumping mine as he gets comfortable.

I wait for him to settle in and try again to focus on my meditation. It's just not happening today, much to my frustration, but I'm too damn stubborn to quit. I frown, scrunching my brow as I do anything at all to delve inward and connect with my dragon, so that she and I can figure this out together.

After a second or two, Tucker sighs again, louder

this time. He even clears his throat once or twice, clearly trying to get my attention.

With my eyes still closed, I sigh and grin, shaking my head as I give in. "What is it, Tucker?"

"Oh, hey, Rory," he says nonchalantly, as if he didn't notice me. "I didn't mean to interrupt you."

I laugh and, groaning, finally open my eyes to find him grinning at me—with those crisp green eyes and dark hair, he's all charm and jokes.

What an adorable idiot.

"What are you doing?" he asks.

"Nothing," I say, waving away the question because I don't want to talk about it. I wrap my arms around my legs and set my chin on my knees as I stare out through gaps in the banister at the city. Lights glow like glittering flames in the desert night as dusk slowly fades into the dark blue night.

"'Nothing' is good," Tucker says with a shrug, leaning back on his palms. "'Nothing' sounds nice."

"Is Levi still mad?" I ask.

When we first got here, Levi immediately shoved his way back into the hall to go secure the building. Drew nearly stormed after him to rein the ice dragon in, but Jace nipped that in the bud with a simple hand on his buddy's chest. With a light kiss on my forehead,

Jace went off to join the ice dragon's angry patrol and keep him from doing anything reckless.

I haven't heard from either of them in four hours. I only know they're okay because I can feel my dragon wriggle and coil as she tracks Jace's movements through the building.

Tucker hesitates, stumbling over his words for a moment. "Yeah," he eventually says. "Definitely still mad."

"I can't blame him," I admit. "Not really. It's hard for a man who has only known the shadows to step into the light."

Tucker snorts irreverently. "When did you get all deep and guru-like?"

I laugh and playfully shove his bicep, and though he leans briefly away from the force, he scoots closer and wraps his arm around me. With a few light tugs, he slides my butt and the towel across the balcony toward him and snuggles close, planting a kiss on my cheek.

"Did you just come out here to keep me company?"

"Of course," he says, feigning offense. "What kind of boyfriend do you think I am?"

I grin, watching him for a moment. Instead of answering, I simply admire the handsome curve of his jaw and the stubble peppering his face. "The best kind."

He laughs and pretends to fan his face. "Oh, you and your compliments."

We sit together in silence for another few moments, simply looking out over Dubai and watching the beautiful city shine and twinkle in the night. Every now and then, I glance over to him, and I notice that his smile begins to falter. It slowly fades, and he tenses his jaw almost nervously the longer we sit in silence.

He's hiding something.

I tilt my head. "Tucker, we can do this the hard way, or you can just tell me."

"Does the hard way involve you naked?" he asks, quirking one eyebrow.

With a laugh, I shake my head. "The opposite, actually."

"*Me* naked?"

I laugh harder and shove his arm. Damn, he makes this so difficult. "Just tell me."

"I don't know what you're talking about," he says, frowning as he runs a hand through his hair.

"The hard way it is, then." Even though I'm wearing a short sleeve shirt, I pretend to roll up my sleeves and rub my hands together gleefully.

He groans and gestures out toward the city. "I have bad news and worse news, Rory. Which would you like first?"

"Oh, good," I say sarcastically. "This sounds fun. Let's make a game of it, and I'll guess which is which."

A half-hearted chuckle escapes him, and he sighs as he hangs his head in frustration. "Fairfax soldiers have been questioning Brett about the orb, just like you wanted. We've been trying to approach it subtly so that he gives us intel without realizing what we're actually after. So far, it's clear he knows something, but he refuses to give any details until he speaks to you," Tucker says, his gaze darting toward me. "And only to you."

I roll my eyes. "I'm not going to talk to him. Not after all of the dojo dragons he killed in that assault."

"Damn right, you're not," Tucker says with a firm nod. "I won't let you."

I laugh. "Like you could stop me."

"Hey, I am quite intimidating, young lady," Tucker says, his eyebrows shooting up his forehead as he waggles his finger at me.

I laugh. "So, what's the other bad news?"

He groans like this is the one he really doesn't want to tell me, and that ruins our little game. Whatever he's about to say is clearly the worse news, and I brace myself for what it could possibly be as he pulls out his phone.

After a few moments of his thumbs racing across the screen, he tilts the phone toward me to reveal a still from a video.

Of Kinsley.

Without an introduction or any explanation at all, he simply hits play.

The still shot of Kinsley begins to move as she sneers into the camera. "There's a war coming," she says, her dark and seductive voice eerily familiar.

We've spoken before, and there's something about her that just sets my nerves on fire.

This is a woman who's used to getting what she wants, and from what I can gather, she throws bloody tantrums if people tell her no.

"There will be dragons against dragons," she says, sitting up straight and looking for all the world like a queen as she stares directly into the camera. "This is going to be the sort of war to end all wars, and humans everywhere can thank Rory Quinn for the bloodshed to come."

"Damn it," I mutter, rubbing my temples in irritation.

I just can't seem to catch a break.

"If you want to end this," Kinsley says, tilting her

head slightly. "If you want to stop this war before it gets really bad, before it kills the people you love, all you have to do is bring her to me." Kinsley pauses, smiling warmly. "It's that simple."

There's a brief moment of pause in the video where she doesn't move. She doesn't speak. She doesn't even blink, and for a minute, I think that perhaps the video froze. It's spellbinding and surreal, drawing me in, and I don't entirely understand what she's doing or how she's doing it.

But I absolutely must hear whatever comes next.

Kinsley leans forward, tapping her elegant finger against her jaw as she sets her elbows on the surface of her desk. "I'm coming for you, little goddess," she adds, her red lips twisting into a sinister smile before the video cuts to black.

When the recording ends, all I can do is stare at the black screen. Her final words echo in my head over and over and over.

Little goddess.

None of the Bosses have called me that before. None of them have even hinted at what Castle Ashgrave has said from the start.

That I'm some sort of goddess.

She's wrong, of course, but it makes me wonder if Kinsley knows more about my magic than she's letting on. Maybe even more than she should know. I suspect she's calling me that as a sarcastic gibe just to drive home that she doesn't think I'm special at all.

That she thinks I have magic I don't deserve.

Tucker stiffens in the silence that follows. After a few moments of me sitting there, utterly still, just staring at his phone, he slowly puts the device away. "What are you thinking, Rory? What's going through your head right now?"

I hesitate because I want to answer him honestly, and I'm still not sure of what to make of all that. So many public videos are being made about me lately that it's hard to even follow all of the threats.

I've never had this many enemies before.

"I feel bad for whatever fools Kinsley sends to their deaths in their attempt to capture me," I admit. "I don't want to kill a ton of people, but I will, and I suspect anyone who tries to capture us is a lot like Viet—they just don't know what they're getting themselves into."

A broad grin stretches across his face. "You're such a badass."

"What?" I chuckle, caught off guard by his comment. I was expecting to brainstorm, or perhaps get a lecture on lying low.

Instead of answering me or explaining what the hell he means, he grabs the back of my head and pulls me toward him, kissing me fiercely. His other hand winds up my waist, dipping below my shirt as his warm strong fingers ignite ribbons of desire clear into my core.

In a single fluid motion, he flips me onto my back and spreads my legs, pressing my knees against the balcony as he dominates me. His strong hands grab my waist, and he tugs me closer to him. My entrance presses hard against the growing bulge in his pants.

With a flirty grin, he watches me. His eyes shamelessly rove over my body as he lifts one eyebrow suggestively. "Have you ever done it on a balcony?"

I just laugh.

What a sexy weirdo.

CHAPTER SEVENTEEN

My fingernails tap rhythmically along the hardwood surface of a dining table in some remote safehouse in Australia. This is one of Jace's houses, actually, and Drew's on the lookout for something a little more secure—a place where we can stay for more than a few days.

I glance out the window at the midnight sky, but I'm wide awake. All this traveling has really thrown off my internal clock. It's been a week since the assassination attempt through the streets of Vietnam, and we've come close to three more.

With a deep frown, I lean back in my chair and stare out the window opposite me. My eyes gloss over as I remember all the bullets hitting the various walls behind me and my men, all far too close for comfort.

I don't have the patience to run for much longer, and I hate hiding.

The longer I live with no shadows, the more I'm coming to despise trying to go unseen. It's surreal, really, and I don't entirely understand it yet. But with every second we spend in a safehouse, I feel like I'm doing something wrong. I feel like I'm playing into someone's hands.

And I'm about done with all of it.

Every waking moment of every passing day has been spent thinking furiously of a plan. Of trying to come up with absolutely any lead at all, any indication or hint of where the orbs might be.

I smack my palm against the dining room table in frustration, and the table shivers under my enhanced dragon strength. I shake my head, irritated, and run my hands through my hair as I set my elbows on the table once again.

Damn it.

I hate being stuck.

I whip my phone out of my pocket and absently check my texts again just to do something, just to feel like I'm doing more than sitting at a table staring off into the sky.

The most recent text is from Harper, and it's simple. Short.

See you soon.

She sent the text last night, mere moments before Jace let me know she's on the way. That she needs to talk about something.

Even though I feel a bit aimless just sitting here at a table, I'm trying to take a moment of respite before what I assume will be a difficult conversation. If she feels the need to do it in person, I can just assume this isn't going to be fun.

Or, hell, maybe she just wants to see me.

I chuckle under my breath, crossing my arms as I lean my head against the backrest of the chair. Yeah, right. Not in Boss Mode. I love her to pieces, but she's all business right now.

Whatever she wants to talk about, this is *not* going to be fun.

With utterly atrocious posture, I slump in my chair and stare at my phone, wondering how badly I want to torture myself right now. My eyes dip in and out of focus as I debate whether or not I want to watch Kinsley's video yet again.

Ultimately, the answer is *why not.*

I pull it up and hit play for the forty sixth time.

It's such a short declaration that I have the whole thing memorized at this point, and I'm not really looking for clues anymore. I'm not even listening. I mute the phone and stare at the screen as her mouth moves.

All I can do is marvel at how similar she and Irena look now. The flowing dark hair. The piercing green eyes that practically glow. Even their smooth pale skin is practically identical.

The only apparent difference is my sister isn't a raging, homicidal *bitch*.

I hesitate, frowning a little as I look off to the left. There are those who would disagree with me on that point.

Nah. I shrug, setting the phone on the table as I run my hand through my hair. Irena only comes off that way to her enemies.

There's a shift in the air, and I peek over my shoulder to find Levi suddenly beside me, stealthy and quiet as ever. He slips his hands in his pockets and simply watches me for a moment, the edge of his mouth curling into a small smile as our eyes meet.

Without a word, he sets his hand on the back of my head and kisses me, our connection opening as a flood of protective love rushes through from him.

It swirls within me like a cool winter day, refreshing and calm, and I can't help but smile.

Have you had any luck with a plan? Levi asks through the connection.

I shake my head in frustration, leaning against my fist as I sigh deeply.

You will, he tells me. *You always do.*

A flutter of gratitude snakes through me, and I can't help but grin up at him. At his confidence in me.

Also, I'm grateful he's not as angry with me anymore as he was in Dubai. Given our track record lately, however, I suspect it's just a matter of time before it happens again.

Footsteps in the hallway interrupt my thoughts, and I strain my ear to listen. Three of the gaits I'm familiar with, and one I haven't heard in a while.

"Guess who?" Harper asks, knocking her knuckle against the open doorframe.

She rounds the corner with Jace, Drew, and Tucker in tow, and I'm grateful as ever to see all of them.

However, I can't help but linger on Harper's face. Her usually smooth and gorgeous skin has lost a bit of its luster. There are soft purple bags beneath her eyes, and her temples are a little red, probably from rubbing them so much. Between the slight slouch to her shoulders and the exhaustion on her face, I figure she hasn't slept much since the battle for the dojo.

With a pang of dread, I wonder if this conversation is going to be even worse than I thought.

Levi leans against the wall behind me while Tucker

slides into the seat on my left. Drew crosses his arms and leans against the doorframe as Jace takes the seat on my right.

The former dojo master props his ankles up on the table, crossing his arms as he studies his cousin. "What's going on, Harper? Why are you here?"

"I can't just want to see family?" she asks, tilting her head slightly as she grins. But with as exhausted as she is, she can barely keep her eyes open, and she rubs them as she speaks.

"No," Jace says simply, grinning. "Not when you're like this."

"Yeah, that's fair," Harper admits, yawning. "Look, guys, I won't sugarcoat this. I need help. It's been hell trying to get allies to go against Kinsley—far more so than I ever thought it would be. No one wants to make this their problem, and none of the Bosses seem to realize Kinsley is going to drag them into this one way or another. She's amassing resources and troops from anonymous third parties outside of the dragon families, and my intel suggests it's probably private human companies that will profit heavily from a world war." She hesitates, rolling her eyes. "Especially if dragons are involved."

"But what do you want us to do?" I ask, not quite following. "I'm not exactly a well-loved public figure,

Harper. Have you seen how many boycotts and anti-dragon marches mention me on a weekly basis?"

"I know," she says, her voice straining. "I know, Rory, and this whole world of publicity and public image is new to you. I get that. I don't need you to garner public support. I need you to talk to the Bosses."

I snort disdainfully. "I'm no diplomat, Harper. Hell, when I first met all of the Bosses, I scarred one of them for life." I pause, letting the point drive home. "Literally."

Drew and I share a tense look, and I can't help but remember the deep scar across Jett's eye after our duel. After he pushed me too far and tried to test my limits.

Hopefully, he won't do that again, but I'm not going to hold my breath.

Harper shakes her head. "I know it seems like they're constantly chasing you, Rory, but the Bosses respect your power. If anything, knowing that you were a Spectre will add fear. They'll listen to you."

I frown, disagreeing. This whole thing sounds like a huge mistake, and I'm pretty sure I'll just make everything worse for her if I go around trying to make friends.

I'm *shit* at making friends, even just political ones. Maybe *especially* the political ones.

But this is Harper, and the Fairfax dragons are family to me.

"If I can help, I will," I promise, not quite knowing what that's even going to look like.

In the end, it doesn't matter. I would do anything for the Fairfax.

I would do anything for *Harper*.

"Thank you," she says, smiling warmly with gratitude despite her exhaustion.

"There's a catch, though," I add. "I need a home base before I can do any of this. I assume Jace has told you about Ashgrave?"

The Fairfax Boss simply nods.

"Then I'm sorry, Harper, but that has to be my top focus. He's dying, and I have to bring him back. Once he's operational, I can help you. This hiding in safehouses thing has to end, and I need the power orb to do it."

Harper's lips part, but she hesitates, her gaze briefly drifting toward Jace in a motion that would have gone unnoticed by most people. It's so subtle. So quick.

But I saw it.

"What?" I demand, a hint of warning in my tone. "Tell me."

"Yeah, Harper," Jace says, narrowing his eyes as he watches his cousin over the bridge of his nose. "What are you hiding from us?"

My shoulders relax slightly as I realize Jace is out of the loop on this one, too, since I hate to think of him hiding things from me.

"Brett has been shutting down," Harper admits, shaking her head in frustration. "He won't eat. He won't drink anything but a few sips of water here and there, just enough to survive. And he absolutely *refuses* to talk. I can't tell if this is depression or a hunger strike. He has so much knowledge, but he won't share any of it unless he speaks to you, Rory. And the more my soldiers dig into him, the more we all suspect he knows quite a lot about these orbs of yours."

I sigh deeply, setting my elbows on the table as I rub my eyes. I just don't trust it. I don't trust *him*. He's a master manipulator, somebody who massages the truth and bends the world to his whim.

But I have absolutely no leads, and Ashgrave is dying.

The fact is I would have to be pretty damn desperate to talk to Brett Clarke, much less trust whatever he tells me.

I won't lie, though.

I'm close.

"Look," Harper says gently, "I need you all to understand this. Kinsley isn't stopping, and neither am I. The Vaer attacked a neutral zone, which is an act of war—one we have to answer if we're going to ever have a hope of defending the way of life we love. This war that's coming is going to get ugly unless we stop it now. We have to do everything in our power to end this before it starts."

"You know better than that," Jace chides quietly, his eyebrows tilting upward in sympathy.

"Yeah, Harper," Drew echoes. "It's too late to stop this."

"Don't talk like that," she chides, her nose wrinkling in annoyance. "There's still time."

"There's not," Jace interjects, leaning forward as his feet drop to the floor. "This is going to be a world war, even for humans. Just look at the players in this game —Kinsley. The Knights. The Spectres. The Fairfax warriors. The *dragon vessel*." He pauses, nodding toward me before he continues. "This could be the downfall of dragonkind if it goes too far. Even if this doesn't kill most of us, it could destroy what little public image we have. It could be what ultimately convinces mankind to wipe us out. You know that. You know how important this is, right?"

"Guys, wait," I interject, lifting my hand to make

them all stop. "The Vaer are only one family, and the other Bosses wouldn't possibly side with them. How can this really be a world war?"

Instead of answering, everyone turns to face me. They watch me in silence with various expressions ranging from doubt to pity. I hesitate as I scan each face, not quite understanding their reaction.

"Right?" I press.

Harper slowly shakes her head. "It's a real possibility that the other Bosses may side with the Vaer just to get to you, Rory."

She lets that sit on the air as I try to process it.

The Palarne. The Darringtons. Hell, the *Andusk*—at war, with someone they wouldn't even acknowledge at their table when I met them—all to get me?

Then again, human agencies were willing to race through crowded city streets after us, firing live rounds into crowds just to get me.

So, perhaps, that shouldn't come as such a shock— even though it absolutely *does,* and I don't want to believe it.

Any of it.

"Any allies we make might not stay loyal to us," Harper continues. "We need to have some kind of test or collateral from anyone who joins our side." She pauses, studying my face as she debates whether or not to continue. "They want your magic, and dragons will do anything to get what they want."

For a moment, I simply stare at her in shock. These Bosses would join a world war, spend millions, even *billions* of dollars, lose their troops, and risk the downfall of dragon kind.

All to get to me?

"In—in *what?*" I ask, truly baffled. "In the hopes of corralling me on the battlefield?"

Harper sighs, her head tilting slightly as she leans her fists against the table. "Your magic is growing, and everyone can see it. But I can *really* see it. Whatever unlocked within you when you shifted, it's unlike anything this world has ever seen, and the Bosses know that. Everyone wants to either steal your power or tame you before you really come into your own. The clock is ticking for them to do that, and desperate times call for desperate measures." She hesitates, her gaze briefly falling. "If I wanted your power, it's what I would do."

"You would join the *Vaer?*" I ask, disgusted.

"I might," she admits without batting an eye, her gaze landing on me. "If it meant I got what I wanted."

I push back from the table, the chair legs scraping across the floor as I stand and pace the length of the room, furious. I can't believe I'm making this war so complicated for Harper and the Fairfax dragons just by existing.

All of this is because of me.

"Rory," Jace says tenderly. "Rory, wait." He grabs my shoulders and roots me in place, his stormy eyes snaring me as he examines my features. "Calm down."

"Don't you dare tell me to calm down!" I snap, batting away his hands.

To his credit, my outburst doesn't faze him. Nor did I expect it to, truth be told.

He sets his hands against my face, those stormy eyes darting back and forth as he looks into mine. "Rory, this would have happened regardless. Dragons crave power. They hoard it like treasure, and nothing you could've done would have stopped this."

I let out a long slow breath and run my hand through my hair as I stare out the window. "That may be true, but I still feel terrible."

"It's not all bad," Harper interjects. "Kinsley doesn't know we defeated the bioweapon and have an antidote ready to go, and that's to our advantage as long as none of the other Bosses tell her. But if they join her, we have to assume they will. As of right now, everyone but Kinsley herself knows about the antidote, and we need to find a way to make that work in our favor while it's still relevant."

"I'm not sure what we can do," Tucker says with a shrug. "Unless she releases the bioweapon, we can't do much with the antidote."

"We'll come up with something," Drew assures us. "In the meantime, Jace and I have gotten the manufacturing of the Spectre tech going."

"That's great," I say, straightening a little bit as Jace's hands slide away from my face. "I thought you couldn't get the materials?"

Drew shrugs. "With a brewing war, we can get materials more easily without raising any eyebrows. Just takes time to find them and manufacture everything."

I nod. Finally, some good news.

"I also have an update on the mole," Drew adds, crossing his arms as he takes a wide stance in the middle of the doorway. "He's been... *handled*," the fire dragon says ominously.

"So, he's dead?" Tucker says, grinning as he leans back in his chair. "Like, *super* dead?"

Drew rolls his eyes, but he can't suppress a grin. "Yes, Tucker. Well put."

"What happened?" I press.

Drew's nose wrinkles slightly in disgust as he briefly shakes his head. "Milo bought off someone I thought I had secured. Most of what my brother threatened to do was just a bluff, but some of it was real, specifically regarding my finances. The financial analyst I was working with managed to track a few of my purchases and take a wild guess of where we would be. It gave Milo the general direction he needed to take." Drew hesitates, his dark gaze fixing on me. "It will never happen again."

Translation—Tucker is right, and the mole is long gone.

"Good," I say with a nod.

We can't afford another spy.

Harper whips out her phone, her thumbs racing across the screen as she texts someone. "There. I've assigned a full tech team to look into these orbs for you, Rory," she says, her gaze lifting toward me as she puts her phone away. "I'll get back to you as soon as I can with any clues or hints. Anything at all."

"Thank you," I say genuinely.

"Of course," she rolls out her shoulders. "I need to get you in Ashgrave as soon as possible, and I need you out there making friends immediately afterward. Speaking of…" She pauses, licking her lips as she trails off and looks out the window, like she doesn't want to finish the thought.

"What, Harper?" I say, tilting my head as I wait for her to finish. "Spit it out."

"If you're open to it," she answers hesitantly, "I have a friend who wants to speak with you now."

I frown, not really liking where this is going or the fact that she saved this for the end of the conversation. "And who is this friend of yours?"

"Isaac Palarne," she says, her soft eye is drilling into me.

Though most of my body remains still, I can't help but slowly shut my eyes in dread. "About what?"

"Your guess is as good as mine, chica," Harper says. "But if you can convince him to join the Fairfax in this war, it could literally turn the tides for us. The Fairfax army is a force to be reckoned with, but Isaac's soldiers are about the only warriors who surpass us. Having them on our side could make all the difference between winning and losing." She hesitates.

I open my eyes to find her staring at me intently, like she doesn't want to ask but needs to.

"If you could go, Rory, this might change everything for us," she admits, her voice almost breathlessly quiet.

Right.

No pressure.

CHAPTER EIGHTEEN

I stand on a plateau two hundred miles from our last safehouse, waiting for a dragon Boss in what's supposed to be a neutral location.

Yeah, sure, and I'm a fairy princess.

This plateau is in a sanctioned neutral zone, much like Reggie's castle. There are accords and treaties, and all sorts of political nonsense set up to enforce this as a place of peace.

In times of war, all of that becomes much less important.

Without the means—or *will*—to enforce it, a treaty is just a piece of paper and a promise. All that means is there's a loose agreement between the Bosses that this place in the middle of nowhere is excellent for clandestine conversations.

With the shifting political climate, it's fast becoming a time of war. And with so many lives at stake if things unravel, neutral zones have less significance than ever before.

Standing out here, with no cover—we're relying on what basically amounts to a pinky promise that no one's going to kill or abduct us.

I stretch out my fingers, doing my best to release the tension in my body as I stand in the center of my dragons. Harper sits beside me in her dragon form, her beautiful violet scales glistening in the setting sun as she surveys the horizon with her wings tucked gracefully against her back.

Truth be told, I'm grateful she's staying for this. As we wait in silence in the stretched rays of the last lingering light of the day, it's comforting to know dojo soldiers are nearby, just waiting for the command to attack in case something goes wrong.

But dragons are fast and brutal, especially the Palarne, and the dojo soldiers are far enough away to go unnoticed. At the very minimum, the six of us would have to hold our own for at least five minutes until they got here.

Levi stands beside me, stiff as a statue as he watches the skies. Drew and Jace flank us, growling softly as they wait impatiently for the meeting to start, and Tucker—bless him— secured an anti-dragon machine gun to an uncovered Jeep parked behind us. He stands off to the side, leaning his elbows on the barrel as he waits for something to happen.

It hits me, then, what all this must be like for him. He's a human amongst dragons. It used to be him and me against the world, the two of us the only humans in a den of shifters.

Not anymore.

Now that I've shifted—now that I have a dragon of my own—he's the only human left in our oddball little family. I can't help but wonder if he ever feels isolated in that.

Tucker's eyes dart toward me as he catches me watching him, and he flashes me a devilish grin. With a quick and flirty wink, his eyes wander my body, and I figure he's probably planning whatever he's going to do to me later.

I smile.

Nah, he's not isolated.

He's Tucker. He's always good.

To my right, Harper leans toward me, her scales brushing against my exposed arm as she briefly opens a silent connection between us.

Don't shift if you can avoid it, she warns me.

I simply nod.

I know.

Harper growls in satisfaction and breaks our link, returning her gaze to the sky.

Though I appreciate the warning, it wasn't necessary. I want to keep my dragon a secret as much as the rest of them do. The longer we can do that, the more she and I can get to know each other before we have to fight the world together.

After all, she's still young, and there's so much more for her to learn.

She twists and turns within me, and I feel a ripple of gratitude come from her. My girl knows I'll always protect her, and I know she'll always protect me.

Behind me, Levi growls, his nose pressing protectively against the back of my neck. Hot air blows down my spine, and a surge of possessiveness bleeds through from him as our connection opens.

I crane my neck, looking up to see the brilliant blue eyes of his dragon watching me from above as his nose presses deeper into my spine.

We sit there for a moment, merely experiencing each other, feeling each other through the connection, and I have to confess it's rather nice. He's been so on edge lately, and though I understand why, it feels like I can't really talk to him anymore, and I miss that.

I miss *him*.

His eyes dart to the side as he looks off into the distance. A low snarl builds in his throat as he breaks the connection and bares his teeth at the sky.

They must be here.

My jaw tenses as I try to find them on the horizon. I don't like this. I don't like the idea of meeting with a Boss right now, even if Isaac is the most respectful of them.

As I watch the skies, dragons slowly appear from the clouds in the distance. As they near, eleven silhouettes blip into existence.

Shit.

He's brought ten soldiers with him, and there could be more on the way.

Shit.

The closer they get, the more I can see—and none of it looks good. These are massive, hardened fighters by the look of their scars. Deep gouges cover one soldier's face, forcing his left eye closed. Another has deep scars across his back and a long gash through the center of one wing. Each shifter is more scarred than the last, all of them proudly displaying their wounds as the badges from the battles they've won.

And then of course there's Isaac, leading the charge as he banks toward us.

It takes a lot to scar a dragon, and the thought of

what these men must have gone through in times of relative peace to get those wounds shakes me. I briefly look at the scar on Levi's underbelly, but I can't let myself be distracted.

Not now.

Harper growls, and so do my men.

"What the hell!" Tucker snaps, his hands grabbing the handles on his machine gun. "He brought an army!"

"I know, Tucker," I say, my voice tense and uneasy as I stretch out my hands once again to prepare myself for whatever is about to happen. "I know."

In a matter of minutes, Isaac reaches us and angles downward. He and his soldiers quickly drop in altitude, each shifter hitting the ground with a heavy rumble that throws me slightly off-balance. I do my best not to let the Palarne Boss see me teeter, and for the most part, I keep my footing.

The battle of the mind has begun, and I don't want him to know he's making us uneasy.

After all, that's probably what he wanted from the start.

The towering, dark green dragon lumbers toward me. I tense, hands balling into fists as I wait for him to do something too bold, too brazen for him.

Part of me wonders if this is it—if this is the

moment I see Isaac's true colors. If he was a conman like the rest of them, all along, and he's brought this show of force to make me obey.

I won't, but still. I'd rather avoid heavy blows with warriors like the Palarne.

Isaac towers over me, his eyes downcast as he studies me from above. His broad jaw and dark scales block out the light, casting a long shadow over my face.

I simply stare him down, daring him to make a move.

After a few tense moments of silence, the Palarne Boss lowers his head respectfully, yet again asking for an audience instead of taking it from me as the others usually do. As his massive head hovers over the ground, his intense eyes rest solely on me.

This is just freaking *weird.*

All of this attention and respect is admittedly strange, given that I'm not the Boss here. Harper is. If anything, he should be devoting his attention to her, negotiating and discussing whatever pressing matter he needs to talk about.

But he doesn't even acknowledge her. He doesn't acknowledge anyone else at all.

Just me.

What an ass.

Furious with his rude dismissal of the Fairfax Boss, as well as the fact that he's clearly trying to unsettle me, I make him wait.

Serves him right.

For several moments, I don't move at all except to scan the soldiers behind him as they all look down on me with a hint of disdain. Slightly wrinkled noses. Snarling. Baring their teeth.

None of them want to be here.

Well, the feeling is mutual, damn it.

To my irritation, Isaac doesn't move. He doesn't huff impatiently. He barely even blinks. He just stands there, waiting for me to open the connection.

This man is too damn patient for his own good.

When the tense silence has gone on long enough, I scowl at the Boss and roughly set my hand against his nose, not bothering to mask my anger. I let it bleed through, let him feel it all, and I barely give him a moment to breathe before I dig into him.

You did this on purpose, I chide him. *You brought too many men. This was supposed to be a neutral conversation, Isaac.*

Laughter echoes through our connection from him, and a few hot breaths roll through his nose as he chuckles. He briefly breaks the connection to nod to Tucker and the dragon killer mounted to the Jeep before he presses his nose into my palm to reopen our connection. *I could say the same for you, Rory.*

I roll my eyes, not having any patience for this nonsense. *Tucker doesn't have fangs, claws, or wings. He's just leveling the playing field, and you know it.*

And you? Isaac presses, unfazed. *What did you bring to level the playing field? You don't seem scared by the fact that I outnumber you two-to-one.*

I narrow my eyes. *I'm never scared.*

He laughs again, surprisingly jovial considering the severity and tension in this conversation. *It appears so, yes. I suppose that's the Spectre training?*

I frown, refusing to answer that gibe, hating that the world knows what I was.

What I can do.

With one of his wings, he gestures toward his men. *I wanted you to see what life will be like from now on, Rory Quinn. Dangerous surprises. Warriors. Tense meetings. Is this the life you want?*

Right. Sure, Isaac, I say, not bothering to mask my sarcasm. *It's all for my benefit, then, and not to shift things in your favor at all.*

He tilts his head, his eyes narrowing slightly in curiosity. *I didn't say that, now did I?*

I lift my chin, looking down at him as I narrow my eyes skeptically. *What do you want, Isaac? Why did you call this meeting? Because if you just repeat yourself yet again and ask me to go with you—*

Come with me, he interrupts, his intense gaze locked on mine. *You need to. Especially now.*

I scoff, too annoyed to deal with this, and break the connection for a moment in my sheer irritation. As I step briefly away, the dragons surrounding us tense and growl. The warriors behind Isaac lower their heads, fangs bared as I disrespect their Boss.

Harper doesn't give them an *inch.*

My friend snarls, her nose wrinkling as she bares her teeth at their audacity. Her stunning eyes narrow as her wings spread, daring them to make a move.

She looks *pissed.*

I figure she's probably used to being in on these conversations. Not knowing what we're talking about must be immensely odd for her, if not downright disconcerting.

Isaac is the only dragon who doesn't move or react. He simply remains where I left him and watches me, those intense eyes never leaving my face as he waits to see what I'll do.

I rub my temple with one hand while the other rests on my waist as I debate my options. He just won't drop this, and now I realize he never will. I yet again question all of his intentions, all of this nobility he claims to have, and I wonder what he actually wants.

Why he's so dead set on getting me to go to his capital.

Gritting my teeth, I gently set my fingertips against his nose so that I can easily break the connection at any moment if I need to.

Why the hell should I? I demand.

He hesitates, breaking eye contact with me for a few moments as he looks toward Jace. In that fleeting moment, I catch the hint of uncertainty that seeps through the carefully constructed walls of his mind.

Hmm.

Interesting.

The sensation is nothing more than a hint of the unknown—just a moment of betrayed emotion—and he quickly resurrects his walls. The whole experience is over in mere seconds as he once more masterfully blocks me from feeling anything on his side.

It could have been a ploy, of course. An attempt to make me think he had a moment of weakness.

Or perhaps I truly did just glimpse into Isaac's mind.

I assume by now you know the truth of the dragon gods, he says, his eyes darting toward me again. *That there were those who served the masters of dragons, and many*

*more who didn't. My family, my people, we have been
among those who protected and honored the gods since the
beginning of time. We have always been loyal to the origin
of all magic, and we consider that to be our most noble duty.*

Interestingly, I note that he says he's loyal to the
gods.

Not to *me.*

The massive dragon takes a step closer, pushing me
gently backward as my palm flattens against his nose.
Have you seen them? He asks, his intense gaze narrowed
on me as he throws me off balance. *Have you heard
them? Are they still alive?*

I almost want to laugh. Like I would ever tell him.

When I don't answer, there's a tug on the back of
my mind.

Strange. I'm not sure what this could be. It's so odd.
So new. At first, I wonder if this is my dragon, trying
to speak to me or use our magic to protect us.

But this doesn't feel right. When she speaks to me,
she feels like home. Family. Safety. With her, magic
can be weird, sure. But never this surreal or uncomfortable.

I carefully guard my thoughts, wondering if maybe
he's trying to push through my walls.

But I'm not fast enough.

There's a surge of pain down my spine as whatever

this is takes over. My body freezes. My fingers curl, my nails digging into the scales on his nose, but Isaac doesn't flinch.

I grimace, falling to my knees as my world swims. For a moment, there's just darkness as my vision fades.

But then there are voices.

Familiar voices.

"Rory," a woman's voice echoes in my mind, everywhere and nowhere all at once.

"Stop," I mutter, slurring as the memory takes hold. "Don't you *dare*, Isaac."

I am sorry, he says, his tone genuine even as he pushes further.

Her voice seems to burrow into me. It takes root, like it wants to live in my bones. Her voice... it sends chills through my body. My intuition flares, and I know in my heart I don't like her at all.

"You now carry great magic," a second voice says. A man this time. "Our magic."

"The power of ancient dragons," another man adds. "The true dragons. The First."

"Others will seek you out," the woman says, her voice still grating on my soul. "They will find you. They will hunt you. Trust no one but us."

"Come to us," the first man orders.

I fight it.

I fight the memory.

This is not Isaac's business. These words, these voices in the mist—I buried this memory for a reason, and he has no right to hear it.

Another jolt of pain shoots through me, and I groan in agony as I fight him.

As I fail.

"Who are you?" I ask the voices in the mist.

They answer, each speaking over the other, but their voices begin to fade. I can only make out a word here and there.

"...ancient dragons..."

"...you can trust..."

"...order of the..."

The gods called to me, back then. I just didn't know it.

I know now who they are, and I know what they want.

They want me.

They want my magic.

They want me to bring them back from the dead and give them the power I nearly died to obtain.

Hell no.

This is mine.

I gasp and break the connection, struggling to reorient myself as my world spins. My ear rings, and as my hands press against the rough grass beneath me, my vision slowly returns along with my hearing.

Everyone around me growls, and when I look up, they're all snarling at each other on both sides, teeth bared. The ground shakes from the thunder of their voices.

Only Isaac and I are still, and we simply watch each other. I glare at him, disgusted, but he got what he was looking for.

I expected better from a man like him.

"That wasn't very honorable," I say as I get to my feet.

A soft growl escapes him, and he brings his nose closer to me, like he wants to reopen the connection.

I snort derisively. "Go to hell, Isaac."

I'll never trust him again.

He huffs impatiently and extends his wing to Harper, who roughly throws her own against it. Isaac growls briefly in irritation at her pushy movement, but Harper doesn't react. Instead, she wraps her other wing around me, opening the connection between us again and acting as a conduit this time.

I don't want to talk to him, I tell her, not even caring that he can hear.

I know, Rory, she says calmly. *You have to.*

I don't have to actually, but I trust her.

I grimace, hating everything that's happening, but I allow it.

For now.

I apologize, Rory, Isaac says, his gaze falling on me. *It was something I absolutely had to know.*

Harper looks warily between us, not following, but I shake my head. I'll tell her later.

You're so full of shit, Isaac, I chide him.

He bristles at my audacity, but I don't care.

I lift my chin defiantly. *If you really value honor—if nobility is truly that important to you—you would've taken my silence as the answer.*

He shakes his head. *For this, it was too important. I couldn't not know.*

Bullshit.

He stiffens, daring me to keep going, daring me to call him a liar again. But I don't press the issue. *You got what you wanted. Now it's your turn to listen to me.*

He tilts his head, his eyes narrowing on me as curiosity gets the better of him. *And what is it you need to say, dragon vessel?*

What you did was dishonorable, but there's a chance to redeem yourself.

Oh? He asks dryly, clearly not interested in redeeming himself to me.

I press on anyway, eager to get this over with. *Ally*

yourself with the Fairfax. I mean, let's face it. You won't want to be mixed up with the Vaer.

I'm not one to take sides in a war that doesn't concern me, he says, his head tilting toward Harper apologetically.

It does concern you though, Harper chides. *It'll swallow everyone in its path. You should know Kinsley's brutal nature by now. She's out in the open, Isaac, with nothing to lose.* Harper lifts her chin, daring him to disagree. *It'll be bloody.*

He hesitates, his gaze shifting to me again. *I'll consider it,* he concedes.

And there's an air of genuine truth to that.

His authentic tone catches me off guard. Even if he did violate what little trust I had in him, I can't deny he truly believes himself to be noble.

There's silence, and it seems the conversation is done—but no one moves. The dragons behind him tense, like they're waiting for an order to strike, and I narrow my eyes skeptically at the Palarne Boss in front of me.

Are you going to force me to go with you? Is that why you're stalling?

Isaac briefly looks like he's considering it, and I summon my magic into my hand to remind him of the consequences of that choice. The white light burns effortlessly over my skin, brighter than ever, and he tilts his head as a ripple of pride streams through the connection from him.

But that doesn't make sense. Isaac shouldn't be proud of *me*. If he truly honors the gods, he knows they're alive—and he should feel disdain that I would dare use their magic so freely.

Yet he doesn't.

My dragon stirs protectively in my chest, gleeful as the magic burns along my fingers, and I force myself not to think about her or the shift. I can't let him read that thought, too. I need to keep her a secret.

Isaac looks briefly at Harper, and there doesn't seem to be any hint of recognition or understanding in his eyes.

I think I'm in the clear. Thank the gods.

You'll come to me willingly, he says, lifting his head as he looks down at me. *As soon as you discover the truth, you'll come. On your own.*

What truth? I ask, admittedly confused.

He's silent, watching me with a knowing expression, and breaks the connection as he takes to the skies. Air from his wings blasts by me, ruffling my hair as the grass trembles from the power of his takeoff.

His dragons follow, the ground shaking as they leap into the air, and fan out into a semicircle. One by one, they spiral into the clouds around us like a vortex, and it'll be tough to get out of here if they don't want to let us go.

We're already in a war against the Vaer. I don't want to start another one with the Palarne.

After a few tense moments of eerie silence interrupted only by the flutter of wings on the air, they take off, slipping into tight formation after their Boss as they fly away.

In minutes, they're gone.

Even with them out of sight, I'm tense. Isaac knows so much more than he should, and I don't think that's going to bode well for anyone.

Least of all me.

CHAPTER NINETEEN

As we stand on the breezy plateau watching Isaac fly away, the phone in my pocket buzzes.

Man, I just cannot catch a moment to myself.

I fish out the phone and look at the screen to find a number I recognize. It's one Irena has called me from before, and despite all the tension from the conversation I just had, I breathe a small sigh of relief.

I press the phone to my ear. "I really need some good news right now, Irena."

"Aw," a man's voice says, the tone dark and familiar. "Is Rory having a bad day?"

I impulsively stiffen, glaring at the ground as my heart floods with dread.

Diesel.

How the hell did he get Irena's phone?

"Your sister is dead," he says, his tone bored and dry. "You're next."

I want to say something. My impulse is to throw some sarcastic quip in his face to let him know he doesn't bother me and that he can never, no matter how hard he tries, get beneath my skin.

But all I can hear are his words echoing dully in my head.

Your sister is dead.

You're next.

Your sister is dead.

My throat tightens, and it takes everything in me to not scream into the phone. I refuse to believe it. I won't.

After everything I've done to protect Irena, I refuse to believe someone could take her from me just like that. That someone would have the *gall* to try. To think that in the blink of an eye my world could shatter—I won't believe it.

I just can't.

In my blurry and hazy confusion as the surreal sensation rocks through me, I hear the faint vibration of Tucker's phone buzzing nearby. He jumps out of his Jeep, his eyes locked on the small device in his hand as he reads something on the screen, and everyone around me stiffens.

The dragons are all alert, unsure of what's going on. Jace spreads his wings, snarling as his claws dig into the dirt, his intense gaze focused on me as if he's just waiting to know who he needs to kill. Drew and Harper growl softly, their eyes darting between me and Tucker, both of them clearly confused as to what's going on.

Only Levi remains still, his intense gaze trained on me as his lip slowly curls in a snarl.

As Tucker nears, he catches my eye and silently mouths *she's fine*.

He hands his phone to me, and I see a group text sent between the five of us from a new number, one I've never seen before. *Douche bag has my phone. Not dead.*

As a silence stretches among us, I briefly check my own phone and see a text message from her as well.

"Wow, I stunned you into silence," Diesel says through the line, shattering my train of thought. "Never thought I'd see the day when I could shut *you* up."

Somehow, Diesel snatched Irena's phone, and now he's just messing with me in an attempt to get into my head and throw me off my game.

A flood of relief nearly knocks me to the ground as I realize how close I just came to losing my sister forever. With my hand on my heart, I close my eyes as I try to regain my composure.

Diesel is messing with me, and I'm going to break him for trying.

"You think this is a game?" I ask quietly, not bothering to hide my anger as it bleeds through my words. "You take Irena from me, and then you call me to dangle it in front of my face?" I add, playing along for now. "Let's settle this, Diesel. Just you and me. Once and for all."

Maybe I can lure him out into the open, slit his throat, and end this. I hate this man. I hate knowing that such a brutal warrior is after me, along with everyone else.

Because I don't have enough enemies as it is.

"Oh, no, honey," he says, laughing. "That's not how this is going to work. You're going to be asleep. You're going to feel a hand over your mouth, and then you're going to feel my dagger against your throat. That's how you die, Rory." He laughs, milking the moment. "Sleep tight."

With that, he hangs up.

"Damn it!" I shout, grimacing in disgust as I crush the phone in my hand. I toss the shattered glass and crumpled mechanics of the phone aside. If Diesel is in any way able to track this number, I need a new phone entirely and so do my men, Harper, and Russell.

Great.

Just freaking *great*.

Tucker's phone buzzes again, and he looks down at it warily. "Unknown number."

We all wait in tense silence as he presses it to his ear without saying a word. With a deadly serious expression, like he's ready to kill the first person he comes across, he looks directly at me.

The distant hum of a woman's voice blurs through the phone, and he relaxes instantly. Without so much as a word, he hands the device to me.

Drew snarls impatiently nearby, probably because he wants to know what's going on, and I suspect none of them have shifted in case they need to fight.

"You guys, it's fine," Tucker says as I take the phone from him. "Look, I'll explain everything."

Thank goodness because all I want to do right now is talk to Irena.

"Why the hell does Diesel have your phone?" I snap through the connection, pressing Tucker's phone to my ear.

"I was trying to get info on the orb for you, baby sister," Irena snaps back. "So you're *welcome*."

"I don't care about the orb if you die trying to get it!" I shout into the line.

She huffs impatiently, like I'm chiding her. "Look, Diesel intercepted me. I got a few scrapes but nothing major. I don't need a lecture, Rory. I just want to let you know I'm not dead."

Even though I'm still furious, I can't deny the relief I feel at hearing her voice. If Diesel got close enough to steal her phone from her, calling her wounds a few minor scrapes is probably bullshit, but I decide not to press it.

After all, she nearly got caught trying to help me. I need to give her a break.

"Thank you," I say, genuinely grateful she called. "If you hadn't called me, I would have…" I trail off because I don't actually know what I would've done.

Gone after Diesel, probably.

Upended my life.

Stopped everything until I had my revenge.

And, honestly, I can't afford that right now. Everything in my life has to be focused on getting Ashgrave operational.

"Stop getting caught," I chide Irena.

"I never get caught," she says, and I can hear the smirk in her voice. With that, she hangs up.

I sigh and pinch the bridge of my nose. We're

running out of time to get this orb, and we have absolutely no leads.

Well... I guess that's not *entirely* true.

I stiffen as I think of Brett Clarke locked in a Fairfax cell somewhere, refusing to speak to anyone but me. I really don't want to oblige him, but I'm starting to think I might need to.

I rub my temples and toss Tucker his phone. He catches it easily, and everyone turns their attention toward me.

"We are at an impasse," I admit, my hands on my hips. "Harper, have you had any leads on the orbs yet? Anything at all?"

The great purple dragon shakes her head, the glowing tattoo on her forehead blurring a little with the movement.

Damn it. I groan in frustration and set my hand against her leg to open a connection between just the two of us because I have something I need to ask her in private.

Mostly because I know exactly how my men are going to react when I suggest it.

How sure are you that Brett has the intel I need? I ask silently through our connection.

A flurry of doubt and unease bleeds through from her as her head tilts toward me. A low rumble builds in her throat as a sort of intuitive warning, and I know she's not going to like the direction this conversation heads. *Roughly seventy percent, based on interrogations.*

I shrug. *Those are decent odds but not great, given everything at stake. What's your opinion of him?*

He's a crafty bastard with nothing to lose, she admits. *I don't even like being in the same room as him.*

Oh, awesome. I sigh and rub my face, breaking our connection as I take a few weary steps away.

Fine.

"We have to talk to Brett Clarke," I say, turning to face the others.

In unison, everyone growls and yells over each other in disagreement.

Tucker is the loudest.

"No," he says simply, pointing to the ground to emphasize his point. "That is absolutely not happening."

"Stop!" I yell, my voice cutting through the thundering rumble of their anger. I'm just not in the mood for any of this. "This isn't helping."

"Rory, I won't stop," Tucker snaps, taking several steps toward me. "I don't care what helps the situation. Brett Clarke represents everything I hate about the Knights. He's a clever, crafty asshole, and I refuse to trust him. *You* should refuse to trust him."

"I'm not saying I—"

Before I can finish my thought, Tucker grabs my arms, pulling me close to him even as he walks toward me, and the motion throws me entirely off-balance. I'm forced to rely on his grip on my arms to keep me upright as I look him in the eye, caught off guard by the sudden movement from my former Knight.

"I can't lose you," he says quietly, his tone laced with a hint of desperation.

"And you won't," I say simply, regaining my balance as I wrap my fingers around his wrists. "Look at the options here, Tucker. The fact is we don't have any. We're running out of time. There are assassins around every corner, at nearly every safehouse. Even the one good dragon Boss not currently on our team just vaguely threatened to kidnap me."

I hesitate, my eyes darting between his as I wait for him to really understand our position, because it seems as though he doesn't. It seems as though he thinks we have other options when we don't.

"We need Ashgrave," I continue. "And we're stuck. I don't stay stuck for long, and all we need to do is come up with a plan. We need to figure out what Brett wants, use it against him, get what we need, and then we'll be done with him forever."

Tucker's jaw tenses, and though he doesn't let me

go, he doesn't throw me off balance again. Instead, he presses his forehead against mine, his body stiff and tense. "I don't like this, Rory."

"I don't either," I admit. "But what choice do we have? Give me something, Tucker, anything better, and I'll listen."

He watches me, no doubt wishing he had another answer, but the fact is he doesn't. None of us do. Irena just nearly got herself killed trying to access intel on these orbs, and I won't risk anyone else's life any more than I already have.

This stops. Now.

I'm speaking with Brett one way or another. My men don't have to like it.

Because, hell, I don't either.

CHAPTER TWENTY

I lean against the tech panel behind a two-way mirror shielded from view in a room much like the interrogation cells of the dojo. Jace sets his hand on the small of my back, and the two of us watch Brett as he sits, still as a stone, in the room on the other side of the glass.

The former Knight is just sitting at a table, his hands in nondescript metal handcuffs as he rests them on the surface and stares at his fingers. After so long as a dragon, with people shoving my hands in special cuffs to block my magic, seeing traditional handcuffs is almost surreal.

Those won't work on *me* anymore.

To my surprise, Brett's cheeks are thin, his arms

having lost some of the muscle definition I saw back when he was captured.

He truly has been starving himself.

A plate of food sits in front of him, filled with bread and cheeses and a big chunk of steak. Little ribbons of steam radiate from the meat, and I'm getting hungry just looking at it.

Brett, however, doesn't so much as glance at the food.

Levi and Tucker lean against the wall behind me, and I peek over my shoulder to find them both scowling at Brett Clarke. Tucker has one leg propped against the wall while Levi simply glowers, immobile. Neither look at me, both too snared by their hatred for this man to so much as move.

Oh, good.

This will be *super* fun.

The door to the surveillance room opens, and both Drew and Russell walk in. Russell nods in welcome as my fire dragon walks up behind him, and we're finally all here.

"It's been a long time since I've seen the lot of you," Russell says.

"It certainly feels that way," I admit.

Truth be told, it's only been about a month—but a

month of constant anxiety and tension has a way of feeling like a lot longer.

With Jace on my left, Russell leans against the panel on the other side of me and sighs in frustration. "This guy is our most promising lead for gaining intel on the Knights, but he won't say much. We've had experts in to read his body language and expressions, and they've given us solid information on how to dig into everybody except this guy."

"What have they gotten from him?" I ask, morbidly curious. "Anything at all?"

"A little," Russell admits with a frown, which means he's clearly not impressed by what they *have* managed to glean. "He hides most of his tells, cues, and signals, which impressed us all. We managed to get little hints here and there that he knows something about Ashgrave and, well, you." The dojo master pauses, looking at me. "He's good."

I nod. None of that is new.

The way Brett carries himself, the way he hides his tells—all of this sounds like how a Spectre would act. I have to wonder if this guy got any training from Zurie.

My eyes drift again to the plate of food in front of him, and I have to confess I doubt he had any Spectre training at all. We were always taught better than to starve ourselves, even in the name of getting what we want. If we starve, we get weak. We lose muscle. And if we're weak, we're less likely to get out of a dire situation should the need to protect ourselves arise.

Rule 103 of the Spectres—when imprisoned, eat whenever you can.

And, of course, my personal favorite...

Rule 104 of the Spectres—if food you're offered is poisoned, pretend to eat it and save it for later. Your captors were stupid enough to give you a weapon.

"When is the next interrogator going in?" I ask.

"Five minutes," Russell answers. "I figured I would take a whack at him today. See if we can make any progress."

"Literal whacking?" Tucker asks, perking up and finally breaking his silence. "Because if you're giving me the chance to break his nose—"

"Tucker," I interject, chiding him with a glare over my shoulder.

He rolls his eyes and glares again at Brett Clarke, his brows furrowed. He's probably imagining all the ways he would like to break the man's bones.

With a heavy sigh, I crack my neck and roll out my shoulders. "You stay here, Russell. I'll go in, but I want to mess with him beforehand. Think you can give Jace control of the panel for a bit?"

Russell tilts his head skeptically, but I don't entertain his silent questions. Instead, I wink at my mate.

Jace grins, leaning against the panel as his eyes rove the various buttons and knobs. We already came up with a plan, and I think this is actually going to be pretty damn fun.

Good. I could use a bit of levity, and if I can have it at Brett's expense, all the better.

"Rory, I don't know," Russell admits, shaking his head. "I don't like this idea. You don't want to go in there. Everything he's done has been to manipulate you into doing exactly that. You would be playing into his hands."

That couldn't be further from the truth, but I don't say anything.

"This is the best we've got, Russell," Jace interjects, crossing his arms as he studies his friend's face. "He'll only talk to Rory, so it's best if she goes in there on her terms to get the upper hand."

And I absolutely *do* have the upper hand.

Since we had to take a charter plane to get here undetected, I spent the entire ride poring over every interrogation video Harper could find for me. I've watched the nuanced twitches in Brett's eyes and around his mouth. I've studied every tell he has, and I will know instantly the moment he's lying.

Most importantly, however, is the fact that he actually has several different tells—and each one gives away something different.

When he's lying, his left eye makes the barest twitch. When he's hiding something, he sniffs and rubs his nose.

But when he's *manipulating* someone, that's where his brilliance really shines.

He *smirks*.

Probably because he enjoys playing with people's minds. Especially dragons.

It's subtle, just the barest twist of the mouth, but it's there—and has been there every time he's tried to get interrogators to give him something he wanted. A phone call. A visit with his fellow Knights. Information on me.

Every time, without fail, the smirk was there.

Brett would have made a decent Spectre, if I'm being honest. He's crafty. Clever. He does everything in his power to appear compliant, all while pulling the strings to the best of his ability.

That's why I'm the best person to go in there. I know how he thinks, and I'll catch him in the act if he tries to mess with me.

And if he attempts to do that, not even the gods can save him from what I'll do to him.

First, I need to catch him off guard. That's where Jace comes in—because we have quite a bit of fun planned for my entrance.

The dramatic entrance is a powerful tool. It can win a fight before it even starts, and I plan to throw Brett off his game. The world thinks I'm supernatural, some kind of magical oddity, and I'm going to let Brett think exactly that.

Jace reaches for the controls on the tech panel, and the lights flicker in the room as he messes with the various knobs and switches across the board. Brett looks around nervously, his brows twisting in confusion and concern before he stares blankly into the two-way mirror.

He can't see us, of course, and there's no eye contact. But he knows we're here, and he knows we're doing something.

The lights come up again, flickering back on almost as instantly as they've gone off, and the goal is to let him think it's over.

We wait until he's calm, until his shoulders relax a little bit and he leans back in his chair, and even then, we wait just a hair longer. Jace and I catch each other's eye, and he flicks a few switches as the lights begin to flicker yet again.

The key is to do this on and off to set him on edge,

to take away his vision and leave him grasping in the dark wondering what's going on.

We repeat this a dozen times, and between each one, Brett's shoulders tense for longer. There's less time for him to relax. Less opportunity for him to calm down between the stretching gaps of darkness.

His breathing begins to quicken.

He leans forward, weight on his elbows as he scans the ceiling.

"Hello?" he asks, glaring into the mirror. "What are you doing?"

In unison, Jace and I grin.

We let this go on for almost an hour. Time stretches as we mess with his mind, taking away his vision for entire minutes at a time. As soon as his eyes begin to adjust, we throw the lights back on.

And never—not once—do we answer him.

The man is used to routine. It's time we throw him off. Everything he thinks will happen, well—we're taking that away.

We want him to think something's happening outside. That the lights are going out because of impending doom—doom that is far outside of his control. We want his mind to race. We want him to be afraid. To wonder how much longer he has left. To wonder how many more breaths he'll get to take.

As the lights flicker yet again, his jaw tenses. His fingers curl around his palms, and his shoulders are so tense a vein pulses in his neck.

That's my cue.

I nod to my mate and gently brush my fingers across Drew's back as I head out the door and into the hallway. There's no window on the door to Brett's cell, so I can't see inside.

It doesn't matter. I trust Jace to orchestrate this perfectly.

Behind me, the lights in the hallway go out. It's pitch black, but my enhanced dragon vision instantly adjusts. The world around me is an ocean of silhouettes, and I easily set my hand on the handle as I wait for the door to unlock.

It's show time.

The door clicks, silent as a breath as it unlocks. With practiced ease from my days as a Spectre, I open it without so much as a sound and slip inside the dark room.

Its pitch black to Brett, but my dragon helps me navigate through the silhouettes and shadows. A cot sits in the corner. The table fills the center of the room. The outline of a figure leans forward in a chair not far off, trying not to panic but failing epically. He leans back, his chair scraping on the stone floor as his breath quickens.

His blood sugar is low since he hasn't been eating, so he's not thinking rationally. Because of his little hunger strike, my game will only set him even more on edge.

That's his problem.

He shouldn't have let himself get weak.

Without so much as a whisper or a breath, I take my seat across from him and let the silence drag on. I get comfortable, as if I've been sitting there for hours, and set my legs gently on the table. Leaning back in the chair, I nod toward the mirror on my left.

The signal.

Instantly, the lights come back on, and I'm already looking at Brett.

His eyes dart toward me. In a flurried moment of panic, the Knight jumps in surprise. The movement scoots him backward, his chair scraping the stone as he stands and lifts his chained hands on impulse to protect himself.

It's a quick and reactive movement that's over in a second, and he quickly clears his throat as he regains his composure.

It's too late though. He can't undo what's been done, and I know he's on edge.

Good.

"I hear you want to talk," I say simply, tilting my head in curiosity. "Speak."

He takes his seat again, his eyes slightly widen as if he can't believe I'm really here. "They refused to ever let me speak to you," he says, swallowing hard. "They said they wouldn't even tell you my demands."

"You don't get to make demands," I remind him. I raise one eyebrow skeptically since I'm not here for small talk.

He stumbles over his words, which surprises me. I expected him to have prepared better for this.

While he figures out what he wants to say, I look down at his plate and pick up some of the cheese, munching on it in front of him as I savor his food. As if taking a cue from me, he grabs the loaf of bread and takes a hearty bite, the savory crust crunching and crisping delightfully as he lets himself enjoy it.

His mouth full, he leans back in his chair as he just watches me in shock.

"I'm a very busy woman, Brett," I tell him. "You're not high on my list of priorities, so I don't have much time for you. If you have something useful to tell me, you need to get on with it because you won't get a second chance."

"Right," he says, nodding as he takes another bite of the bread. "Right, of course." He shakes his head a little like he's dazed and trying to clear his brain. "With all the beatings, I'm just a little woozy," he adds, the tone genuine and a little sad.

And there it is.

The tell.

The corner of his mouth tilts upward as he lies to me. As he tries to manipulate me into feeling compassion for him.

I already knew this would happen. The Fairfax have been incredibly kind to him and his men given what they all did, and for him to so brazenly lie to me right to my face just pisses me off.

Time for him to see who he's messing with—and what I refuse to allow.

I lean forward as he takes another bite of bread and set my finger on the loaf, letting as little magic through my fingertip as I possibly can. Several arcs of white light pulse through me, too wild, and I briefly wonder if I just screwed up. If I let too much through.

Shit.

Doing my best to rein in the magic, I grit my teeth and snap my finger away. Thankfully, just enough of my magic pulse through me to do what needed to be done.

In a flash, the bread dissolves into ash in his hand

and mouth. He gags, spitting out bits of black saliva as the ash lands on his tongue.

"Brett, I want you to listen to me," I say as if I'm bored. "If you lie to me again, I will punch you in the nose. Do you understand me?"

He grins like I passed some sort of test and nods. "Okay, dragon vessel. I won't."

I frown as he uses the title other people gave me, and I wonder if it's meant to be sarcastic. There wasn't a hint of mockery in his tone, but with Brett, I can't be sure.

Ugh, fine. Let's get this over with.

"Why are you so insistent on talking to me?"

"Because I have nothing left to lose," he admits, leaning his elbows on the table. "I can never go back to the Knights. My whole life, my whole career, everything's gone. The General would kill me instantly the moment I tried, since no prisoners of war are allowed back." He hesitates, shaking his head slightly. "All thanks to Tucker."

I don't answer for a moment, simply watching him and imagining what Tucker must be doing right now on the other side of the glass. He likely just cussed under his breath, maybe even slammed his fist against the wall.

It seems these two men hate each other equally.

"I've always had the Knights," Brett continues. "For pretty much as long as I remember, killing dragons was a calling. A purpose," he adds, looking at the floor, his eyes glossing over.

There's no smile on his face, no sense of nostalgia. He speaks as if there's no emotion at all, like he's just telling me facts.

It takes everything in me not to grimace with utter disgust.

He runs his chained hands through his hair. "The Knights are imperfect, Rory, but I really thought they were doing good work. I thought they were men of honor and nobility protecting mankind."

I snort derisively. "You actually believed that bullshit?"

Brett pauses, looking up at me with a deadly serious expression. "I did," he admits. "I really and truly did."

I hesitate, admittedly snared by the morbid honesty on his face. "What changed?"

"These people," he says, gesturing toward the two-way mirror. "I was always told they're brutal and merciless assholes. That they would beat me senseless to bleed information out of me, and once I was no longer useful, they would snap my neck." His shoulders slump as he stares at the table. "It's what everyone thinks. Every human, anyway. Because that's all we ever see—dragons abusing their power, taking advantage of the situation, manipulating humans against each other to keep us busy and keep us fighting. I really believed that no one saw the real threat," he admits quietly.

"No one but the Knights," I add, not bothering to mask my sarcasm.

"That's what I thought," Brett confesses, rubbing his eyes. "But the Fairfax have been—well, Rory, they've been kind," he says, utterly baffled. "I slaughtered eleven of the dojo dragons in the battle, and yet I'm still alive." He looks at me, his eyes wide and weary. "I shouldn't be. They should have put a bullet through my brain and thrown me in a mass grave. That's what I was expecting. When they dragged me away, I thought I was going to my death." He pauses, leaning toward me as he makes his point clear. His finger taps briefly on the surface of the table. "I shouldn't be alive right now, and I am. That has shattered me. It has destroyed everything I thought I knew about dragons."

Through his confession, I continue to look for the tell-tale signs of a lie or manipulation. To my utter and complete surprise, there isn't one.

He's telling the truth.

He groans and rubs his face, his long beard unkempt from the month of neglect. "How do you do it?" he asks, his voice weary and tired. "Just… just tell me that, okay? Just be honest. I've been honest with you."

"Do what?" I ask dryly, taking the bait.

"Enchant people," he answers with another gesture toward the mirror. "How do you get people to do what you want? How do you bend them to your will like you do? I don't understand."

I frown in confusion, knowing full well that it's breaking through my mask and that he can see it on my face. But I legitimately don't know what he's talking about. I look again for the tell that he's messing with me, but it's not there.

By some weird twist of fate, he actually believes I enchant, charm, and bend people to my will.

I roll my eyes in irritation, not sure how much longer I can talk to this guy.

"Please," he says quietly. "Just… if nothing else, tell me that. I have to know for my own peace of mind. I mean, how could you sway Tucker from the General? From his own father? How could you get Jace to leave the dojo? How did you get Drew to abandon his family and his wealth?" Brett scoffs. "Hell, how could you tame a feral dragon? How do you do any of that?"

I rub my temples, not even sure where to start with such stupid questions.

"And how did you snare me?" Brett adds.

I impulsively stiffen, looking up to find Brett watching me with intense and baffled eyes. He's waiting for an answer and utterly serious.

What the *hell* is wrong with this guy?

I frown, my feet dropping to the floor as I lean toward him. "You will never be one of my men," I say, giving zero fucks about his feelings. "You have done too many horrible things that you must atone for before I can even consider you worthy of the air you breathe, much less one of my *allies*. You have a lifetime of horrible deeds that should leave you begging for forgiveness from every single dragon you see. You should be on your knees, every second of your *life,* asking those you have wronged to find compassion in their hearts not to kill you. Because you, Brett Clarke, do not *deserve* it."

He stares at me in somber silence for a moment. The silence stretches on, and his wide eyes only get wider.

No one's ever spoken to him like that before.

I stand, my palms on the table as I glare at him, daring to disagree.

After a moment, he stares down at his hands. A

deep and wounded scowl breaks across his face, and he slowly shakes his head. "Don't you think I know that? Don't you think I know what a revolting monster I am?"

I know that's what he is, but I doubt he believes it.

I wait, but, yet again, there's no tell.

It would seem that I'm hearing what he truly thinks of himself, and if that's the case, he's been fighting with the demons of his past the entire time he's been down here. His time in this cell has broken him, and if what I'm seeing now is real, he's just trying to rebuild from what's left.

The problem is he's doing a shit job of it on his own.

"I'm trying to make sense of all this," he continues, unable to even look at me. "I'm trying to understand—"

"I didn't *tame* Levi," I interrupt, not bothering to mask my contempt for Brett's choice of words. "I helped him heal. I didn't lead Drew astray," I continue, rolling my eyes. "I gave him a voice. I didn't steal Jace from his destiny. He chose me." I tap my finger on the table as I make my final point. "And I didn't seduce Tucker away from the General. I gave him a way out. That's what I do, Brett. It's all I've ever done. I ask the people in my life to be themselves and live up to the expectations they have of themselves, to challenge them to be the best version of who they are while they do the same for me. There's no spell. There's no trick. And while it may be hard for you to fathom, there's certainly no game."

For a moment, the silence settles on us. I expect Brett to look up at me, to answer, to do *anything*, but he just sits there, silently processing everything I said.

And I wait.

My men and I don't play games with each other, but this, here—this moment with Brett most definitely *is* a game, and I must play my cards carefully.

After a while, Brett shakes his head, like he can't quite believe it. "But you *did* something."

I scoff disdainfully, about done with this. "I just *told* you—"

"No!" He shouts, smacking his hands on the table as he looks at me. "No, dragon vessel. Up there on the roof, in the heat of the battle, you were magnificent. You roared into the sky and unleashed a hailstorm of lightning. Knights turned tail and *ran.* They were horrified. They knew what you are, at least partly. They knew what you could do to us."

"And?" I ask dryly, waiting for him to make a point.

"But I wasn't afraid," he admits wistfully, almost lost in his confusion and disbelief. "I wasn't scared at all, dragon vessel. I was just in awe." He pauses, wrinkling his nose in disdain. "Of a *dragon*. I didn't even know it was you until much later. I didn't realize you were the one I couldn't stop watching until I was down in these cells, and one of the guards let slip a clue as to who the diamond dragon was. I pieced it together from bits of info and still couldn't quite believe it when I figured it out."

I watch him in stony silence as his confession drags on, and after a month of silence, it would seem I've finally cracked Brett Clarke open.

Now, he can't *stop* talking.

"A human becoming a dragon." He leans back in his chair, hands in his hair as an utterly confused expression haunts his face. "You're everything I thought could never exist. You're proof that everything I knew about dragons is wrong. The way I've been treated here, the way we have all been treated—it violates everything we've ever been told about what dragons stand for. With every day that passes down here, I have slowly been forced to admit I was wrong, and if I was wrong about the dragons and how they treat us, what they think about us…" He trails off, shaking his head as if he doesn't want to finish the thought. "Then what else in my life is a lie?"

I let the broken man in front of me sit in silence

because I don't have an answer for him. He's having an existential crisis, the kind of train wreck that can only be watched.

Brett has to decide between two paths—the one that will save him, or if he doesn't want to change course, the one that will destroy what little remains of his life.

"There's nothing left for me to lead," Brett admits, his gaze on the floor. "I was going to take over for the General. I was going to be a Commander. A man of purpose and mission. I was idolized. Respected. Obeyed. I had everything I ever wanted, but now that dream is dead. With nothing to lead and no one to follow, I have no purpose. I have no direction. I have no hope and no clarity, and somehow all I can think about is you," he says, his gaze darting toward me again. "Up there in the battle, you weren't just a dragon. You were a *queen*."

I frown, hating how often that word is coming up. I resist the temptation to look at the two-way mirror, knowing full well that Drew is already staring at me. That great big twit is probably smirking in victory that someone else finally said it besides him and a deranged castle.

Brett leans forward, his elbows on the table as he

looks intently at me. "That's why I need something new. I need a new purpose. Someone else to follow."

Whoa.

What?!

You have got to be kidding me.

"Let me bow to you," he says intently, almost breathlessly. "Let me be loyal to you, and I will tell you everything you need to know." He hesitates, briefly licking his lips in anxious worry I'll reject this offer. "Give me a purpose again, Rory."

I scoff. "You mean you want me to let you out."

"If you want." He shrugs without so much as considering the option, like he doesn't care what happens. "If you want me to rot down here, that's fine too. But I hope that's not the case," he admits, taking a deep breath. "If you let me follow you, I'll do whatever you ask, even if it means staying here."

"Uh-huh," I say, not quite believing him. "Look, Brett, that's not how I work. You have to prove you're—"

"You want the orb, right?" he interrupts.

My eyes dart toward him before I can help myself, and I'm utterly caught off guard by the fact that he knows how badly I need it.

"It's locked away," he continues. "In our most secure vault in the most secure fortress we own. That's where the General lives. Where I used to live," he adds with a grimace. "That's what you wanted, right? I could tell from the questioning, from the way power sources kept coming up. They asked without asking to see what I knew, and I know all of it."

I impulsively stiffen, both thrilled by and dreading this conversation. He knows what I need, which proves it exists and gives me a lead. But he's also a Knight I can't bring myself to trust.

It's a delicate conundrum.

"We've had it for eons," he says, shrugging. "It's one of our oldest artifacts. It's stored in that secure vault within a vault with the most valuable items the Knights have ever owned. We have two of them, actually."

I blink rapidly in surprise, letting just a hint of shock bleed through my mask. I almost can't believe it. Going from no leads to two, suddenly.

It feels too good to be true.

He leans his elbows on the table, his hands splayed in breathless anticipation as he waits for me to say something. The way he's looking at me, it makes me think he's waiting to find out if he passed some kind of test.

I don't say anything. I want him to keep guessing.

To keep wondering. To keep feeding me information in the hope that he can impress me.

"What else do you want to know?" he asks desperately, his smile fading as his brows knit in confusion. I'm sure he can sense that I'm about to leave, and he doesn't want me to go yet. "Do you want to know how to destroy the Knights? Is that enough?"

Now *that* catches my attention.

He nods, apparently picking up on the subtle hints in my face that he has my interest.

Damn, he's *good.*

I have to be more careful.

"Look," he says eagerly, shuffling forward in his seat. "Listen, okay? There's data logged in the network that could dismantle them. Identities, plans, access codes, kill orders, everything. It's a full record of all names and identities, all safehouses, all plans and all detailed records of past terrorist events falsely attributed to dragons and dragon sympathizers."

He rattles off the list, and from the way his eyes dip in and out of focus as he recalls each thing only confirms that he's actually seen this information. He's actively recalling a list rather than throwing words at me.

"It's the truth," he insists. "If it were released, it would cripple all future recruitment while also undercutting the safety and loyalty of current members. It would destroy them, I promise."

"It would also destroy you," I point out, crossing my arms as I look down at him skeptically.

He groans, rubbing his eyes as he pauses. He sits with my words, leaning into them, living them. "There's nothing left to destroy, Rory."

I gently bite the inside of my cheek, watching the withered husk of what was once Brett Clarke, wondering exactly what is left of the man.

When I came in here, I figured I would be playing a deadly game of chess. I still am, of course, but my opponent isn't who I thought he was.

That means the stakes have changed.

"There would be nowhere for any of them to hide anymore," Brett continues, looking me dead in the eye. "There would be no possible way for them to go unnoticed for long. Releasing that to the world lets the governments who have been after them for centuries finally make some headway. The only reason the Knights have stayed ahead of the law is by keeping secrets and tying up loose ends. Releasing all of this would cripple them."

"By tying up loose ends," I echo, shaking my head with disgust. "You mean by killing people? Anyone who knows those things?"

"Yes, exactly," Brett says quietly, nodding. "But if we release this information, they're done."

I raise one skeptical eyebrow. "Who said anything about *we*?"

He swallows hard, still breathless, like he knows he's losing his one chance to impress me. It's astonishing to see him so desperate for my approval, and I almost start to wonder if my dragon did put some kind of spell on him.

There's a lot of information to process as he pours his soul out to me, and I'm still not quite sure if I believe him at all.

I slowly walk away from him, about done with this entire conversation. "Brett, I want you to answer any and every question the interrogators have for you to your fullest ability. Do you understand? If I discover you've been holding out at all, well…" I pause, milking the moment. "Let's just say I won't be as impressed anymore."

"Yes, ma'am," he says immediately.

I hesitate, trying not to show my surprise. He's a good seven years older than me, and yet he just ma'am-ed me.

I don't really like that at all.

I turn my back on him, mostly as a power play, but I can tell it's not what he wanted. His chair scrapes over the ground as he abruptly stands. The sudden movement sets me on edge, and my hand curls into a fist as I prepare to punch him in the nose if he tries anything at all. I track him in my periphery, but all he does is lean his palms on the table.

"An attack is coming," he warns. "And the Knights are going to blame you for it."

I pause, my back still turned to him, but I listen.

"It's designed to mirror your magic, and the Knights will blame you specifically. They've been studying your abilities anytime a public incident of your magic is tracked, and they've managed to replicate it convincingly. It's not perfect, and it's not actually something they can weaponize. All they can do is recreate the overall effect."

I frown.

Shit.

If he's telling the truth, that's really, *really* bad.

"The attack is going to be designed to spark anti-dragon protests," Brett continues. "Specifically, they're targeting you. Hundreds are going to die, and you're going to take the fall for it."

I look at him over my shoulder, trying not to let a hint of emotion through. "What else?"

"The General will no doubt be changing specifics of the plan since several who knew about it have been captured," Brett says, licking his lips nervously as he speaks. "But the fundamental attack won't change. I can tell the interrogators everything I know. But please…" He pauses, his eyes glancing briefly over me. "Be vigilant. The General wants nothing more than to torture you and give you a slow death. He hates you with a passion, and that ardent hatred has broken the will of some of the strongest people I know."

I don't answer. I know this could be a trap, but I don't know if I'm willing to risk letting hundreds die just to test his honesty.

Most of all though, I can't help but be baffled by Brett's sudden change—well, sudden to me, anyway. He's been down here with nothing to do but reflect on his life, and it's possible I just spoke to a changed and broken man.

Possible, yes. But certain? Absolutely *not*.

I don't trust Brett Clarke. Not yet.

And, hell, maybe not *ever*.

CHAPTER TWENTY-ONE

I lean back with my foot propped against the concrete wall, tapping my fingers impatiently on my arm as I wait.

And wait.

And *wait.*

Once again, I scan the empty building in the heart of Washington, D.C. as wind howls past holes in the open windows. Ladders and loose cables fill the large stretch of space, and there aren't even any walls up right now. The top floors of this building are empty and bare as renovations go on, and today the working crew was mysteriously given a day off and an extension on all project deadlines, courtesy of Drew pulling a few strings.

After all, we had to get them out of the space.

Twelve dojo soldiers pace the edges of the open floor, keeping close to the few panes of glass covering the wall as they scan the streets below us. We're about six floors up, and we're careful to keep to the shadows.

No one can know we're here.

Beside me, Jace is stretched out over the ground, a sniper rifle against his shoulder as he peers through the scope through a small hole we broke in one of the floor-to-ceiling windows. Once again, I follow the direction of the barrel to the parking garage across the street.

The parking garage where Brett warned us the attack would happen.

I kick off the wall and pace behind my mate, scanning the room as I try to imagine which direction the Knights will come from. Levi looks up at me from the opposite end of the massive space, his cool blue eyes settling on me before he returns his attention to the streets below, always keeping a vigilant eye out when danger might be near.

I can't even remember the last time he was relaxed.

Well, I guess that's not totally true. The last time he was completely relaxed, I was in his arms, and we were enjoying the sun in a warm Florida manor. Back before Zurie told the world who I am.

Back before all hell broke loose.

I sigh and rub my jaw, taking to the nearest window and scoping the streets below as dozens of people walk across the sidewalks and jaywalk through the painted lanes in between cars.

Drew and Tucker are on patrol across the street, mostly keeping an eye on the garage as we wait for Knights to descend. After all, someone has to be there to apprehend the General's men when they show up.

If they show up.

Each of my men has a half dozen dojo soldiers with him, and it's been eerily silent for the last five minutes.

"Teams report," I order into the comm in my ear, pressing my finger against it as I wait for someone to speak.

"Alpha Team in position," Drew says, and I chuckle quietly to myself. Of course he chose the alpha team.

"Bravo Team secure and returning for shift change," Tucker says, his tone stiff and stressed. My smile falls, and I know he's still irritated about all of this. He doesn't trust Brett, and if it were up to him, Brett wouldn't even be breathing.

I wanted to go on patrol, of course. Do my part. You'd think I asked to get a tattoo on my face or walk through fire, though, with the way they all reacted. Pretty much everyone but Jace threw a hissy fit, and just wasn't in the mood to deal with any arguing.

Ever since my discussion with Brett, my mind has buzzed with the hundreds of ways this could go wrong.

Cops could converge at any moment in a sting operation designed to catch dragons operating outside their jurisdiction. After all, none of the dojo soldiers should even be here, much less staking out possible terrorist activity, and neither should I. Everything we're about to do is highly illegal, even if it's for the greater good.

Or, the Knights could trap us somehow, lead us into some sort of trick designed to lure us out into the open so that they can put red scope dots on our foreheads.

Or—somehow—we could all get off scot-free with the Knights in custody.

I frown, not quite willing to believe it could be that easy.

This experiment will let us know if we can trust Brett, and honestly, I won't even if he is right about everything. There are too many ways a manipulator like him could play this to his advantage. He could give us this event to make us trust him, only to betray us later. He could use this to lure us into a trap we can't even see.

But every time I start to doubt him, I remember

sitting across the table as he desperately ached for my approval. To serve me. I remember watching his mouth for tells of a lie and seeing nothing.

It's just hard to believe he, of all people, could be telling the truth.

There's the shuffle of footsteps up the stairwell. The echo up the stairs is soft and barely audible, and of everyone on this floor, scoping and on edge, only Levi looks over.

Moments later, Tucker and his team enter the room. With his shoulders tight and tense, the first thing he does is scan the open floor until his eyes land on me. He lets out a small breath so subtle most people wouldn't even notice, and he rolls out his shoulders to ease the tension in his back.

Without a word, Jace stands. It's his turn to patrol. Lifting the sniper rifle, he extends his hand and offers it up. With Tucker between the two of us, it looks like he's trying to hand it off to Tucker, and I suppress an irritated eye roll at my protective men.

Tucker reaches for the sniper rifle, his attention already trained on the window as he prepares for his next shift.

Instead of handing it to Tucker, however, my mate walks around the former Knight and sets the rifle in my hands. He flashes me a mischievous grin and winks on his way out.

That delightful scoundrel.

I have to admit, I love the weight of a gun in my hands. It feels like a safety blanket, almost. Like security and comfort. To know that if anything happens, I have yet another means of protecting those I love.

As Jace leaves, six dojo soldiers flank him. "It's an honor to work with you again, sir," one of them mutters beneath his breath.

My smile falls.

They really miss him.

Jace grins at the soldier and nods, more relaxed than I ever saw him at the dojo. I like to think he enjoys mated life, and as he heads toward the stairwell, he flashes one last grin at me over his shoulder before disappearing down the stairs.

Beside me, Tucker's jaw tenses in annoyance as he stares after the former dojo master. Knowing Tucker, he'll try to snatch the gun from me, and it's probably best if I proactively keep him from even going for it.

Wordlessly, I take up Jace's spot on the ground. I peer through the scope with the butt of the gun against my shoulder, the heavy weapon filling my palms as I all but sigh with nostalgia.

I have *missed* this.

Tucker lays on his stomach beside me, grumbling to himself as we stare out at the garage across the street. It's still, only half-filled with cars in the mid-morning heat, and I wonder why the Knights chose this location. I mean, I *guess* it makes sense. This is a district frequented by businessmen and packed with restaurants. They can get in and set up before the lunch rush, before everyone pours out of the dozens of office buildings around the garage. It's mostly empty, too, since this structure belongs to an elite and private law firm nearby, which gives them cover and a hint of anonymity.

The more I think about it, the more I realize it's the perfect location for a bomb.

"I don't want you screwing Brett," Tucker says suddenly. "I can't live with it, I can't condone it, and I can't deal with it. I can't imagine him inside you."

My cheeks impulsively flush, and I quietly gag. "I think I threw up in my mouth a little bit."

Tucker glares at me, the full force of his gaze hitting me hard, in no mood for jokes.

I roll my eyes. "Tucker, I don't want Brett. I made that clear in the interrogation room. In case you forgot since, you know, you were *watching* it."

For a moment, Tucker doesn't say anything or even move. His gaze shifts back to the garage. For several minutes, he stews in angry silence, like he's actively imagining Brett railing me from behind.

I shutter, absolutely disgusted with the thought.

After a moment, my weapons expert finally sighs and relaxes. "I know, Rory. I know you don't really want him, even if he obviously wants you."

"He wants someone to follow," I correct, peeking through the scope as I survey the parking garage.

"You are so adorably naïve sometimes," he says with a derisive snort.

Peeking away from the scope, I briefly glare at him in annoyance.

"You're gorgeous," Tucker says plainly, like it's an obvious fact not up for discussion. "You're powerful. You're imposing. You're strong. You're a leader unlike anything anyone has ever seen, and you have a growing, devoted following. Brett wants to capitalize on that, and if he can get in your pants in the process, bonus."

"Tucker," I say, my voice tense with warning.

"He will try anything to get you in his bed," Tucker continues, apparently oblivious to my tone. "I just know it. He wants what's mine, and if he can take you from me—"

"Gods, Tucker, just stop." I shake my head, lowering the gun as I try to snap him out of this catastrophic spiral he's going through. "No one could *ever* take me from you."

"I—I just—" Tucker groans and runs his hands through his hair in frustration. "I know, Rory," he adds, his voice calmer as he takes a deep and steadying breath. "I guess—I don't know. Even if you forgive him, I can't. I'll never be able to."

Even though I'm on scope duty, I can't help but watch Tucker for a few seconds. It's a distraction, something Zurie would have never allowed. But I'm not under her thumb anymore.

I reach toward him and gently brush my forehead against his, and even though it's a quick and subtle movement, flickers and sparks of delight snake through me at his touch. He looks at me again, his gaze softer this time, and I even get a little smile out of him.

"I understand where you're coming from," I admit, returning my attention to my scope as I scan the mostly empty garage. "Brett is devious, and he represents your old life. Everything you hate about it. Everything you were supposed to be. You don't ever have to like Brett, Tucker. I'm never going to ask you to. And I will *never* fuck that man, so you don't have to worry about that. As for him taking me from you—

well, he can never get under my skin. The moment he tries, I'll just kill him."

For a few moments, there's only silence. But after a second or two, Tucker reaches for my lower back. He gently rubs his fingers along my spine, and even through the shirt, I feel the tingle of desire at his loving touch. I smile, grateful for him. Grateful he can trust me with these things and be honest with something as difficult to wrestle with as his feelings.

I feel the weight of someone's gaze on my back, and I look over my shoulder briefly to find Levi standing at a nearby window. Our eyes meet, and his jaw tenses.

There's meaning, here. In that look. In his expression. Something he wants to say that he doesn't have the words for.

My lips part, ready to tackle this head on, ready to finally begin to understand what's going on for Levi, too. Just like Tucker, he's wrestling with something massive—maybe larger and more difficult to process.

But I don't get the chance.

In my periphery, there's movement through the scope. My eyes dart toward the black blur as a van speeds up to the top of the garage.

I smirk.

Gotcha.

"All teams converge," I order into the comm. "Black van on the first level quickly heading toward the top. White scuff on the back right bumper."

"Roger," Drew says into the comm.

"On it," Jace echoes, and I hear the click of a gun cocking.

I wish I was down there. I hate being all the way up here, nothing but glorified surveillance. Camping out just isn't my forte, and I'm not going to stay in the safe zone even if I do have a rifle.

Besides, even I can admit Tucker's the better shot.

"All right, everyone. Let's go," I say, standing. The rifle clatters gently in my hands as I offer it to Tucker, who nods as he takes it from me.

"I'll stay here," he offers.

"Thanks," I say with a small grin

The man is brilliant with a weapon, and if anyone's going to cover the men I love, it's going to be him. I can set my pride aside long enough to admit that.

He takes my spot by the window, the sniper rifle settling into the crook of his shoulder as he peers through it, giving Drew and Jace cover.

"I don't suppose I can tell you to stay here, too?" Levi asks, the ice dragon suddenly beside me as I head toward the stairs.

"You're cute," I banter back, chuckling under my breath as I jog down toward the basement.

It's a nice way of saying *hell* no.

A half-dozen soldiers charge down the stairs after us, while the other half stays behind to watch over Tucker. Guns drawn, hackles raised, all of us prepare for war.

These assholes will be lucky to make it through the day.

Our unit bolts down the stairs, all of us racing toward the secret walkway in the basement that connects our renovating building with the garage across the street. The tunnel carves under the road, and we managed to lock these doors along the bottom floors.

No one gets in or out.

With every step, another burst of adrenaline tears through me. We've timed this, and the entire route takes a grand total of thirty-three seconds. With my heart thundering in my ears, I'm ready. I'm ready for a fight. I'm ready to break noses.

Hell, I'm more than just ready. At this point, I need it. I need to burn off some energy. I've been itching for a way to do something, to do more than run and hide and plot and plan.

I need to make a difference, and ever since Zurie's

announcement, everything I've known has been thrown aside. I've been forced to step into a new world, to work in a new way, and it pushes my limits in ways I never thought possible.

By the time we scale the stairs to the top floor, the van is already sitting in the middle of the parking lot with its back doors open. Four men in all black lay on the ground in cuffs with red gags across their mouths as they squirm and fight, the dojo soldiers pinning them to the floor.

"Aw man," I mutter, shoulders slumping as I skid to a stop. "I missed it."

Jace digs his knee into the nearest Knight's back and grins mischievously at me. "This was actually pretty fun, Rory. The way we descended on them, their expressions—you would've liked it."

"Well, don't rub it in," I pout.

Four silver vans drive up, and though they have no markings, I recognize one of the drivers.

A dojo soldier.

Within a matter of a few seconds, dojo dragons discreetly carry off the Knights, loading them up into the various vans before the tires peel as they drive off.

Technically, that was a kidnapping. The Fairfax family has no jurisdiction here, and the Knights are

American citizens. Since these are terrorists, however, I don't think anyone will really mind.

Drew's leg hangs out one of the back of the van as he fusses about in the shadows cast by the blacked-out windows. His foot twitches slightly, and I hear him muttering to himself, though I can't quite make out what he's saying.

White lights flair to life within the van, and very suddenly, we're faced with a massive black box that glimmers and shines, occasionally beeping as I stare at it in surprise.

I tense on impulse, slipping my weight onto the balls of my feet in case we need to grab Drew and run. After all, this could be a remote-activated bomb for all we know.

There's so much risk, and I hate that almost everyone I love has their life on the line right now.

"I've got it," Drew snaps, and his hand waves in our general direction as we slowly approach him. "Everything's fine. This is just new to me. I've never seen anything like this before."

"Can you defuse it?" I ask.

He peers around the device and arrogantly smirks at me. "Who do you think you're talking to? Of course I can diffuse it."

I chuckle and smack his leg. "At least feign some modesty."

"Nah," he says, brushing my thought away with a flick of his wrist as he returns to his work. "There. Remote access disabled," he says, tapping the side of the van as he scoots out and sits on the edge of the bumper.

I breathe a sigh of relief, setting my hands on my hips as I scan the strange machine. "You scope the van?"

"Yeah, of course," Drew says with a nod. "There's a shitload of explosives strapped to the bottom."

"What?" My eyes go wide, and I shrug, wondering why I'm the only one who seems to be upset by that little note.

"It's fine," he says, chuckling. "I disabled the remote connection, so we have nothing to worry about."

"Uh-huh," I say, only relaxing a little.

"What even is this?" Levi asks, nodding toward the strange black box in the van.

Drew shrugs. "As far as I can tell, it's some kind of modified tesla coil, but I need to study it further to know for sure. Well, not me, honestly. I need my tech guys looking at this since this is way more advanced than anything I've seen before. From what I've gleaned so far, this creates arcs and light that imitate your magic, Rory." He pauses, looking at me. "It doesn't actually do anything, which means the actual destructive power comes from the TNT strapped to the bottom."

Huh.

So, they can't actually replicate my magic, which is a good thing. They can, however, make a lightshow convincing enough that people might *think* it's me—and that is very much *not* a good thing.

Man, they must have a ton of these machines if they're willing to just blow it up.

More importantly, however, this means Brett was right. He said there would be a terrorist attack here, and we caught them before they could hurt anyone.

There's a chance this was meant to be a trap to capture me, or it could still be a trap to get me to trust him. Either way, I may be able to use Brett to my benefit.

A flicker of white light radiates along the horizon. It's brilliant and bright, and I instinctively wince as it burns through my peripheral vision. "What the—"

Before I can even finish my thought, an explosion rocks the other side of the city. The rolling echo of an earth-shattering boom shatters glass nearby, and a blast of air rolls toward us from the river.

The ground trembles. Around us, the structure

groans as it takes the brunt of the shockwave. We're all thrown off balance, and I grab one of the van's doors to keep from falling.

A hand is instantly on my waist, holding me in place. Levi's tall, imposing frame towers over me as he's instantly at my side.

Oh, no.

Tucker.

With my heart in my throat, I look warily at Tucker's building. Dread rocks me as I wonder if the building can withstand the force. We're in a parking garage, a solid structure designed to weather any storm—but he's in a glass tower actively under construction. If one of these goes down, it's more likely to be his.

It holds.

As the aftermath of the explosion settles, we all race to the side of the garage and stare out into the city to figure out what happened. A huge plume of smoke billows over the historic buildings not far off, the cloud thick and dark as smog. Sirens blare through the streets, and I can hear the faint shrill screaming of panicked bystanders in the distance.

We caught *one* bomb.

It would seem we missed the *second* one.

In my utter, unrelenting fury, I freeze. I just shut

down. My rage burns through me, hot and white, and I lose all sense of feeling.

With my hand on a pillar at the edge of the garage, my fist slowly tightens. I don't feel the concrete crumble beneath my touch, and I don't even notice it until dust falls through my palm.

I can't believe this.

We failed.

Those *bastards*.

Something takes hold of me, and all I can see is red. It's just like when Zurie stole away my shadows. It's that sense of failure, that overwhelming dread that takes hold of me and tells me I should have done more. It's all-encompassing, almost numbing, to the point where the only thing I can feel anymore is the rage.

"We have to help." My voice is dark and tense, allowing for no disagreement as I head toward the stairwell.

"No, Rory, you can't," Levi snaps, grabbing my wrist.

I instantly counter, twisting my hand out of his hand without so much as looking his way.

"If you go, you'll be seen near the event," he snaps, grabbing my shoulder. "That will confirm it for people. You cannot be seen, Rory, even if you're just trying to help."

I'm not listening.

It's almost like I can't.

People aren't going to die because of me. Most likely, people already *did* die, and I should have been there to save them.

I can barely think as the rage churns and burns within me. My only desire is to make this right.

Though his fingers dig into my shoulder, I shake off his hand. It's effortless. Easy. Practiced a thousand times in my duels and sparring matches with Irena.

If I want something, no one can stop me.

Except, perhaps, my men.

Levi grabs my arm in one fluid motion, apparently done with words. I twist and slide out of his grip yet again, rotating his arm until I pin it behind his back. His icy blue gaze falls on me, and he frowns.

Something changes, in that moment. It's fast and brutal, sudden and severe, but I don't pause to figure out what it is.

He leans backward, throwing his weight against me to set me off-balance, but I'm ready. I drop into a fighting stance, taking the full weight of his body as he twists out of the arm pin. He grabs my forearm and curls it around my body, pinning my arm to my chest as he holds my back to his strong torso.

He and I haven't truly sparred before. He's watched me, of course—but he doesn't know what he's up against.

I curl my leg under his ankle and knock him backward. His grip loosens, but it's not gone.

He's not done, and neither am I.

"Rory, enough," Drew says.

Though my vision is still blurred and red, thick with rage and fury, I hear the shuffle of his gait across the ground.

I don't want to fight them, but I will.

Before I can move, he wraps his arms around my shoulders and lifts me, pressing my back against his chest as my feet come off the floor. Levi stands, shaking out his shoulder where I pinned him, and I wish these two could just understand what I'm trying to do.

I writhe in Drew's grasp, trying to break free even as the big, dumb, stupid, strong fire dragon keeps me pinned with his insane strength. I wrestle with him, furious, and though I can hear his voice, I can't make sense of any of the words.

"Rory," Jace says calmly, his voice echoing through my brain.

In a second, Jace is in front of me, and my heart calms the moment I see his face. He grabs my jaw tenderly, his thumb brushing my lip as our eyes lock, and that alone pierces my rage.

It's like a cloud passes, and I can finally think clearly again.

My heart settles, and I stop struggling. But as the rage passes, I'm forced to face the pain it masked—and my entire soul breaks.

I failed.

Me.

I'm not *allowed* to fail.

With a cloud that big, I can guarantee people died, and it's all my fault. I just want to destroy something, to decimate someone, to burn off all of this anger.

And I can't.

"Thank you," I say quietly, my eyes darting from Drew to Jace and then finally to Levi. "I wasn't thinking clearly, and that's not like me."

Deep within my chest, my dragon stirs, still furious. It takes only a moment to realize what happened —she took over.

That can *never* happen again.

I snap. My fury and rage funnels abruptly toward her, and in that moment, she stills. It's like I slapped her, like she wasn't expecting me to disagree, but she needs to understand.

Her rage, when unchecked, can get the people I love *killed.* It could get *everyone* killed.

I still trust her. I still love her. But she can never have control like that again. After all, she's still a baby, and her emotions can get the best of her sometimes.

She coos gently, the soft apology so unlike her. I can practically feel her brush against my soul, and I think she gets it.

"We need to go," Levi says, gesturing for me to come with him. I nod and follow, feeling kind of guilty about knocking him onto his ass, but nothing between us has changed. He doesn't glare at me. He doesn't give me the cold shoulder. He simply resumes, ready as ever to protect me, and I have to admit I'm grateful.

It would seem he has forgiven me already.

Tires squeal through the garage, and seconds later, another silver van rounds the bend. The silhouette of the driver leans back as he hits the brakes, and after a few seconds, I recognize Tucker at the wheel.

"Get in!" he shouts at us, waving for us to hurry up.

We don't argue.

One by one, we duck into the back of it as Drew tosses the keys to the black van to one of the last remaining dojo soldiers. Within moments, the bomb is out of sight, and my men are all safe.

As our getaway car pulls out of the garage, however, I can't pull my gaze away from the black smoke barreling into the sky.

Brett didn't lie to me, but it seems as though he didn't quite tell the whole truth either. There were two bombs planned for today, and this feels suspiciously like a trap.

If it is—if he somehow fooled me into walking into the General's plot—I'm going to kick his ass.

CHAPTER TWENTY-TWO

B rett might well have led us into a trap, and I am
in no mood for pretense.

No games.

No tricks.

Not anymore.

As I stalk through the hallways of the Fairfax
capital holding cells, all I can do is silently fume.
Russell has said that Brett has been forthcoming since
I last spoke with him, and it's basically impossible to
get him to *stop* talking now.

Russell doesn't mind that, of course. As far as I'm
concerned, however, Brett is not in the clear.

I kick open the door to Brett's cell to find him
sitting at the table with his hands clasped in front of
him. This time, he isn't wearing any handcuffs. As the

OLIVIA ASH

door flies open, he instantly looks up, shoulders tensing as his lips part with surprise.

Initially, he smiles, his eyes lighting up as if he's happy to see me. But that quickly fades once he has a few seconds to study my face. I stalk toward him, slamming the door behind me, and with every step, his brow furrows deeper and deeper with concern.

Good.

He should be worried.

Without so much as stopping to say a word, I grab him by the collar and lift him out of his chair with my enhanced dragon strength. He hits the wall hard as I slam him against the stone. His legs dangling, I lean in, our noses mere inches apart as he gasps. His eyes dart between mine, like he has no idea what's going on or why I'm angry.

That only pisses me off more.

I can barely contain my rage. I have to keep my dragon at bay because she wants to eat this guy alive.

I won't lie. I'm kind of tempted to let her.

"You have two seconds to tell me the truth," I say, my voice dark and dangerous. "I want to know what was planned for the attack. What was really *planned.*"

To his credit, he looks genuinely confused, but I don't trust this guy. Maybe he planted the tells. Maybe he was an even better manipulator than any of us knew, and he tricked me into thinking I understood all of the ways he could lie. All of the ways he can manipulate.

When he doesn't answer, I shake him. His head briefly rattles as my strength takes over. "I want to know what your game is. What you're playing at. Trying to get me to show up at the site of a terrorist attack designed to mirror my power. Is that what you were doing? Trying to pin me in the heart of it all?"

"You *went?*" he asks, his voice breaking with dismay as his brows twist upward. "Rory, why wouldn't you send people? You must have an army. Why would you go?"

"Shut up!" I snap, my voice echoing in the small space.

In the silence that follows, I simply watch him, and he looks genuinely concerned—not for himself. Not for the death toll.

But for my *safety.*

"Rory, you should never have gone!" He frowns, like he's scolding me. "I told you about the plan so that you could send people. I can't *believe* you went. Why would you be so reckless? You should have been with witnesses, where you would have an alibi!" His eyes dart between mine, his hands tenderly weaving around my wrists as his feet continue to dangle over the floor.

No.

I don't want him to *touch* me.

I throw him aside, knocking him on his ass as he slides over the stone floor. He grimaces, curling briefly as I walk slowly toward him.

"You are never to give me an order," I warn him, my voice low and deadly. "You are never to give me a demand. And Brett Clarke," I say, waiting for him to look at me. When he does, he's tense and wary, like he isn't sure what he's looking at. "Brett Clarke, you are never to speak to me like that again."

He hesitates, still on the floor, still holding his stomach as he recovers from my rage. After a moment, he nods, and it's very clear that he finally understands.

To my utter surprise, however, a small smile creeps over his face. "You're even more incredible than I thought," he admits.

Flattery won't get him anywhere. That's Tucker's forte.

"I mean no disrespect," Brett says, apparently trying again. "But I did warn you there might be changes to the plan. The General is crafty and distrusting. I knew about that one machine, but they must have found a faster way to replicate the technology if they had two."

I study Brett for a moment, looking down at him over the bridge of my nose as I square my shoulders and wait. I let the silence settle between us as he watches me with a hint of desperation, like he needs me to believe that he's telling the truth.

There is a chance that the General banked on Brett telling me about the attack today. Anyone else would have changed locations or altered the plan significantly, maybe even stopped it altogether if there was a chance the intel got out.

But not the General.

I'm starting to suspect he used it as a trap to lure me in. After all, the General ultimately wants the world to hate me. It would probably be worth it to him to set an easy trap for me to walk into if it meant exposing me publicly. If it meant luring me into a place I shouldn't be at a time when I shouldn't be there.

That could explain why it was so easy to get a hold of the van. The General wanted me to be there, and he didn't want any human witnesses, like the police, to place me at some spot away from the other attack.

The General might have been banking on me being there. He might have been relying on me trying to help, on dashing into the danger and letting myself be seen.

Because then everyone would blame me for what happened.

There is a real chance that this attack wasn't Brett's fault at all, that it was entirely the General.

Hmm.

I stretch and curl my fingers absently, my thoughts racing as I piece everything together. But one simple thing stands out to me. Brett helped the Knights build that machine. Not only that, he knew all along—for ages—while he was down here. He knew exactly what they were planning, and he didn't tell anyone until I sat down in front of him. He used human lives as a tool for bartering, and he withheld valuable intel that could have saved them.

"Did they tell you how many people died?" I ask, finally bringing myself to look at Brett again.

His shoulders slump, and he stares at the floor as he sits against the wall and leans one elbow on his knee. "No."

"Four hundred and three," I say, my voice hard and tense. "Including fifty-three children on field trips in the area. Children, Brett. They hit a subway station two hours before lunch. There were families on vacation, business people—everyone was in the line of fire.

They didn't kill or even injure a single dragon. Every death was a human life, Brett. *Humans.*"

I let the word echo in the room, waiting for him to show the remorse I think he should feel. I want to see him crumble beneath the guilt and shame. I want him to know exactly what his hatred has done. What this organization he said he used to believe in has done.

What he helped them do.

"Is that what you stand for?" I ask, taking a threatening step toward him as my eyes narrow. "Killing your fellow humans? Just to make dragons look bad?"

He hangs his head and sighs deeply, rubbing his temples as his shoulders droop. I've seen that look before plenty of times—hell, I've worn it more than once.

That, right there, is real and honest shame.

"I used to," he admits quietly. "I really did believe it was for the greater good, that those were sacrifices made to make the world better. But the longer I've been down here, the more I'm changing my mind." He hesitates, groaning as he sets his head back on the stone wall.

He won't look at me, and that's probably a good thing. I'm pretty sure I could ignite paper with my rage right now.

"It's toxic there," he says. "I got caught up in it

because there was no room to question it. There's no disobedience or doubt allowed. You either follow eagerly, or you die," he says, listing off the two options on his fingers. "Tucker knows that all too well."

"Don't bring Tucker into this," I warn him, seething.

"I'm sorry," Brett says, his gaze drifting toward me as he starts to stand.

"I didn't say you could get up," I snap.

Brett hesitates halfway off the floor, watching my face in a bit of shock. I wait, looking for any signs of dissent or disgust or frustration, anything at all to hint at the feelings beneath the shame, at the chance of another possible manipulation.

There's nothing. He simply sighs and sits back down on the floor.

"I should just kill you," I say, taking slow and steady steps toward him as I tower over him. "Everything you've done is unforgivable, and I'm still not sure you're in the clear with this whole near-miss."

His chest stops moving as he watches my face with terror. His eyes go wide, his brows twist upward and his lips part as if he's debating what he could say to get himself out of this.

But the terror is brief.

After a few moments, he simply hangs his head,

shoulders stiff. "If that's what you think is best, Rory," he says quietly.

And he waits.

I have to admit, I wasn't expecting that reaction.

I wait for an intuitive hint that he's lying to me, but nothing comes. I simply watch him, waiting for him to peek through his arms, looking for any signs or tells of a manipulation at all. I call on all of my training. All of my experience.

I wait, and I watch.

He simply sits there, surrendering to my judgment.

I sigh in frustration, rubbing my eyes. I'm not actually going to kill him. I'm not that cold-hearted. I just wanted to put the fear of the gods into him, and apparently, it worked.

Maybe a little too well.

"I'm not going to kill you," I say with a hint of irritation, turning my back on him.

He breathes a heavy sigh of relief. "Thank you."

I don't even reply. I can't look at him. I'm still too furious. I snap my fingers and point to the nearest chair, giving him a silent command.

His feet shuffle over the floor, and the chair legs drag against the ground as he obeys.

I pace the length of the room, lost in thought, wondering what I'm going to do with this man.

"I know I'm on thin ice here," Brett says after a few moments of silence. "But I have an idea."

I snort derisively. "Of course."

"Expose the Knights," he says, his voice tense and urgent. "Give the world the truth. Show the world who you really are, and they'll fall in love with you just like everyone else."

I hesitate mid-stride and look at him over my shoulder, wondering what he's playing at with all this flattery. He should know by now it doesn't work on me.

Flattery aside, however, he does have a point.

Exposing the Knights would be the best way— maybe the only way—to destroy them. I don't know about the whole showing the world who I really am part, but I do know the Knights are probably the world's number one terrorist organization, and everyone wants a piece of them.

All I have to do is give the world the keys to the Knights' organization, sit back, and watch it burn to the ground.

Right—*all*. Like it's easy. If this data exists at all, it's in a remote and secure location that's easily the most heavily guarded fortress the Knights possess.

"Why are you so keen on seeing them destroyed?" I ask, probing to see if I can peel back the layers in

Brett's mind. "That's twice now you've brought this up."

Every question I ask gives me a chance to test his honesty. It gives me a chance to watch him try to manipulate.

More importantly—every question is a chance for him to mess up, and for me to catch it.

"I'm just trying to redeem myself," he says quietly. "I've killed so many. I screwed up so much that I don't think I can save myself from damnation." His gaze drifts to the table, and he studies his hands. "But I want to at least try to atone for what I've done."

As he loses himself in his apparent shame and misery, I simply watch, wondering if he could really change. I'm not stupid enough to blindly trust anyone, least of all a man like Brett. My trust is earned.

To my surprise, Brett might be slowly earning it.

Slowly.

Bit by bit, and just maybe.

But there's a chance.

"What exactly do you have to go on, Brett?" I ask, pacing once more. "So far, you have no proof of anything you've said. There's no proof the orb is in this facility. There's no proof this data that we want even exists."

It's a bluff, of course. He knew about the orb

without us even hinting at what it was, so I know he's telling the truth there. But this is more so to flesh out proof about the intel he's dangling like a carrot in front of my face.

After all, if he's lying, this is a classic ploy. Give you opponent something useful in order to make your other claims seem more believable. If you lead with a bit of the truth, people will believe almost any lie.

"I can't give you proof," he admits, shaking his head as he watches me. "All I can do is tell you what I saw."

I lean my hands on the table. "And what did you see?"

"The first time the General gave me access was the day he nearly recaptured Tucker," Brett admits, his shoulders slumping. "It was a safeguard in case the General didn't come back, since he would also be meeting with three Spectres and a ghost in training." Brett's gaze drifts briefly toward me, and I frown. "And that's not all, of course," Brett continues. "He would be meeting with the dragon vessel and three powerful dragons. He kind of assumed that would be the day he died, but he had to try. He truly loved Tucker." Brett grimaces slightly, exposing a hint of his deep-set jealousy. "The General was heartbroken when Tucker left."

"Focus," I chide.

Brett nods and clears his throat. "He took me into a room with a hundred screens. He showed me everything. It all went by so quickly because he was just trying to let me know it was there. Profiles flashed across the televisions. Safehouses. Blueprints. Everything. It was a sort of lockbox he could leave to an heir and know that everything would continue as he wanted it to. It is his contingency plan."

I have to confess, it sounds plausible. After all, it's what Zurie did for Irena. Why wouldn't the General, who operated closely with Zurie in many accounts, not do the same?

With a sigh, I rub my eyes and briefly glance at the two-way mirror. My men and I need to reconvene before we make any decisions, and I figure they probably have plenty of opinions on everything Brett's saying. They're watching in the other room, and I'm sure they might have even picked up on things I'm missing.

We're done here, but first, it's time to make sure Brett knows where he stands with me.

I lean forward, glaring at Brett as I get close. "You know what I think you're doing?"

He shakes his head, breathless as I near.

I wrinkle my nose in disgust. "I think you're trying to get me to let you out of here. I think you're trying to trick me, and it won't work. You want to redeem yourself, but to whom? The General? You think you're going to lead me into the lion's den, where you can betray me and hand me over to the General himself?"

"No, Rory. No," Brett insists, leaning backward, bringing his hands between us as his eyes go wide.

I grab his collar and drag him close, not giving him room to breathe. "If you betray me, Brett Clarke, there will be no mercy," I warn him, my voice dangerously low. "There will be no kindness. There will be no forgiveness. Just pain. Just blood. And then, nothing at all. You don't have to join me. You don't have to obey me. But you absolutely do have to tell me the truth. You're playing with fire here, and I will burn you to dust if you test me."

Any sane, mortal man would be afraid. He would watch me with wide eyes and tremble beneath my hands.

Brett doesn't.

A thin, wry smile pulls at the edge of his mouth as he watches me, clearly impressed. Instead of tensing, eh relaxes into my hands as his eyes rove my face. "I wouldn't dream of betraying you, Rory Quinn."

It takes everything in me not to drop him on his ass. It takes all of my training and experience to simply watch him with a stony expression when all I want to do is wrinkle my brow in confusion.

Brett Clarke is many things, but he's no coward—and he's no idiot, either.

He knows he's playing with fire. The question is, what am *I* playing against?

CHAPTER TWENTY-THREE

My men and I sit in relative silence at a war room table in the heart of the Fairfax palace. This is serving as the temporary dojo grounds while the dojo itself is being rebuilt, but I haven't even had a chance to explore. Short of flying in and out for brief moments, we never stay here long, and never during the day.

The Fairfax already have enough to deal with. I don't want witnesses to confirm I'm spending time in their Capital. That might start an orchestrated attack not even the dojo dragons can stop.

Levi stands at the window, looking out over the city below. He always is lately. He's always watching, always alert even in friendly territory.

Beside me, Drew and Jace pour over a laptop, Jace

frowning the more Drew mutters about production schedules for the Spectre tech Irena stole. They keep running into hitches, nuances of the design that are more difficult to implement than previously expected, and I figure this is probably what Zurie dealt with when she initially set up production herself. Little hitches. Little setbacks. Little slowdowns.

They add up.

Tucker paces the length of the room across the table, furious as he fumes over Brett. He rubs his jaw, eyes to the ground and glazed over as he walks. Every now and then, he'll look up at me, and I wish I had the energy to smile and console him.

But I'm still fuming as well.

I lean back in my chair, arms crossed, my heels on the table as I stare up at the ceiling, mind wandering. All I can do is remember Brett's terrified expression as I loomed over him, threatening to kill him. His wide eyes as I lifted him and shoved him against the wall.

Everything about it felt so genuine, but this is Brett Clarke. He can't be genuine.

…can he?

The double doors to my left burst open, and Russell storms in with his arms full of rolled papers and printouts. He drops them on the table, the papers rustling as he begins to open them all. In a matter of a few seconds, he spreads a map across the table, followed by blueprints of a fortress I've never seen before. Dozens of highlights and circles litter the page, each paired with little notes and arrows written in a handwriting I don't recognize.

Enter here.

Weak point, next to a circled door.

Vault. A star, circled three times, sits next to the word. An arrow points to a small unassuming square in the middle of the map.

"Let me guess," I say, dropping my feet to the floor as I look at the papers. "That's Brett's handwriting."

"Yeah," Russell says dryly, frowning as he rubs his jaw, staring at the papers.

"Where's Harper?" I ask, my eyes darting again to the door. "Is she going to join us?"

"France," Russell says flatly.

I frown, not entirely sure what the hell she's doing out there, but there are endless Andusk palaces and manors spread across the French countryside. It's not hard to guess who she went to see.

"I'm surprised you're not with her," I admit. "Especially given how crafty and dishonest the Andusk can be."

Keeping her safe is his top duty, after all. I suspect there are responsibilities here that he must tend to as the dojo master, even though all he wants to do is be with the woman he loves.

His gaze drifts toward me, and he seems to catch something in my expression that I hadn't quite meant to give away. "Don't worry," he says. "I secured a contingency squad to trail and keep an eye on her."

I smirk. Of course he did, and I bet she doesn't have a clue they're with her.

"So, here's what we figured out," Russell says, shaking out his shoulders as he surveys the maps and blueprints in front of him. "Everything we need is apparently in this one fortress. This facility is called Ravenwood, and according to Clarke, this is where the General keeps the most important information and resources available to the Knights. It's their main base, so to speak. I don't know if I buy it. Intel suggests their main facility is actually Alpha Prime, the one they have in Montana."

"That was a decoy," Tucker says, shaking his head as he looks over Russell's shoulder at the blueprints. "Ravenwood was always Father's favorite."

Russell grimaces, setting his palms on the table as he looks at Tucker without a word.

We all do.

"What?" Tucker asks as his eyes scan the lot of us. "No one asked, and it was never relevant before now."

"It's the *Knights*," Russell snaps. "It was always rele —you know what, never mind." The dojo master groans impatiently and rubs his eyes before returning to the papers. "This is a secluded fortress, and little is known about it except that it does in fact seem to be managed and owned by the Knights. Therefore, we can confirm that, if nothing else, the General does occasionally go here."

He waits, turning his attention toward Tucker again as the former Knight paces the wall behind him. Tucker hesitates, his gaze darting between the dojo master and me. "What?"

"Nothing to add?" Russell asks sarcastically.

"Carry on, Jeeves," Tucker says with a cheeky wave of his hand.

Jace and Drew chuckle nearby, the former dojo master hiding his mouth behind his hand.

"Right," Russell mutters, clearly annoyed. "This place is huge." He taps the paper, shutting his eyes as if the very thought overwhelms him. "It has immense defense measures built into the cliffside, with every anti-dragon and anti-anything weapon known to man. As far as I can tell, it's impossible to get in unseen."

"Lovely," I say dryly, rubbing my eyes in irritation.

"According to Clarke, the orbs are in the vault here," Russell continues, tapping his finger on the little square I noticed earlier. "And the data drives are in the command center's lockbox, which is a secured room stored behind a labyrinth that involves five steel doors. It's basically a vault with four other vaults in it."

"I guess we know which is more valuable to the General," Jace quips.

"No kidding. I mean, just look at it." Russell taps again on the paper, this time at the opposite end of the building, and I stand to get a better look.

With the two things we need that far apart, it's clear we can't go in as a single unit. We won't have time to mobilize. Unless we split up, we would have to pick only one target.

Yet again, my Spectre training flares in warning. Divide and conquer, another excellent technique to weaken your enemy. If this is Brett's attempt to take us down, he's not only trying to get us into the most secure Knights location in the world, but he's also trying to make sure he splits us up when we're in there. That makes us weaker and limits our ability to disable any enemies we encounter.

Oh, that's just *fantastic*.

"So, we need two teams," I say, running a hand through my hair as my mind buzzes with options. "We have to make this quick. That means we divide and conquer. Two teams, running simultaneously. We go in, we get what we want, and we get the hell out."

Russell doesn't answer. Instead, he simply watches me, his palms still flat against the surface of the table and his mouth set in a grim line.

I scan the room to find everyone watching me in grim silence, and it's hard to process their expressions. There seems to be a blend of wariness and concern, but no one wants to say anything.

"What?" I ask tensely.

"I'm not sure about this," Russell admits. "Going into the lion's den? It feels like it could be a trap."

"Obviously," I say, shrugging slightly as I gesture toward the blueprints. "But listen to your gut, guys. Are any of you actually having intuitive hits about this? Is any of this a trap?" I pause, honestly asking and waiting for somebody to share their thoughts on it, because my dragon is giving the all-clear despite my Spectre training. "Do any of you think Brett's really lying?"

"Honestly, I can't even stand to look at his face," Tucker admits, shrugging as he leans his back against the wall. "Just seeing him makes me want to kill something. So, I have to admit I haven't actually paused to look for any signs of a lie."

"That's very…" I hesitate, looking for the word. "Honest."

Tucker shrugs, still frowning.

In the silence that follows, no one else answers because we all have the same strange unease. We all expect him to lie. We all expect him to be full of shit and to try to lead us into some sort of trap.

What's strange, however, is that it very much seems like he's *not* lying. That's almost more disconcerting because it's not what any of us expected.

"I don't like any of this either," I admit, gesturing again to the plans. "But it's not like the information we need to dismantle the Knights is going to be easy to get. They're going to guard it like gold."

"Is this even a priority?" Levi snaps, finally joining breaking the silence to join the conversation.

"What do you mean?" Jace asks, his eyes narrowing in suspicion. It would seem my mate senses something off about Levi—the same odd coldness I've been feeling from him for a while now.

"This," Levi says impatiently, gesturing toward the blueprints. "The Knights. Who cares? They've always done terrible things, and they always will. Is getting this information going to matter? Is putting our lives on the line going to change anything? Get the orbs.

That's what's important. Get Ashgrave operational and get a home base."

"They're coming after Rory, man," Tucker says calmly. "They want the world to hate her, so yeah. They're pretty damn important."

"The world does hate her," Levi spits back. "It hates all of us already. We need a secure home base to fight them off."

"We may not have time," Drew says, leaning his elbows on the table as he looks Levi straight in the eye. "There's new chatter about the Knights, and now it seems like they're mobilizing. Something big is coming, and it's coming soon."

"Exactly," Jace says, crossing his arms. "Even if we do get Ashgrave operational, the Knights were the core piece of the puzzle to dismantle the gods in the first place. What's to stop them from doing it again?"

"Because the gods were idiots," Levi says. "They trusted their stupid Oracles. They got lazy. They had servants. They got weak and let people pamper them. Rory would *never* let anyone into Ashgrave. She would never make that mistake."

Drew's jaw tenses, and he and I share a brief glance. I can tell he's barely holding back a biting comment, and I wonder what it could be about. Most likely it probably has something to do with his queen theory.

I sigh, rubbing my eyes in frustration. I need to stop this before it all unravels.

"Emotions aside, guys, let's look at the facts," I say calmly, setting my fingertips on the table as I lean onto the surface. "The Knights are coming after all of us, but they especially hate me. Long ago, their ancestors destroyed Ashgrave, and they're trying to destroy it again by doing everything they can to expose and weaken me now. We can't simply dismiss them just because they're human or not as disciplined as the Spectres. They are dangerous. They are desperate. What's worse, they're out for revenge. They're killing people. *Innocent* people." I pause, shaking my head in disgust. "I won't overlook that."

For several moments, no one says anything. I can feel the weight of several gazes on my shoulders, but I don't look up. I simply study the plans, my mind churning with ideas on how we can get in and out without dying.

There aren't a ton.

"What are your thoughts on all this, Tucker?" I ask, looking up at my former Knight. "Are either of these carrots Brett's dangling in front of us even real?"

Tucker groans, setting his head back against the

wall as he shuts his eyes. "I don't trust Brett worth a damn, but it's clear he has access to information I was never given." Tucker pauses, biting the inside of his cheek as he slowly shakes his head. "Father told me about the vault where the orbs are apparently stored, but he never told me what was inside. He just said there were secrets there and that when I was ready, when I was worthy, I would get to see it all."

I sigh. "So, it's real."

"It's real," Tucker confirms. "And as for the lockbox, well..." he trails off, staring at the closed doors as if they're going to give him an out from this conversation. "It makes sense. He never trusted anyone. He recorded interviews of new recruits confessing their darkest secrets, all so he could use them as collateral if they ever betrayed us. He did everything in his power to own the lives of every Knight under his control." Tucker sighs. "He's an authoritarian control freak. So, no. It wouldn't surprise me if the lockbox is real."

"It's settled then," I say, standing and rolling out my shoulders. "We're getting both the intel and the orbs. We're doing this."

Levi grimaces in disdain and disappointment, looking out the window as if he can't even bear to look at us right now.

My heart twists at seeing him so angry, especially

with me. He's a hunter, and I just won't give him back his shadows. He and I need to talk through this, and it's becoming more and more clear that it can't wait much longer.

No matter how exhausted we are after this meeting, he and I are going to discuss it. I have to confess—even though I've faced explosives and life-threatening traitors, a heart-to-heart with Levi daunts me more than any terrorist.

Ugh. *Feelings.*

"What about Brett's idea?" Jace asks, his chair grating against the floor as he stands and looks at me. "The one to come forth and tell the world the truth?"

I frown in confusion and point to the papers spread across the table. "That's what we're doing, Jace."

"No, about you," he says, quirking one eyebrow skeptically.

I laugh. "Yeah, right. Let's deal with that another day, okay? One death-defying stunt at a time."

"I don't think it should wait," Jace admits, his intense gaze landing on me. "I don't think it *can.*"

"You can't be serious, Jace!" Levi snaps.

"I am," Jace says, his stormy gaze passing briefly to the ice dragon before it returns to me. "I hate Brett with a passion, Rory, but the man has a point. If the world sees you for who you really are, they won't believe the Knights, the Spectres, or the Vaer anymore. They won't believe the lies."

"Some of them will," I point out. "Actually, a lot of them will."

"I think people will surprise you," Jace admits, sitting a little taller in his chair. "Brett's full of hot air, but he's right about one thing. People will love you if you just let them see who you really are."

I snort derisively and chuckle under my breath. "You already mated with me, man. You won me over. You don't have to flatter me anymore."

He chuckles. "It's not flattery, Rory. It's the truth."

I shake my head and return my attention to the specs, but my eyes gloss over. I can't help but consider it.

Back when Zurie shared her lies with the world, I decided I wasn't going to run anymore. No more shadows. No more lies.

At the time, I thought that meant fighting back. Refusing to run. Refusing to play nice.

Maybe I was wrong.

After all, what's the alternative? Being seen? Letting the world know the truth? Who I am? What I can do?

Throughout my life, I've always let people underestimate me. It was safer to go unseen. There was less I had to worry about. The less people knew about me, the more I could get away with. The longer I would live.

Now that I've had a chance to see the world for what it truly is, however, I have to admit there's a limit to what staying in the shadows can do. There's only so much you can achieve when you hide, only so much available to you, and the limit is especially glaring now.

I can let the world talk about me, say whatever they want and pass judgment. I can let them believe the lies that they're being fed.

Or I can step up and share the truth. If I let the world see me as I am, it gives me back some of my control. It lets me tell the story, instead of my enemies.

I groan, pinching the bridge of my nose. "Politics. Publicity. All of this is so foreign to me."

"It's not foreign to us," Drew points out, gesturing between him and Jace. "We can help you, but you have to be the one to lead the charge on this. It's not something we can do for you."

"Guys, slow down," Tucker says, raising his hands as he gestures for us all to chill the hell out with this conversation. "I don't think I like this. We're talking about giving away information to the people that want her dead, right? Like, are you guys thinking this through before you talk, or—"

"Of course we are," Jace interjects. "Not everyone wants her dead, Tucker. Not everyone wants to manipulate her. There are people like that secretary who are simply excited she exists. They want to know who she is. What drives her. The world can't help but be curious. Are we going to let them make assumptions, or are we going to tell them the truth?"

Levi slams his fist against the wall, and the entire room shakes. Glass in the window shatters, raining down to the ground below.

"That was expensive," Russell says dryly.

"I can't believe what you all are saying," Levi snaps, ignoring the flippant remark as he glares at all of us. "I'm disgusted. I really am. You're going to let her walk into harm's way like that? It's reckless. You're supposed to care about her. Protect her. How could you *possibly* keep her safe if the world knows everything about her?"

"Levi," I say gently, trying to calm him down. "Take a deep breath and—"

"No, Rory," he snaps, practically shaking with rage as his gaze darts towards me. "I can't sit by and listen to this."

"We're not throwing her to the dogs," Jace says, a

little insulted. "We all have a stake in this. We wouldn't let anything happen to her. You know I wouldn't let her die, Levi. Do you think I'm an idiot?"

"I think you're reckless," Levi snaps back. "You don't control what the world does to her. Especially not if you're letting all of her protection simply disappear."

"We wouldn't—"

"I won't lose you," Levi snaps, his voice booming through the room as he smacks his fist against the table, the full weight of his gaze on me. A crack splinters through the wood, and Russell just sighs in frustration as we break something else of his.

I sigh in frustration. "Levi, you're not going to lose me."

"I will," the ice dragon says tensely. "If you go out there, you become prey, Rory. You're already prey. You're hunted at every turn by people you can't even see because they stay in the shadows where *you* should be." He points his finger at me, his body tense as he frowns. "They hide until they strike, and then they return to continue their hunt. Those are the brutal ones. The deadly ones all of us can't even see right now."

I've never seen him like this. He's barely said this much in one go, much less with so much zeal. All of us are awestruck into silence, utterly and completely snared by his passionate anger.

Over *me*.

"Kinsley. Jett. Aki Nabal," Levi continues, listing off my enemies on his fingers as he speaks. "You think those people are just lying low? You think they've given up?" Levi shrugs, gesturing wildly as he asks the rhetorical question with utter disgust and disdain. "They tried to strike before, and they failed, so they returned to their shadows to wait. The longer they go unseen, the better their chances of success next time because they're hoping we'll get soft. That we'll get complacent and comfortable because we forgot about them." He taps his finger against his hard chest. "But I never forget, not when it comes to the hunt. Not when it comes to you. And your list of enemies is far too long. It's probably longer than any of us even knows. There are wiser hunters, *smarter* ones who haven't even made themselves known yet." He hesitates, looking at me with utter confusion. "And you want to just walk out into the sun with a target on your back?"

In just a few powerful strides, he crosses to me and holds my face so that he's the only thing I can see. "If you do this, I will lose you. If I lose you, I'll lose my dragon." He hesitates, shaking his head. "If I lose you, I lose everything, and I can't allow it. I won't."

The room is silent, and I can feel the weight of every gaze on me. I want to speak, but I'm utterly dumbfounded. I'm not used to Levi speaking to me like this.

When I don't answer, his brow twists in frustration. His soothing touch disappears from my face, and he storms out, slamming the door behind him.

In the surreal silence that follows, I can hear my pulse in my ear. Without Levi in front of me anymore, I can see the glowing lights of the Fairfax capital through the window. It's a city I haven't even been able to admire except for the late-night flyovers. It's a string of glittering golden windows in the desert night, hot and dry, filled with dragons whose brothers, sisters, and children are putting their lives on the line in a war people started just to control me.

It's all clear, then. In that moment.

Deep within me, something changes. It locks and immortalizes, and I know I'm changed forever.

I'm not alone in this. I never was. However much I was raised in the shadows, I don't get to live there anymore.

My choice is clear. Either I hide in my tower and lie to myself, saying the shadows are fine—or I step into the light, and I show the world that I am not prey at all. I'm a hunter so fierce that I will *decimate* any fool who comes for me.

That, at least, is an easy choice.

Deep in my chest, my darling dragon stirs and coils with glee.

It would seem we're in agreement.

We are, after all, the *hunters*.

CHAPTER TWENTY-FOUR

I quietly shut the door to Levi's suite as something shatters in the bedroom. I frown as his shadow crosses through a thin moonbeam in the short hallway that leads to his bed, and I wonder if he's throwing things. That's so out of character.

He already knows I'm coming. After all, he's the one man who seems to hear me even when I mask my movement, so I don't try too hard to be silent. I cross the small living room in his suite and lean against the doorframe to find him cursing under his breath as he kneels over a broken vase—the same one that's in all of our rooms. Bent hydrangea stems lie in puddles of water as he quickly picks up the broken shards of the vase.

He tosses the fragments in the trash can and rubs

his face, frustrated. "I don't want you to see me like this, Rory."

"It's okay, Levi," I say calmly, giving him space.

He shakes his head. "No, it's not. The great master of stealth can't even keep from knocking over a vase." He gestures at the broken stems with disgust and turns his back to me, running his hand through his hair as he stares out the window.

I do my best to hide my smile. He's so damn endearing, even when he's mad.

I know he probably wants to be left alone to silently fume and lose himself in his anger, but I don't indulge him. Instead, I walk up behind my ice dragon and gently set my arms around his waist.

With the movement, he flinches gently in surprise.

I know he heard me coming, so he must not have been expecting me to hold or comfort him in any way. He probably thought I would launch into a lecture or chide him on how he's acting, or just yell at him until we get to the truth of everything.

But this just feels right.

I expect him to pivot, to hug me back and hold on tight. This is the sort of moment when we can heal things, when we can be real and honest.

He doesn't.

In a movement so fast I barely register it, he spins

me around and pins my back to the wall. With his hands on my waist, he presses his hard body against me as our noses touch. His eyes snare me, his gaze locks on mine.

The entire movement is so intense. After all, he's still boiling with anger. The steam from all the things we haven't talked about since Zurie's broadcast is quickly taking over him. Everything that has been shoved down, pent up and saved for later.

He's about to blow, and I feel like he's at a breaking point. I just don't know what that means. He's never been like this, and I don't know what to expect anymore.

"Levi—"

"You know what's at stake, Rory," he says, practically growling as he doesn't even give me a chance to speak. "You're putting yourself in harm's way, but it's not just you. It's Jace. It's me. It's everyone who loves you. Everyone who needs you to stay alive."

Before I can reply, he grabs my throat, his thumb gently brushing my jaw as our connection opens through the fluttering sensation of skin on skin.

No words come through the mental link. Instead, a torrent of emotions flood from him, overwhelming me.

Possessiveness.

Hurt.

Love.

Devotion.

Lust.

Everything about this is overpowering. His hand on my throat. The heightened sensation. The tsunami of feeling. His grip around my neck is so dominating, so possessive, that it's kind of turning me on right now.

Truth be told, it's hard to focus on anything he's saying because what he feels is so *intense*.

He grits his teeth, bracing himself for something. I expect him to keep going, to keep talking, to keep telling me why we have to stay small.

Instead, he presses his mouth roughly against mine, kissing me as he holds my throat.

For an ice dragon, this man is *hot.*

I've got to be honest—between the yelling, the anger, the kiss, and the hand on my throat, I'm having trouble following his intentions here. I'm not even sure what he wants out of the conversation anymore.

Whether he wants to fuck or fight me.

I seriously can't even tell.

With one hand still on my throat and the other on my waist, his grip on both tightens. It's not painful, but there's no denying the pressure he's gently applying to my windpipe.

"You know what I want," he says simply, his lips hovering over mine.

"You want me to stay out of the public eye," I answer.

"But you won't," he says darkly, his fingers pressing into my hips as he frowns.

"No, I won't," I confirm. "We're too big for the shadows, Levi. We couldn't stay in them even if we tried."

He goes still, and for a moment, he barely even breathes. His brows knit slightly upward as he stares at me, his cool blue gaze darting between my eyes, and he looks absolutely tortured. I expect him to disagree, to fight me on this, and I prepare myself for the worst.

Everything about this moment feels shattering and life-changing—that could be for the better, or it could decimate everything I know and love. I don't know what's going to happen, but I know we have to do this.

No matter how painful it might be.

I swallow hard, and even though I know we have to talk about this—even though I know this conversation absolutely has to happen—I don't know if I'm ready for the consequences of whatever might come.

"Don't you think I know that?" he says quietly.

My eyes widen briefly in confusion. "What?"

"I *know*," Levi says intensely, leaning against me, his grip tightening as he breathes me in. "I know you can't stay small."

He squeezes his eyes shut, grimacing as he presses his forehead against mine, and the thunder of his thoughts is too loud, too rough to follow. He's fighting something I can't even see, and it takes me a moment to realize this isn't *just* about everything we're facing after Zurie's broadcast.

This is just as much about him. We've been fighting the same demons, and we didn't even know it.

"You lived your whole life in the shadows," I say, finally piecing it together. "You tried so hard not to be noticed or seen. Being recognized by Kinsley and your commander…" I trail off, shaking my head slightly as I realize what a devastating turn of events that must have been.

Being recognized by those in power is often the big break most people wish for their whole lives. For Levi, however, his talent destroyed his family and got his sister Daisy killed.

"Up until I met you, I tried so hard to go unseen," he admits, his eyes downcast as he stares at the floor. "It was the only way to survive."

"Levi," I say gently, trying to get him to look at me.

Instead of that, however, he gently leans his cheek against mine, tilting his head as he lightly bites. The soft and subtle movement is so distracting that I almost lose track of my thoughts, and his chest rumbles slightly as he all but growls.

With his hand still around my neck, he lets go of my waist and sets his hand on the wall instead, looking at me. He's so passionate, so serious. As I watch his face, something shifts for him—just like it did in the forest.

Something in him just changed, and I have to admit I'm terrified he will leave me. Leave *us*.

"I can't ask you to play small anymore," he says, shaking his head. "It's not who you are. It's not the life that works for you."

My lips part, and for a moment, I can't find the breath enough to speak. "Are you going to leave?"

His powerful blue eyes lock on me, and his body goes stiff. There's no answer, just silence, and after a heart-wrenching moment, a small smile breaks across his face. "No. For you, Rory, I can give up my shadows. For you, I can do anything. I didn't want to face this. I didn't want to look at it, but I realize now that hiding in the shadows is an old belief that used to serve us both but doesn't anymore. Fear doesn't serve us anymore. The fear of the unknown, the fear of losing control…" He trails off, shaking his head. "In the shadows, hiding from the world, you can simply observe, but I guess it's time for us to live."

I smile, almost not willing to believe that this is really happening. "You mean it?"

He nods. "I'll always worry about you, and I'll probably do stupid things in the name of keeping you safe," he admits, laughing. "But me trying to keep you small —that's nothing more than me holding you back, and I won't do that to you again. You deserve better than that. You deserve more."

I can't help myself—I sigh deeply with relief, leaning against him as the sensation floods through my body. Every fingertip, every toe relaxes.

I almost can't believe this is happening.

With the way he was acting, I was so worried I might lose my precious ice dragon.

Once again, he wraps his fingers around my neck and holds me gently as his lips brush against mine. "You make me better, Rory. You push me. You break my boundaries. And it sucks," he adds, chuckling. "But you help me be a better man."

I laugh as his rough kiss deepens. I love the sensation of his thumb on my jugular, of knowing he has control over such a vulnerable part of my body—and, more importantly, knowing without a doubt that he would never abuse that power.

His other hand snakes up my shirt, and I almost don't recognize him. He's dominating. Controlling. With a rough shove, he slams his hips against mine, rooting me in place against the wall as his mouth hungrily explores mine. His fingertips trace along my abdomen, trialing upward toward my breasts, exploring every inch of me and savoring the experience, like all of this is new.

In one flawless movement, he spins me around and presses my chest against the wall. Seconds later, he plants delicate kisses along my cheek, almost in apology for being so rough, but the sweetness quickly dissolves as he weaves his arm under mine and reaches up to grab my neck yet again.

I've never seen him like this—both dominating and doting.

I freaking *love* it.

His other hand trails down my waist, dipping between my skin and my jeans as he traces his way toward the zipper. I squirm with delight, and he gently bites my jaw, almost like he's punishing me for moving.

His fingers reach the button on my jeans and deftly unclasp it. The zipper lowers. My pants loosen, sliding over my hips as he grabs the fabric and yanks it toward the floor. The denim hits the carpet, and my underwear follows seconds after.

A cool breeze flows over my legs as he exposes me in his dark bedroom, just feet from the window. I expect him to throw me on the bed, or maybe hoist me over his shoulder and carry me into the shower, but his fingers simply rove across my entrance as he presses my chest against the wall.

I hum with delight as he plays with me, his fingers brushing across my clit as he nibbles my ear. He presses his hips against my ass, the denim rough against my skin as he dips his fingers roughly into me. I moan, pressing my palms flat against the wall as he takes control. With each of his movements, his biceps brush against my shirt, hiking it up a little higher as he toys with me.

I'm completely at Levi's mercy.

It's *divine.*

For a moment, his hand disappears, and my body and dragon both ache for him. Though his intoxicating touch around my neck still makes me buzz with delight, I can't stand the thought of him moving away.

There's the rustle of a zipper, and the shuffle of denim as he undoes his belt. With one fluid motion, he slaps the belt leather against my ass. I gasp, laughing as the sharp sting radiates through my thigh, quickly receding to utter pleasure and delight.

Before I can say a thing, he winds the belt around my waist and buckles it. The strip of leather slides down to my hips, hanging loosely off my body with nothing to hold up and no purpose to it—until he grabs the belt and roughly tugs me closer to him, treating it like a handle he can use to manipulate and control my body.

I gasp and laugh with shock and delight as the sharp sting recedes into pleasure. "What's gotten *into* you—"

"Hush," he demands, practically growling in my ear.

His thick cock dives between my thighs, the tip brushing against my entrance as he rubs the length of him between the sensitive folds from behind.

Every inch of him feels hungry. Insatiable. Impatient. With my jeans around my ankles and his cock sliding toward my entrance, I finally realize what he's up to.

He's going to ride me with most of our clothes still on. He's too hungry to even wait for us to undress.

His strong, thick fingers return to my clit, toying with me as he kisses my cheek. His hand tightens around my throat as he pushes past my sensitive folds from behind, his thick cock moving slowly into me. He takes his time, in no hurry at all, and it's almost agonizing how slowly he slides inside of me.

Inch by inch, he fills me. Stretches me. As his fingers rub my clit, spurring my desire, I surrender to him completely. I can't help it. He's utterly in control, and I don't even *want* to take it back.

When he finally presses his hips against my ass, his jeans scratch against my skin. His cock stretches my pussy, filling me entirely. I gasp, his hand at my throat as I squirm beneath him, loving this.

Once he's inside, he holds himself within me, savoring the first thrust. His cool breath slides down my spine, beneath my shirt, as he leans his forehead against my hair.

It's like a switch flips, and he roughly pulls out of me—only to buck into me again immediately after. I gasp with delight, pressing the full weight of my body into my palms as they flatten once again against the wall paper. I arch my back as he dives into me once more, riding him as much as I can from this position.

"Come for me," he demands in my ear.

Gladly.

I close my eyes as he rails me from behind. I love this. I love everything *about* this. My whole body trembles with every thrust. His cock fills me again and again as his fingers rub my clit, driving me wild.

I can't last long. Not when he's pounding me like *this.*

With every bucking thrust into me, my head pushes against the wall. I lean my cheek against the wallpaper as he nails me again and again. His fingers briefly leave my clit as he pulls hard on the belt, keeping my waist flush against his with every thrust, dominating me completely.

Every now and then, he peppers sweet and doting kisses between the fierce ones. He bites my jaw, only to gently caress my cheek afterward.

It drives me wild, and I lose all sense of time.

All I can feel is *him.*

My orgasm slowly builds, the blissful sensation brewing in me like a blizzard, ready to break. I gasp, unable to contain or silence my moan as it rises in my throat. I arch my back, angling my thighs against him, riding him, giving in to him completely as he takes me.

"I'm with you to the end, Rory," he says as I tighten around his cock. "If we're going out there—if the world wants to know you—we're doing it together."

That's it.

I'm done.

I can't hold back the orgasm anymore—not with a declaration of love like *that.*

I moan as I come on his thick cock, but he doesn't pause. He only rails me harder, riding me through it all. It rocks me, and I dig my nails into the wallpaper, dragging streaks through the pinstripe design as I give in to my climax. We ride it together, his belt around my bare waist as he bucks into me, ever stronger.

It's heaven, and I don't even know how long I'm lost in the blissful sensation.

When the orgasm slowly fades and I finally relax my cheek against the wall, he thrusts into me a few final times before I feel the surge of his own orgasm burst within me. It ripples through me, filling me all over again, and I hum with pleasure. The belt slides down to my hips as he releases it, and he wraps his arm around my waist as he growls with pleasure. He bites my shoulder, only to pepper it with kisses seconds later.

He leans against me, his chest to my back as we try to catch our breath. There's a few breathless moments where all I can feel is his chest rising and falling against me, his powerful lungs sucking in air as he recovers.

After a few moments, he adjusts. His hips slide

forward, his cock delving deeper into me, and I gasp in surprise and pleasure with the sensation.

He never even pulled *out.*

Levi kisses my neck as his strong hands grab my hips. He thrusts hard against me, the sudden motion throwing me off balance. My breasts nearly flatten against the wall as his hips pin me once more to the wallpaper. His bare cock slides fully into me, already hardening yet again.

Oh *gods,* what this man does to me.

We're dragons, about to charge into an army of Knights—but we do what must be done. Always have. Always will. And with Levi at my side, I know I'll have everything I need to succeed.

He hums with pleasure, interrupting my thoughts as he reaches again for my clit. His strong fingers toy with the sensitive bud, shooting ripples of warm and lust through my thighs as he prepares for round two.

I smirk with mischievous delight. We'll do whatever it takes.

CHAPTER TWENTY-FIVE

There's only one way we're getting into this fortress, and that's if we have an invitation. With all of the weaponry and advanced military hardware the General has procured over his years as the Knights' commander, the only way we can get in is if they open the door for us.

Brett is going to be that invitation, whether he likes it or not.

I pull out the chair across from him and sit at the table, both of us silent for a moment as he blatantly tries to gauge my mood. I rest my elbows on the table, studying his face, and there are two reasons that I don't say anything.

One, this is an intimidation tactic. I am one

hundred percent in control of his situation, of his life, of whether or not he ever gets out of here.

And two, I'm getting a baseline, refining my ability to detect a lie or manipulation on his face.

With Brett, I can't be too careful.

Once I get my baseline, I lean back in my chair, getting as comfortable as possible. I drape my arm over the back, lifting my chin slightly as I look down at him. "Do you know how easy it would be for me to kill you?"

He swallows hard. But to his credit, keeps my gaze. "Given what you did to the loaf of bread?" he asks. "Yeah, I imagine it would be pretty easy."

I smirk, keeping his eye, and I decide to do something that I haven't so much as *considered* in the past— really showing him what he's up against. What kind of fire he's playing with. I stretch out the fingers of my right hand, studying them as I debate whether or not I really want to do this.

Ultimately, the answer is yes.

Just as I did on the mountaintop when Milo attacked, I focus my energy and magic into the palm of my hand, envisioning the dagger I grew up with. White light buzzes across my fingers, sparks fizzing across my skin as the knife slowly starts to take shape.

After a few seconds, it flickers into existence, and the weight of the dagger weighs on my palm.

Every time I summon it, I feel a little stronger, and even though I expect it to fizzle out, I want to play this to my advantage. People always underestimated me before, and now I need them to overestimate my control of my power.

My enemies need to fear me.

Brett's lips part as he gapes at the dagger in my palm, and I lift the magical blade, examining it as it glints in the low light. Deep down, I'm exhilarated that it hasn't faded yet, but I don't let an ounce of that excitement show on my face.

I can't give anything away.

My chair legs scrape across the stone floor as I slowly stand, studying the blade as I take slow and purposeful steps around the table until I'm behind him. He stiffens with every step. Once I'm in his blind spot, he sets his palms flat on the table as if he's bracing himself for something.

I lean down, holding the magical dagger to his throat. I press it gently against his skin, and my blade actually holds for a few moments.

But I'm not going to kill him. The will isn't there, and so the magic doesn't hold.

The white light dissolves into crackling sparks before everything fades into the air, and instead of slitting his throat, I simply press my fingers against his neck.

He lets out a sudden sigh of relief and squeezes his eyes shut, his breath shaking slightly.

Damn, that worked even better than I imagined it would.

"What would you do if I let you leave?" I ask him, continuing my circle around the table, this time with my hands behind my back.

"Leave?" he asks, baffled.

I point to the door. "What would you do if I open that? Right now?"

He hesitates, frowning, clearly looking for the trick in this question—which is smart, because of course, there is one. I study his face, waiting for him to trip up. For him to get too excited and show his cards.

Brett thinks about it, licking his lips lightly as he eyes the door. But after a moment, his shoulders droop, and his eyes fall to the floor. "I would probably ask to stay."

I quirk one eyebrow skeptically. "Stay?"

"Maybe not here," he laughs, gesturing around the cell. "I'll work in exchange for room and board if you guys are willing to let me stay in perhaps a slightly nicer area."

I lean against the wall, propping one leg against the stone as I roll my eyes. "Do you think I'm an idiot?"

"You're no idiot, Rory." He shrugs like he doesn't care if I believe him. "I have nowhere else to go. I'm not a Knight anymore. What else can I do?"

I frown, crossing my arms as I study his face. Yet again, I find no tells of a lie. Not even a hint.

How weird.

It would seem that he has possibly changed his allegiance after all, but I'm wary against trusting a Knight I barely know.

Stiff as a board, I simply watch him for a few moments in silence. I'm churning through all of the ways he could play this, all of the possible scenarios where he gets out of this not only alive, but also gets his rank and authority within the Knights back. However, given what I know of the General, I just don't think that's possible.

After all, when we first captured Brett, he begged us to just kill him because the General would if he ever tried to go back.

"What are you thinking?" Brett asks quietly, his fingers woven together as he leans on the table and watches me intently.

Instead of answering, I shoot him a withering look. He doesn't get to know that. Ever.

"Okay," he says, lifting his hands in subtle surrender. "You don't have to tell me."

"Damn right, I don't."

I look toward the mirror, giving my men the signal. Time for phase two of this little plan. While I can't say that I trust Brett explicitly, I'm convinced he isn't lying to me. For the moment, at least.

Moments later, the door to the hallway swings open and both Tucker and Levi enter. Levi carries a small folder in one hand, and both men glare daggers at Brett Clarke.

Tucker slams the door behind him, his gaze never lifting from his father's former second-in-command. Brett stiffens the moment they lock eyes, his jaw clenching, and I wonder if I'm going to have to stop a fight.

It's no question, of course. Tucker would win, but I need Brett in one piece.

For now.

"It's funny, you know?" Tucker asks without a hint of humor in his voice. "I heard all the chatter when I left. You were too happy about it, Brett. I was finally out of your way. No more competition to take the General's place. You were the son he always wanted." Tucker's gaze drifts over Brett as if he's trying to size him up. "You were all too happy to take my place when I left, but you expect me to believe you won't go back? What changed?"

Brett sighs, rubbing his temples as he stares at the floor. "Everything."

Tucker scoffs like he doesn't believe it, and I don't blame him. "If it were up to me, Brett, you'd be dead. Don't you ever forget that."

"I'm glad it's not up to you then," Brett snaps, eyes narrowing.

"Don't push your luck," I chide.

At that, Brett shuts up, his jaw clenching as he examines his clasped hands on the table.

Levi slams the folder he's holding on the table's surface, all business. A few pages slip out and slide toward Brett. "The Knights are mobilizing for something big, and we need to know what it is."

"I've told you everything I know," Brett admits, barely glancing at the folder. "The terrorist attacks he has planned, the locations, all of it."

"And Ashgrave?" Tucker presses, settings his hands on the table as he glares daggers at Brett.

"Ashgrave," Brett says wistfully, like the castle's nothing more than a pipedream. "The General knows the vague location of where Ashgrave is thanks to some ancient journals that have been passed down from the beginning. That's all I can think of. The area that he has marked on the map is a wasteland, and he won't go there unless he has to." Brett shakes his head. "The General has been hunting for the exact location and was close to finding it when I left for the war against the dojo." He hesitates, hanging his head in shame as he briefly glances toward the mirror. "But I don't know if the General actually found the location or not. If he hasn't, he's close."

I frown, not liking the idea of the General knowing where Ashgrave is, even if it's just a general guess. If he wanted to spite me, he could simply bomb the shit out of the entire area and destroy my new home before I can even get it operational.

Levi pushes the still-closed folder toward Brett. The former Knight reluctantly opens it, flipping through the pages to appease us.

I cross my arms, watching him rifle through the papers. They're mostly benign blueprints and other data he's already given us, but I planted a few lies in there to test him.

Brett hesitates on one of the pages and pulls it out, frowning as he stares at a set of blueprints. He lays it down, tracing the outline of a facility in Canada, skimming the information on it that's written in the top right corner. "This isn't ours. We never had a base in Toronto."

"It's a new acquisition," I lie, knowing full well I'm not giving any signs or tells on my face.

The Spectres trained that out of me.

And here's his test. If he wants to mislead us, he could just go with it. After all, the more false intel we have, the better off he and his Knights will be.

However, if he's really telling us the truth about keeping our best interests at heart, he'll fight this. If he cares about whether or not we live or die—which he needs to if this plan of mine is going to work—he's not going to let us believe this facility exists.

"No," he says, shaking his head as he looks at me imploringly. "I think whoever gave you this is feeding you false intel." He taps his finger on it as he scans our faces. "Please, just look into this person a bit more, okay? The General already has a facility close by, so a second base of operation this close to the first..." He shakes his head, trailing off for a moment. "It just doesn't make sense."

I briefly look at Levi, but we don't reveal anything on our faces. It looks like Brett passed our little test.

Time for phase three then.

I rifle through the pages in the folder until I find the blueprints for Ravenwood. The page that has Brett's handwriting scrawled across it. I set it in front of him and tap the paper. "What would happen if I just walked into this fortress?"

Brett balks, his eyes widening slightly as if I'm crazy. "I'm not going to tell you because I won't let you do it."

"You *will* tell me," I say with a small grin, daring him to disagree. "Because you don't get to give me orders, Brett Clarke."

"I'm not helping you commit suicide," he insists, leaning back in his chair as he crosses his arms.

Good. Wow, he passed another test.

Of *course* walking in would be suicide. We've scoped it and we already know the three dozen ways I could be shot or captured. A manipulator trying to get me into the General's clutches, however, would have tried to convince me to do it anyway.

"Is that because you already know I told them everything?" Tucker asks, his hands on his hips as he glares at Brett. "Everyone would be treated as a high-level threat, even you. The General wouldn't trust anyone and would immediately separate or just kill us all."

Brett hesitates, watching Tucker with a strange blend of emotions—something between disdain and concern. "There have been changes to the code since you defected."

"Changes?" I prod.

Brett hesitates, his nose flaring slightly as he stares at the blueprints. "The order is to kill Tucker on sight. Same with all of your men." His gaze briefly flits toward me. "They would take me in for questioning before killing me, and you would…" He trails off, rubbing his messy stubble and apparently unable to finish.

"I would what?" I ask calmly.

He clears his throat, clearly uncomfortable. "The General would want to see you first," he says. "In person. And when he was done with you…" Brett trails off again, unable to meet my eye. "Everyone would get a turn."

I can't help it. I wrinkle my nose in disgust and shake my head.

The General is a sick bastard.

The energy in the room changes very suddenly. The air becomes tense and angry, and none of us wants to speak. Tucker grabs my waist possessively, his hands tightening.

I brush my fingers along his arm to soothe him briefly before I continue. "That won't happen."

"No, it won't," Brett agrees. "Because you're not going in."

For a moment, I'm utterly disarmed—because the

concern on his face mirrors that which I've seen on Russell and Harper's faces anytime they think I'm putting myself in harm's way. It's frustrated. A little angry.

But underneath it all, there's concern. Compassion. Protectiveness.

With Brett, that concern just doesn't make sense. Well, not yet anyway. It's starting to, the more I talk to him, but I'm not going to take any chances.

"I'm sure they've changed your access codes by now." I casually change the subject, shifting gears as I move into phase four. I straighten my back and roll out my shoulders, preparing to poke and prod until I get what I want. "There's no way you can get in."

"Exactly." He nods, still refusing to look me in the eye.

I set my hands on my waist, grinning slightly. "And I'm sure you wouldn't have any backdoor access codes that you managed to preserve, say in an emergency situation where you were locked out and needed to get back in?"

Seeing as he had high-level access, it makes sense that he would create something like that for himself. Not in case the General disowned him—which was certainly not even a *possibility* in his mind back then—

but more so in the event he got locked out by the enemy and needed to get back in to save everyone.

It's what I would have done.

Brett smirks. "Damn, you're smart." He shakes his head. "Too smart for your own good."

I cross my arms, waiting for him to continue.

"Yes," he admits reluctantly, rubbing his temples. "I have backdoor access codes I procured in case of emergencies that the General doesn't know about, but I can't guarantee they'll work. At the very least, it would notify Central Command within sixty seconds of the moment they're used. Even if you got in, there would be a rush of soldiers at the location almost immediately."

"Those are shit access codes then," Levi admits.

"It was the only way I could do it," Brett admits with a shrug. "However, the code is a skeleton key. They can't block it, and it will grant you access to anything." He hesitates, frowning. "Well, almost anything. Probably."

Tucker groans and rubs his eyes. "Almost anything? *Probably?*"

"That's why you pointed out these tunnels," I say calmly, unfazed as I point to the blueprints. To the hidden passageways between the core areas of the building that he circled earlier. "Your plan—should

you have ever needed it—was to slip in and immediately dart into the tunnels before anyone could find
you." I tilt my head, daring him to disagree. "I bet most
of the soldiers don't even know about those tunnels,
do they? Only a handful of the best." I pause, daring
him to lie to me as I study his face. "The elite."

He chews the inside of his cheek as he watches me,
his eyes narrowing slightly as he debates whether or
not to give me this information.

But he's going to.

"That was the plan," he eventually admits. "You
would need a diversion, though. Something to distract
those in central command. Something bigger than a
possible error in the observation software. Something
that would split attention and get most people over
here, on the other side of the fortress." He points to the
entrance.

I nod. "I already have something in mind for that."

He frowns, looking deeply concerned, but I have
what I need.

We'll slip in. We'll use a void to take out the
cameras, and then we will immediately dart into the
tunnels—or, at least, *most* of us will.

Some of us, however, will have another job to do.

First, there's one last little thing to do.

"Brett, do you know what this is?" I ask, fishing a

small box out of my pocket. I open it to reveal a little black square, roughly the same size as the head of a pin. Small silver lines trace the top of the thin device in the vague shape of a spider.

"No," he admits, looking warily between me and the little device.

Of course he wouldn't. I don't expect him to.

I lift the little device out of the box, examining it in the low light of his prison cell. "This is Spectre tech. I implant this in you, and it gives me the ability to remotely detonate enough of an explosive to hotwire your entire nervous system."

Brett makes a small choking sound, his mouth parting as he stares at the tiny thing. In my periphery, Tucker smirks, his brows furrowing as he stares at the former Knight across the table from us.

I'm full of shit, of course.

This little device is nothing but a prototype—advanced tech Zurie was desperately trying to force into being. It was a failure, but the design itself was easy enough to quickly produce.

As much as I would like to shove a bomb into Brett's spinal cord, the best I can do right now is bluff.

"You won't feel it," I say calmly, almost like I'm bored. "Our surgeons will implant this against your cervical spine, and if you betray us at any point, I pull the trigger." I look at him over the small device between my thumb and pointer finger, highlighting the full weight of the threat. "Got it?"

He swallows hard, his breath shallow as he stares at the small device. Eventually, however, he nods. "I have a long road to earn anyone's trust, so, yes. I understand."

Tucker scoffs, like the very idea of Brett earning anyone's trust is downright laughable.

I brush my knuckles against the wooden table, knocking three times as I end the conversation. "The guards will lead you to your new room," I tell him. "Get a shower. Shave. You have thirty minutes to look presentable. If you impress me, Brett, you won't have to stay in this cell anymore."

"What do I need to look presentable for, Rory?" Brett asks with a hint of terror in his voice. "What do you have planned?"

"We're taking you on a little vacation, Brett." I smirk. "And when we're done, there won't be anything left of the Knights to follow us."

CHAPTER TWENTY-SIX

I n the past, I would have simply slipped into Ravenwood, ideally unnoticed and through a side door. I would've spent months preparing, of course, since a fortress like this is no joke. Between my Spectre tech and experience, I would've stolen access codes and used voids to steal my way through the fortress and get what I wanted.

And I would have probably died trying.

This place is too big. Too heavily guarded. Besides, I'm missing half the tech I usually need to make that happen.

So, as a virtual celebrity and hated person number one on the General's shit list, I'm going to walk in the front door.

After all, Brett said it himself. The General wants

dibs. He wants to break me, and he wants to do it himself. He won't let anyone do anything to me until he's done. As disgusting as that is, I can use it to my advantage because it buys me time.

There are two ways this could go—either the General is home, and I have significantly less time to work with; or, he's off trying to find Ashgrave and screw me over.

Though I hate leaving anything to chance, I'm hoping for door number two.

Brett drives me along a winding road past a sheer cliff. To our left, the canopy of a thick forest sways below us as the road cuts along the mountainside, giving us a pristine view of a stunning valley. Fog weaves through the trees below us, crawling up the mountains on its way back to the sky.

We're in the middle of nowhere, just how the General likes it. Any second now, we'll pull up to Ravenwood—or, at least, the gate that should lead us there.

Provided we're not blown to hell at first sight, of course.

Brett's knuckles bleach from his tight grip on the wheel, his shoulders tense and nervous as he acts as both my captor and chauffer. With a dark blue base-ball cap planted on his head, his gaze keeps drifting toward the rearview mirror as he looks back at me time and time again—instead of watching the damn road like he should be.

I frown, my fingers flexing in the fake cuffs around my wrists. They're identical to the ones Harper used on me in Russell's test. Though they don't work at all, they'll convince anyone who doesn't look too closely that I am, in fact, bound and unable to use magic at all.

Absently, he scratches the small scar on the back of his neck where we pretended to implant the fake bomb. It's already healing, the thin cut barely even visible anymore, and I suspect it's more so the idea that he has a bomb in him that's making him itch at it.

"Stop scratching at it," I chide him.

"Sorry," he says, planting his hand on the wheel again. His jaw twitches as he stares ahead, his gaze slowly wandering again toward the rearview mirror.

Gods alive, this man is a shit actor.

I hastily bump my cuffs against the back of a seat. "Chill out," I chide, gritting my teeth as I scan the forest around us. "You're going to give us away if you look nervous."

"I'm not sure about this, Rory," he admits, shaking his head. "It's not too late for you to reconsider. We can turn around right now, and we'll just look like lost tourists." His gaze drifts once again to the rearview mirror, his brows knit with concern.

Either he's doing an incredible job of reverse psychology, or he actually cares and thinks my plan is going to fail.

Either way, he's about to realize just who I am and just what I can do.

"We're not stopping," I say, glaring out the window. "Too much is riding on this to back out now, including your life," I remind him, my eyes darting toward the rearview mirror as our gazes connect.

"I know," he says, nodding, returning his attention to the road. "But I'm not even sure my access codes work, Rory. There are too many unknowns in all of this."

I don't answer because truth be told, there really aren't. I've planned everything.

Irena managed to confirm that Brett's access codes work, though I would never tell him that—and she wouldn't tell me how she knew.

Harper and Russell are on backup with a full Fairfax army waiting and practically salivating at the chance to destroy the Knights. Every Fairfax dragon alive wants revenge for the war on the dojo. Hell, even dojo dragons who are on break or vacation came back just for this attack, in the off chance they would be needed.

I grin. I love the Fairfax dragons. They're absolutely amazing, and they have my same penchant for revenge.

I settle into the seat, going over my plan in my head once again just to make sure I didn't miss anything. But I didn't.

Irena told me not to make a move until she could bring some Spectres as backup, but we don't have the luxury of time. She wanted me to wait a solid week while she mobilizes everyone, since her rebel organization is still relatively small.

There's just no possible way we could wait. In a week, the Knights could be ready to blow up every major capital, for all we know.

We need to act as if every second counts here, because it does.

The road angles downward and curves through the forest, winding away from the cliff. Before long, we rumble up to a gate. Barbed wire covers the chain-link metal entrance that blocks the road. Massive concrete walls extend from the forest and meet in a single steel-plated door that's bound shut.

I expect to encounter soldiers manning the entrance, but the only hint that anyone is at home is a small screen to the left of the road with a camera on top of it. The camera rotates with the car as we near, tracking our every move.

This is the moment of truth.

After this, every movement will be tracked. By now, my men should be using the backdoor access codes to go undetected into the secret passageways through the fortress—according to Irena, their entrance will appear as nothing more than a blip on the radar, a possible error in the detection software that security will slowly dispatch someone to investigate. By the time anyone arrives, they'll be safely in the tunnels, moving undetected through hallways no one monitors.

Protected by the dark tint on the windows, I slip my gag on, ready to play the part of captured damsel.

As Brett rolls to a stop by the camera and screen, the unmistakable click of guns cocking rolls through his opening window. I scan the walls, and it takes me a moment to see the two massive automatic rifles mounted on either side of the road. They're hidden back behind the trees, but now that we're within their line of fire, their barrels are trained on us.

I quickly examine them, trying to figure out what we're looking at here. Unfortunately, they're mounted to full-circle rotational platforms—which is bad for us.

These guns can fire in any direction and probably for quite a considerable range.

There's no turning back now.

I impulsively stiffen, but Brett looks unsurprised as he leans his elbow on his door and tilts his head toward the camera as it trains on him.

I keep expecting the video screen to flare to life, for us to see a Knight or for someone to menacingly stare us down, but it remains dark.

"Name, rank, detail," a mechanized voice blares through the speakers.

"Brett Clarke," my captive answers. "Lieutenant General, here to see General Chase."

For a moment, the line goes quiet, and I wonder what that means.

"I have a present he'll want to see for himself," Brett adds.

The video screen finally snaps to life. Instead of some nameless soldier, however, the General himself appears. His glare trains on Brett, his nose wrinkled in disgust and irritation.

Brett flinches subtly, almost imperceptibly, and it's clear that he wasn't expecting the General to answer either—at least not right away.

Tucker's father squares his broad shoulders, his salt-and-pepper hair distinguished against his tanned skin. No wheezing. No limping. Strong pecs and biceps press against his shirt as he stands, legs spread and his hands behind his back.

Crap. He healed faster than we thought he would. And if he's actually here in the fortress, then I don't get the bought time I was planning on.

It takes everything in me not to groan with dread.

"Hello, sir," Brett says calmly.

"Tell me why I shouldn't blow you to hell now, boy," the General snaps, skipping any pretense. "What present could possibly be worth your life after spending so long in captivity?" The General grimaces disdainfully. "I assume you've gone native, too? Just like my son?"

"No, sir," Brett says with a cocky twinge to his voice. "In fact, quite the opposite."

He rolls down my window to reveal me. The camera above the screen pans toward me as I glare angrily over the gag, playing my part.

The General quirks one eyebrow. It's the only hint of reaction to any of this besides brazen anger. "And what do you want in exchange?"

"Back in," Brett says simply. "This place was my life, sir, and I just want my life back."

As Brett speaks, I watch him in the side mirror, looking for the tells of a lie on his face. Even though his eyes are trained the entire time on the General, I notice his mouth twitch slightly. It's subtle, almost imperceptible, but it was there.

The smirk. His tell that he's manipulating his opponent and playing a familiar game.

He's lying to the General.

Hmm.

Brett's definitely not a Knight anymore, and that's still kind of hard for me to fathom. However, I still don't know what he really wants, and that's just as dangerous.

"And how did you capture her?" the General asks skeptically, like he doesn't quite believe it.

It's clear he can smell the ambush. He just can't see it yet.

Ideally, he won't be able to see my little trap until it springs and it's too late for him to run.

"I tricked her into trusting me," Brett says, his tone even. "I got her alone, and I took her out. She only woke up about 15 minutes ago. I used her codes to escape, and they're probably all still scrambling, trying to find us. I don't have long before they manage to though, sir," he adds, hinting that we should be let in. "I stole a car to mask our movement, but she's hard to hide for long."

I almost smirk, but I manage to rein it in. Nice touch.

The General hesitates, glaring down Brett as if he's waiting for the man to crack. To Brett's credit, he doesn't.

After a tense silence, the General grins. "You always were a master manipulator, Clarke. It's one of your greatest skills and assets. We'll let you in, but I need to talk to you before you do anything else. Welcome home, boy," the General adds, his eyes narrowing slightly. "I knew you had it in you."

The video cuts out, and I wonder what he could possibly mean by that.

"Your meeting with General Chase is in twelve hours," the robotic voice says as the gate buzzes and opens.

I almost let out a sigh of relief but manage to keep it at bay. This is important—*drop-everything* levels of important. For the meeting to be in twelve hours, it can only mean the General isn't even here. He has to book it out to the fortress.

Even though it's not good that the General is recovered enough to travel, at least he's not here. That's still in our favor. Technically, that gives me twelve hours to do what I need to do, but we need to be long gone before the General gets here.

Brett drives through the gate as it's still opening, his side mirror missing the edge by barely an inch. He takes the road quickly, the tires squealing now and then as he rounds the winding curves that cut through the forest.

I lean against the car door to keep my balance, wondering if something has changed in him. Wondering why he's suddenly in such a hurry.

He's probably just as eager to get this over with as I am.

Maybe.

The road levels out, and as the trees whiz by, the forest thins to reveal a massive tunnel carved into the cliffside. The road angles toward it, leading us down into the fortress.

This is it.

As we drive into the darkness of the main tunnel, the shadows lit only by the occasional yellow light bulb along the wall, I shake my head. "You Knights and your underground fortresses."

Brett shrugs. "They're less likely to be discovered and observed. Easier to hide. It works in our favor."

I don't answer. After all, he has a point.

The road winds downward, the steep angle taking us deeper and deeper into the ground before it finally levels out into a massive parking garage with ceilings easily three stories tall. Jets line the far wall, and eight missile launchers clutter the edge of the massive lot.

Oh, man. It would be so much fun to blow this place up.

Dozens of Knights armed with rifles wait for us in the center of the lot, spread out across the asphalt as their heads track our movement.

Brett doesn't waste a second, pulling the car toward them and rolling to a stop barely ten feet from them. The moment he parks, he sets his hands on his head. He doesn't even bother opening the door—and no need.

The dozens of soldiers around us instantly swarm, throwing open every door. They scope the car with their guns, their barrels pointing in every direction as several of them grab me and Brett, hauling us out of the sedan.

To really sell it, I struggle with them, trying to shake off their grip even as their fingers tighten around my biceps and waist. One shoves me hard in the middle of my back, and I stumble forward. With my hands clasped in the cuffs in front of me, I almost fall.

Dick.

Without so much as a word uttered between them,

the soldiers usher me and Brett down a hallway—
according to the blueprints, this is the primary hall.

Just as Brett told us they would.

This path will branch up ahead, and after that,
there's no telling which route they'll take us down.
They'll probably split us up the moment the hallway
forks, but they *have* to take this route to get to the
wing of the fortress with the interrogation cells.

So, that's what we banked on.

My plan hinges on this next moment. Most of the
guards remain in the massive holding bay as backup,
the barrels of their guns trained on us as we're led
away by eight soldiers. We weren't sure entirely how
many soldiers would follow us in, but we planned for
this.

The soldiers lead us down the hallway, and this
stretch has no cameras since it's the main thorough-
fare. According to our intel, the command center
watches the ends and branches of the hallway instead
of the center. In a fortress this big, you have to be
strategic with your cameras—yet another benefit that
works in our favor.

As we're shoved down the blank stretch of hallway,
we enter the cold stretch of metal walls. There's
nothing along this corridor but the smooth sheets of
metal interrupted by the occasional ribbon of divots

holding everything in place. Our boots tap against the black tile floor, and the only other sound is the rustle of the soldiers' guns.

The one thing the Knights didn't plan for is the fact that the secret tunnels go parallel to this hallway. There's one access point almost too close to the monitored hallways to even use, but we're just going to have to make it work.

We can't let them see us.

Brett's supposed to signal the moment we reach the access point, but this is just another test. I already know where it is.

The hallway snakes to the left, and I recognize this stretch from the blueprints. Sure enough, Brett scratches his nose, stumbling a bit as the guards push him forward, urging him faster.

The signal.

It's weird to think he might really be on our side. I still can't quite fathom it.

So I don't. After all, I need to focus on the men we're about to kill.

The key here is to not let them fire off a single bullet because the thundering boom of the gunshot will attract the wrong kind of attention. We need to take them out, and we need to do it quickly.

That means I can't use my magic. It's still too wild. Too new.

I have to beat their asses the old-fashioned way.

A hidden door in the wall opens, the hinges and edges hidden perfectly along the divots and lines of the uneven metal wall. The guards cock their guns, distracted, and Brett and I take our chance. I elbow the nearest soldier in the gut, and he doubles over. I use his momentum against him as I rail him in the face with the cuffs around my hands.

He goes down like a sack of bricks, his rifle clattering on the floor.

All at once, silent chaos breaks through the hallway.

The two Knights nearest to me train their guns on my back as my allies flood out of the access panel. Drew darts out first, already wearing a Knight's uniform, and breaks the neck of the nearest soldier. It's effortless, like snapping his fingers, and he's already on to the next.

Four seconds in, and two Knights are already down.

Beside me, Brett grabs the nearest Knight's rifle and twists his arm expertly, ripping the gun from the man's hands before his finger can tighten around the trigger. He punches the Knight in the face, and the man falls onto his knees. He groans in agony before Brett whips the rifle around, hitting the man in the temple with the butt of the gun.

Huh. Not bad.

As I sweep out the legs on the nearest Knight, taking him to the ground, Levi bolts out of the access panel. Jace and Tucker are hot on his heels, each man grabbing one of the few remaining soldiers. Beyond the occasional grunt or groan of pain, the Knights don't even have the chance to make a sound. Bodies fall to the floor as our enemies are taken out in quick succession. Between all of us, the guards are on the ground before a single gunshot can be fired.

I roll out my shoulders. "Time for phase two."

Brett nods and wordlessly grabs the hat off the nearest Knight laying on the ground. He tugs off the man's jacket and pants while I check on my men.

"Did you guys get any intel on where they're supposed to take us?" I ask, my eyes darting briefly to the cameras down the hall, grateful they're still pointed down their respective side passages and not at us.

"You'll be heading to the left," Drew says with a nod toward one of the hallways. "In that direction. Brett's supposed to be taken to the right. Each to holding cells."

"Good," I say. "We can work with that."

Tucker ruffles his hair, making it look messy and unkempt, much the way Brett's hair looks right now. He's dressed in identical clothing, and he grimaces as he gives his former nemesis a once-over. "I can't believe I have to dress up as him."

"Technically, you don't have to," I say with a shrug. "But it's really helpful."

Tucker's eyes dart toward me, and he grins. "Well, we both know I'm incredibly helpful."

"And modest," I say with a brief nod.

"Let's hide these guys," Jace says, clapping his hands together before he grabs the nearest downed soldier and drags him toward the secret passageway. Silhouettes move within the tunnel, and hands reach out to take the soldiers as Jace, Drew, Levi, and Tucker drag them over.

Dojo soldiers.

"Cooper, Rogers, and Sanderson, you're up," Jace says into the tunnel, nodding into the hallway as he gestures for the soldiers to come forward.

Three dojo soldiers dressed in Knights uniforms jump out, moving quickly and efficiently as they take the place of the soldiers we just knocked unconscious.

Everyone already knows their jobs. Drew, Tucker, and those three are going to head off to the right, toward the command center. Their goal is to find the intel on the Knights.

The rest of us have to figure out where the hell those orbs are.

Since Tucker has knowledge of the fortress's layout, as well as an understanding of how to get deeper into the command center, it only makes sense that he goes with them—even though he didn't want to leave me alone with Brett.

Technically, I won't be alone with him at all, but none of my overprotective men wanted me to be near him in the first place.

I can't really blame them. After all, Brett *has* tried to kill all of us multiple times.

Once Drew and his team drop off "Brett" in the interrogation room—or, at least, Tucker *dressed* as Brett—Tucker will change quickly into a Knights uniform and funnel out with Drew and the rest to get the data. Hopefully, whoever is watching the monitors at that point doesn't pay too close attention to the body count of who leaves. Ideally, they'll just be looking for a cluster of Knights, their faces and identities protected under their hats as they walk away.

Tucker plants a blue baseball cap on his head—the same one Brett's wearing—and brushes a kiss along my nose before he trots off down the hallway.

Drew grabs my waist and plants a rough kiss on my mouth, shooting a glare at Brett before signaling to his team that they need to leave.

With them slightly ahead of us, Jace, Levi, and Brett stay with me, but we need one more soldier to complete my entourage.

I frown, surveying the few of us left in the hallway as Drew and his team disappear around the bend. "Jace, who else—"

Before I can finish the thought, Russell steps out of the secret access panel with a bag draped over one shoulder. "Ready to go?"

"What are you doing here?" I ask, my eyes scanning the Knights uniform he's wearing. "You should be on backup."

He laughs, adjusting his hat. "You guys don't get to have all the fun."

Jace briefly checks the fake cuffs on my wrists, and when he's satisfied that they're still on convincingly enough—and namely, won't fall off, since I used them as a weapon—he winks at me. Sure, they have a little dent in them, and they're going to break a little more easily the next time I use my magic, but they'll be fine for now.

After all, I really shouldn't use my magic—not in the tight, underground confines of the Knights' fortress.

But if any of these people come for the men I love —well, I can't be held accountable for what I do to them.

For what I'll do to them *all*.

CHAPTER TWENTY-SEVEN

We hurry off down the hallway, only about forty-five seconds later than they're expecting us, and we take the route to the left. I briefly look over my shoulder as Drew's team rounds a bend, and Tucker shoots a fleeting smile at me just before he disappears around the corner.

Levi sets his hand possessively on my shoulder, guiding me through the hallway even though I already know where we're going. I'm sure this is just as much for him as it is to comfort me, but on the cameras, it should look for all the world like he's just another Knight soldier getting a little pushy.

They maneuver me toward my holding cell, and thankfully, Jace has the coordinates for the right room so that we don't set off any alarm bells—at least, not yet. After all, it would look highly suspicious if they led me into the wrong room.

The door unlocks automatically as we reach it, which proves that they are in fact watching us. Even though I was expecting this, I roll out my shoulders a little bit to ease my nerves. It also doubles as a distraction, since the more I move, the more people watching the security feed will pay attention to me rather than scrutinizing the identities of the soldiers around me.

As the door opens, the first thing I notice is *red*.

The wall, the carpet—everything is a deep red color and embossed with golden inlay. A soft mural of clouds covers the ceiling, and as my eyes sweep the room, I notice a four-post canopy bed draped with a rich red satin canopy. Elegant heavy drapes cover fake windows on the far wall, and I can't help but figure out that this room feels entirely out of place with the cold grey hallways.

But I'm not here to enjoy the décor.

As Levi shuts the door behind us, I frown as I make quick work of my disguise. I break the cuffs, kind of wishing I'd gotten a chance to shatter them with magic instead. It's just so much more fun. They crumble to the ground, nothing but shards and fragments now.

As Jace and Levi quickly sweep the room to ensure we're alone, Russell digs into his bag and yanks out another Knights uniform. I tug it on over my clothes to give me a bulkier appearance—at least one convincing enough for the cameras—and then tug on the hat, doing my best to shove my hair up into it to hide my flowing curls.

It's not perfect, but it should mask me on camera, and that's all that matters—especially if I stay in the center of the others as we walk through the hallways.

Russell offers me a small comm link, and as I shove it in my ear, I take a deep and steadying breath to prepare for what's coming.

Everything about this plan is risky. No matter how much we prepared, no matter how much intel we stole, everything could unravel in an instant. All it takes is somebody walking down the hallway to recognize us despite our disguises, or someone on the camera's feed being a little more inquisitive and aware than they should be.

We're in the heart of a den of dragon killers, and every single one of them has been ordered to fire on sight.

No pressure.

"All right, guys," Brett says tensely, his hand hovering over the door handle. "We won't have long to make this work. You ready?"

His eyes drift toward me, and I simply nod.

He leads us into the hallway, and Jace and I share a brief glance as we both notice he's heading in the right direction. We already know the entire route. This isn't something we were willing to leave up to chance at all.

Yet again, we're testing him—and, to our utter shock, he continues to pass.

We weave through the corridors for far longer than I would like, but with this much at stake, every second feels like an hour. If we run, we'll look suspicious, and we have to do our best to go ignored.

After seven flights of stairs and two steel doors, we finally reach the vault. To my surprise, it's nothing more than a thick steel door set into the wall, perfectly seamless with the rest of the metal. Brett tenses at the access panel, staring at it briefly before turning to us. Levi scans the hallways, our momentary lookout as we regroup and prepare for whatever might come.

"After this, we won't have long," Brett warns, his fingers hovering over the keypad. "This code will give us a small advantage, but eventually, the backup systems will kick in and alert the command center. We have maybe sixty seconds to get in and out before we set off the alarms."

I nod. "Do it."

Brett takes a shaky breath, watching me as if he's

hoping I'll change my mind. He's smart enough to know I won't, especially not when we're this close.

His fingers quickly hit the code into the keypad. The word override flashes a few times on the screen, and the door screeches as it slowly opens.

Beyond the door, we discover a massive room easily two stories tall. My training kicks in, doing a rough sweep as I look for what I need.

The floor is covered with carefully laid out stacks of gold bars, silver bricks, and neatly bound piles of cash in every currency I've ever seen—and then some. Three rows of shelves line the walls, each covered in identically sized glass displays filled with a wide array of valuables. Ladders mounted to a set of rollers lean against every wall.

I tense, wondering if the orbs might be up there, and do a quick scan of the treasures. Framed letters with stained paper and cracked ends, implying they're ancient. Jewels. Crowns. Ming vases. Large diamonds.

No orbs.

The Spectre in me is tempted to grab a few treasures—hell, some of those letters may contain valuable intel, especially if they're framed and hoarded in an anti-dragon organization's primary vault.

But that's not why we're here.

A second door sits nestled in the middle of the far

wall, flanked on both sides by shelves littered with priceless artifacts.

The second vault.

The one I want.

As I jog toward the second door, eager to get this over with, the comm goes fuzzy. I hear Drew's voice, but I can't make out anything he's saying. I narrow my eyes, glaring at Brett, wondering if he knew this would happen, but he doesn't even look my way. He doesn't have a comm so he can't possibly know what we're hearing.

"You never told me the connection's bad in here," I say, my voice ominous.

"Is it?" he asks absently, his focus on the keypad as he taps in another code. "I've never had to wear a comm while I was in here, so I didn't know."

I'm tense, and I hate relying on a former enemy. Even more than that, I hate surprises in the heat of the moment.

Without a connection to Drew and Tucker, we don't know if they've been caught. We don't know if they're okay. If they're stuck. If they need help.

I don't even want to be in here the full sixty seconds. We need to get the hell out of here, and *soon*.

The door to the second vault screeches as its hinges come to life, hissing a little as the seal is broken.

The second it opens, I feel my heart *sing*.

It's like home and heaven, all in one. The sensation floods me, like everything is right in the world. My dragon stirs, delighted, connected to something that is undoubtedly *us.*

There's something in there. Something connected with my magic. Despite the ticking clock and the gravity of what we're trying to do, I start to let myself believe that maybe this really will work.

Just maybe.

"Hurry," Brett says, gesturing for me to enter ahead of him.

Ha.

Hell no.

I shake my head and nod for him to go first. I'm not taking any chances, especially not this close to the finish line.

You never know when there might be a trap.

He runs in impatiently, and I follow. The small room is sparse, without much in it at all except for three pedestals laid out in the center of the twenty-by-twenty room. Glowing orbs that spark and fizzle with brilliant white light sit on two of the pedestals.

In my heart, something clicks into place.

Brett was telling the truth.

The third pedestal, however, has an oddly familiar

crystal on it roughly the size of my forearm. My jaw tenses as I recognize the beautiful weapon that Zurie used to nearly drain me of my power. It looks identical to the one I shattered, and my chest clenches at the mere sight of it.

There really are more.

Shit.

My impulse is to destroy it, and as much as I want to break the thing in half, I refrain. We need to study it. To understand it. That's the best way to protect yourself against something—to know it inside and out.

Even as I stare at the crystal, the men around me are a flurry of activity. Within seconds, Jace and Levi both grab the orbs—and Russell, to his credit, grabs the crystal. In mere moments, all three artifacts are in the bag on Russell's back.

"We have ten seconds," Jace says tensely, nodding back to the main vault.

We run, not wanting to risk getting caught in here. Before we can so much as reach the door, the alarm screams through the air like a banshee.

Damn it.

The doors to the main and secondary vaults roll on their hinges as our only way out slowly disappears.

The movement is a slow and steady hum, like a draw-bridge falling.

The gap is closing, and we might not make it.

Russell dives through first, with Brett hot on his heels. Jace maneuvers behind me to make sure I go ahead of him, and I dive through. I roll, my shoulder hitting the far wall hard as the small gap gets smaller behind me.

Through the closing gap, Jace and I catch each other's eye. My heart skips beats. If he and Levi get trapped in there, it ruins our whole escape plan.

Everything.

They have to get out.

Jace dives through the closing gap, his shoulder scraping against the door as he pushes through. He rolls, grunting in pain as he lands, and Levi dives through after him. My ice dragon lands hard on the ground as the vault seals behind us, his foot mere inches from being sliced clean off in the closing door.

After all, I doubt they have security measures in place on a vault protecting that many valuable artifacts.

I let out a sigh of relief—only to see movement in my periphery.

A dozen soldiers skid to a stop at the far end of the

hallway, the barrels of their rifles raised and pointed at us as their gloved hands tighten around their triggers.

Shit.

Somehow, in the flurry of activity that was our exit, I ended up between everyone else and the oncoming soldiers.

I'm the frontline, the only thing between the people I care about—and, well, Brett—and an oncoming onslaught of dragon-killer semi-automatic weapons.

Time slows as I scramble for a plan. Impulsively, I lift my hands, my flattened palms the only thing between me and the approaching soldiers who have been instructed to fire on sight.

In the flurry of anxiety burning in my chest, my magic surges. Sparks burn across my skin, the only hint at what's about to come. Pain splinters through me as my dragon tenses with dread.

"Rory, no!" Jace shouts from behind me.

It's too late.

I couldn't stop this if I wanted to.

My magic rips through the air, arcing off the metal walls as it surges wildly. The uncontrolled blast of white light blinds me as the deafening thunder of gunfire booms through the hall.

The lights around us flicker. The ground shakes. The entire fortress trembles beneath my power.

Men scream, and then there's only an eerie silence —and the blinding white light.

As the surge fades, color and definition return to the world around us. I look up to find ash floating across the hallway, settling in piles along the floor. A few rifles lay on the ground, somehow escaping the line of fire, but otherwise we are alone in the hallway.

The only thing that remains of the men who tried to kill us are the bullet holes in the wall just above my head.

"Shit, I'm glad I'm on your side," Brett says, chuckling.

"For the moment," Jace says, his voice tense with warning as he glares at the former Knight.

The fizzling pop of the disrupted communication link suddenly returns in my ear. "Shots fired!" Drew shouts. "Get the hell out of here. Shots fired!"

A second alarm goes off, blaring through the building. It would seem we've been discovered, and Drew's right.

We need to get the hell out of here.

CHAPTER TWENTY-EIGHT

We bolt through the hallways, all of us trying to get to the rendezvous point before all hell breaks loose.

Which should be about any second now.

I grip two handguns tightly—a little present Russell brought for me. Jace and Levi carry two of the rifles from the small army I just obliterated, while Jace has a third rifle draped over his shoulder. It was all we could salvage. Russell carries a handgun as well, and Brett—well, we all decided it was better if he remained unarmed.

He didn't like that.

We didn't care.

The cold metal walls whizz past me, each panel identical to the last. Thanks to my Spectre training, however, I know exactly where we are. We're about a hundred feet from the nearest access panel to the secret passageways that wind through select portions of this fortress, and we absolutely have to get there before we encounter any more soldiers.

Out here in the hallways, we're exposed. We have limited ammunition and only a handful of weapons, so we are clearly at the disadvantage here. It would be effortless for the Knights to outnumber us, and it's really just a matter of time.

If we give them the chance, they'll overwhelm us, and every last one of us will die.

I cannot let that happen.

We round the corner only to find two dozen soldiers amassed and waiting. The front row kneels as I skid into the hall—right into their line of fire—and they block the entire hallway.

Their barrels raise, aimed right at us.

I slide against the tile, my boots squeaking as I drop to the floor. The soldiers open fire, and several bullets whiz over my head as I duck with seconds to spare. The guys throw their backs against the walls in the hallway we just came through, taking cover as I scramble to join them.

Levi and Jace grab my shoulders, dragging me out of the line of fire as the torrent of bullets sails past me.

Once we're behind cover, we pause for a moment. Adrenaline floods my veins, heightening every sensation as I rest my forehead against Jace's. Levi holds me tightly, the three of us taking only a moment of respite after that *very* close call.

These two saved my life.

I'm so grateful for them.

But this is war, and we don't have any time to waste.

I lift my handguns, one on either side of my face as I return my attention to the hallway. The bullets die down, a brief lull—probably to lure us into the open.

Ribbons of white light burn across my skin, and I want nothing more than to unleash hell on all of these guys. I press my back against the wall, debating whether or not this is a good idea as sparks dance across my body.

In my periphery, Jace weaves his hand around my waist. His touch instantly soothes the fire in my soul, despite the situation we're in.

We lock eyes, and he simply shakes his head. "Every use is dangerous, Rory."

He's right, of course. Back when the soldiers attacked us near the vault, we got lucky. The surge burned away the enemy, but it could have just as easily burned away two of the men I love most in this world.

I grit my teeth, rolling out my shoulders to dispel the magic. The white light dissolves into the air, but I know it won't last long. With the surges of power I've been feeling lately, I'm going to blow sooner or later.

I just want to make sure the people I care about aren't in the line of fire when I do.

With hallways this small, especially hallways coated in metal, there's a high chance that any power surge I have is going to cook everyone around me. Back when we left the vault, my intuition took over, and we got lucky.

To make matters worse, we can't shift down here. If we try, we could bring tens of thousands of pounds of debris, metal, and rock down with us, burying us alive.

I don't want to risk their lives again, so I'll just have to do this the old-fashioned way.

Fine.

Time for some good, old-fashioned Spectre fun.

With my handguns raised and ready, I drop to the ground as I wait for a momentary lull in the fire. Out of the corner of my eye, Russell and Brett both eye me warily.

It's fine. They'll see what I'm up to in a minute.

All I need is one opening.

Across from me, our hallway continues on the

other side of this corridor. The bullet-strewn corner is dented, but it'll give me enough cover if I can get across the line of fire.

I can make this work.

In the hallway, men bark orders, something about moving forward—probably to flush us out.

Nope.

Not today.

Briefly, I set one handgun on the ground and grab the hat off my head. With a quick flourish, I toss it into the hallway and grab my other handgun before it even hits the floor.

Down the hallway, men shout. Gunfire erupts once again, tearing the hat to bits and shooting ribbons of fabric into the air as it's decimated.

Good. I want to catch them off guard.

The hail of bullets subsides for the briefest of moments, and I take my chance. They won't be ready to fire so soon, and I'll have a split second or two in my favor.

Laying on my shoulder with both guns raised in front of me, I kick off the nearest wall and slide across the slick ground toward the other side of our hall. As I come out from cover, I open fire on the line of soldiers, firing seven shots.

With my careful aim, every bullet hits.

OLIVIA ASH

Seven soldiers go down. Twelve left. The clamor of their bodies and guns hitting the ground is almost ear-splitting as it echoes through the metal corridor.

"Fire!" One of the soldiers says, his red cap standing out from the other black ones. I assume he's a Captain or some other high-ranking official. "Fire, damn you all, fire!"

The survivors obey almost immediately. Barrels train on me as I slide across the floor, never once pausing. They don't have much to aim at, however. As their bullets sail through the air, I'm already sliding toward the other end of the hall, taking cover behind the far corner across from Jace, Levi, Russell, and Brett.

Safely behind cover, I slam my back against the wall and take the chance to reload.

As the thundering hail of gunfire rocks the small space, I look over my shoulder to find all four men watching me, each wearing a different expression.

Jace smirks with pride.

Levi has one eyebrow cocked, as if he can't believe I would be so foolhardy.

Russell is chuckling under his breath.

And Brett... well, his lips are parted in shock and awe.

"Get back to work," I mouth to them, knowing I

won't be heard over the gunfire. To emphasize my point, I nod toward the soldiers still firing on us.

That seems to snap them out of it.

Levi, Jace, and Russell move into gear. Russell kneels, inching the barrel of his gun around the corner. Levi follows suit, slouching slightly as he takes the middle ground. Jace, several inches taller than any of us, takes the high ground. Without any weapons, Brett scowls and crosses his arms, looking anxiously over his shoulder in case anyone comes up from behind.

The gunfire pauses, and the clatter of ammunition shells hitting the ground echoes through the corridor.

Time for us to go.

Simultaneously, all three dragon shifters dart around the corner and fire into the line of soldiers. As I finish reloading, I can hear the thud of bodies falling to the ground, and by my calculation, there should only be about seven men left.

"Can I please have a gun?" Brett yells. "I feel useless!"

"No," Jace and I snap in unison.

"Fall back!" one of the Knights snaps, ordering his surviving soldiers to take cover. I cock my guns and lift them, one on either side of my face as I dart into the hallway. Through a gap between Jace and Levi, I catch the soldiers running toward a side hallway about ten feet behind them.

That's good. It's not a full retreat, but it's progress. I scan the hallway, making sure I know where we are.

Gunfire has a way of disorienting you.

There—the access panel, about twenty feet away. It's almost imperceptible, hidden in the metal wall halfway between us and them.

I don't get the chance to celebrate, though. Several barrels peak around the corner where the Knights took cover, and our survivors open fire yet again.

The idiots aren't even aiming. They're just trying to hit *something*.

Jace, Russell, Levi, and I fall back and take cover. Rolling my eyes in irritation, I press my back once more against the corner as bullet holes rock the wall opposite me.

Damn. We're so close, and yet so far.

A flurry of gunshots chips away at the bottom of the corner opposite me, which means they're aiming at where they think I am on the ground.

They must think I'm the bigger threat. Take me out, and the others will go down easier.

Ha. Poor fools. No one here is the weak link. Well, except maybe for Brett.

I stand, jumping a little to loosen up my muscles as

I eye the wall opposite me. There aren't many options here, but I need to take out at least half of the remaining soldiers before reinforcements arrive. As I jog in place, warming up my muscles, I debate whether or not I want to run a little maneuver I used to use every now and then in the Spectres.

As the gunfire booms through the hallway, I think that yeah, this might be a great idea.

My guns still firmly rooted in the palms of my hands, I take a few steps back to get a running start and bolt toward the opposite wall. The momentum carries me upward, launching me almost entirely to the ceiling. I keep close to the top of the hallway, where they'll least expect me to be, as I sail across the open corridor.

I'll only have a few split seconds to fire, but that's all I need.

As I sail through the air close to the ceiling, I take aim once again. I fire five shots, and four bodies hit the ground. The fifth bullet hits the far wall, and I curse under my breath.

Wasted bullet.

Damn.

With my enhanced strength, I launched myself just a hair too far. I soar over the four men on my side, joining them in their hallway once again as I roll to catch myself. I slide a little on the finish, skidding to a stop as I check my clip.

I don't have many shots left. From here on out, every bullet counts because, after this, I have no more ammo.

"We have to get to the access panel." I shout, standing as I cock my guns.

"You are so damn *hot*," Jace says, smirking as he stares at me.

I grin and shoot him a dashing little wink.

Levi chuckles. "Focus, kids."

"They just keep coming," Russell says as he briefly glances out into the hallway. He whips his head back as another hail of gunfire reigns across the walls opposite us. "Drew says reinforcements are on the way. Ten more Knights, headed in our direction."

"Damn it," I mutter. "Drew. Tucker. Check in," I say, pressing my finger against the comm as I try to catch their attention.

Gunshots rattle in my ear. "I'm a little busy, babe," Tucker snaps. "Call you later?"

The soldiers in our hallway open fire again, and I cuss under my breath. "Yeah, same."

Keeping low, I peek out into the hallway to gauge how many soldiers we have left, at least for now. The longer we stay here, the higher the chance that the

Knights will just send more soldiers. We can't make our last stand in a hallway, and we absolutely must get to that access panel.

The secret passage is our only chance to get out of here, and it's the only one within range of us.

As I survey the hallway, it's mostly corpses and spattered blood. Ten rifles litter the floor between the downed soldiers, and four barrels peek around the corner.

Just four. I can handle that.

With both my pistols raised and little in the way of options, I dart into the hallway, taking the risk I'm fairly certain will pay off. The closer I get, the more powerful my shots will be and the greater the chance I can bust through the metal edge of the hallway. After all, we've been slowly chipping away at it this entire time.

I concentrate my fire on the corner. On each barrel that's pointing out at me.

I fire.

My first bullet lands in the barrel of the gun at the top, and the weapon flies backward from the force.

That's one.

My second and third bullets hit the next highest gun, throwing it backward.

That's two.

I expect gunfire. Hell, I figure I'll probably take a bullet or two—but it's for a good cause.

They fire. The bullets sail past me. One hits my thigh. I wince, grimacing as I fire again. A shoulder peeks out from around the corner—the idiot.

Don't shoot me and then show me where you are.

I fire again.

My bullet hits a vein.

He grimaces, falling into the hallway. Our eyes meet, and he grits his teeth with hatred as he lifts his gun toward me.

He doesn't get a chance to shoot.

My next bullet takes him out.

The final barrel disappears. Seconds later, the clatter of a gun hitting the floor mixes with the footsteps of a soldier running away, apparently abandoning his post.

Of them all, I think that guy was probably the smartest.

I look over my shoulder and point toward the access panel, which is now just five feet away from me. "Move, guys, move."

"Rory, you've been shot," Levi says, chiding me as he races toward me. His eye drifts to my leg, and then to my shoulder.

A ribbon of pain bleeds through my arm, and I

look down to see blood pooling on my shirt. Damn, I didn't even notice.

Adrenaline is powerful.

"I'm fine," I say, only lying a little bit as I nod to the access panel. "Get it open."

As the four of them near, I check my clips again. I'm almost out of ammo. Damn it. I only have a handful of shots left, and that's not going to do much good if soldiers descend on us once again.

Instantly, Levi and Jace are beside me, guns raised as they cover Brett. The former Knight bangs his fist against the wall, exposing a small keypad as he furiously types away at it.

The echo of boots and men hollering orders ripples down the hallway, and I grit my teeth.

We don't have much time.

"They're coming from this way too," Russell says, and I peek over my shoulder to find his gun raised at the opposite end of the corridor. I strain my ear, and he's right. I can hear the echo of boots from both directions.

Shit.

The door opens just as soldiers round the corner, and I empty both guns into the approaching line of Knights. Levi and Jace open fire with me.

"Go," Brett says, and in my periphery, I see him

gesture for us to enter the now-open door. "We need to get out of here."

"Come on," I say, backing up and nodding toward the door as my gaze drifts from Levi to Jace. "Let's go."

Levi's gun clicks as he runs out of ammo, and he gestures for me to go first as he tosses his empty gun aside and reaches for one of the rifles strewn across the ground.

I back toward the door as I fire my final shots, my full attention focused on the soldiers actively trying to kill us.

There's a hand on my shoulder, and the tight grip throws me off-balance as my final bullet leaves my gun. I'm thrown into the tunnel, and my back hits the far wall hard. I grimace, my head briefly spinning.

When I get my bearings once again, I look up to find Brett watching me intensely from the doorway.

Time seems to slow, and I watch as he grabs a rifle off the ground.

One of the Knight's guns.

Moving on impulse, I lift my handgun to take him out, but the clip is empty.

And his isn't.

Brett turns his head down the tunnel and fires, and I hear several bodies hit the ground.

For a split second, my horror gets the best of me. I

wonder if he could possibly have just taken out Levi and Jace.

The thought is paralyzing.

Seconds later, familiar silhouettes dart into the light, blocking my already limited view of the hallway.

To my relief, Levi ducks into the tunnel, followed closely by Jace and Russell. Brett's the last one through, and once he jumps into the secret passage, he slams the door shut behind him. Working furiously, he quickly types a code into the keypad beside the door. The words 'override lockdown' flash on the screen as soldiers bang on the exit, trying to open it.

The whole thing took at most five seconds, but in my paralyzed state—lost in the dread of possibly losing two of the men I love most in the world—it felt like a lifetime.

With the door secured, Brett lets out a shaky breath of relief. "We don't have long before they get that open. Let's go."

Though he turns to leave, I grab his collar and slam him against the wall. My bullet wounds scream in agony, but I push through the pain.

The man needs to get something straight.

"Don't you ever do anything like that again," I warn him, my voice deadly. "You ever interrupt my shot again, I will pistol whip you in the *face*."

He hesitates, his brow twisting briefly in confusion as soldiers bang on the door behind us.

We don't really have time for this, but I need him to understand that even in the heat of the moment, he doesn't ever get to control the situation.

I let him go, hating that we had yet another surprise thrown at us at the last minute, but at least this one worked in our favor.

"Go in front," I demand, my eyes drifting to the gun that's still in his palm.

I don't trust *him* with a gun to my back.

He lets out an uneasy breath and complies, darting ahead as he leads us through the passageways. We race through the labyrinth of barely lit corridors, headed to the rendezvous point so we can finally escape this dreadful place.

The entire time we're running, the pain in my shoulder and thigh screaming at me for rest, I grit my teeth and glare at the back of Brett's head. Even though I can feel Jace and Levi's gazes on me, I never once look away from our former enemy as he leads us through one of the most dangerous places on earth.

Mostly, I'm replaying everything that just happened over and over.

Tucker told me not long ago that Brett wasn't the

best marksman. That his skill was as a sniper, not in close combat.

However, Brett only fired two shots, and two bodies hit the ground. It was a perfect sweep, and he took out those soldiers with ease.

His former allies. Hell, the people he used to *lead*.

Shot dead without a hint of remorse.

It's clear he's been practicing with close-quarters combat, and that's both an interesting and very important little detail that Tucker needs to know.

What's more, however, is that he saved both Levi's and Jace's lives. Sure, I could have done it, but he stepped in and stepped up.

And however much I despise being tossed about like a ragdoll, I can't deny that in the heat of the moment, Brett did something good.

He saved the men I love, even when he didn't have to.

I just don't understand *why*.

CHAPTER TWENTY-NINE

We're almost out of the Knights' fortress.

Just a little farther, and we're finally done with the lot of them.

If we make it out alive. And that's a big if.

"Tucker and the rest of the team are through," Drew says, his voice piping in through the comm in my ear. "I'll meet you at the rendezvous point for our grand exit."

"You're not with them?" I snap back, my throat tightening with dread.

That was the plan. He was supposed to leave with them.

If the plan changed, that could put our entire exit at risk.

"It's fine, Rory," he says simply, the line crackling.

I frown. If he won't tell me what he's doing, it's definitely *not* fine.

Even though Drew is clearly up to something, I can't deny that this next part of the plan is the one bit of this whole thing I've actually been looking forward to.

Provided Drew doesn't try to play the hero.

Because I refuse to leave without him, and his vague assurance is setting my nerves on edge.

The hallway ends in a ladder that seems to go up forever, and we race up the bars as fast as we can. Brett leads the way, and as we reach the top, he throws the strap of his rifle over one shoulder as he reaches for the wheel on the ladder cover. He grits his teeth, his biceps flexing as he throws his back into it, and the rusty wheel slowly begins to turn.

"Any day, Clarke!" Russell snaps from underneath me.

"Sorry I'm not as big and strong as you stupid dragons," he snaps back, glaring down at the dojo master as the lock finally clunks open. The cover pops ajar slightly, and he sighs with relief now that it's open. Carefully, he peeks through the gap. "Shit," he mutters.

"What?" I ask, skeptical.

Instead of answering, Brett grabs the rifle. I tense, half-expecting him to fire down at me, but he throws his shoulder into the cover and launches it open. The hinges squeak as he pops his head through and lifts his gun, his eyes briefly scanning the world I can't see as he fires off eight shots.

I grit my teeth, and I can't deny that I feel pinned. With all of us below him, clinging to the ladder for dear life, we're easy pickings.

Well, I can do something about *that.*

I wrap my leg around the bar by my knee and lift my hands, ready to blow him to hell if he tries anything. A thin ribbon of light blisters across my body, ready to fire.

Deep down, I really hope he doesn't do anything stupid. If I fire my magic in this thin, vertical tube lined with metal, there's an even higher chance I'll hurt Jace, Levi, and Russell than there was back in the hallways.

"Come on," Brett says with a brief glance downward as he climbs out.

I climb to the top, and Brett gives me his hand to help me out. Before taking it, I briefly scan the world around us.

Six bodies lie on the ground, still as death.

One helicopter hums with life, the blades swirling above it.

The four other choppers are quiet, and there's only one other access door about a hundred feet away.

He actually cleared the area.

Huh.

I glance at Brett's hand, and even though I don't need to, I take it.

He helps me onto the helicopter pad as I scan the world around us. At least forty anti-dragon guns have been mounted along the cliff wall, and for the moment, they're all silent.

I can guarantee they won't be silent for long.

One by one, the others file out of the ladder tunnel, and I examine the still-running chopper a little more closely to see if it's a decent getaway car for Tucker.

In the cockpit, someone stirs. It's only the barest hint of a silhouette, just a whisper of movement, but the guns mounted to the side of the helicopter slowly pivot toward us.

Nope.

My magic burns along my skin, and this time I don't hold it back. Out in the open, it's safer to fire, and I unleash the full brunt of every ounce of magic I've been holding back this entire time. The white light blasts through the air, sizzling and crackling through the sky as it hits the chopper.

The helicopter explodes, shooting debris through the sky, and we all duck as one of the helicopter blades flies overhead.

"Warn us next time," Russell chides me. He can't fool me, though—not with the broad grin on his face.

He liked that.

I chuckle, rolling out my shoulders. "I've just got to keep you on your toes, man."

The access door nearby swings open, slamming hard against the wall behind it. I lift my hands impulsively to blow anyone who comes through to hell.

"Me," Tucker says, waving his hands to get my attention. "Just me."

He and the three dojo dragons who first went with him file out onto the helicopter pad. They're worse for wear, and one of them limps as he runs. Blood drips down another's neck, and Tucker grimaces as he holds his hand to his shoulder.

They took heavy fire, and Drew's not with them.

"Aw, man! Rory, you blew up the best one," Tucker whines, gesturing at the charred remnants of the chopper with frustration. "You were supposed to save one for me, babe!"

"I'm sure you'll figure something out," I say, shaking my head at him. "Where's Drew?"

"He got caught up giving the rest of us cover," Tucker admits, and his gaze darts once again toward me. There's a hint of concern on his face, and with the way his jaw flexes, I can tell he's trying to hide his unease.

Dread sinks clear through me. If these Knights hurt Drew, no amount of revenge will ever be enough to satiate me.

If the Knights *kill* him, I will never heal.

The crackle of energy and magic burns through the air as the dragons around me shift. Jace changes first, giving in to his dragon as the dark thunderbird towers over me. Levi and Russel follow suit, as do the other dojo dragons. Before long, six dragons perch on the landing pad, snarling and ready for a fight.

Because a fight is coming, and there will be no stopping the bloodshed.

But Drew's still not here.

Jace snaps at me, his teeth biting the air as he urges me to hurry up. Russell stomps on the ground, destroying the comm links that popped out of their ears when they shifted.

I can't shift, though. Not yet. Once my dragon

takes over, I'll no longer have a way to talk to Drew. Comm links don't fit in dragon ears, after all.

I press my finger against the comm. "Where the hell are you, Drew?"

"Leave," Drew orders, out of breath. He must be running. Gunfire cuts through the line, and he curses under his breath.

"I'm not leaving without you."

"I promise you won't," Drew answers tersely. "Now go."

Levi takes to the air, circling me as he hovers nearby, and Jace growls impatiently.

I don't think Drew would be the kind to sacrifice himself, but if push comes to shove, I know that he would.

And he had damn well better not.

I don't want to shift until I find Drew. Until I'm sure he doesn't need any help.

But I need to trust him.

With little in the way of options, I close my eyes as my dragon pushes against me. She wants to shift. She wants to help, and with the others covering me, I give in to her. It still takes me longer than them to shift, so I need a few protected moments to give in to the change.

The anti-dragon guns whir to life around us, and I

grit my teeth to keep from looking at them. I need to focus on shifting. As my body changes and reshapes itself, popping as my joints and bones grow, ripples of pain tear through me. My thigh and shoulder scream, and I know that even in my dragon form, they won't fully heal for awhile. It's agonizing, but relief quickly follows, and there's even a hint of pleasure as my claws dig into the asphalt on the helicopter pad.

I shake out my body, stretching my wings as I roar into the sky.

The signal.

All hell is about to be dropped on this place, and I have no mercy for any of them.

A helicopter nearby whirs to life, and my eyes snap open. I snarl instinctively, magic burning along my scales as I prepare to fire, but I notice a familiar man sitting at the controls.

Tucker.

The blades chop against the air as Brett races toward the helicopter and hops in the passenger seat. Tucker glares daggers at him briefly before arming the guns. As the weapons warm up, the helicopter lifts into the sky, and Tucker officially joins my other men in the air.

With a deafening boom from somewhere deep below, the ground trembles. I launch into the air with the others, wondering what fresh hell this is and preparing for the worst.

A massive crack tears through the asphalt, launching a rock slide down the steep cliff above us. Seconds later, Drew's red dragon breaks through the falling rock, roaring and spewing fire as he takes to the sky. Explosions tear through the building, and I wonder what kind of trouble he got himself into.

I don't really care though. Not as long as he's safe.

The anti-dragon guns lock on us, springing to life along the cliff, and I snarl. My magic brews within me, and Jace roars to the others in warning to get out of the way.

He probably knows I can't hold this one back, not after holding back the entire time I was in the Knights' fortress.

I let loose, and the blast arcs of blistering light across each of the guns. Several of them fire, missing me by mere inches. One bullet lodges deep into my side. Pain splinters through me, and I roar louder—which only makes my magic stronger.

My lightning rips them apart.

As the white light fades, dozens of explosions rock the edges of the cliff. Boulders along the top of the mountain shake loose, tumbling across the stone toward the gaping hole below.

The Knights' fortress is deep, and there are several reinforced vaults and safe areas. There will be survivors when we're done with them but not many—and those that are left won't last for long.

Not with what we have planned for them.

There's a whistle through the air, and it sounds eerily familiar to the missiles that nearly killed me in the battle for the dojo.

But I know what these are, and this time, they're on my side.

Dragons descend from the thick clouds above—hundreds of them, all led by a single dragon with brilliant lavender scales. She screams into the air, snarling as she lets loose a powerful bolt of lightning into the gaping hole in the Knights' fortress.

I twist in the air, rounding to join her as blood drips from my wounds. Russell, Drew, Levi, and Jace all flank me, and the four of us join the legion.

The full might of the Fairfax army is on display, and there will be no mercy for those below.

The first wave of dragons fires on the fortress as bullets whiz into the air. Artfully, we bank aside to let the second wave fire. Line by line, we dip and circle, sending bolt after bolt against the fortress mixed with the occasional blast of ice and fire.

Every weapon that appears, we destroy. Every

plane that tries to take off, we shoot down. We fire in a relentless and never-ending line, never giving the Knights a chance to so much as breathe.

The Knights started this war, but we've come to end it.

And end it we shall.

CHAPTER THIRTY

Even though I want nothing more than to get to Ashgrave now that we have the orbs, I'm forced to stop at the Fairfax capital.

Because *blah, blah,* wounds. *Blah, blah,* bleeding. *Blah, blah, "*Rory we don't want you to die."

Ugh.

The fact is we were riddled full of bullets in our onslaught through the Knights' fortress, and if we push through now, we might push too far. I'm more than willing to risk my life, but not the lives of my men. Not the lives of the people who are risking everything to help me.

So, despite however much I want to power through and get to Ashgrave, I let Harper redirect me to the medical ward deep in the heart of the Fairfax capital.

The doctor she gave me, however, could use some refinement on her technique.

I inhale sharply through my teeth, gritting through the pain as the doctor digs into the hole on my side. Deep in there, buried in my muscle, is the bullet that shot me as a dragon—and it's a hell of a wound. Shifting with bullets in you is never a good idea, but there wasn't a ton of choice here.

With my shirt held high, the doctor leans in, the light on her forehead shining on the open wound as she sets to work. Loose hairs frizz around her face as she focuses, a magnifying glass attached to the glasses covering her face as she peeks through one eye. The sleek silver tweezers in her gloved hands rummage around inside of me, the wound ripping ever so slightly as she digs deeper, and I groan in pain.

Harper crosses her arms, my only company in the room as the hospital shouts and rushes men on gurneys through the hallways beyond our open door.

I'm beginning to wonder if I made a mistake in offering up my place in the operating room. I figured it would be easy to get a few bullets out, even if we didn't have the full setup a doctor would traditionally have. With the wounds and casualties of the battle against the Knights, the hospital is swamped—even though they had prepared for a surge of wounded after the battle. There are only so many rooms and doctors to go around.

I thought I was helping. Now, however, I'm wondering if that was the best choice—or if this is just going to slow us down.

My doctor's utensils dig into me once again, and I grimace. Ribbons of white light dance across my skin with every burst of pain. Harper shifts her weight, propping one foot against the wall as she watches with a small smile on her face.

"This entertains you?" I ask, gritting my teeth again as the bullet wiggles against the muscle at the base of my wound.

"You're such a badass that it's kind of fun to see you wince," she admits, her grin widening.

I laugh. "You're such an asshole."

"Yeah," she says, chuckling.

A familiar figure walks past the open door—my stoic fire dragon, his intense gaze sweeping the hallway around him as he hunts for something. Or, perhaps, *someone.*

"Drew!" I shout, trying to catch his attention.

Even though he passed our door already, his shadow on the floor hesitates and pivots. His hand grabs the doorframe as he peeks in. "*There* you are."

The bullet wiggles again, slowly dislodging as the

doctor digs into me. I groan in agony, resisting the impulse to punch her as I try to distract myself. "Have you gone through any of the Knights' information yet?"

He laughs and shakes his head. "Woman, we just got the data about twenty minutes ago."

"Yeah," I say, shrugging. "So, what's the holdup?"

Drew laughs, shaking his head harder. "You know me too well."

"I really do," I admit, quirking one eyebrow while I wait for the brain-dump of what he knows. Or, rather, whatever I can get him to share.

"Jace and I are still going through it," Drew admits. "However, I wanted to see how you're doing and how much longer you have before you're ready to go again."

"Hopefully, not long," I say with a nod toward the utensils sticking out of the wound. Warm blood oozes against the gauze the doctor presses against the opening, which is actually a good sign—she's probably got the bullet in her sights and is trying to stem the flow of any torn blood vessels once she gets it out.

"There are only two bullets left to get out," Harper says. "Then we can go."

Yay me.

"What about Levi and Tucker?" I ask, my eyes darting between Harper and Drew. "How are they?"

"Levi is almost done," Drew says, leaning against the doorframe as he crosses his arms. "Tucker's still in surgery."

I frown, not liking the sound of that. "And Russell?"

"Is fine," the dojo master answers, his footsteps thudding against the ground as he joins Drew at the doorframe. "Thanks for asking."

Russell peeks in, and his gaze darts immediately to Harper. They share a fleeting glance, both of them relaxing slightly as they look at each other, and I know that expression—relief. They're both glad the other is alive.

I'm tempted to give them shit for their obvious attraction to each other, but I decide to be nice.

This time, anyway.

Familiar footsteps echo down the hallway, and I sit up a little straighter as I recognize Tucker's gait. A sharp pain shoots up my side as the doctor tugs out the bullet and holds it into the light, examining it while she presses the gauze to the open wound. I groan, my fingers curling as I try again not to hurt the woman who's helping me, but *damn* it she makes that hard.

Ow.

"Hanging out with dragons is bad for my health," Tucker says, running a hand through his hair as he squeezes between Drew and Russell to enter the room. He isn't wearing a shirt, and a white bandage wraps around the entirety of his torso. His strong biceps catch my eye, and though I have to admit he's gorgeous, I'm still concerned that he took so many hits.

There were far too many close calls on this mission, but we all knew the risk and we had very little choice.

"That's out," the doctor says calmly as she sets the bullet on a metal table beside her. It clatters against the tray, and I let out a sigh of relief despite the pain.

Almost done.

I lay back down so that she can get the last one in my hip. I try to stare at the ceiling and tune out the pain, but the familiar patter of footsteps in the hallway catches my attention.

Jace.

And he's running.

My dragon curls within me in warning and worry, deeply concerned for our mate, and my impulse is to jump out of bed and run toward him to find out what's wrong.

Instead, I force myself to stay in place so that the

doctor can get the last bullet out. "What is it, Jace?" I yell, hoping he can hear me over the manic den in the hospital halls.

"Bad news," he shouts, darting between Drew and Russell as he shoves his way into the room. His disheveled hair is a wiry mess, and his urgent gaze darts between me and Harper. "The Knights are on the move. I've been rifling through their data, and I just found proof that they know exactly where Ashgrave is. Right down to the gate. All activity indicates they're on the way there."

"Shit," I snap, darting up just as the doctor dives into my hip to get the bullet. Her metal tools hit the bone, and I grimace in pain. White sparks shoot up my arm, and I press my nails hard against my palm to keep my magic at bay.

"I'm so sorry, dragon vessel," the doctor says, shaking her head. "Please. I need you to stay still."

"I know," I say through gritted teeth. "I'm trying."

The room buzzes with the low murmur of overlapping conversation as everyone tries to decide what to do.

"...we have to beat them to..." Russell says, his words trailing off as Drew and Jace get into a heated debate and drown him out.

"If we go now, we might make it," Jace snaps.

"Not likely," Drew counters. "It's a remote and isolated area, sure. But this is a big deal, and they're going to send everything they have."

"…and what's actually moving?" Tucker asks. "They don't…"

Harper's voice briefly drowns out the others as she gestures toward the window. "…where can we possibly…"

"Stop!" I shout. "Everyone shut it for *two seconds*."

Harper and Jace frown with irritation, but everyone eventually looks my way. They pause, a brief silence settling on the room as they wait to hear me out.

I take a deep breath to steady myself through the pain in my hip. "Jace, are you sure they're mobilizing?"

"No doubt," he says, shaking his head. "The command center is currently tracking their movements. As far as we can tell, every known Knights unit, missile launcher, plane, or tank is headed to the same spot. To Ashgrave."

"Obviously, this is his last stand," Russell says, squaring his shoulders. "He knows exactly what you took, Rory. I can guarantee it."

"Do we know where they're headed *specifically*?" a familiar voice asks from the doorframe. Drew and Russell step aside to reveal Levi leaning against the frame. His shoulder presses against the entrance, his arms crossed as he watches us calmly.

Stealthy as ever, he didn't make a single sound as he approached.

"As far as we can tell, they're amassing outside the entrance into the mountain pass," Jace says. "Before any of Ashgrave's enchantments take hold."

"They must know how dangerous it is once you go through," Levi says, chewing the inside of his cheek as he looks at the floor, lost in thought.

"We could wait them out," Harper suggests.

"Not a chance," Tucker interjects, shaking his head.

Levi's ear twitches, and he looks off to the side as Tucker speaks. He frowns, his eyes narrowing as he sees something I can't.

"The Knights are too stubborn," Tucker continues. "Father would have supplies and be willing to wait as long as necessary. If all else fails, he'll just blow everything up out of spite."

"Tucker's right," Brett says from the hallway behind Levi.

Several heads in the room turn to look at him, but Levi's already glaring daggers at the former Knight. Brett's shirt is gone, and a few bandages around his bicep cover a few wounds he got in the hallway stand-off. After weeks of starving himself, however, he's lost much of his muscle definition, and he looks like a twig compared to the other muscular men in the room.

Tucker groans. "Didn't we leave you behind on the roof?"

Brett grimaces in annoyance. "I was agreeing with you."

"That doesn't mean I like you," Tucker counters, frowning.

Brett rolls his eyes, turning his attention toward me. "The General would probably blow Ashgrave to hell before walking away from it. He's been amassing huge amounts of TNT after dealing with the Spectres a few times."

I frown. Smart move, but one that does not play into my favor.

Once again, everyone launches into conversation, talking over each other as I try to tune them out. Ripples of pain shoot up my leg from the doctor's attempt to get the bullet as she pinches and maneuvers the metal prongs through my leg.

I'm not usually one to ask for help, but this is bad, and I need to swallow my pride.

After a moment or two of awkwardly rummaging through my pocket, I tug out my phone and text the last number Irena called us from.

I forgot the eggs, I text her. *Ask RK.*

It's a pretty simple code, one that's intentionally short. Usually, when we send it, we don't have the luxury of time.

I really need your help. Russell Kane can tell you when and where.

I sigh with frustration, knowing that she probably won't be able to join us. Even with the urgent attack on the Knights, she needed a week to amass her Spectres. By now, she knows what I've done, and she probably knows the hell that's coming for me. That might be enough of a motivation to get her to bring whatever she has, but the truth is I simply don't know if she can get there in time.

Ashgrave is in the middle of nowhere, after all.

I sigh, pinching the bridge of my nose as I debate my options.

"What do you want to do, Rory?" Harper asks, her voice cutting through the clamor.

With that simple question, the room goes silent, and I look up to find everyone looking at me. I scan their faces, more resolute than ever.

I know exactly what I need to do.

We've come so far. Sacrificed so much. So, no, I'm not going to let my home be destroyed at the last minute by a vengeful asshole.

"We fight," I say simply. "We carve a hole through

them if we have to, but we take this orb to Ashgrave and we give him his power back."

The doctor fishes out the final bullet, and I sigh with relief as it leaves me. There's no point in stitching any of these wounds up. After all, when I shift, they'll heal—at least for the most part. Especially now that the bullets are out.

I stand, gritting through the pain as my body splinters with agony from the open wounds, but it's time to move.

After all, I need to go save my evil butler.

CHAPTER THIRTY-ONE

Helicopter blades chop against the air as our carrier takes us closer to Ashgrave. I look out the window, the thick headphones on my ears muffling only a portion of the noise as the cold tundra stretches below us.

Harper and Russell sit across from me, both leaning over a tablet in Russell's lap. Jace sits beside me, his hand on my knee as he stares intently out the window to my left. Levi sits beside him, while Drew types furiously onto a laptop propped on a shaky metal table that vibrates with the whirl of the helicopter blades above us.

Tucker scowls in his seat beside Drew, his arms crossed as he glares out the other window at the thick-ening snow, preparing to go to war against his father and everyone he used to begrudgingly fight for.

I figured it was best to leave Brett back at the Fairfax capital under heavy guard. True to my word, I didn't have him locked in his cell again—but he *is* on house arrest in a much nicer room a few floors up.

We're not taking any chances.

All of us have been flying for hours, doing our best to race toward Ashgrave and get whatever upper hand we can, but it's not looking good.

It's almost as if this was the General's plan all along, and he's simply escalated the urgency of his attack.

Everything was ready. Everything was waiting. Deep down, I'm beginning to suspect that he was waiting for me to come back to Ashgrave. Somehow, he knew my next move.

I suppose I should have expected this, honestly. He and I have been enemies for eons. We're simply picking up a war started ages ago—by other Knights. Other generals.

Other gods.

He wanted to catch me off guard, but now it's more personal than ever, and he doesn't care if I know what he's doing. All pretense, all subtlety is gone.

Tucker's father just wants me dead, and he doesn't care how he does it. Not anymore.

The General really is making his last stand, and a man who takes his last stand is desperate. He doesn't care about collateral damage. He doesn't care about consequences. All he cares about is revenge. Getting what he wants and damning as many people to hell with him as he can.

Like Zurie, the General is a dangerous enemy, one I've been fighting for a while. I already killed her, and now I'm ready to end this—come hell or high water.

"This isn't your fight, Harper," I say into the mic attached to my headphones. My voice echoes in the headset, connecting us through the little black cable plugged into the wall.

"Of course it is," she says tensely into the mic, her eyes flitting toward me as she speaks. "The Knights came after us, too. There isn't a dojo soldier alive who wanted to stay behind. We need this, Rory, just as much as you do."

"You've already done so much," I insist, shaking my head.

I don't know if I can accept her help—not with the hell that's waiting for us at Ashgrave. I peek out the window again to see dozens of other choppers, each filled with twelve dragons or more. Other carriers hoist weapons, missile launchers, and anything the Fairfax Army could gather with such short notice.

We aren't just bringing an army to the General's last stand. We're bringing the entire goddamn armory.

But the specs that we've managed to glean so far from the General's sensitive data, as well as satellite images, show that the General is not going to go down easy. He has easily two hundred missile launchers and anti-dragon, high-caliber weapons mounted already across the entrance into Ashgrave.

The only one entrance into the snow-covered peaks of my new home.

Of *course*.

This man has armed choppers, jets, and basically every weapon known to man—as well as an assembling army of thousands.

Tonight, a lot of people are going to die. It guts me to think of the dojo dragons taking a missile to the back. Of them careening toward the snow.

Especially if they do it for me.

"It's not negotiable," Russell says, squaring his shoulders as he leans his elbows on his knees. "Even if I ordered the dojo dragons to stand down, Rory, I doubt most of them would. They're thirsty for blood, and they're out for vengeance. The best we can do is guide them and give them cover to make sure they don't die in the process."

I shake my head, looking out over the choppers, wondering how many of them won't be going home tonight.

"This is war, Rory," Jace says, his voice tense and low.

Though his presence soothes me, there's something so final about the way he said that. So certain. I lift my chin, catching his eye as he looks down at me. He studies my face, a calm expression on his features as he lets the silence stretch between us.

He wants to make sure I understand.

Deep down, I do. Though we're fierce, Spectres aren't really ones for war. We're assassins that run through the night, hidden and overlooked until it's too late to do anything. Until it's too late to run.

But in war, your enemy knows you're coming. Worst of all, this expedition is a full-frontal attack. The General not only knows we're coming, but he has his guns trained on the sky. He can guess our moves. Our approach. Our tricks.

This is a hardened warrior—a career soldier with a vendetta against everything that has scales.

He's deadly.

"Can we plan to have any help from your friends?"

Harper asks, her eyes narrowing as she shoots me a subtle, knowing look.

The Spectres.

"I don't know," I confess, rubbing my temples as I look once more at the window.

"Have any of Ashgrave's defenses kicked in?" Levi asks, leaning toward Drew.

Drew shrugs. "It's hard to tell for sure. The weather masks most movement through the area and makes satellite imaging difficult. As far as we can tell, none of the Knights have actually gone into the mountain range. They're all amassing outside Ashgrave's domain. It's like they know exactly where the line is," he adds, his gaze darting toward me.

I frown. That's not good.

I hate how much the Knights know about my home because the more they know about it, the more likely they are to destroy it.

My gaze darts toward the bag at my feet, the one filled with the two orbs we stole from the man who's trying to kill me. I left the crystal back in Fairfax for now, safely guarded in the Fairfax vault because I can't risk it breaking.

We need to study it, and that's not something to bring into a war zone.

"The orbs are supposed to restore some of

Ashgrave's power," I say, trying to work through the best course of action as we near the battle zone. "I just don't know what that means, or how much of him will come online with just one or two."

"Ashgrave didn't even mention two," Jace points out. "He really just needs the one."

I shrug. The list of unknowns in all of this is far too long for my taste.

The tablet in Russell's lap beeps and flashes to life. He lifts it, his finger is darting across the screen as he sorts through whatever data just popped up. "Oh, great," he mutters.

"What now?" I ask wearily.

"Looks like he just managed to get a hold of another thirty anti-dragon launchers, fourteen missile launchers, seven tanks," he adds, grimacing in confusion—probably because tanks aren't really beneficial in the snow. "And they've built a makeshift shelter to protect them from the blizzard." Russell shakes his head, groaning. "This is a full-on war zone, and they're just waiting for something to shoot out of the sky."

I pause, something clicking in my brain as his comment sparks an idea.

"Drew and Levi," I say cautiously, my finger tapping along my jaw as I piece my thoughts together.

"Can you combine your magic to create a cloud cover too thick to see through?"

"Yeah," they both say at the same time, with the same wary tone.

"What are you up to, woman?" Drew adds, his eyes narrowing in suspicion.

Instead of answering, I grin.

"If they're expecting a massive air assault, then let's surprise them," I say, my grin widening as I speak. "Let's throw them off their game."

Throughout the chopper, everyone starts to look at each other, clearly cautious of the plan I'm concocting. It's fairly clear they aren't sure if they're going to like it.

"What do you mean?" Tucker asks.

I just smirk. "I think you're going to like this, babe," I admit. "There's going to be lots of blowing shit up."

He laughs. "Then I'm in."

I chuckle. I knew he would be.

In fact, I think the only ones who *won't* like my plan are the Knights—and I can absolutely live with that.

CHAPTER THIRTY-TWO

As I soar through the thick cloud cover Drew and Levi created, I can barely see my own wings. The swirling white fog practically clings to me. At any moment, I could ram face-first into a mountain.

But I listen to my dragon, and she guides me.

I impulsively bank to the left, and seconds later, a mountain peak soars into view mere inches from me. Tucker shifts at the base of my neck, strapped in tight to my scales and carrying supplies we'll need for Ashgrave—including the all-important orbs—in a pack on his back. His fingers brush across my scales, sending fluttery sparks of delight through me as he opens our connection.

You've got this, he tells me.

Instead of answering, I send a flood of gratitude back to him. I really have to stay focused, and I have to listen as closely as I can to my dragon as she guides us through the gray gloom.

Everything about my plan—everything about the safety of my men, my friends and the Fairfax soldiers waiting on standby—depends on the element of surprise.

The only problem is the enemy knows we're coming, so the only surprise I can have is our method of attack. All we can do is set them on edge and let the enchantment of the snowy mountain range set their nerves on fire. My magic should do the trick—but for me to use the wild magic in my dragon form, no one else can be nearby.

It puts me at risk, but I can stir up some chaos on my own. Once they're scrambling—when they think I've come alone and are least expecting it, the others will descend.

All of us.

All at once.

It's risky. They seem to know firsthand to stay out of the mountain pass itself. After all, they've amassed at the entrance, at the only way in that's not shrouded in fog, snow-capped peaks, or air too thin for even a dragon to breathe. Everything about Ashgrave's location is strategic, and I suspect that's why the original gods chose it. That's why Ashgrave has remained hidden all these years. That, and its enchantments.

But with an enemy at the pass, what was once a defense is now an obstacle for us to overcome.

There's a flare of warning in my chest, the over-whelming surge of sudden danger nearby, and I know I've reached the battlefront.

And except for Tucker, I'm alone.

I take a deep breath, bracing myself for everything that's about to come, but it all hinges on this moment.

It all hinges on me.

No pressure.

My chest rumbles as I summon my magic, but I can't give myself away. I'm only giving myself the barest head start, just enough to get the ball rolling. My magic crackles along my teeth, white light shim-mering across my scales, and I hope it's still hidden by the cloud cover.

Bracing myself for whatever might come next, I break through the fog and descend like a missile through the wind.

Almost instantly, the mist clears. An ocean of men and rocket launchers appears before me. They shout, their voices panicked and shrill on the wind as I summon the full force of my magic. Spread out across the snow below, thirty missile launchers adjust, each of them slowly maneuvering toward me as they prepare to fire.

I snarl fiercely as the final surge of magic swells within me, ready to disintegrate whatever poor souls lie in its path. Though it's tempting to dive lower, my dragon and I have only just recovered from the battle with the dojo. Even just a couple hits from those guns could very well kill me, not to mention Tucker.

I scan the ground, looking for any hint of Tucker's father, but I can't see him.

That doesn't mean he's not here, Tucker says through our connection, apparently reading my thoughts.

That's true, I admit.

The magic burns and swells within my throat, and though I'm still nervous to let loose with Tucker so close, I have very little in the way of choice.

Let's do this.

I roar over the crowds as I pass them, the wild arcs of white lightning and brilliant light shooting from me as they sail through the ranks of my enemies. Men scream. Seven rocket launchers explode, and the ground shakes from the force of my attack.

The mountains tremble, and an avalanche breaks across the nearest slope. The snow tumbles and roars as the Knights below try to outrun it, and I bank over the avalanche as it swallows two more of the rocket launchers.

Almost instantly, another wave of Knights—easily two hundred or more—pour out of several passes through the snow.

Backup.

Several armored vehicles race down makeshift roads hastily carved into the snow, and it won't take long for them to assemble.

But I was just the first wave.

Almost instantly, dragons descend from the cloud cover, each of them blasting their magic across the army below.

And my men lead the charge.

Blasts of ice cut through the air, freezing everything they touch. Rocket launchers, men, vehicles—everything becomes a block of ice as Levi makes his way over the soldiers, unleashing his fury.

To my right, a blazing blast of fire cuts through the sky as Drew joins the battle. The snow hisses and fizzles under his fiery breath, and my red dragon streaks through the air as he decimates a squadron of Knights aiming their weapons at me.

I circle, looking for my opening. I wish I could attack again, but my magic is still too raw. Too wild. I was merely the diversion, letting them think I'd come alone. Now with everyone distracted, I need to make my move.

The only way to end this is for me to reach Ashgrave, and the only way for me to reach Ashgrave is to find an opening through the soldiers and rocket launchers so that I can dart into the pass.

My dragon curls within me as Jace nears, and I feel him long before I see him. There's a whistle through the air, and I tilt my head as my black dragon dives from the murky white clouds above, blasting his brilliant magic at one of the rocket launchers currently taking aim at me. It explodes on contact, and his magic chars the snow with black streaks.

Several rocket launchers along the slopes fire. The missiles take to the air, and to my dismay, most of them are still aimed at me. I swerve as best I can, and several explode just below me. It throws me off balance, and for several seconds, I lose altitude before shakily recovering.

I think I might barf, Tucker says through our connection.

I growl in apology, but it's the best I can do right now. I still haven't mastered flying. Hell, I barely had two seconds to breathe since Zurie's announcement, much less refine this new skill and this new body.

But I'll figure it out. I always do.

Drew, Jace, and Levi circle, flanking me as we race toward the pass. Levi blasts one of the remaining rocket launchers in our way while Drew rains fire on the soldiers as they lift their rifles at us. Jace lets loose a mighty blast of his lightning, and it arcs toward the final rocket launcher between us and the pass.

But when I go, I have to go alone.

If anyone's going to follow me into the pass, I want it to be the soldiers. That way, Ashgrave's wisps and other booby traps can kill them—but my men would be just as vulnerable to the enchantments as anyone else, and I can't risk them getting hurt.

Only Tucker, tied to my back, can withstand the magic of the mountains. Even though I told Ashgrave not to harm my men, I don't know how much control he truly has over the booby traps and various enchantments throughout the mountain range in his weakened state.

It's not a risk I'm willing to take, and I've warned all of my allies to stay out of the mountains.

The sound of helicopter blades on the air catches my attention, and eight armed choppers descend from the cloud cover above. Since Harper ordered her choppers to remain behind, these can't be ours. In the distance, I hear the scream of jets approaching, and none of this bodes well for us.

The choppers fire on us, and I bank to protect Tucker, taking a few bullets to the underbelly. I roar, snarling in pain, furious that someone could distract us so close to our goal.

Levi fires a blast of ice that hits one of the choppers. Its blades freeze as it falls to the ground. Drew and Jace blast several of the others, but one breaks through the thundering hailstorm of magic and heads toward me.

It's like they're banking on me not using my magic with my allies so close, and that just pisses me off.

He fires, and impulsively, I roll, flying upside down as I race toward him to protect Tucker from getting hit. At the last second, I dive toward the ground, my tail swinging behind me as it breaks through the helicopter and snaps it clean in half. With the ground quickly approaching, I roll again, my wings tearing against the air as I try once more to get airborne.

I can practically feel Tucker's nails digging into my scales as the straps keep him bound to my back.

He's not enjoying this part.

Sorry, I tell him.

Just glad I'm not dead, he says back, and I can practically feel a surge of his nausea burning in his throat through the connection.

The scream of jets approaching gets louder, and I take the chance while I have it.

For this moment—and perhaps this moment alone—the pass is clear.

With one glance over my shoulder at Drew, Jace, and Levi, I soar toward the opening between the mountains. Jace and Drew roar in encouragement, but Levi watches me with a tortured expression. He's my protector, and I know he hates letting me go into danger without him being there to look over me.

But he has to, and he trusts me.

Our eyes meet as I sail into the pass, and he disappears from view.

As I fly into the mountain range, the snow pelts against my face. The longer I fly, the thicker the fog gets as the endless blizzard of the Ashgrave mountains rolls through the slopes. I turn inward, listening to my dragon, letting her guide us around every peak and valley.

I can't help but wonder if the Knights know about the enchantments here. I assume they must if they set up outside of the pass, but there's always the chance they don't. There's always the chance they'll follow me in and succumb to the wiles of the mountains.

A girl can hope.

The scream of jets gets louder, and I peek over my

shoulder as three of them descend from the cloud cover. The sleek black jets look like they were stolen from the military, and given the General's connections, that might very well be the case.

They open fire, and I snarl in frustration as I dive, trying to protect Tucker. Seven bullets dig into my back, one dangerously close to my weapons expert, but I take the hits instead of him.

Rory, are you okay? he asks through the connection.

Fine, I lie, trying to focus.

Good. Because I want a jet, he says. *You can get me one of those, right?*

I snort in annoyance, but I can't help how much I love this adorable idiot.

With an intuitive bend of my wing, I bank right, and the jets follow in tight formation. They move like a cohesive unit, and I wonder how long they've flown together. I wonder why they hate dragons so much, and why they're willing to dive into such a dangerous blizzard just to get me.

I also wonder if they're willing to die together—because that's exactly what's about to happen.

Trying to shake them, I sail to the left this time. My goal is to fly so close to the slopes that the jets can't help but hit one and lose control.

Curve by curve, I careen through the pass ever

faster. Up ahead, there's a tight gap between two mountains, and I growl in anticipation.

Rory, don't, Tucker says.

It's happening.

Rory, please, he says again.

Trust me.

The thin gap approaches blindingly fast, and I let my dragon take over as she tilts us to the side, flying perpendicular to the ground as I cut through the impossible opening. A flurry of white powder hits me in the face and sails off the tip of my wings as I fly through.

I look over my shoulder as the pass quickly disappears from view, just in time to see a bright orange fire tear through the opening as the jets hit it. The explosion rocks the slopes, sending a flurry of avalanches down several mountains nearby, and I growl in victory.

Maybe I'm not so terrible at this whole flying thing after all.

The scream of jets through the air catches my ear yet again, and my growl of victory becomes one of frustration. One of them survived, and he cuts around the other side of a slope as he heads toward me yet again.

I snarl, wishing these assholes would die already. I

wonder if perhaps I can use my magic now, but it takes all of my attention to just fly through this difficult pass. The thought of trying to control a burst of magic enough to not kill Tucker is more than I can manage.

Damn it.

That's pretty, Tucker says absently, almost like he doesn't know I can hear him through the connection.

There's a momentary pause of confusion as he leans too far to the right, throwing me slightly off-balance as he looks over my wing into a chasm below. I briefly glance downward to find a flickering blue light shimmying along the slope.

A wisp.

Well now—*that* could work.

I dip toward it, mostly just to make sure the pilot flying the jet behind me can see it. Even though this route takes me slightly away from Ashgrave, I think this detour is probably going to be worth it.

Wings tense on the blustering wind, I abruptly tilt toward a cliff. The violent motion shakes me on the rough wind, but I manage to hold my ground as I roll through the air and double back the way I originally went.

Here it is.

The moment of truth.

The jet flies past me, and for a moment, I can see into the cockpit. I expect the pilot to be glaring at me, to have his full attention on me as he tries to follow my movement.

Instead, he seems fixated on the little blue light deep in the chasm below.

I feel a flicker of pity for him that he's about to angle his plane into a pit. He's a skilled pilot diving toward his own death, and part of me can't help but think it's a waste of talent.

Then again, this is one of the Knights who has been hell-bent on killing me from the start. So, whoever it is, this is just karma catching up to him.

I push myself faster, urging my dragon to take us to Ashgrave as quickly as possible. As I round the nearest mountain, the muffled explosion of a jet hitting a wall rocks the mountainside.

We need to go down there, Tucker says, snared by another wisp's magic.

I look down to find two more shimmying below me, and I try to simply tune him out. He's enraptured by the enchantment, and nothing I do will shake him of that.

To help him, I need to get us out of here. And to do *that,* I need to simply focus on my flying—and the beating pulse of Ashgrave's beacon, guiding me home.

I cut through the mountains as Tucker repeatedly urges me to land, to let him look at the lights, to follow them, and it's difficult to ignore his voice. He is Tucker after all, a man I deeply respect and love. I never want to ignore him, but in this case, I have to for his own good.

We're almost there.

I can feel Ashgrave getting ever closer, his heartbeat snaring me and pulling me close. It's overwhelming, almost dominating every one of my senses and driving me blindly forward.

We're *so* close.

As I round a bend, I see the gate. I see the familiar cliff with its runes exposed, and my heart leaps into my throat. All I have to do is get down there, give Ashgrave the orb, and he can join us in the fight. Hell, maybe he can even *end* it.

Through the howling wind, the muffled and distant click of a weapon arming catches my attention. Furious and baffled, I scan the endless snow, trying to find whatever I missed.

No one can be all the way out here.

That's not possible.

And yet there, by the gate, almost perfectly matched to the snow and the misty fog, are two rocket launchers. Dazzled by the promise of being so close to my goal, I missed them when I first scanned the slope. Hidden deep within the snow bank, the weapons are almost impossible to see—but that's no excuse.

Not with this much on the line.

They lock, taking aim—at me.

Somehow, by some twist of fate, the Knights reached Ashgrave first. I don't even know how they managed to get in here without succumbing to the wisps, but they did.

The rocket launchers fire, and two missiles scream through the air.

Toward me.

Toward *Tucker*.

And we are *screwed.*

CHAPTER THIRTY-THREE

My world is blurry.

A sharp ring in my ear dulls the other sounds around me as I slowly come to. Explosions rock the mountains, the thunder faded and distant, almost like they're explosions from another life. The snow is soft and cool beneath my fingers—not the biting chill I would expect from a blizzard.

When I open my eyes, I only see splotches of white and blurry silhouettes. Black spots cloud my vision. Everything slides in and out of focus.

My world spins as I try to make sense of where I am and what happened.

I lay in the snow, the white powder like a mattress beneath me. Carefully, I lift and examine my hands against the cold sky, turning them every which way as I slowly piece things together.

Crap.

Wait.

Hands?

At some point, I must have shifted back.

I press my hands into the snow, teetering as I try to stand. My blurry vision surveys what little around me I can see as I look for any signs of Tucker, hoping against all hope that he's okay. I can't even let myself consider the alternative.

My knees give out, and I fall to my palms as the snow gives out underneath me, soft and unsteady. About twenty feet away, a familiar dark green jacket with a tan fur lining lays in the snow, still as death. My heart thuds in my throat.

Tucker.

After a moment of paralyzing dread and howling wind, he groans. The jacket shivers in the frigid wind as he rolls onto his back and stares up at the sky.

I sigh with relief, trying again to stand so I can run to him. Bit by bit, my vision returns—but only partially. My periphery is foggy and mostly black, but I catch sight of the backpack he was wearing.

And I leave it.

Tucker is more important.

Pain splinters through my body—from the missiles, from the bullet wounds, and from the fall. With each step, I stumble. With each stumble, my head spins. A surge of nausea rises to my cheeks, and I fight to keep it at bay. The ringing in my ears fades as I get closer and closer to Tucker, and the world outside slowly begins to return as I come to my senses once again.

The crunch of boots in the snow sails by on the wind, and my intuition flares in warning. I look over my shoulder, but I'm a second too late.

A familiar man with salt-and-pepper hair and broad shoulders lifts a gun, the barrel aimed at my torso—and he fires.

The echoing boom of a single gunshot cuts through the mountains, and the bullet hits my bicep. I yell in pain, my hand pressed against the bleeding wound as the snow beneath me slowly turns red.

That asshole—he made me *scream.*

That is *unforgivable.*

I glare bloody murder at the man standing over me, white sparks burning along my skin as I boil with rage.

And he—that *jackass*—grins, like this is fun.

"You're an animal," he says calmly. "This is what my father taught me to *do* to animals."

The barrel of his gun tilts slightly to my other side and he squeezes the trigger yet again. The second bullet rips clear through my other shoulder and hits the snow with a dull thud.

A second scream builds in my throat, but I grit my teeth to silence it. Despite the pain, despite the agony, I refuse to show him the depths of my misery even as my blood carves hot rivers through the white powder beneath me.

"You know what we do when an animal goes rabid? When they're a danger to the greater good?" he asks, raising one eyebrow as if he's waiting for me to answer. "We put them down."

Through the rage, the anger, and the pain, I summon my magic. White light simmers across my skin, the sparks crackling between my fingers as I prepare to blow him to hell.

The General merely clicks his tongue in disapproval, unfazed by the threat of being burned to ash. "Do you really want to start an avalanche? You might survive, but Tucker won't." The General nods to his still unconscious son lying just ten feet from me.

This bastard is using his own son's life against me.

A half-dozen soldiers appear from the thick fog around us, the barrels of their guns cutting through the mist as they approach. Every rifle is aimed toward me, and with no other option, I summon the dagger into my palm. It flickers, the weight coming and going for a few seconds before it settles into my hand. Definite. Certain.

And not much of a defense against all those guns.

Four gunshots cut through the air, and I wonder if this is it. If—when I was so close to winning, so close to giving Ashgrave what it needs to power on—I failed.

I'm not *allowed* to fail.

And I *don't*.

The soldiers look behind them as the gunshots continue railing through the sky. They yell, their tones panicked, and start firing into the mist at something the General and I can't see. The General grimaces, glancing between the fog and me as he tries to decide which is the greater threat.

All I need is a clear opportunity and a hit of adrenaline to slit his throat.

"Damn it," the General mutters, lifting the gun toward my head.

He fires, and with every ounce of fire left in me, I throw myself aside at the last second. The bullet careens into the snow between the two thick red splotches I left behind—and if I hadn't moved, I would be dead.

He fires two more shots, the barrel trailing me as I do my best to keep out of the line of fire, and both bullets miss me. With each passing second, I get more of my bearings. With each surge of the howling wind, I force a little more of my brain to clear.

To my delight, a surge of adrenaline hits me hard. In a sudden rush, my vision clears completely. I can see him perfectly—every wrinkle on his face and the twitch of his lips as he glares at me and lifts his gun.

I grip my dagger tighter, naked and exposed in the snow, and yet I can't bring myself to care. This is life and death.

I may have brought a knife to a gunfight, but that's all I need.

Even against a man like him.

Before I can attack, one of the General's soldiers races toward him. The sudden interruption throws the General's aim off, and his bullet sails into the fog.

"Sir, get down!" the man shouts.

A gunshot cuts through the mist, and the soldier falls to the ground. His momentum leaves him sliding across the snow and instantly dead.

The General cusses under his breath and bolts for cover with his other soldiers as they dip in and out of the fog. He glances over his shoulder at me with all the fire of his hatred as he retreats and disappears from view.

The barest hint of footsteps crunch across the snow toward me, and in the thick fog, I can barely see the General as he retreats. I know this momentary pause in his fire won't last long, and I know he'll be nearby.

And yet the footsteps continue, their path headed toward me.

Whatever's coming, I hope it's on my side.

A silhouette appears in the mist, and I lift my dagger, putting myself between the shadow and Tucker. With no cover, I have little chance to protect us, but I won't let anyone touch my man.

"Why are you naked?" Irena asks, frowning as she materializes out of the fog. Her brows knit in confusion as her gaze drifts over me.

Thank the gods above.

I let out a deep sigh of relief, and I can't even bring myself to answer. I simply shake my head, the knife in my palm dissolving as I lose my killer focus.

"Come on," she says, apparently not needing an answer. Though she reaches for my shoulder, her gaze drifts across the wounds, and she hesitates. Her nose wrinkles in disgust and she glares once more into the fog.

"I already have dibs," I say darkly, taking the chance to run toward Tucker. "The General is mine."

"Not if I kill him first," Irena says, seething as she looks again at the gunshot wounds. "Here," she adds, pulling out a few bandages from a pocket in her black cargo pants as she nods for me to kneel beside my weapons expert.

As I kneel beside Tucker, Irena sets to work rolling the gauze over the wound to stop the bleeding, but I don't even care. I can't even think about it. Not really. Though it stings and the agony splinters through me with every breath, all I can think about is my man, lying unconscious in the snow.

I press my hands against his jaw as I check for signs of breath and life. His chest rises and falls in steady rhythm, and his eyes flutter like he's trying to wake up.

That was a hell of a blow, even for a dragon. It could have killed him, and the fact that he hasn't woken up yet means it nearly did. If he spends any longer in a coma, there could be serious brain damage or internal bleeding.

He *needs* to wake up.

Now.

Three more silhouettes appear in the fog, and I grimace as I prepare for war, ready to take on the

Knights again. I summon my dagger once again, the adrenaline making it easier to manifest, and I'm ready to kill.

"Wait, no," Irena says, shaking her head. "They're with me."

Seconds later, three men dressed in white military camouflage dart out of the mist with rifles pressed against the butt of their shoulders. They kneel in front of us, turning their backs to me as they aim the barrels of their guns into the mist in the direction the General and his men had gone.

They're our cover.

"By the way, baby sister," Irena adds with an annoyed glare at me. "Can you *please* get your magic castle to stop trying to kill my soldiers?"

"Sorry, he's kind of…" I trail off, not sure how I can word this. "He's a little *fuzzy* right now."

She rolls her eyes.

"I can't believe you made it," I admit as she finishes the second bandage. I wince, grimacing in the agony of the many bullet holes in my body, and my delicate flower of a sister shoves a loose pair of pants and a coat into my hands.

"Of course," she says with a small grin. "I'm not about to let you die."

I smile in gratitude as I tug on the clothes. After all,

there's no reason to give the Knights a free show. "How long do you think we have before the General regroups?"

"Sixty seconds?" Irena asks with a shrug. "At this point, you know him better than me, Rory."

"We probably have about thirty," I admit, tapping my hand against Tucker's cheek to wake him up.

"How do you like your eggs?" Tucker asks groggily, his eyes slowly opening even though they're dazed and out of focus. "Fertilized, I hope?"

I chuckle, shaking my head, just grateful he's alive. "Irena, take care of him. If either he or I die, I'll haunt the *hell* out of you. I'm going in."

Irena does a quick scan of the foggy snow bank around us going. "In *where*?"

I nod to the exposed cliff, to the symbols carved against the wall—the markings that will glow the moment I touch them. "I need to get over there. Once I make it, I need sixty seconds of cover to get the door open."

Irena snorts derisively, scanning the bare cliff and squinting her eyes. "There's a door?"

"Just trust me," I say impatiently, rifling through the backpack to find the orbs.

They're both there, and thankfully they didn't

shatter in the fall. They're a lot more durable than I realized. Thank goodness.

I swing the pack over my back and nod to her, our silent signal that I'm ready.

"We'll cover you," she says, slipping into boss mode as she raises her rifle and aims it into the fog.

"Can I get a gun?" Tucker asks deliriously, rubbing his temple as he leans up.

"Stay down," I tell him.

The General is trying to intimidate me. Throw me off. Make me slip up. He wants me at his feet, begging for mercy—but that's a dream that will die with him.

Because, in the end, he's going to be the one with a gun to his temple.

Ultimately, this is what I do best—carve my way out of impossible situations. And, damn it all, I'm going to have *fun* with it.

In a sudden and painful surge, Ashgrave calls to me. It's overpowering, and the summons to the door is so strong that I can barely think.

Though, admittedly, that might be the concussion.

At first, my feet move on their own, darting through the snow as I race toward the cliff, the pack swinging slightly as I run.

I have to get to the door.

I have to get to Ashgrave.

As I reach the cliff and set my hands on the nearest symbol, golden light cuts through the rock. The first time I saw this, I thought it was beautiful—but with an army behind me, trying to kill everyone I love, now all I can think is that it's moving too damn slow. I wait with bated breath for the door to appear as the light slowly trails through the carvings.

"Come on, damn it, come *on*," I mutter under my breath, looking over my shoulder into the mists.

A familiar rectangle cuts through the rock, and after a few painfully slow moments, the door creaks open. My head spins briefly, my brain still disoriented from the fall, but I grab the rock to keep from falling. When my world stops spinning, I run into the stairwell.

When my foot hits the first step, I get a flare of intuition.

Turn around.

Duck.

I obey, but not fast enough.

The gunshot echoes through the sky, railing off the mountains like an omen. Something hits me hard in the back—dangerously close to my spine—and I fall.

The momentum carries me down the stairs. My body hits every step as I careen down the staircase. My nails drag against the walls, gouging the stone, but it's not enough to stop myself.

My body screams for rest, and so much of me hurts that I can't place where it's coming from anymore. Everything stings. Everything aches. Everything in me tells me I should sleep, that closing my eyes would fix this, but that's a trap. This wounded, falling asleep might be the last thing I ever do.

So, as I fall, I fight to stay conscious.

Two more gunshots cut through the air above me, and as I roll, another hits me in the side. Splinters of sharp and biting pain tear through the growing numbness, and I groan in agony.

I just cannot catch a freaking break.

In the Knights' fortress, I got shot three times, and on the way here, I've taken five more hits. There are at least two bullets in me right now, and I'm still dealing with the fallout of yet another concussion.

I've never been one to keep count, but I'm pretty sure I was injured *less* as a Spectre.

I hit the bottom step and tumble across the floor. Even though I'm not moving, my brain still spins as it tries to catch up with me.

For a moment, I can't even breathe. Blood trickles down my side and down my back, and there's a strange numbness along my spine that can't be good. I squint through the blood streaming across my face, and even though my vision still swims, I recognize a familiar pedestal. It glows with the faint blue light of a fading pulse and a dying castle.

"MY QUEEN," I hear Ashgrave say, though his voice is raspy and distant. "YOU ARE HURT."

"Yeah, no shit," I mutter, crawling across the floor as I try to get to him. All I can do is hope the orbs haven't broken.

If they can survive a fall from the sky, they can survive stairs.

My knees and elbows scrape across the stone floor as I slowly make my way toward the pedestal, pushing myself past every limit I've ever had.

Footsteps echo down the stairs behind me as my brain goes fuzzy, but I refuse to pass out.

Twenty feet to go.

I won't let a monster like the General win, no matter the cost to myself.

I just can't.

And I *won't*.

CHAPTER THIRTY-FOUR

With every second that passes, my stalker and I make equally slow progress. I move a few inches forward, my head still spinning, my body in agony as I try desperately to get to the pedestal. And he—clearly wounded—plods down the steps behind me. His gait is hurried and hurt, and every few steps he shuffles, his shoulder hitting the wall as he tries not to tumble down the steps. There's an occasional groan of pain that echoes down the stairwell, and I honestly don't know which of us is going to reach our mark first.

Ten feet away.

The pedestal is so close.

My ear twitches as my stalker's footsteps near, dangerously close now. I shake my head, trying so hard to clear my thoughts. To get to my feet. To force myself to get up and finish this.

I get to my knees, and my world pivots. There's no sense of up or down, and if gravity is working, it's not working in my favor. A surge of nausea hits me hard, and I fall yet again. I strike the ground hard, my elbow scratching across the stone floor as I catch myself.

Damn it all, I refuse to go out like this.

I stand again, my knees shaking as I try to catch my balance, but I merely stumble forward. I fall to my hands and knees, and I'm so very close.

Five feet away.

"Ashgrave," I say quietly, my words slurring. "Kill him. Kill the man on the stairs."

"AS YOU WISH," the castle says gleefully, the pedestal roaring to life.

Gunshots cut through the air, and the glass around the pedestal shatters. The machines across the walls hum and catch, whirring and clicking as they sputter, close to death.

"No!" The word grates my throat, scratching my soul as it leaves me.

I roll onto my back, the orbs pressing against my spine as I force myself to sit up. On impulse, I summon my magic, and the ribbons of white light ripple over me as I can barely contain it. The power wants so desperately to break free, and my dragon wants to destroy everything in her path. In her pain—in her anger—she has almost no control, and it takes everything in me to rein her in.

If we fire now, we could destroy Ashgrave himself. This is his heart. Everything he is and everything that's left is in this room. My magic is still too wild and too untamed to give in to it now.

I wince as my body ripples with pain and force all of the magic currently burning through me into my palm, summoning my dagger once again. It glows in my hand, ready to deal a final blow to whomever is unlucky enough to be underneath its blade.

The General walks out of the shadows of the stairwell, the barrel of his gun aimed at me as he limps forward. His other bloodstained hand presses hard against his side. Blood oozes between his fingers, and his nose wrinkles in disdain as he glares down at me.

"You dragons are monsters," he says through gritted teeth as he stumbles toward me. The gun in his hand shakes, and I can tell he wants to fire. He's just waiting for a good shot.

I force myself to my feet, teetering as I lean against the shattered pedestal—or at least what remains of it—for balance. "I'm the monster?" I ask, utterly astonished at his twisted brain. "What have I done to *you*?"

"I'm just stopping you before you have the chance to destroy what little good is left in this world," he says, the barrel of his gun briefly pointing at the floor as he tries to take aim. "It's what all of you are, what all of you are destined to do. You have too much power, too much control over the world. You all take whatever you want. You kill whoever stands in your way. My only purpose was to take that away from you and give this world back to mankind."

He fires a shot, the bullet ricocheting off the stone floor by my feet as it rebounds into the wall behind me. I teeter, trying to get my balance and knowing that when I do attack, I'll only have one chance to get close enough to end this.

I have to make it count.

"You dragons," he seethes. "You stole everything from me. You, woman—you stole my son. And others like you stole my *wife.*" He spits out blood, his eyes never leaving me. "I couldn't even go on assignment. I couldn't even do my *job.*" He fires another shot, and it also ricochets off the ground and into the wall behind me.

With each shot, my brain clears a little more as adrenaline floods through me. My vision slowly begins to crystallize again, and second-by-second, I can see the man more and more clearly.

"I went on tour, and when I came home, my wife was dead," he says, tears burning in his eyes as he swallows hard. The trembling gun in his palm raises as his hate fuels him. "Dragons broke into our house, took what they wanted from her, and slit her throat." The General shakes his head as he stares at me bitterly. "And that's what you all do. That's the way you all think. It's the reason none of you should exist."

The barrel of his gun stills, pointed directly at my heart, and even though I'm not ready, I know this is it.

I won't get another chance.

To throw of his aim, I feint to the right and dart toward him. He fires, the bullet soaring through the air and brushing my temple, but it only grazes the skin. My ear rings as the bullet screams past me, and I drive the dagger into his side. It digs deep, the magic holding strong in my palm for several seconds before it fizzles and flickers. I try to twist it, but the dagger disappears from my fingers just as the General punches me hard in the jaw.

I fall to the ground, rolling with the momentum of the blow, but Zurie used to hit me harder than *that*. I use the momentum to push myself awkwardly to my feet. I teeter briefly, summoning the dagger once again, determined to make this work because it's all I have. Though his gun is still trained on me, he holds the second gaping wound in his side, his hand now permanently red from all the blood he's lost.

"How are you still standing?" I ask, my grip tightening on the magical dagger in my palm.

"I can ask the same about you," he says, his eyes briefly scanning me. "I've shot you, I've blown you to hell, and yet here you are, a freak of nature still on your feet. This is why you dragons don't deserve to be alive. You're unnatural."

"No," I say, smirking, unable to resist the chance to piss him off. "I'm just stubborn."

He grits his teeth, snarling with disgust as he fires three shots at me. I dart toward him, trying to roll my shoulder to keep it out of the line of fire. The first bullet sails past me. The second trails too far to the left.

But the third hits.

It pierces my chest—just above the lungs, thank the gods—and throws me off balance. I fall to the ground, rolling and gasping for breath. My vision flashes red and white as I try desperately to push through the pain, but it's overwhelming. It burns through every nerve, every brain cell, and I can barely feel my fingertips, much less stand.

Blood trickles down my side. Down my shoulder. Down my back. It drips from me to the floor, staining the edges of the coat and pants that Irena lent me as small pools of red gather on the cobblestone.

"You want to know why I'm still standing?" he asks, his voice cutting through the hazy ring in my ear. I look up as he approaches, his silhouette blurring as my vision doubles. "I took adrenaline *just* for the occasion," he says, shaking his head. "Just to kill you. My heart will go out before the day is over, but it's worth it. You won't end the Knights. You won't destroy what I've built, even if I have to die defending it. All of this," he says, gesturing back up the stairwell with the barrel of his gun. "All of that is *worth* it to end you. You know why?"

"I bet you'll tell me," I slur, goading him even to my last breath.

"Because when you die, so does the dragon dream," he practically snarls. "You mean so much to so many. If a human kills you, other humans will take that to heart. Other humans will realize they can kill dragons, same as I did."

"You haven't killed me yet," I remind him, my vision slowly clearing.

The first thing I see is the barrel of his gun, aimed right at my face. "I've accepted my fate today, little girl," he says. "So why won't you just lie down and die?"

"Zurie did," I tell him, forcing myself onto my palms as I push through the pain. "In those final moments, she looked peaceful," I add bitterly, angry that someone as vengeful as her could have even a moment of tranquility.

It seems so unfair. Zurie hardly deserved serenity, even in her final moments.

The steady drip of my blood slowly hitting the floor beneath me fills the space for a moment as we merely glare at each other, wondering if this is really how it ends for us both.

He's already accepted his fate. He said so himself.

But this isn't where I die.

I shift my weight onto my knee, pressing the ball of my foot against the floor as I prepare to charge him one last time—my final stand with nothing but the dagger in my hand.

He cocks his gun, his finger on the trigger as he aims it at my forehead.

A gunshot cuts through the air, and before I can so much as move, the General gasps and drops his gun as he holds his chest. He stares down in shock, lifting his palm to reveal a giant red stain.

He's bleeding, and I didn't give him this wound.

The General turns around, and as he does, we both see Tucker leaning against the doorframe at the bottom of the stairs. He teeters, the barrel of his gun trained at his father.

Tucker and I lock eyes, and though he briefly winces in pain, he nods.

He's as ready for this to end as I am.

With the General distracted, I force myself to my feet and stagger toward him, driving the magical dagger in my palm deep into his gut with all of my remaining rage and all my fury. The weapon holds in my hand, fueled by my hatred, and I twist it in a maneuver I learned from Zurie herself.

It's a guaranteed kill, every time.

The General falls to his knees, grabbing my arm. His tight grip takes me down with him. My knees hit the stone hard, and though I grimace in pain, I'm in so much agony that it barely registers compared to all of the bullet holes currently in my body.

The Knight holds me tightly, glaring at me as he tries to form words, but I don't give him the chance.

"You seem to hate women and dragons with equal passion," I say, practically seething. "I guess it's only fitting that I get to kill you."

I twist the dagger again, driving it deeper, wanting this to be over.

Wanting this man to finally be done.

The General falls back, his grip on my arm loosening as he hits the cobblestone. His head arches backward as he watches Tucker, and to his credit, Tucker holds the man's eye as he dies. For several moments, the General merely wheezes his final breaths until he finally goes still.

I stand, my legs shaky as I stumble toward Tucker and hold him close. He holds me tightly, both of us leaning against the doorframe as we teeter off-balance.

"Are you okay?" I ask, pressing my forehead against Tucker's.

It's a weighty question. After all, he helped me start a battle, was ensnared by a deadly enchantment, took the brunt of a missile, fell from the sky, was used as bait and leverage against me, had a terrible concussion, and shot his father.

All in the last hour.

At first, he doesn't answer, and I open my eyes to find him watching his father's corpse. Though I don't have much strength left in me, I hold him tighter in comfort and solidarity.

Both of us escaped lives we were never given the choice to live, and both of us had to kill those who raised us. With Zurie, my old life died, and I realize now that Tucker is experiencing something similar.

His gun clatters to the floor. "I thought this would be harder," Tucker admits after a second. "I thought that, when the moment came, I wouldn't know if I could pull the trigger." He shakes his head, turning his attention toward me as he holds my face with bloody fingers. "But when he had his gun trained on you, when he was ready to kill you, I didn't think twice."

I smile, holding the former Knight's wrists tenderly as I look deep into his green eyes. "Thank you, Tucker."

"Thank *you*, Rory," he corrects, kissing my forehead. "You saved me. And as much as I would like to carry you off to a bedroom somewhere to celebrate, we're not out of the woods yet."

In the distance, an explosion rocks the mountains, and he's right.

We're not.

I turn my attention toward Ashgrave—toward the shattered pedestal at the center of the room—and briefly scan the trail of blood cast across the cobblestone floor from my battle with the General. I study the loose shards, wondering if there's anything left.

Or if—like the General—Ashgrave is dead.

CHAPTER THIRTY-FIVE

For a tense moment, all I can do is look at the General's corpse as I hold Tucker close. There's a sense of disbelief that filters through the pain rocking my body and my brain—a surreal sense of relief mixed with the irrational fear that at any moment, he's going to spring back to life and shoot me.

"Rory," Tucker says gently, teetering slightly from his wounds. "We don't have long."

He's right, of course.

I swing the pack off my bloodstained shoulders, limping toward the splintered pedestal as blood drips down my leg with every step. As my bare feet brush the cobblestone, my toes slide sometimes along the puddles of blood I left across the floor in my fight with

Tucker's father. But I persevere and grit my teeth through the splintering pain and the foreboding numbness in my spine.

When I reach the pedestal, I kneel and run my fingers along the fractured blue glass. The pulsing light is gone, and dread sinks clear through me as my hands brush across the bullet hole that shattered everything.

But there, deep in the pedestal, is the barest hint of a glow as the castle's heartbeat slowly fades.

I try to fight the rising tide of hope as I rummage through the bag as quickly as I can, grabbing the first orb I see.

Not that one, a delicate voice says, her sweet words echoing clear into my soul. The sensation is smooth and soothing, like honey and heaven.

My dragon.

I pause at the surreal sensation of hearing her voice echo through my brain. It's sweet and soft, not quite what I was expecting, though I have to admit I wasn't expecting my dragon to speak to me at all.

But I listen.

I lift the other orb—a blistering white sphere that churns like a storm cloud. Tiny arcs of lightning cut through it as the eternal storm rages on. Once again, I scan the pedestal, wondering how the hell I'm supposed to give this to him.

"Ashgrave, can you hear me?" I ask.

"I HAVEN'T MUCH TIME," the castle says, his voice fading and almost gone completely. "DEATH WAITS FOR ME AT THE DOOR."

Because I'm a dark and twisted person, my impulse is to chuckle. We're all at death's door, and he's being dramatic.

"Where do I put this?" I prod.

There's a sharp hiss and a dull pop as the shattered pedestal trembles beneath my hand, and a small drawer opens at the base. It slides slowly out, shaking as it runs on broken mechanics. There's an indent at the base of it—just a little divot that would hold an orb—and I set the glass-encased lightning storm into the drawer.

It fits perfectly.

I slam the drawer shut, hoping I'm not too late. Hoping that all of this wasn't in vain. After all, my castle took a bullet to the heart, and that would kill even a dragon.

But something in me tells me he's tougher than that.

At first, nothing happens, and the shuffle of Tucker's feet across the bloody floor as he joins me is the only sound in the empty room. He kneels at my side, one hand holding his waist as the other rests against the small of my back in comfort and solidarity.

My ears ring as I wait, refusing to believe I didn't help him in time. I strain to listen in the silence. A distant explosion rocks the mountainside, and I wonder who's winning.

Because everything came down to this—to bring Ashgrave online. It was a wild, risky bet, and we went all-in. If he's dead—if it's too late—then we've lost.

I set my palms against the pedestal, wondering if I can do anything to help this along. Wondering if he needs me to say something or give him an order.

"You're not allowed to die, Ashgrave," I tell him calmly. "There are so many people you have to smite for me."

He chuckles, the sound distant and echoing—and almost a little sad.

Deep within the pedestal, a mechanism whirs and clicks into place. The blue light hums and glows stronger than ever, growing stronger with every second.

What was once the distant echo of a dying voice becomes a thundering boom as Ashgrave's laughter grows louder and louder. It becomes the maniacal cackle of a madman. Of a man who has been returned to his former glory. Of a man who can see everything clearly once again—and who, in just an instant, finally got the upper hand.

I impulsively tense and frown, and there's a flicker of doubt deep in my soul. The risk in bringing Ashgrave back online was twofold.

One, yes, we weren't sure if we would be able to do it at all.

But two is the fact that he obeys the *gods*.

And I am not a god.

The ground beneath us rumbles, shaking and trembling as the room around us springs to life. The gears and mechanisms along the wall roll faster, their halting click becoming a seamless and continuous movement as they all resume their steady pace—the pace they haven't had in ages.

"Of all the things to get his attention," Tucker says in disbelief. "Knowing he had to smite people for you was the only thing that brought him back?"

"I guess we'll see," I say, not entirely convinced.

My stomach churns as the floor moves, and it feels for all the world like we're on an elevator, rising high into the sky. The force is overpowering, knocking both of us to the stone as we struggle against it. For several moments, we have to simply lie there as we're propelled into the sky.

550
OLIVIA ASH

To my surprise, the rough walls become windows peeking out into the clouds, into the misty blizzard that's overtaken the entire mountain range. The floor's upward momentum slows, and the moment I can stand, I limp toward the window and look out onto a warzone.

It's chaos.

Dragons dive in and out of the fog. Explosions shatter the mountains. The scream of dying soldiers lingers in the air, and I can't for the life of me tell which side is winning.

As I watch the warzone, several other towers shoot into the sky from the ground around us. Any snow touching the emerging castle begins to melt, revealing frozen grass and meadows that surround us on all sides. The blizzard begins to fade, rolling back into the sky and revealing gorgeous mountains covered with evergreen trees. Waterfalls form from the runoff of melting snow.

I almost can't believe it. It's a patch of Eden in the tundra.

And it's mine.

I look over my shoulder at the glowing pedestal as the cracks along the glass fuse together into a seamless sheet once more. He's healing himself, and the power in the orb is everything he needed.

Now, to see if he still needs me.

"How are you feeling, Ashgrave?" I ask, my body tense as I do my best to remain calm.

"BRILLIANT, MY QUEEN," he says, and I can hear the joy in his voice. "I FEEL CAPABLE AGAIN. I CAN FEEL THE ROOTS OF THE CITY DEEP BENEATH THE MOUNTAIN. EVERY ENCHANTMENT, EVERY DEFENSE, IT'S THERE. NONE OF IT LEFT."

"Good," I say, squaring my shoulders. "Because we have a war to finish."

"OF COURSE, MY QUEEN," he says gleefully. "WHO SHALL I KILL?"

"Anyone with the Knights emblem on them," I say pointing to the General's body. "Anyone who works for him."

"AT ONCE, MISTRESS."

"He's such a good evil butler," Tucker says, grinning as he leans on my shoulder.

I wince as his elbow brushes across one of my wounds.

"Oh, sorry," he says, holding my waist as he looks me in the eye for a moment. We slowly lean into each other, my eyes drifting toward his lips as I pause to savor our victory, but his fingers close around one of the wounds in my side.

I groan in agony, my eyes fluttering shut.

"Damn it, *sorry*," he says genuinely, lifting his hands so that he doesn't touch me or hurt me anymore.

With a few deep breaths to ease the rising sting of pain, I open my eyes and study his face for a few moments.

It doesn't take long for us to burst out laughing.

"Maybe wait until the bullet holes have healed," I say.

He rubs his eyes and nods. "Yeah, that's fair."

Through the windows, the war rages on, and for a moment, I wonder what Ashgrave is waiting for.

It's almost like he read my mind.

Mechanized arms dart from the ground near every missile launcher and tank within view. Hundreds of gears whir along the enchanted structures in perfect harmony as hundreds of mechanized fingers grab tanks and soldiers with wild abandon. Missile launchers are hurled into the sky. Soldiers are crushed in the fingers and dragged into the ground.

One by one, every last remaining Knight succumbs to the fury of my castle.

To my relief, the Fairfax dragons are left alone. Though I can't see Irena or her Spectres, I trust they're staying out of harm's way.

In moments, the Knights are gone or dead, and only my allies remain.

"I'VE BEEN WAITING EONS TO DO THAT," Ashgrave says, gleefully murderous. "THAT WAS QUITE FUN, MISTRESS."

I survey the carnage below, noting that most of what's left of the Knights is just the occasional dropped gun or shattered piece of metal.

There's nothing left.

"Good job, Ashgrave," I say with a smile, looking back at the pedestal.

"BUT, OF COURSE, MY QUEEN," he says, a hint of hesitancy to his voice.

I frown. "What? What is it?"

"AH, WELL…" He hesitates again.

"Spit it out," I demand.

"I AM NOT USED TO RECEIVING COMPLI-MENTS, MY QUEEN," he says. "YOU ARE QUITE A CURIOSITY TO ME. I SHALL ENJOY GETTING TO KNOW YOU MORE."

I chuckle, setting my hands on my hips. "The feeling's mutual."

I reach into the bag and pull out the other orb as a blue storm rages within the glass. "What's this one for?"

"ALL IN GOOD TIME, MY QUEEN," Ashgrave says, to my surprise.

I had assumed he would want to immediately bring something else online, but his patience just confirms for me that he's not the power-hungry madman I was concerned he might be.

"LET'S CHECK ON YOUR SERVANTS, MY QUEEN," he says.

"Yes," I say, laughing. "Let's."

Evil butler, indeed. I really like this guy.

CHAPTER THIRTY-SIX

I almost can't believe it's over.

I lean my wounded shoulder against the glass window as I stare out over the surreal patch of green in the middle of a snow-covered mountain range. The boundary of Ashgrave's magic cuts a clear line through the powder, the green reaching for several miles in every direction before it abruptly becomes white. From this vantage point, I can't quite get a full view of the castle itself.

But I do see the dragons.

The Fairfax dragons soar through the air, diving and roaring in victory as they swarm above the circle of green cut through the snow.

To my relief, I spot a familiar red dragon in the crowd. It takes a moment longer, but I also spot a familiar blue one as well. Deep within, my dragon stirs with delight as Jace cuts through the swarm and banks toward me, like he already knows where I am.

Probably because he does.

I set my palm against the glass as I lean toward him. He cuts sharply to the left as he nears, our eyes meeting briefly before he disappears around the tower.

"Lead us out, Ashgrave," I order.

As I step away from the window, my bloody hand-print remains on the glass. I frown as the splintering pain in my body slowly becomes a numbness, and I should probably see a doctor.

It would be really great to not have so many near-death experiences anymore, but with my new place in the world, I'm not going to hold my breath.

Tucker wraps my arm over his shoulder, supporting me as we limp for the nearest archway.

"THIS WAY, MY QUEEN," Ashgrave says, his voice booming and vibrant. The wheeze is long gone, and he speaks with all the strength I would imagine a magic castle to wield.

It's a nice change.

Sconces flare to life nearby, illuminating a new archway and a stairwell that winds downward. Fire springs to life in the sconces down the staircase, lighting the way into the darkness.

Tucker and I quickly make our way down the stairs, leaning on each other for support as we follow the lighted path through the endless corridors of Ashgrave. The stairs become hallways, and over time, the identical stone walls slowly widen. With each new hall, the ceilings become gradually taller, arching above us as we make our way through this magical labyrinth.

There's so much to explore and discover, but for now, I have only one mission.

Find my men.

Our hallway ends in a vast corridor easily wide enough for five dragons. The ceiling arches high above, easily tall enough to fly through. I strain my neck as I look upward, and as I scan the dark ceilings, dozens of glimmering chandeliers roar to life. They hover and float in the air, suspended and glistening like a galaxy of light and glitter.

It's surreal to think this is my castle. That this is my home.

To my left, a massive set of double doors glistens in the magical light. They tower above me, easily two stories tall and inlaid with elaborate gilded carvings.

Sconces roar to life on either side, and I limp toward it, assuming this must be the way out.

"SHALL I ANNOUNCE YOU, MY QUEEN?" Ashgrave asks.

"Oh, gods no," I say, laughing. "Just open the door."

"OF COURSE," he says, and I can hear a hint of disappointment in his voice.

I sigh in defeat, figuring it's only fair to let him have his fun. "All right, Ashgrave. Go ahead."

"DELIGHTFUL," he says.

There's the briefest pause before I hear his voice again, only this time it's distant, muted by the thick doors in front of me.

"WELCOME TO THE VALLEY OF THE GODS, OF THE ONE QUEEN OF THE SNOW AND ALL MAGIC," Ashgrave says, his voice booming through the mountains.

"Oh, no," I mutter, rubbing my eyes.

I instantly regret this.

Tucker just laughs. "He's fun."

"I PRESENT TO YOU THE ONE TRUE QUEEN OF ASHGRAVE," my castle shouts into the mountains as the doors swing dramatically open. A crowd of dragons gather across the grass and lingering snow, all intently watching and waiting for whatever happens next.

They're all watching me.

"I'm never letting him do that again," I mutter to Tucker.

"Aw, why not?" he asks, grinning. "I liked it. Is that how I should talk to you in bed?"

"BOW BEFORE YOUR QUEEN," Ashgrave shouts.

"Don't you dare bow!" I tell the crowd, pointing a threatening finger at them.

Laughter ripples through the dragons, and I scan the faces of the assembled soldiers, looking for my friends and my men. Still in their dragon forms, Harper and Russell make their way through the crowd, the dragons around them slowly parting to let them through. Both of them lower their heads toward me, growling happily.

With a groan, I shake my head. I'm pretty sure they're dragon-bowing.

As Harper's beautiful lilac face nears, I set my hand on her forehead.

Thank you, I tell her, the gratitude burning through me like a flame, and I hope she can feel it all. *I wouldn't have been able to do this without you.*

It's what friends do, she says, tilting her head as her eyes wrinkle with joy.

I smile. It's still such an odd feeling—having a friend, much less one who would risk her life for me.

Russell and I catch each other's eye, and we both nod to each other with respect. He and I don't need any mushy gooeyness. He knows I appreciate him, and vice versa.

My dragon stirs and tugs on me, urging me to turn around. As I indulge her, three dragons bank around the massive tower above us all. They land behind me, between me and the open doors, and I smile as I recognize my fire dragon, my ice dragon, and my thunderbird.

My men.

They brush their foreheads against me, a flurry of thoughts and emotions burning through me with every open connection, and I just laugh.

I'm fine, I tell them. *Are you?*

Of course, Drew says, snorting a little as black smoke rolls from his nose. *I'm a badass. Remember?*

I just laugh.

"COME, MY QUEEN, TO YOUR THRONE ROOM," Ashgrave says, his voice echoing through the sky.

"We are *really* going to need some ground rules," I mutter, shaking my head, utterly mortified at this whole queen-thing he keeps pushing on me.

A murmur of excitement burns through the crowd behind me, and I figure we might as well go inside.

They're probably all just as morbidly curious as me, and they deserve full access to the castle after all they did to help me get here.

I can't wait to explore this place.

As I head in, the prickling feeling of someone watching me tickles my neck, and I look over my shoulder to find a familiar woman with dark hair and bright green eyes resting her foot on a nearby rock as she leans her elbow on her knee. Our eyes meet, and she smiles at me.

I nod to my sister in gratitude. She briefly salutes and jumps off the rock, disappearing down a steep slope and gone in an instant.

It's the Spectre way.

My smile fades, but that's what she needs—at least for now. I'm grateful she made it here to help us. That she came when she did and sacrificed so much to be here. Even though it feels like she's gone, I know she will never really leave me, and she will always be there when I need her—just like I'm there for her when she needs me.

I take a deep breath and square my shoulders, doing my best to hide my limp as I walk through the vast entry of my new castle. Elaborate pillars made of marble and carved with ancient symbols I don't recognize lead the way into a vast throne room.

In the heart of the massive chamber, a dozen steps lead up to a platform with three elaborate thrones covered in gold. The ornate chairs loom over the empty court below as we file into the room.

Three thrones.

Three gods.

It's a surreal reminder of those who were here before me—of those who built this place, and the origin of the magic that burns through my blood. All of this was theirs, and if they're still alive, I suspect they'll want it back.

Well, if they try to take it from me, there will be a bloodbath.

"You should really see a doctor," Tucker says, still holding my wrist tightly as he keeps my arm rooted around his shoulder for support. "Hell, we both should."

"Give me a minute," I say, grinning up at my throne, wondering which one I'll take.

"ALLOW ME TO FIX THIS FOR YOU," Ashgrave says, his voice thundering through the room.

Two of the thrones crumble instantly to dust, the base of the platform swallowing up the rock as they leave only the center throne behind.

Huh.

That gives me an idea.

"Make it five," I tell Ashgrave.

"Five?" Tucker asks.

Still in their dragon forms, Levi and Jace watch me suspiciously, their eyes narrowing slightly in confusion.

Drew, however, chuckles. The hot breath of his laughter rolls through his nose with ribbons of dark smoke, and it's clear he knows what I'm getting at here.

I slowly climb the steps, careful not to fall as four more thrones dart immediately from the platform, flanking the center throne.

"I got here with you," I say to my men as I reach the top, turning to face them as I take the center chair. "And we'll rule our little patch of snow together."

Jace and Drew growl approvingly, and Levi play-fully rolls his eyes. I figure he's not really the ruling type, and his throne probably will go empty more often than not. But I figure it's the thought that counts.

I settle into my chair as the Fairfax dragons roam and wander the castle freely. I close my eyes, and with a happy sigh, I finally relax.

Home sweet murderous home.

CHAPTER THIRTY-SEVEN

I sit on the roof of my new bedroom, admiring the view. The cool wind whips through my hair as I scan my little patch of green in the middle of the snow, and all I can do is smile.

Ashgrave's land is stunning, and as I sit on the black shingles of my tower roof, a flock of white birds sails by. A waterfall rumbles in the distance, tumbling toward a river I haven't explored yet, and the massive castle stretches around me on either side in the shape of a crescent moon.

My new tower is at the heart of it, looking out over it all, and the dozens of spires and archways that comprise my new home stretch on either side of me. A beautiful cobblestone road cuts through the center of the castle, headed toward the front doors, and all I can do is savor the taste of magic on the air.

These are enchanted lands, full of ancient power that I can feel right down to my bones.

As the beautiful day stretches on, the sun beating down on my back, I breathe in deeply. The numbness has finally faded from my spine, and the bullet holes are mostly healed now that the bullets are out. It'll be a while before I recover from the concussion, but for the most part, I'm back.

I curl my arms around my legs and set my chin on my knees as I enjoy the view. It reminds me so much of the dojo, and yet it all feels so incredibly different.

It's new and unknown, but somehow comfortable and right.

Two hands appear on the edge of the roof, and I flinch slightly in surprise. Since I didn't hear him coming, I figure this is probably Levi.

Sure enough, his gorgeous face pops over the edge of the roof as he drags himself onto the shingles with me. He smiles warmly and jogs to sit at my side.

"I see why you like it up here," Levi says, his eyes scanning the castle around us. I follow his gaze and notice a hole in the roof along the buildings in the outskirts.

Huh. I frown, wondering just how much work is ahead of us to repair this place.

"Brett arrived this morning with the crystal," Levi adds absently.

I already know, of course. I heard the chopper when it delivered him, and I wonder what it must have been like for him to stay back as we killed his former boss. "I'm still not sure I trust him."

"That's one of the reasons you've lasted this long," Levi says with a wicked little grin as he looks at me through the corner of his eye

I chuckle. "Thanks… I think."

"Tucker's probably off giving the man a black eye," Levi admits, setting his elbow on his knee as he stares out at the stunning mountain range around us.

"Probably," I admit. "I take it Drew grabbed the crystal the moment it landed?"

"You know it," Levi says with a laugh. "He says he has a few theories on what it is and what it can do. He may have even found the trail of the person who originally secured one for Zurie."

I bite my lip, wondering whose head I need to bash in for trying to steal my magic and kill my dragon.

My girl stirs within me, happy and joyful as she curls around herself with delight.

Jace, she says.

There's a whistle through the air, and I look over my shoulder as my mate flies by. He roars in triumph and rolls, the brilliant glow of the magic in his body blurring in the air as he shows off.

I'll probably join him in a bit.

"Rory?" Harper asks, her voice catching on the wind. "Where the hell are you?"

"Watch this," I say mischievously under my breath as I jump to my feet. Levi follows behind me as we head to the edge of the roof. A draft hits me hard in the face as I look over to find Harper on the balcony of my bedroom, scanning the sky.

With a quick and fluid motion, I jump down onto the balcony. She gasps, her hand on her chest as she flinches.

"Gotcha," I tease the Fairfax Boss.

"Damn you," she mutters, laughing.

I chuckle as Levi lands beside me without so much as a sound.

"Are you ready?" Harper asks, nodding into the room.

"As I'll ever be."

I take a deep breath, squaring my shoulders as I follow her inside. A camera with a bright light around the lens stands on a tripod in the middle of the living room in this master suite. Several doors jut off to other rooms, and through the nearest open doorway, I spot the elaborate four-post bed draped with blue silk that I still can't believe is mine.

It's a long way from sleeping on the floor in safe-houses on my missions with Zurie.

I take a deep breath and sit in the overstuffed armchair across from the camera. Several papers lay on a small table beside the chair, and I rifle through my notes on the Knights' data for the hundredth time. I memorized it all on the first read, and by now, this is more of a nervous tic than anything else.

"Are you sure about this?" Levi says without a hint of doubt in his voice. He watches me calmly, and it's clear this is his attempt to comfort me without me realizing what he's doing.

I nod, forcing a little smile. "We need to broadcast the General's files and make all of his lies public." I hesitate, my gaze drifting again to my notes. "And they all need to know the truth about me, too."

"You've got this," my ice dragon says, tucking a lock of my hair behind my ear as he kisses me gently on the forehead. He joins Harper behind the camera, and she signals to me to begin when I'm ready.

Drew seems to think I'll be a Boss. That I'm some kind of queen in the making. I'm not so sure—I mean, hell, I don't even *want* to lead. I just want to live.

I can't, however, deny that I'm the only one of my kind. A diamond dragon with the power of the gods.

If anyone had told me a year ago that this was my fate, I would have laughed in their face.

But that's what I am, now.

A warrior. A fighter.

A *dragon.*

I take one more deep breath and look dead into the camera. "My name is Rory Quinn," I say. "You've been told quite a few lies about who I am, what I want, and what I can do." I pause, my gaze briefly drifting toward the papers beside me, but I don't need them. "I'm here to set the record straight. I'm here to tell you the truth."

After all, I'm in the light now—and I'm never going to hide again.

**Rory, Levi, Tucker, Drew, and Jace will return in
Death of Dragons, available for preorder on Amazon.**

**Join the exclusive, fans-only Facebook group to get
release news & updates.**

Read on for a special note from the author.

AUTHOR NOTES

Hey, babe!

I HAD SO MUCH FUN!!

This book swept me off my feet. It's the sort of story that leaves me breathless, and I found myself writing late into the night. Diving into Rory's tale. Exploring this new world with her. Conquering the Knights. Finding Ashgrave.

Everything about this book just stole my heart, right down to Rory's murderous butler. Seriously, who else here is #TeamAshgrave? Because *swoon.*

I mean, who *doesn't* want an evil butler?

Rory faced a new kind of foe in this book—herself. Namely, her need to stay in the shadows. I enjoyed the metaphorical dance she and Levi had in this story as they both fought with their inner demons and stepped into the light.

In *Reign of Dragons,* for the first time in her life, she defied her master.

In *Fate of Dragons,* she learned how to give up a bit of control. How to compromise.

In *Blood of Dragons,* she learned what it means to have family. To trust, to let down her guard to her inner circle, and grow as a person.

In *Age of Dragons,* Rory finally accepted who she is: a dragon, a warrior, and someone worthy of being loved.

And in *Fall of Dragons,* Rory realizes she's not prey —she's a hunter, one who doesn't *need* the shadows to survive.

All while remaining her beautiful badass self, of course.

Tucker just steals my heart. Even when he's close to death, he's snarky, adorable, and horny as hell. Our resident weapons expert makes me laugh nearly every time I see him.

Drew knows so much more than he lets on, and in this book, we get to see him channel all of that powerful knowing toward Rory. Namely, he has a vision of her new life—and what it means to be a queen. If anyone can put Rory on a throne, it's him.

Jace gives me happy shivers. His confidence, not just in himself but also in Rory, brings me so much joy. He loves her, heart and soul, but he's his own man—a powerful warrior who doesn't take shit from anyone. Not even our resident badass babe!

And Levi really grew in this book. He pushed himself past the limits he thought he could never conquer, and he became an even better man for it.

As for the universe of the Dragon Dojo Brotherhood? I loved exploring the Bosses and other world players in new and exciting ways. Getting to know more about the Palarnes, seeing Milo try to manipulate Drew, and watching Zurie briefly come back from the dead—Rory certainly has a long list of enemies, doesn't she?

Those poor souls don't know who they're messing with. Not really.

Of course, I couldn't play in this world so much if you didn't love reading it. So, from the bottom of my heart, *thank you.* Thank you a million times over. If I ever get to meet you in person, I'm going to give you *such a big hug.*

You truly are such a gift to me!

I know you're probably chomping at the bit to learn what happens next. That crystal has come back —could it be we're finally going to figure out how tried to steal Rory's magic in book three? What are the Darringtons up to, since we know they never lie dormant for long? Will Brett try to betray them, or is he truly her loyal servant now? Where are the other orbs, and what do they do?

Lucky Rory and her men are such brilliant fighters. They won't let anything come between them. Whatever lies ahead, they're ready.

Are you?

The next book will be available in four short weeks! That's right, babe, you can even order it *now*.

The next book will be available in two short months. Make sure you **join the exclusive, fans-only Facebook group to get the latest release news & updates.**

Until next time, babe!
Keep on being your beautiful, badass self.
-Olivia

PS. Amazon won't tell you when the next Dragon Dojo Brotherhood book will come out, but there are several ways you can stay informed.

1) **Soar on over to the Facebook group, Olivia's secret club for cool ladies,** so we can hang out! I

designed it *especially* for badass babes like you. Consider this as your invite! We talk about kickass heroines, gorgeous men, our favorite fantasy romances, and… did I mention pictures of *gorgeous men*?

2) **Follow me directly on Amazon**. To do this, **head to my profile** and click the Follow button beneath my picture. That will prompt Amazon to notify you when I release a new book. You'll just need to check your emails.

3) **You can join my mailing list by going to** https://wispvine.com/newsletter/olivia-ash-email-signup/. This lets me slide into your inbox and basically means we become best friends. Yep, I'm pretty sure that's how it works.

Doing one of these or **all three** (for best results) is the best way to make sure you get an update every time a new volume of the *Dragon Dojo Brotherhood* series is released. Talk to you soon!

Dragon Dojo Brotherhood

Reign of Dragons

Fate of Dragons

Blood of Dragons

Age of Dragons

Fall of Dragons

Death of Dragons

War of Dragons

Queen of Dragons

Myths of Dragons

Vessel of Dragons

Gods of Dragons

A Legend Among Dragons

Blackbriar Academy

The Trials of Blackbriar Academy

The Shadows of Blackbriar Academy

The Hex of Blackbriar Academy

The Blood Oath of Blackbriar Academy

The Battle of Blackbriar Academy

The Nighthelm Guardian Series

City of the Sleeping Gods

City of Fractured Souls

City of the Enchanted Queen

Demon Queen Saga

Princes of the Underworld

Wars of the Underworld

Sentinel Saga

By Dahlia Leigh and Olivia Ash

The Shadow Shifter

ABOUT THE AUTHOR

OLIVIA ASH

Olivia Ash spends her time dreaming up the perfect men to challenge, love, and protect her strong heroines (who actually don't need protecting at all). Her stories are meant to take you on a journey into the world of the characters and make you want to stay there.

Reviews are the best way to show Olivia that you care about her stories and want other people discover them. If you enjoyed this novel, please consider leaving a review at Amazon. Every review helps the author and she appreciates the time you take to write them.